E. CHRIS A

THE ASSASSIN'S THRONE

A BONE GUARD ADVENTURE

ROCINANTE

Table of Contents

Chapter One..1

Chapter Two...7

Chapter Three...11

Chapter Four...17

Chapter Five..23

Chapter Six..28

Chapter Seven...33

Chapter Eight..40

Chapter Nine...45

Chapter Ten...52

Chapter Eleven..59

Chapter Twelve..64

Chapter Thirteen...70

Chapter Fourteen..75

Chapter Fifteen..78

Chapter Sixteen...81

Chapter Seventeen..85

Chapter Eighteen...90

Chapter Nineteen..93

Chapter Twenty...99

Chapter Twenty-One..103

Chapter Twenty-Two...108

Chapter Twenty-Three..112

Chapter Twenty-Four..115

Chapter Twenty-Five...123

Chapter Twenty-Six...130

Chapter Twenty-seven...134

Chapter Twenty-Eight...139

Chapter Twenty-Nine..143

Chapter Thirty...147

Chapter Thirty-One...152

Chapter Thirty-Two...157

Chapter Thirty-Three..161

Chapter Thirty-Four..165

Chapter Thirty-Five..167
Chapter Thirty-six..172
Chapter Thirty-seven..176
Chapter Thirty-eight...181
Chapter Thirty-nine..184
Chapter Forty...189
Chapter Forty-one..195
Chapter Forty-two..201
Chapter Forty-three..203
Chapter Forty-four...207
Chapter Forty-five..211
Chapter Forty-six...216
Chapter Forty-seven...221
Chapter Forty-eight..224
Chapter Forty-nine...230
Chapter Fifty..234
Chapter Fifty-one...239
Chapter Fifty-two...242
Chapter Fifty-three...245
Chapter Fifty-four..248
Chapter Fifty-five...253
Chapter Fifty-six..255
Chapter Fifty-seven..259
Chapter Fifty-eight...262
Chapter Fifty-nine..264
Chapter Sixty...268
Chapter Sixty-one...272
Chapter Sixty-two...275
Chapter Sixty-three...278
Chapter Sixty-four..282
Chapter Sixty-five...288
Chapter Sixty-six..295
Chapter Sixty-seven..299
Chapter Sixty-eight...303
Chapter Sixty-nine..307
Chapter Seventy...311
Chapter Seventy-one...316

Chapter Seventy-two..319
Chapter Seventy-three..323
Chapter Seventy-four...327
Chapter Seventy-five..330
Chapter Seventy-six...333
Chapter Seventy-seven...336
Chapter Seventy-eight..339
Chapter Seventy-nine...344
Chapter Eighty...347
Chapter Eighty-one..350
Chapter Eighty-two..354
Chapter Eighty-three..359
Chapter Eighty-four...361
More by This Author...365
About the Author...367

CHAPTER ONE

After slipping on his signet ring, Blaise Lebreque donned the silver mask of the King of Jerusalem and prepared to meet the machine. He wore a black suit as a mark of his penitence, a crisp white shirt beneath with silver cuff links. A deep purple cape flowed from his shoulders, the garment perfectly weighted to strike the balance between tradition and impression. Blaise stepped from his vestry, and a pair of knights came to attention, half-capes allowing their sword-hands free movement. Haldan's eyes flared just a hint and he drew himself up taller, his ruddy mustache and beard twitching as he adjusted his demeanor to befit the honor of his role. Chloe swallowed hard, her gaze lifted to the mask, then away.

"Show me this alleged lion of truth that I may judge its value," Blaise said. The mask gave his voice a hollow effect and Chloe stiffened, her hand shifting on her sword-belt. It was only her second service. She would adjust. Blaise had faith in her.

"Yes, my lord." Haldan took the lead. "The vendors arrived about an hour ago, and we've left them in the temple with Darius."

"I helped to carry in the device, my lord," Chloe piped up from behind. "But it hasn't been tested."

Blaise nodded. "We'll see to that." As they walked from the smooth marble and sleek steel of the building's addition, they walked back through its history, down an early twentieth-century staircase, through an Ottoman-era doorway rich with carvings, and into a passage of medieval stonework.

Blaise relaxed into himself, wearing the impassive face of judgment. Their footfalls echoed in the arched corridor, and torches lit Haldan's form only to cast him back into shadow a moment later. As might be said of any man. At least Haldan and the other knights repented of the shadow they brought upon themselves. Haldan heaved open a massive wooden door, its base jagged by years of damp. Carved into a niche above, two knights rode a single horse, the age-old sign of the Knights Templar.

Darius stood alert to one side, hand on his hilt. At the heart of the round chamber, two people swung about, shoulders high and eyes wide. They drew closer together as Blaise entered, their gazes fixed to his mask.

"Welcome, good people. If you are honest and repent of your evils, you have nothing to fear in my chambers." Blaise's Turkish carried a faint French accent even after twenty-four years, so he spoke carefully, lest he be misunderstood. The cape rippled out behind, then swirled at his ankles as he stopped before them, gazing down at them from the empty eyes of his silver mask.

The woman chuckled, glancing to her companion, who nodded too many times. Perhaps this mode of entry lacked benevolence. Blaise smiled. They couldn't see the expression, but it would ring in his voice. "I understand you have brought me something?"

"Uh, yes, sir?" The woman said. She prodded the man, and he tried a smile of his own. They were in their twenties, without the bearing of academics. Perhaps they had inherited the device. He hoped, for their sake, they had not stolen it. Or carried it to him as a false offering from his enemies.

"It's a lion," the man blurted, raking dark hair out of his face as he took a few steps back. On the table behind them sat a large bundle wrapped in a blanket. "I don't really know what it does." He tugged the blanket away from the treasure it concealed: a seated lion with the blocky form of Byzantine sculpture, its contours covered in gold. No, not gold. Blaise grinned behind the mask and moved forward. This gleaming surface held chips brighter and valleys darker. Better than gold: orichalcum, the gilded bronze of the ancients. Few forgers would go to such trouble. The right leg showed unusual grooves in the surface. Jointing. Blaise imagined the diagrams of similar constructions he'd seen, and found a notch in the statue's base. He gently tugged at it, pulling a concealed lever.

With a soft, well-oiled groan, the lion raised its paw, drawing up a shield. The couple startled back from the table, and Haldan gave a quiet sound of delight as the lion moved. The shield bore an inscription in Greek: *Who speaks the truth fears no justice.* So similar to his own words, he wanted to reach out and give the creature a pat on the head.

On the table, the lion's head about reached Blaise's chest, its ears flattened back and broad mouth parted in a snarl. When he squatted down, he could see into the creature's dark throat where the mechanisms hid, anchored to a framework of wood. A thin metal tongue lolled inside the open jaw. His heart quickened. The restoration work was excellent. It had to be the work of a museum, possibly taken over the border from the wreck of Syria or another troubled nation. "It's quite remarkable. May I ask how you came by it?" Blaise cocked his head to look up at them. This position made him into the supplicant before the Lion of Truth.

The couple shared a glance, and the man wet his lips. "My father used to have a shop. He died, but I kept some of the stuff."

"We heard you pay for old machines?" The woman put herself forward, her lipstick too bright and clothes too tight. He wondered what she made of Chloe, a model of virtue and modesty.

"Automata," Blaise corrected. "Did your father perform the restoration?" He rose and prowled around the table, appearing to examine the lion from all angles, and really examining them. They brought him an exquisite piece, museum quality...honest inheritors? Desperate thieves? Or Nizari Isma'ili?

"I don't know," the man told him. "But it's good, right?" He flapped his hand toward the marvel between them. "It moved and everything."

"It remains to be seen how good. So, you didn't test the mechanism, but you knew it's not just a statue."

"Look, if you don't want it, we can find another customer," the woman said, and Haldan cleared his throat, calling attention to her rudeness. She glowered at him. "That robot woman, she's in town, I heard she likes this stuff, too."

Really. Blaise made a note of that. "Oh, no need to move on." He made sure to smile again as he rounded the table to stand by the lion's upraised paw. "If the inner mechanism is in working condition, my price doubles."

That brightened her face. "How do we test it?"

"One of you needs to place your hand into the lion's mouth and speak the truth." He gestured toward the creature. "Silly game, I know, but indulge me?"

The man fidgeted, and the woman gave him a nudge. "You go. It was your father."

"I mean, what does it do?" He eyed the lion sideways.

"Back in the Day, it might have released fumes, or roared." Blaise laughed warmly. "As I said, a parlor game for wealthy Byzantines."

"Fumes? Like poison?"

Blaise regarded the creature affectionately. "I was lucky the lift mechanism still worked after a thousand years. It's unlikely anything hazardous could have lasted for so long." He shrugged. "Ah, well. I can still give you something—"

"He'll test it, won't you? For double?" The woman prodded her man toward the table.

The man glanced toward the elevated paw, then the mouth, then back up to Blaise's impassive mask as if he tried to get a glimpse of the mechanisms there, too. "Sure. Parlor game." He yanked his hand out of his pocket and placed it in the lion's mouth. "I love you, babe!" he announced, and started to swipe his hand away again.

Blaise braced the man's elbow, making sure his palm touched the lion's tongue. "Where did you get this?"

"I told you that." The man's gaze Danced now, his arm jerking back against Blaise's grip.

"Tell me again." Blaise lost his smile, letting his hollow voice go deep.

"Hey," the woman said, but Chloe stepped up to her.

"You know how far that money could go," Chloe said, woman to woman.

"My father's shop!" the man said in a rush, then his body thrashed and he shrieked, the smell of something roasting emerged from the lion's mouth with a curl of steam.

Blaise let go immediately, but the frisson of power had made his skin tingle, even through the layers of clothing. A Baghdad battery triggered by a sweaty palm. How intriguing. The young man dropped to the floor, spasming against the mosaic. A thief, then. Nizari would have shown greater control.

"Altu!" The woman pounced toward the stricken man, then stopped. "Will it get me?" She pulled back her hands.

"Are you telling the truth?" Blaise inquired, but he did not wait for an answer. He knelt at the young man's side. "I suggest you repent of your wrongdoings," he said softly.

"Get away from me! Are you fucking crazy?" Bloody spittle flew from the young man's mouth. "Who the hell do you think you are?" He cradled his burned hand and tried to dig in his heels to push away from Blaise.

Blaise pinned the young man with his palm to the beat of frantic heart. "The heir to the throne of Jerusalem. It is my burden to bring peace to this troubled region. If you submit to penance and move forward in humility, that peace could be yours as well."

Altu spat at the mask, trying to roll away. Pity. The future needed strong young people to rebuild all they had lost. Blaise scooped an arm beneath him as if to help Altu off the ground. The young man stilled briefly, and Blaise grabbed his face, shifting his other hand to the nape of the man's neck. He wrenched Altu's head to the side, feeling the snap and grind, pulling hard to be sure he severed the spine, a merciful death.

Blaise remained on one knee, holding the body as the eyes rolled back, the lungs failed, the frantic heartbeat stuttered.

The woman started screaming and Blaise heard the commotion around him as his knights caught her and brought her near. She struggled and wept. "No, please, no! I repent! Whatever—don't kill me, praise to

Allah, please don't kill me!"

Chloe lowered the woman to her knees, steadying alongside the body of her companion. Sobs wracked her form, exaggerating the thrust of her breasts in her immodest clothes.

Blaise held out his hand. "Kiss my ring in token of your repentance." The dead man's head drooped toward the ground, blood dripping on the mosaic.

She grabbed Blaise's hand, eager now to show her faith, and kissed, then flinched as the barbs pierced her. She pulled away, hand to her lips, finding a trace of blood. Her eyelids fluttered, and she sagged into Chloe's arms.

"Darius? Bring her to our allies. She is of their faith, and perhaps they can bring her back to the fold."

"Yes, my lord." Darius helped Chloe take up the unconscious woman and bear her away.

Haldan stood nearby. "Will you sit in vigil, my lord?" The knight's fingers tapped on his sword hilt.

"I will cleanse myself of this, but there is no need for you to stay." He lifted his masked face to gaze at the knight. "After all, you've a party to attend, with that robot woman."

"Yes, my lord. May it bring us that much closer to your reign."

"Amen," said Blaise, and his guard departed, leaving him to sit in penance for the unrepentant dead.

CHAPTER TWO

Four meters under a mosque in Istanbul, Grant Casey stood at parade rest, watching himself work the room in a way he'd never done in his life.

The other him was good at this, sticking close by the client's side, suppressing his gregarious nature as he deflected questions about Genghis Khan's tomb and that thing in Arizona—can't really say much until the trials are over, leaning in conspiratorially to one of their local contacts, you understand. The client, Kyra Akbulut, kept glancing toward the conservation room barred off from one wedge of the octagonal chamber. Bookshelves spread out in rays from the central opening where she waited, impatient for her big moment, while the imitation Grant Casey at her shoulder played at being a bodyguard. He scanned too quickly, not proper technique, but good enough to fool the average observer. In the dim light of the medieval archive, with his hair raked across one side of his face, he could even pass for Grant from twenty or so paces. Up close, he could've been a Bollywood star. Vivek Destry, actor, playing the role of Grant Casey. Maybe Grant should keep him on payroll. Meantime, Grant kept scanning. Man with a limp, two women keeping close to the encircling bookshelves, skinny young reporter trying to work out the settings for his camera, not allowed to use a flash in the vault. The place smelled musty, as if two millennia of mites and moisture conspired in the gaps where the ancient building settled deeper into the contested earth, making a claim to its place in a city that could barely keep the same name for more than a century.

Across the room, near a temporary dais that intruded among the books and scrolls, Nick matched Grant's pose. He wore an identical bespoke suit with a subtle Bone Guard logo stitched in at the breast pocket. What would be next, pocket squares? It looked good on him, though, black from his buzz-cut head to the shiny toe of his leather shoes—until his teeth flashed in a grin, his gaze tracking the other Grant.

Grant muttered, "Nick, eyes on the prize, okay?" The ear piece he wore picked up his voice even that low. He'd have to compliment D.A. on the upgrades.

Nick dragged his eyes from the actor to the barred door opposite, where the star attraction would soon appear. "Dang, Chief, that is one good-looking man. Better looking than you are, for sure."

Grant shot him a brief glare, then continued to scan the room. Nicely dressed men and women, some with head scarfs, glasses of champagne in spite of the ranks of rare books that climbed the ancient shelves toward a distant ceiling. "If somebody hires you a promotional stand-in, you don't pick the ugly one."

Nick laughed, nodded to one of the passing women. "This is a fine gig, Chief, but I hope I can get some of that champagne once this party's over."

Two servers doled out drinks from a makeshift station, an open case of bottles beside them. "I'm sure Ms. Akbulut would be happy to provide." She'd already given them two days of sight-seeing on top of the situational briefing—hard to object to that kind of treatment. His scan caught for a moment on a familiar face, or so he thought.

"See something?" Nick shifted a little as if his necktie were pinching, allowing him to glance in the direction of Grant's hesitation. Excellent wingman, as sensitive to Grant's expression as the mic was to his voice.

"Negative." Still made his heart race at the idea of seeing her. The Phantom. Flickering pseudo-candles made the whole archive hard to scan and cast so many faces into shadow. Shelves receded back in octagonal symmetry to walls of stone he remembered from their earlier circuit, but now could not discern.

"Told you, Chief, details, not ops. Every time you get an op, it gets us in trouble." Nick straightened and cut the chatter as the room gathered to attention around the podium.

Their host, the archive's curator, stepped up to the podium, and Kyra Akbulut moved quickly to join him, her thick, black braid swinging against the silk of her shirt. She did everything quickly, with an efficiency of movement that recalled her most famous creation, the Homedroid. When they first met, he wondered if she cultivated the style deliberately, drawing herself closer to her machines. Good marketing. Hence this whole publicity thing. Hence the other "Grant Casey" who stood at her shoulder, a visible suggestion of several layers of power, not just the strength of former warriors, but also the wealth it took to fly them to Turkey just to stand around at an event like this.

"Thank you all for coming," the curator began. "And thank you, Ms. Akbulut, for your generous support of the library that will allow us to conserve so many of these ancient works, and create a suitable display space so that we may, at last, open our doors to the public."

Kyra smiled and nodded, offering a little wave at the polite applause. At her shoulder, the other Grant stifled a smile and twitched to wave on his own behalf, as if the audience were there for him. Actors.

"And so, as a measure of our gratitude, Ms. Akbulut, allow me to offer you the unprecedented opportunity to transport for conservation and study one of our rare works, the so-called Crusader Codex. From our examination, we find that this compilation includes a number of accounts of the siege of Constantinople during the Fourth Crusade, including what appear to be diagrams of the legendary Byzantine automata some crusaders claim to have seen. Neglected for years, due to its poor condition, the content of this manuscript has only recently become known, and I am sure it will open many new avenues of inquiry for scholars near and far. I will welcome its return along with the results of your scientific analysis." The archivist gave a short gesture.

An old man emerged from the locked wedge of the library, beyond the barred door. He carried a handled wooden box inscribed with carvings and edged in the black accumulation of centuries. Tickets to Istanbul, cases of champagne, all that stuff Grant could take or leave. The chance to be among the first to view the codex after its discovery? Yeah, he was on board. The old man shuffled nearer, holding up the box, and Kyra's smile spread.

"Thank you, Curator. I've engaged Grant Casey, and the Bone Guard, to ensure the safety of this valuable text during its transportation." Kyra tipped her head toward Grant's stand-in, and Vivek accepted the box on her behalf, then—reluctantly—stepped back from the center of attention. "I can't say how much it means to me to be given this chance to view evidence of medieval practitioners of the robotic arts." She smiled, cameras clicked and bloggers murmured. "I will look forward to—"

Another click, small but distinct, and distinctly out of place in the crowd. Grant turned sharply. Toward the back, a man's arm raised, a short staff in his hand.

"Nick! Five o'clock. Cover the prize!" Grant lunged forward.

Even as he moved, the other Grant Casey staggered, blown backward. He crumpled to the floor around a rush of blood.

CHAPTER THREE

G rant's gut clenched as if he had, indeed, absorbed the impact. "Take care of the target, I'm on the perp!"

"On it," Nick replied. Each of them moved with military speed and accuracy while around them, civilians scattered.

"Give him space! The rest of you, get down!" Grant shouted, repeating the message in two other languages. He pointed toward the archive's own security guard. "And call an ambulance."

The guy with the rod took a step forward, still aiming at Vivek. One of the women rammed into his side so his shot went wild. He spun about, swinging the rod for her head, but she was already gone, scattered like the others—or not. Ducking his swing and turning sharply, she swept her foot around for his knees. The guy leapt her, making for the stacks.

Grant dodged the crowd, vaulted a low shelf into the aisle where the man had gone. When the perp spun about, Grant caught the man's wrist, squeezing hard as he yanked the arm up, aiming the weapon toward the sky. The man grunted, turning with the woman's assault and now finding himself pinned between them. "Drop it!" No guns allowed in the library, but Grant slid a knife from his belt, the point pressing into his captive's spine.

The woman pivoted, recovering from the perp's speedy escape, and her eyes flicked up, pale green, flashing in recognition and surprise. Her glance darted toward the podium, toward the fallen man. He hadn't seen her for more than a year, but he would never mistake her. The Phantom.

As if aware of the brief distraction, the assassin rocked himself backward onto Grant's knife, overbalancing them both and crashing into a bookshelf. He wrenched his arm downward, turning hard. Ignoring the knife carving into him, he landed a flurry of blows. He fought in silence, in spite of the blade, his narrow face grim as Grant blocked the blows aimed at his head and stomach. Where had she gone? No time to wonder. He ducked a back-handed swing of the rod, then slammed that hand against the shelf. Still the guy didn't let go of his weapon.

A high kick slammed Grant's side and he twisted back to solid footing. The guy's other hand dropped to his pocket, and Grant dodged, expecting a gun. Instead, the shooter produced a butane lighter. He snapped it on and swept the flame along the nearest shelf. The yellowed paper of exposed pages curled and crackled. Shit.

The lighter swung toward Grant's face, searing his cheek before he turned aside and brought his knee into the other man's crotch. Yeah, no sympathy for that kind of bastard.

Even that the man absorbed in silence. He dropped to his knees, pulling free from Grant's grip to tumble away. He swept the lighter along a woman's dress as she tried to flee the scene and she screamed. Then the perp was up, his weapons vanishing under his coat. Grant's knife clattered to the ground as the guy fled, pushing through the bewildered crowd and lunging up the stairs. Pursuit or damage control? Grant took in the scene. Books burned behind him, the woman's gown flared up ahead, a horrible beacon in the gloom. No question his choice of action.

"Down, get down and roll!" Grant moved toward the woman, but the Phantom was already there, calling out to the victim, clasping her. Turning aside, Grant stripped off his suit coat to smother the flames that crackled along the texts. He left his jacket there and sprinted past the shelves back to the open space where Nick crouched over the other Casey, stabilizing a shaft that thrush from his lower abdomen. Vivek choked and gasped.

"How bad is it?"

"I won't be you anymore," the actor panted, as tears streaked his face. "I quit. I won't be Grant Casey if it means getting shot."

And beaten, bound, gagged, stabbed, blown up, and occasionally thrown into a cactus. "Sometimes, buddy," Grant told him, "I'm right there with you. Nick's taking care of you—you're in good hands."

Kyra Akbulut paced on the other side of the barred door, the curator huddling nearby, each of them on a cell phone, each speaking a different language. Before it opened, that door stopped anyone from grabbing their goodies, it wouldn't stop a bullet. She froze when she saw him and covered the microphone. "Where's the box? The codex?"

He swept a glance across the floor: blood, Vivek's thrashing form, Nick tearing away the actor's clothes to work on the wound. The box was nowhere to be seen.

"We're good here," Nick said. "Go!"

With that, Grant ran, sliding between the scattering crowd as they stumbled upstairs and spilled onto a cobbled street. The bleat of foreign sirens reverberated from thousand-year-old walls. Far ahead, stumbling as he ran, the assassin moved away from the sound of police—and his hands were empty. Shit. Grant spun about. Seventeen women, twenty-eight men in the archive. One of the women was the Phantom, one of the men was the shooter. Could the Phantom be here to steal the book he was paid to guard? A handful of cars stood along the narrow street, and a few people piled into them, more than the people who'd arrived in them. Grant blocked the first one, slamming his hand on the hood. "Security! We need to search—"

Their eyes looked round and terrified as he popped the doors. Nothing. Moved on to the second vehicle. Where the hell was the box? How could it be concealed so fast?

"What are you doing? You're not security." A beefy man behind the wheel of the car, glaring over a red-gold beard.

The sound of a motorcycle starting up. There! Fifty yards beyond, the rider had a bulky parcel under his arm, and another twenty terrified curators, collectors and librarians wailing in between. The rider could be her: he'd mistaken her for a man the first time they met. "Let me through!" Grant rocked into motion, then a sudden flash in his eyes, and he tripped over someone.

"Wasn't that your boss who got shot?" A thin kid thrust a camera in Grant's face. Grant swiped the camera easy and started shooting, zooming in on the escaping biker as he streaked up the street toward a sharp turn.

"Hey! You can't do that!" The kid's hands grabbed for his camera, making Grant feel like a mean big brother.

"Someone's been shot, and something's been stolen. Take it up with Ms. Akbulut, but get out of my way."

"Okay—but I want the story."

Who did he think he was, Jimmy Olsen on the track of Superman? "You won't get it from me."

The cycle spun around the curve and Grant tracked it in his head. That road came back around to join up maybe two blocks north. Yanking the camera strap over his wrist, he pivoted and started running, alert for the sound of the motorcycle as it curved toward him. He dodged the approaching ambulance, put on a burst of speed as the bike's engine grew louder. They reached the corner at the same time, the biker taking a minimal pause to check traffic.

Grant surged and leaped, slamming into the biker and toppling him to the ground. The bike whined in a half circle and scraped into a lamppost, wheels spinning. The biker rapped Grant with his helmeted head and scrambled to his feet. The helmet turned, scanning, and they both spotted the bundle, the ancient box revealed beneath the scarf used to wrap it. The biker pounced and Grant swept his ankle, bowling him into the street.

Tires squealed and a black sedan lurched to a halt between them. Shit. But the box remained. Grant grabbed the handle and hauled it toward him, the dangling camera clattering across cobblestones. He tucked the box like a football. Beyond the hood of the car, the thief staggered through a crowd of tourists and vanished. Grant aimed a glare at the car that had enabled the getaway.

"That's an alley! I know where it goes!" shouted the guy inside, in accented English. "Get in!"

Grant swung open the door to find the bearded man who had shouted at him earlier.

"You're not security," the guy said, "I am."

He looked familiar from Grant's scanning, and from the earlier security briefing. Grant dropped into the seat, box on his lap, and the guy hit the gas almost before he'd closed the door. They squealed around the tourists and the car roared down a narrow street. Cars parked half on the sidewalks to both sides, and a delivery van pulled around a corner toward them, only to stop and reverse as Grant's driver gunned his engine. They shot past the delivery van and accelerated down a brief straightaway before turning hard across a narrow alley left over Roman times. Empty.

The driver slammed his fist against his steering wheel, breathing hard as he slumped back in his seat. Grant popped his door and stood up from the car, taking advantage of a higher view to scan the streets around. Minarets and domes interrupted the stacked old houses and twisted paths, with a steeple here and there just for variety. Lots of people: women shopping, vendors hawking, tourists gawking. Nobody limping in a conspicuous hurry. Damn. At least he had the box. Grant sank back into his seat and shut the door. "Thanks for trying."

"Doing our job, right?" The guy grinned at him. "At least you retrieved the chest." He put the car into gear and started off at a more careful pace, heading away from the archive. Probably looking for a place to turn Probably.

"Michael Donahue," Grant said, using the assumed name he'd taken for this op. "With the Bone Guard working for Kyra Akbulut. Who're you?"

"Haldan Brunelle." He glanced down at the ancient wooden box under Grant's arm. "Do you want to put that in the back? Might as well be comfortable."

"I think Ms. Akbulut would be more comfortable if I hung onto it. She's very concerned about the codex." He shifted it into his lap. Brunelle

15

presented as an ally and drove like an operator, heading resolutely away from the archives. He didn't appear to be armed. The squint at his eye and the sheen of sweat at his temple suggested the guy was going off script and doing his best. Grant wasn't too worried. Yet.

"So will the archive be, naturally. They were hesitant even to reveal they had it, much less its location in the vault." As Brunelle turned the wheel, a cross tattoo on the inside of his wrist peeked out from one shirt cuff.

"Your accent. Not Turkish or Greek. Sounds Germanic. Do you mind my asking?" Grant ran his hands over the box, worked-iron hinges, iron handle, truncated triangle for the lid, a classic medieval shape A piece of wood had cracked at the back with what appeared to be fresh damage. The box felt light, dried out over centuries. Or...

Brunelle chuckled. "I think of myself as Varangian Guard—you've heard of this?"

Nice. Didn't address the question, but Grant flashed a smile of his own. "Vikings in Byzantium in defense of the empire. What's not to love? Pull over, would you? I need to check something."

Brunelle's hands tightened on the wheel, then he gave a nod and pulled over alongside a souk, packed with stalls, vendors, tourists and scammers. So, Brunelle was an operator, but not experienced with abductions, confirming Grant's suspicion that they were both improvising. In ten seconds, Grant could disappear into that crowd and never been seen again. In the meantime, he wiggled free the thousand-year-old latch and opened the lid.

"Are you sure you should expose—?" Brunelle stopped abruptly and both men stared into the empty box.

CHAPTER FOUR

Kyra Akbulut aimed her hardest of stares as Casey rushed out the doors, efficiently streaming past the others to do as she asked. Some security guard or another shouted for calm, and nobody listened. Panic and anger echoed off the stone walls to beat at her ears. Behind the gridded door in the heart of the archive, Kyra paced like a jaguar. Nobody was supposed to get shot. Take some photos, write a large check, and walk out of here with the key to proving her father's legacy. Hire in some flashy mercenaries to add gravity to an otherwise routine exchange of favors. It wasn't the sort of thing someone got shot for, until suddenly one of her hirelings lay on the floor in a pool of blood while two others worked clean-up for the disaster. And she had just gotten off the phone with her lawyer to make sure she wasn't criminally liable.

The wounded man cried out, and Kyra flinched. Bile rose in her throat.

"Stay here, Miss. Let the security take care of everything. Everything's going to be fine," said the curator next to her. He patted her hand and tried a smile that trembled in all the wrong ways.

Stay here, and cower like an old man. No. Kyra straightened her back, tossed her braid over her shoulder and strode out into the chamber. The old man yelped behind her. "Miss Akbulut! Please!"

All he wanted was the money. That was all anyone ever wanted from her, the money, or the technology that created it. The danger had gone, fleeing up the stairs a few paces before the Bone Guard went after them, but even Casey hadn't seen them take the box. The smell of burnt manuscripts tinged the air now, a swirl of smoke obscuring the upper shelves. A woman with a blackened dress sat sobbing on a chair while one of the champagne servers offered comfort.

Kyra turned on her heel and stalked closer to the stricken man. "How is he?"

The big, Black man—what did Casey call him? Nick?—knelt awkwardly with his right leg stuck out along the body. Not the body, the victim. Destry. As she watched, Nick unzipped his pantleg up to the knee, with a zipper worked invisibly into the seam. Underneath, a sleek, state-of-the-art carbon fiber prosthetic showed above an ordinary sock. He pried up a panel on the side of his leg and slipped out a knife with his right hand. The lack of two fingers on his right hand was obvious, the prosthetic, much less so.

"Where did you get that?" Kyra said before she could stop herself. She squatted alongside them. "Sorry, that's the wrong question. I wasn't aware you had a prosthetic."

He shot her a look, gave a slight shake of his head, and got back to work. His left hand still braced the short shaft that emerged from Destry's side. Now his right hand deftly slit the shirt away from the injury. "First question you asked was the better one, Ms. Akbulut. How is he?" Nick smiled down at Destry. "Well, he's in some pain, as you'd imagine, but I hear an ambulance on the way already, and I'm an army-trained field medic. I've seen a lot worse than this."

Destry grimaced back up at him with a desperate nod, and Kyra studied Nick's face, trying to determine if he was lying. She brought up her cellphone again, sliding through a few screens to find the right app for that. He radiated warmth through his baritone voice and carefully paced words, then glanced at her again with an edge like that knife in his hand. "If you're not busy, Ms. Akbulut, you could ask if they have a proper first aid kit."

"I wouldn't think so," she replied. A frown pinched her mouth. The app was having trouble reading his features. An effect of the dim lighting, the smoky air, or the simple fact that, once again, the developers had trained their software only on other Silicon Valley pasty faces.

"Put down the phone and find out."

She didn't need an app to read his hostility. Kyra pushed to her feet and peered around the room, trying to find anyone competent. "You!" she called out in Turkish, pointing at one of the archivists who held a discarded Bone Guard suit coat in one hand and a singed manuscript in the other. "Yes. Put those down and find a medical kit."

"Right! Of course." The man hurriedly complied. Or perhaps just hurried out of view, the jacket flapping in his grip.

Kyra's phone quivered in her hand, and she glanced at it. One new message.

>*Bad time? Jemma626*

Perfect time, really. >*Someone's been shot > with some kind of Dart*

>*Not by me > who else is interested?*

>*none I know of*

>*think again*

Kyra's jaw clenched and her thumbs hovered over the keyboard like raptors, but she could not think of a reply before another message popped up.

>*price is rising*

"Ms. Akbulut, if you could—"

Kyra shook her head. >*so you have it?*

>*considering an auction*

No auction, just name the new price. Kyra hesitated, then replied >*Do you have it?*

>*I control it*

A black hand wrapped the cellphone and twisted it from her grip. Kyra yelped. "What are you doing? That's private."

Nick ignored her as he slid the phone into an inside pocket and stripped off his tie. "You hold or you wrap." He thrust out the tie.

"What are you talking about? You need to give back my phone. You people have already ruined this event, and I won't stand for—"

Nick caught her elbow and drew her down beside him, forcing her to meet his eye. "Did you sign off on the combat clause? In the contract? Because none of us got on board for assassination. Not me, not the Chief, and certainly not Vivek." He bunched the tie in his hand, then stretched his fingers out again, as if he had to forcibly restrain himself—from what?

"I thought I was signing on the most competent crew I could, and now I see I was wrong. This is hardly the time—"

"Damn straight. When the Chief gets back, he will read you chapter and verse, and don't say a damn thing about competence, Lady, or I will not pull my punches. You knew what you were setting us up for, and you didn't tell. As of now, we're making double. Him, too." He nodded to Vivek. "So. You hold or you wrap. We need to get this thing stabilized for transfer to the hospital."

Kyra glanced down again at Destry. Sweat beaded his face, and maybe tears, his skin gone ashy. She likely didn't look much better. She swallowed hard. "I—I have a problem with blood." Her glance cut away toward the rough mosaics of the floor. Even there, tendrils of red crept between the tiny stones.

"Really."

In a rush, she said, "I have a problem with blood. My father died of a hemorrhagic fever. I have a problem with blood, I told you!"

Nick's demeanor shifted as if he were taking off a mask. Was he in his right mind? He toggled from tough guy to tender heart so quickly, as if he ran two programs simultaneously on different channels of his mind. "Hey, hey, it's okay. In that case, you hold. You keep your eyes averted, I guide your hand. You game?"

Game? What even—Destry gave a whimper, and Kyra clenched her jaw, still tracing the patterns of the mosaic, trying not to follow the patterns of blood. She held out her hand to the side. Nick grasped it firmly, gently. "Here," he directed, placing her hand against the damp heat of Destry's side, some sort of cloth already wadded there. At least she needn't touch the blood directly.

"Press down, hold here." He wrapped her thumb and forefinger around the shaft, holding her hand in place a moment as she took over. Kyra nodded, her braid slithering down off her shoulder. She cried out, imagining its dark tail dipped in the stranger's blood. Nick squeezed her hand, then let go. He flicked her braid across her neck to the other side, then shifted around, working at something.

Destry moaned softly, and Nick crooned to him, "Don't worry, we're taking care of you. Chief and Ms. Akbulut, they're gonna make sure you get the finest care. Hey, do something for me, Vivek, if you would?"

"What?" A rough whisper.

"You keep playing your role. Last thing we want right now is the enemy knowing they got the wrong guy."

"The enemy?" Destry stammered, more clearly this time, and Kyra's head lifted at the same moment. She hired them for the projected menace of military men—for their brawn, not their brains. What could the man possibly be thinking?

"We're gonna find out what's behind all of this, Vivek, and it'll be a lot easier if they think our boss is in the hospital, understand? Sure you do—you're not just a pretty face, I know that. You've got a thousand things going on behind those incredible eyes."

Excellent. Now he was flirting. What else had she not known about these men?

Destry gave a soft whuff of something like laughter.

"Clear the way!" Someone shouted in Turkish, then a pair of uniformed men rushed down the stairs with a box of medical supplies and a folded stretcher. "Where's the patient?"

"He speaks English," Nick reported, easing his leg back, preparing to rise. At some point, he'd re-zipped his pantleg, concealing the prosthetic, and who knew what else.

"Can you tell me the name?" the first responder asked carefully in English. "Yours?"

"Grant Casey," Vivek murmured. "The Bone Guard." Kyra caught a glimpse of his movie-screen smile, tremulous though it was.

"That's a good man," Nick said. "You'll be alright. We'll be over as soon as we can, Casey." Nick brought up his arm, guiding Kyra back, and the two of them rose, Nick's hand now cupping her elbow.

As the emergency crew got to work, Kyra caught a glimpse of Nick's tie, expertly wound around Destry's middle, with the actor's own tie, working together to keep the shaft from moving. Perhaps she'd gone slightly off course by impugning the men's competence. Though she still had no word of Casey and the box. "May I have my phone back?"

Nick handed it over without a word. Which Nick was he at that moment? His face looked too calm, not the stern warrior nor the soothing counselor. If she could work out how Nick controlled his features, it could rip the Uncanny Valley problem wide open.

"You told him Ca—that your crew would work to find out who did this." She lifted her chin, trying to command Nick's gaze, glad of her thick heels for the extra few inches they gave her. It still wasn't enough for parity.

His gaze shifted incrementally across the chamber, taking in the blood, the commotion around the downed man, the cluster of archivists near the burnt books. "Hemorrhagic fever? That's rough."

Kyra regretted saying anything, regretted that her filters so often failed her just when she needed them most. "Can we please focus on the matter at hand? Given what's happened here, I presume that the Bone Guard will be stepping aside to allow a proper investigation by the Turkish authorities."

Nick pursed his lips. "Really. You planning to be just as honest with them as you were with us?" He shook his head slowly. "Hurts like an SOB, you know, getting shot."

"I imagine it would, and I hope I never find out." Her cell phone buzzed softly and her fingers itched to bring it up to her face. She tucked her hands under her arms cell phone and all. Give him no excuse to cross that line again.

"I hope so, too, Ms. Akbulut. But you know what hurts worse?" He swiveled to face her, and the mask hid everything beside his eyes, deep-brown pools of sorrow. "Knowing somebody else took a shot meant for you. You think the Chief's done here, and I'm telling you, he's not even begun."

CHAPTER FIVE

laise sat in front of the table, legal pad on his lap, ankle crossed over his knee. He wore glasses he didn't need because they made him look more engaged, and gave him something to remove when he wanted to shift to a more intimate register. The small conference room gave too strong an impression of corporate unconcern, so he had moved the proceedings to one end, himself with his back to the big table, the occupying chairs he had placed a careful angle from which they could see each other, and him. Out the window behind them, the exquisite skyline of Istanbul glowed in the late afternoon sun, minarets pointing the sky as if to indicate God's presence, church domes resting like warm eggs underneath, and the squared-off structures of everyday living filled in all around them, a jostling, beautiful gathering of humanity, rather like the pair before him. Brothers, estranged by their father's death.

After the eldest trailed off a moment ago, his younger brother sitting in stony silence, Blaise allowed the silence to grow, regarding his notepad full of irrelevant remarks. Finally, he replaced the cap on his pen, and removed his glasses, tucking them in his pocket and leaning forward, fingers pressed together. "Thank you for agreeing to meet under these less formal circumstances. It is clear to me that each of you prizes your father's legacy—"

The younger immediately began to speak, but Blaise held up his hand, and the man subsided into a glower. "Mavi. You perceive your brother's desire to change the business and move on to new markets as an attack upon your father's memory."

"Yes! Yes, exactly." Mavi crossed his arms and shot his brother a look as if Blaise had just confirmed everything he believed in.

"It's not so! Father and I talked about this plan when he was alive. You'd know that if you had—" Aziz started up again, but he subsided when Blaise directed his gaze, and his comforting gesture in that direction.

"Aziz. You stayed very close to your father during the last months of his illness. You regard yourself as the keeper of that legacy, and you hope to carry on his wishes with your portion of the business."

Aziz jabbed a finger toward him, then toward the heavens. "Just as he would have wished."

"You both agreed to arbitration because you don't wish your father's business to be torn apart by these proceedings, but at the same time, each of you believes he is the one to best carry that business forward." Blaise wheeled his chair slightly forward. "I am not here to tell you what to do, but to help you listen to each other, and understand together what is best for you both, and for the legacy your father left you. It is my task to make clear to you the things you might not speak aloud." He spread his hands, opening the moment to them both. "What you must know, Aziz, is that Mavi didn't stay away from the hospital because he was so eager for money that he disdained your father. To him, his work as the buyer meant preserving the relationships with your vendors which struggled already because of your father's decline. Mavi's work was how he showed his love."

Mavi's arms folded more tightly, and he glanced upward, his eyes sparkling. Aziz blinked a few times, and seemed about to speak, but refrained. Awkward for them both to have their emotions laid out by a virtual stranger. Awkward in a way that would draw them together, if he treated them carefully.

"This is not the court of Solomon where I say I will cut the business in half, and the one of you who loves it more will give up his half to the other to see it preserved." Blaise smiled gently. "It is very clear to me how much each of you loves what your father has made, and how much each of you wishes it to continue."

"Fine, we both love it," Aziz snapped. "How does that help us if we can't agree what to do with it?"

Blaise drew a deep breath. "Curious to say, but the first step will be to part yourselves from your father's plans. You both wish to uphold his legacy, but that does not mean you must adhere to his instructions. Aziz is hopeful for change and growth. Imagine that he takes that hope into a new arena, expanding the store's offerings and seeking new partners. Yes, your father appointed you as the floor manager, and you have done very well, but you see beyond the shop doors. Mavi, on the other hand, strives to preserve. If he were to return, taking over the daily operations, he would ensure a strong platform from which new ventures might set forth, and to which the family can stay close if those risks don't quickly show benefit."

Aziz puffed a derisive breath. "You're saying we trade roles. We keep the business intact, and simply—what—change ourselves."

Mavi's crossed arms parted at last, open almost in a prayer. "You could go to the trade shows, see what else is out there. You would love that, Aziz." His smile faded a little, and he said, "Wouldn't you?"

For a moment, the elder surveyed the city outside the windows. "You'd be stuck here, in the shop, talking to the same customers, every day, the same conversations with the tourists."

When Mavi laughed, Blaise sat back in his seat, withdrawing from the conversation. Mavi waved away his brother's objections. "That's what I do—talking to people, having the same conversation, but making it better and stronger every time. So Babi gave us these jobs, he groomed us for this, but imagine we could both be happier, and still keep his memory. Don't you think he would rather see us together?" Mavi put out his hand, reaching.

After a moment, Aziz took it, nodding, but still refusing to smile. "We'll need a contract, a plan. If this doesn't work out..."

Blaise said, "I shall ask the lawyers back in to help you with the terms. It's been a pleasure working with you. I wish you both every success." He took each of their hands in turn, laying his free hand gently over and pressing, meeting their eyes. "If you'll excuse me," and walked a few paces to the far end of the table, his phone vibrating in his pocket. Haldan. Blaise tapped to ignore the call for now. Haldan would be patient.

Blaise stepped out the door where the lawyers were waiting.

"They went from daggers out to shaking hands—did you just do us out of a hundred billable hours?" Baris Ozan, one of the senior partners asked, then squeezed Blaise's shoulder. "You ever thought of running for office?"

Blaise demurred with a wave of his hand. "I don't wish to be beholden to a single side of any conflict."

"I'm so glad you're coming to Cyprus next week, for the Davos-ME. The region could really use someone like you," said Ozan, his grin widening as if he planned to devour Blaise along with the clients. "Have you heard about the yacht the Arabs are bringing? It's as big as a hotel, but lying down —They're hosting Thursday's dinner."

"To help the wealthy celebrate the spoils of the wars they fund? I can hardly wait." Davos-ME, for Middle East: the premier Mediterranean marketplace of heads of state and figureheads, and the men who bought and sold them. Those men wanted to pretend they were world leaders, like the people who gathered at Davos in Switzerland, when in fact, they were the men who ruined the Middle East, riding it into the ground for their own gain. He would be there—but not in the way Ozan intended.

"Ah, you're an idealist? How long have you been living here, and you still think there's any other way?" Ozan laughed, his tie flapping against his belly. "At least you don't mind fine dining at the billionaires' expense."

"Sometimes, the lion must lay down with the lamb, Baris." Ignoring the partner's puzzled expression, Blaise ushered them in to the room he had left. Then he returned the call.

"Tell me," he said in French. Blaise strolled the corridor, swapping waves and signs of approval with the rest of the team as he made his way to a balcony where he could get some privacy.

"Empty," Haldan told him. "The box was empty. Another man there, one of those Bone Guards, chased down the retrieval agent, in spite of my efforts to stop him. When he got hold of the box, I offered a ride in case we needed to take him in, but we opened it and found it was already empty."

"He couldn't have taken it without your noticing?"

"No, sir. He thinks me a buffoon, for how I got in the way, but the agent had dropped the box. The agent had no chance to hand off the codex either. The entire event—sir, it was chaos, just as we planned." He briefed Blaise on what happened at the archives, then added, "I was by the stairs the entire time, and I'm sure the box went from storage to the Bone Guard, then to our agent. Nobody opened it until I had it in my car."

Beating the rail softly with his fist, Blaise contained his frustration. Davos-ME began in just a few days. His allies wanted to go ahead regardless of whether he was ready. Prior to the discovery of the codex, he'd been inclined to agree, but this chance was too exceptional to pass up. "I presume our agents are on the way to the temple?"

"Yes. The police have pictures. But who would intervene like this? Hardly anyone knows about the codex, much less cares what it contains."

"It must be the Nizari—who else? The Assassins will do anything to stop me."

"We'll make sure they never get close, my lord." He dropped to sotto voce for the title, and Blaise warmed with the knowledge of this man's loyalty. This man, and all of his other knights.

"This Bone Guard. Do you think he trusts you? Could you get him to? We need to know what they're doing. Also, we need word from the hospital."

"Yes, sir. I've also asked Chloe to step up her involvement. What else?"

What else indeed? Blaise rested his hand on the rail, gazing toward the Sea of Marmara—Syria, Iran, Lebanon, Israel—all those warring factions in need of a common vision of peace. In Cyprus, they would gather, looking to wealth to lead them, not knowing it would merely shackle them in corruption and apostasy. The key had been within his grasp, only to be stolen away by the agents of fury, those who reaped what vengeance sowed. "I shall ask the head. Baphomet may have another secret for me."

CHAPTER SIX

After too little questioning by the local police, Grant and Nick escorted their client, by limousine, to her house on the outskirts of the city center, a ride hardly long enough to justify the luxury. Grant kept his eyes on Nick, watching for a break, while Akbulut kept her eyes on her phone, texting furiously. Nick raised his eyebrows and tipped his head in her direction, then rolled his eyes, and Grant gave the slightest nod in reply. A tech millionaire attached to her device. Imagine that. Nick's tie had gone and a streak of blood marked his right cuff. Grant's humor faded as quickly as it flared. A cushy job gone wrong. Imagine that.

The uniformed driver held the door for the client, and Grant stepped out first, stepping straight into vigilance. He'd lost his jacket to fire control, and his knife to the local authorities. Well, one of his knives. Still he slid into the familiar role as if he were putting on his favorite jeans.

In a square, beige structure, a pair of patterned blue doors carved an impressive entry. Shuttered windows to either side. A family strolling with baskets in hand, a woman consulting a guide book and glancing back down the street, frowning.

"Come." Kyra Akbulut stepped from the car, but Grant put a hand in front of her, still silent, and shot her a look. She scowled in response, dark brows turned theatrically down. "It's my own house, Mr. Casey."

"Donahue," he corrected. "Casey's in the hospital."

With an exasperated sigh, she slid past his hand and kept walking.

Nick emerged behind her, a little awkward as he stood up.

"You alright?" Grant asked.

"Battle ready." Nick gazed after the client as she approached the huge door and passed inside. "Bit of a pain, sitting on floors."

"I hear you." Grant waved to the driver, who shut the car door, and climbed back in to park the massive vehicle somewhere else. The family heading home from market let themselves into a modest square door across the road. One of three pedestrian doors, four garage bay doors with line of site to the client's home. Few first floor windows, shutters on the second. Lost tourist now absent. Interesting. Grant set off after Akbulut. "When do you think she starts to worry?"

"You think she ever worries?" Nick strode along with him. "I mean, aside from worrying about the stock market and the launch date for the next I-crap."

"Somebody wanted me dead."

"And you're not worried."

"Are you?"

Nick moved his right hand, dispelling a bit of the tension that edged every line and muscle. "Chief...that setting, musty and dim, the man I'm meant to serve flying back from the impact—almost went straight back to Afghanistan, to seeing you die all over again."

Grant bumped his wingman with his elbow. "You didn't break. You went straight to saving his life, like I knew you would."

"Near thing, though, and you—" Nick gave a snort, drawing Grant's eye. "You're pumped, aren't you? Old adrenaline kicking in already."

Grant shook his head. "We've got a job to do; protect that book. Now it's gone." They passed into the shade of the mansion, and he flashed a grin. "Admittedly, the job just got a lot more interesting."

Nick elbowed him back, harder. They passed from the shade of the thick gateway into a sunlit courtyard with a central fountain, and the door whirred shut behind them, an electronic lock engaged. Four doors and a staircase wide enough to drive the limousine up. Akbulut conferenced briefly with a man dressed in a tunic who immediately rushed off to do her bidding: Adem Kazaz, her personal assistant.

"Are we allowed to talk now?" Grant called after her.

She pivoted on her heel, arms folded. "I do not appreciate your attitude, Mr. Casey. You are the one who insists upon securing everything, and now you're upset I asked for silence in the car?"

"If your decree of silence had anything to do with security, Ms. Akbulut, you wouldn't have been texting the entire time. Do you have a secure line?"

"I have the highest level of encryption on every device I own."

"And it hasn't been out of your hand all day?"

"Only when your man took it."

"And when you left it in your purse while you were being photographed in front of the archive, then on a shelf in the secure chamber for a second round of photographs inside the archive. When you accepted a glass of champagne, you placed it on another shelf, and momentarily forgot where it was when that old colleague of your father's approached you."

Her eyes widened during this recitation, but rather than be impressed, she shrugged. "So you saw where it was all the time—why ask me?"

"Because I wasn't paid to guard your cellphone, ma'am, and I am not willing to state in a court of law that nobody had access to it. Outside of those moments, I had eyes on the crowd, not on your device. I'd highly recommend replacing it as soon as possible." Grant stood at parade rest, regarding his client. "Who else wanted that manuscript?"

"Nobody." Her glance flicked away.

"Bullshit." She flinched, and he said, "Sorry, did you want that in Turkish?" He gave her a long moment. "The man we hired to pretend to be me was shot two hours ago and the target was stolen. I don't expect clients to let me into their intimate lives, but I do need to know what we're facing to do a proper risk analysis. Who else wanted it?"

Her crossed arms tightened, and she glared at him. "Is the manuscript valuable? I suppose it is, but, like your services, it's rather niche. Most of the codex is the usual Latin drivel. It's only the part about the automata that's likely of much interest, and then, only to the right audience."

"Got it. Make me a list. Nick?"

Nick took a step forward. "Yes, sir?" All soldier, all over again. At least he never made the break into sniper mode.

"Reach out to D.A. We need to define the niche for that kind of material. I also need to know about the weapon I was shot with, and—" he stopped short.

"What's up, Chief?"

He was on the verge of mentioning the Phantom, but no need to reveal that detail for the client, not unless it proved relevant. "We need a full work-up on the security man, Haldan Brunelle."

"He's the dude helped you out, right?"

"He interceded, anyhow, but not for my own sake. Seemed as likely to become an abduction as an assist, right up until we opened the box. And he has a tattoo, a small cross." Grant indicated the inside of his wrist, and Akbulut cocked her head.

"Well, if ink's a reason to be suspicious, Chief, you're the prime suspect."

"Your man is a knight," Akbulut said. She stared at Grant as if he, clearly, were not.

"Looked more like a Viking," Nick observed.

"Look, Mr. Casey," making a point of saying his name, "as I told your associate, I hired you to guard and escort the codex, and now, it's been stolen on your watch. So far as I am concerned, that constitutes severe dereliction of duty, and—"

"That's how you're playing this? With all due respect, ma'am, I don't think stopping an active shooter situation, fighting a fire, and chasing a thief while Nick saved a man's life adds up to dereliction. If we determine that you've been withholding information that we required in order to adequately perform our job, I think I can win that lawsuit with about 40 witnesses willing to testify, including the knight."

Her lips compressed, and her eyes flicked as she calculated the odds or considered how to lie, her impersonation of righteous anger on pause.

"Do not play games with me, Ms. Akbulut, and I will continue to play straight with you."

Nick chuckled softly. "Told you," he said softly, and she cast him a look a little more gentle than anything she'd shown to Grant. Interesting.

Finally she flipped back her braid. "Very well, Mr. Casey. What do you advise?"

"You expected something to happen, so I advise you to tell us what and why. At least two other parties are interested in that manuscript. From here on out, no security theater. We've got a man down, a shooter and a thief on the loose. It's not about appearances, it's life or death. You need a new cellphone, for one thing. And no duplication of that device. Anything you want off of it, you transfer manually."

She took two steps toward him. "Do you have any idea what you're asking?"

"You're not the one who got shot."

At the top of the stairs, Adem Kazaz reappeared, keeping his distance.

"Neither are you." Lips still parted, Akbulut absorbed what she had said and broke off with a crisp nod. "In that case, make yourselves comfortable in the grand salon. Adem will assist you and I'll send up the drones."

CHAPTER SEVEN

The two men strolled toward the stairs, Casey slowing his pace to match Norton's. Kyra had no one who could match their pace to hers. She was used to living at 1.4 speed compared with everyone else. What might it be like to have someone walk beside her? Her father used to. Nobody had kept up with her since his death.

Kyra opened an access panel concealed in the tile work next to the entrance and folded down the workstation. A monitor fitted behind the panel showed a split screen and she toggled to the view behind her. They mounted the steps toward Adem, following him around the corner. She toggled again, getting a view along the upper stairs. Casey lifted his hand and Norton stopped along with him, the two facing opposite directions, Casey's glance flicking toward her. He didn't trust her. She glared at his image on the screen. The more time she spent with him, the more insufferable he became.

She keyed in her personal code and a small drone emerged from the dovecote high up in the courtyard. It shot swiftly upward, then moved in a careful pattern over the rooftop, across the yard and back again. Given the other systems in the house, the drone was likely superfluous, but she preferred to have redundant systems rather than be exposed to unwarranted risk. Her cellphone sat atop the console, numbers flicking higher on her message icons. Discard her phone? Absurd. He had no idea what really happened, he was just trying to earn the exorbitant amount she was paying, plus the so-called "action" bonus now that there had been shots fired. If she didn't know better, she might guess he hired the shooter himself in order to inflate their own worth. Kyra rolled from her heels to her toes and back again. The actor was felled not by a bullet, but by some sort of lengthy dart, and only a single one. She made a note to review the contract language and see what triggered that clause. In the meantime, she keyed instructions for surveillance in the guest suites, took up her cellphone and closed the console.

She hesitated a moment, then slid open an app, to find a message waiting.

>*should be no mercenaries involved*

An apt description, though they preferred the term "private security." As if the person she corresponded with were any better. >*Add'l security clearly warranted >disregard other interest, I have prior claim.*

A minute passed, then >*I'll be in touch*

Kyra slid the phone into a concealed pocket at her waist. Security firm indeed. They were mercenaries, no better than the Crusaders sent by the Venetians to trash Istanbul back in 1204. Armed men who understood nothing, and cared only for the booty they hoped to acquire. Might as well have hired the Templars themselves. At least now she would know who to contact if she required the slaughter of innocent Muslims. Kyra swept her hands over her silk suit, tugged down her jacket, and swept up the stairs. Marble and tile in cool, contemporary shades lined the walls, a perfect union of ancient style with modern ways.

The smell of rich coffee lured her into the long chamber where she found Norton patiently explaining to Adem the difference between coffee and tea, while her assistant stood to one side, looking vaguely amused. Casey looked up from the bookshelf at her approach and executed a military pivot. "Interesting titles, Ms. Akbulut." He tipped his head toward the shelf.

"They belong to my parents. I trust Adem is taking care of—"

The double doors at the near end of the chamber flew dramatically inward and her mother entered, head held high. "Darling, you didn't mention bringing home company," she said in Turkish. "Won't you introduce me?"

Norton rose from the sofa, but remained where he was, a hint of strain edging his smile. Even a top-quality prosthetic like his would be difficult with all of the transitions he'd gone through in the last few hours. Casey stepped up along with him, both men waiting with a sense of readiness. Kyra forced a smile as Mother swept past her. With every year, she resembled the woman even more, high cheekbones, intense gaze, dark hair twisted back to emphasize the face. Behind and below that face, however, they couldn't be more different. Mother wore a flowing garment with rich colors like an antique rug, a sharp contrast for Kyra's cool suit. At Mother's appearance, Adem hurried off to fetch the mint drink she preferred before she got querulous.

"My mother, Irene Akbulut," Kyra announced. For her mother, she reverted to Turkish. "These two men are among those I hired to assist with the manuscript this afternoon. That's all you need to know."

Norton's gaze shifted toward her, then he smiled, white teeth glinting in his dark face. "Pleased to meet you. May I call you Irene?" He put out his hand, palm up, and her mother hesitated, her gaze toward his missing his fingers, then finally hovered her palm over his. He kissed the back of her hand and she gave a shiver.

"So handsome, and so polite," Mother purred. Finally, she switched to English. "You may. I was named for one of the three holy virtues: Sophia, Irene, Dynamis. Wisdom, peace, and power." She intoned the list with a dramatic flourish of her hand, then sank into a chair not far from where Norton had been sitting.

"Nice," Norton said. "Is there a Hagia Dynamis as well?"

His pronunciation was dreadful, but the question lured her mother in. Mother's plucked eyebrows rose. "So you already know of the Haya Irene?"

"Well, of course, but I haven't had the chance to visit. Is it as lovely as you?"

Kyra assumed earlier that the man was gay, but perhaps he just flirted with everyone. Well, everyone except her. "It's not a social call, Mother. These men are here to discuss what to do now that they've lost what I paid them to defend."

"Oh, dear." Mother plucked a slim remote from the parquet table at her side and tapped a button. From across the room, a prototype personal bot a little larger than a hatbox whirred to life and glided across the floor to position itself in front of her chair. It gave a tone to indicate readiness for orders, and sparkled a series of colors through the Mangam logo on its front. Mother tapped the button again, replaced the remote, and leaned back, propping her feet on the low, molded plastic exterior. "Thank you again, darling. It's the perfect height."

Kyra hardened like thermoplastic herself. Her mother was meant to be testing the bot in a real-world setting, running it through its functions and establishing its capabilities. Not using a hundred-thousand-dollar prototype as a footstool. Norton seemed amused, but Casey glanced to her mother with a speculative expression.

"I'm glad you could join us, Mrs. Akbulut," Casey said. "I understand many of these books are yours—some in more ways than one. Eight volumes on the literature and history of the Byzantine period. I'm intrigued."

Fuck. He read Turkish. Did he speak it as well? Was the whole conversation meant to tip her off to what he already knew? And how had he noticed her mother's titles that quickly? Kyra strode between them to snatch a cup of coffee from the tray Adem had abandoned in his readiness to please her mother.

Speaking of which, Mother laughed, a tinkling little sound. "Why, I'm flattered. I also have a number of co-authored works, of course, but you know how it is with those things."

"The men get listed first." He gave a nod, and raised his cup to her. "Congratulations on your dedicated scholarship."

Mother's eyes sparkled, and she locked onto him as if she longed for her magnifying glass. "Did Kyra tell you? It was I who brought the codex to her attention. It's not often that our interests coincide, but in this case, I learned of the discovery from a colleague who specializes in the Latin invasions."

"Honestly, Mother, I'm glad you could join us, but we do need to talk business."

"Oh, of course, I'm just waiting for my tea." Mother waved a hand to dismiss Kyra's interruption and faced the men fully. "It was her father who got her into all of this—" a gesture toward the robot at her feet. "He was somewhat obsessed with ancient machines."

Casey's glance flicked to the bookshelf, then to Kyra, who had long since removed her father's collections to merge with her own. She explained, "He was an archaeologist. I'm an engineer. Rather different things. What are our next steps?"

"Facial recognition. I assume you've got something?" Casey slipped something out of his pocket. "I had this off the photographer outside the archive. We need to know who else was in that room."

Adem re-entered with another tray and a glass cup of tea in a filigreed silver holder which he offered to Mother.

"Adem? Would you bring my laptop? The brick, if you don't mind." The steam of her coffee helped to take her attention from her mother's foibles.

"Ancient machines are certainly intriguing." Casey settled onto the sofa opposite Mother, the embroidered cushions and bright colors shifting him from an American into someone more ambiguous. "So many people, especially in America, I'm sorry to say, don't give other times and nations much credit for innovation."

"That is certainly the truth." Mother raised her glass in his direction. "But there is a balance to find between the denigration of others, and the sort of Orientalism that pervades so much of the supposed research. Take my late husband. He grew so eager to prove the brilliance of the East that he bought into every legend—"

"Mother, would you mind—"

"—Every legend," she repeated, yanking her feet from the robot to lean forward in her seat. "Even the most preposterous. Visitors to the

Byzantine empire expected to be impressed, and so they were, but not by a flying emperor or a veritable gauntlet of golden animals."

"Mother!" Kyra stalked closer, but her mother only leaned in more, and Casey leaned in to meet her.

"The most ridiculous stories, which he claimed to have seen the evidence for. Statues that could judge truth from lie, seats that only a righteous man could sit on. The Latins invented all kinds of riches to exaggerate their own exploits. A few jeweled trees or fire-breathing griffins and they begin to think we're magical. Not at all. My husband had part of a doll he found in a landfill. Where did that go, anyhow?" Mother swiveled around, flapping her own hand. "An arm..."

Kyra forced her fingers straight. "You must forgive my mother. It's an academic rivalry, nothing more."

"Indeed. Much more reasonable to think the emperor sat on marble and gold and ivory than that he could rise into the air and be defended by swords that no hand held. You didn't bring the book, though? I am always ready to be proven wrong, and if this new codex really contained sketches of Solomon's Throne, well, I shall go do penance at your father's grave." Mother cocked her head.

Kyra squeezed her core so tight she could have taken up pointe ballet. The book was missing. Her father's dream, ever elusive, receding once more from her grasp, and these two men who had no right to know any of this clearly taking it all in like a pair of automated vacuums. She could almost see the dollar signs that flickered in their minds. Mercenaries.

Across the room, Adem cleared his throat. "Where should you like it?" He held up the laptop.

Anyplace but here. Back in Sacramento would be lovely. "Excellent. Thank you. Mr. Casey? The card?"

He rose smoothly, with a bow of the head toward Mother. "If you'll excuse me. I'll look forward to chatting again some time."

He kept to her shoulder as they crossed the room and Kyra slid a desk surface out from a converted antique buffet near the street side. "Who's your designer? D.A. would love that."

"They're all custom. The card?"

Adem provided her a chair, but only one—Casey remained standing as she booted up. "Perhaps you and your associate should get cleaned up? Back at the hotel?"

"You place that much trust in your security system? All the electronic eyes in the world won't stop a bullet, and a drone that calls the cops can't help you if it takes twenty minutes for them to get here."

Leaning in, one hand planted on the desktop, he finally produced the SD card. She swiped it from his hand and jammed it into the slot. "There's no reason to believe my life is in danger."

His voice dropped low. "Because you hired the assassin who tried to kill me."

CHAPTER EIGHT

C lad in his regalia, Blaise walked through the antechamber of the Hagia Dynamis, pleased to see that the effluvia from his last visitors had been cleaned in his absence, that unfortunate young man who refused to recognize his sins. Blaise paused outside the next door, and one of his knights stepped forward to activate the organ. This wasn't a proper throne room of course—he required the throne for that—but still, adopting some of the awe due to the Kosmokrator invigorated the enthusiasm of his knights and set the proper tone for visitors. The ancient mechanism hummed as the knight cranked air through the pipes. It moaned softly, then opened full-throat in a chorus as if a host of patriarchs acclaimed him. The door slid open and Blaise stepped through in a square temple shaped into a cross by clusters of pillars that supported a fine early Byzantine dome. Four knights knelt inside, heads lifted and eyes shining, their half-capes brushing the inlaid floor. Their eyes tracked him eagerly as he crossed to the center of the cruciform chamber. Arched windows above illuminated the space with the warm glow of LEDs through smoky glass. Defenders of the faithful must be defenders of Creation as well. Pity they could not allow true daylight, but their day would come. When he secured his throne and invited the various Children of Abraham to join his council, then would his knights stand proudly in the light of the sun. In the meantime, he had work to do.

The other two occupants glanced at each other uncertainly. One of them leaned heavily against a pillar, his arm clamped over his side, cleaned and bandaged, but no doubt still painful. He did his best to nod at Blaise, then sank toward one knee. Blaise moved swiftly forward and took his elbow, guiding him onto one of the carved stone benches at the corner.

"Thank you, my lord," the man said thickly, but Blaise waved this away.

"I understand that your target survived," he said softly.

"Forgive me, my lord. There was a woman, a stranger who fouled my shot, and that other mercenary assailed me as well before I could fire again." He gulped a breath, his head drooping.

Haldan had mentioned no woman. Another Bone Guard?

The man spoke into Blaise's hesitation. "My lord. If my penance is at an end, I understand. Your campaign can tolerate no failure." Again, he moved as if to kneel, but Blaise held him back.

"It is the mark of true penitence that you would even say so, but stay. For the moment, take your rest." Blaise rose and swept his cloak in a circle as he took the center. Carefully aimed lights reflected off of his silver mask and caught the glints of gold all around him, highlighting the symbols of Holy Power. "Do you know, my companions, why our movement grows in this city?" He aimed his look at the thief, who shifted a little, but only shrugged.

"My lord," said Chloe—the one who ran their outreach program for street youth—and Blaise gestured for her to speak. "My lord, we penitents returned to the scene of knighthood's greatest crime. It was here in 1204 that the crusaders who swore to defend the Holy Land attacked and destroyed the kingdom of their fellow Christians instead. That's when the throne went into hiding, because those who professed to goodness violated their oaths." She stumbled a little over the words, but it was almost word-for-word what he told new recruits, and he gave her a partial bow.

"Indeed. It is here we perform our greater penance, on behalf of our spiritual forebears, to remind ourselves what we shall not do. Our battles shall be righteous, our might directed toward those despoilers who swear an oath before Lord and country, and refuse to uphold it. Mere orders are not enough reason to bend your nobility. Money is certainly not sufficient. It corrupts those who crave it, and those who offer up their honor for a price." He returned his attention to the would-be executioner. "Because of this I asked that Grant Casey should die. Why have they come to this city save to plunder it once again? If we cut off the head of this small viper, we break the strength of the body and may overcome its corruption. It was to be a symbolic blow in the midst of the sale of our patrimony for personal gain."

"Forgive me, my lord," the man said again, and Blaise gestured for him to rise.

"Go to the hospital not as one who seeks to overcome the pain of the body, for the body is merely what carries the heart. Go, rather, as one who would strike off that head." He clasped the man's elbow, and the man's blue eyes sought his behind the mask. Blaise imagined that he could send his strength and will along their joined arms. "I know what I'm asking will place you in danger. The police are looking for you, and the man's companions may be vigilant."

"My lord, I'm not afraid to die."

Blaise released him. "Take what you need from the arsenal and go with holy power at your back."

"Thank you, my lord." The man held himself as proudly as he could and limped through the arsenal door. Blaise doubted he would see the man again. Too much risk lay along his path, but he fervently hoped the task could be accomplished first, and either way, the man performed his penance with the grace that chivalry demanded.

Turning back to the thief, Blaise strolled closer. "I understand the mercenary caught you. Almost caught you twice, in fact, in spite of Haldan's intervention. Is this true?"

"My lord, I was told to be casual, to draw no attention to myself. I wasn't trying to race at first. I don't know how he—"

"Don't give me excuses. We are the Knights Penitents. The first thing we do is to accept responsibility for our mistakes."

The man scowled. "It's not like I wanted to get caught, sir."

"I'm sure that's true. And when you did, what then?"

"I tried to fight off the guy, but he fought back. Haldan pulled between us, and I realized the box was gone." The man shrugged. "It seemed like Haldan could handle it."

"And if he could not? What if his assailant were armed? He'd already proven himself more than your equal, he spotted you in spite of your casual guise." Blaise pointed to a relief sculpture embedded in the wall. Weatherworn and chipped through its thousand year history, the piece depicted two knights mounted on a single horse, the classic symbol of the Templars.

The thief scowled. "Well, we got it anyway, didn't we? Haldan got the box."

"I just sent a man to his death because he sought forgiveness and accepted his charge. It is not merely results that matter, it is the means with which we achieve them. Do you understand me?"

"What do you want me to say? I'm sorry? I got attacked, the guy was good! Haldan helped me out. Give me something else to do, alright?"

For a moment, Blaise bowed his head, facing the unrepentant, his heart grown heavy, but he knew what he must do. Blaise withdrew, standing aside from the man and shouldering back his cloak. "Run."

"Excuse me?"

With a sweeping gesture, Blaise drew his knights to their feet. "You take no responsibility for your failure. Your heart is not strong enough for the burden of repentance. You ask for something else to do, and I give you the chance to help your fellow knights with their training." He spoke again with resonance, letting the mask echo his voice. "I said run."

Steel sang from sheaths as the four knights drew their swords.

"Jesus!" The thief yelped and scrambled backward.

The knight who had spoken earlier lunged and her blade bit the thief's ribcage as he spun away and fled, not toward the arsenal—he wasn't that smart. No, he fled toward the arches. The four knights ran after him, dividing at the entrance by silent accord to take two different pathways. Would he run to the cistern? Blaise hoped not—that area connected more closely to the secular world beyond his walls, and someone might report the footfalls of creatures larger than the usual vermin. Blaise listened carefully.

The sound of the thief's pleading turned toward the buried corridors, a hundred ancient arches domed and stooped from the intervention of earthquake, fire and riot. Somewhere in the dark beyond, the thief shrieked again, then the sounds receded into the depths of the sunken fortress.

Moving toward the far corner, to the shrine, Blaise lit a genuine candle and sank to his knees. The Lion of Truth occupied a niche to one side, a beautiful union of ancient wisdom and power. Should he have chosen full knights, dedicated penitents, for the mission at the archives? Perhaps that would have given more surety of success, and yet each man must have his chance for redemption. Blaise would meditate on that.

He gazed up at the shrine's focal point, the head of Baphomet: a gilded face with ivory eyes and a silver tongue, its neck crudely severed from the wood and bronze body that once supported it. Quite a wonder it must have been, this ancient figure standing guard over the emperor's chamber. Did it hold a sword to dispense justice? Or had it once contained pipes and vials to breath fire or spread poison? A hundred years after its theft from this very city, a single Templar, tortured to the point of speech, betrayed the order and spoke of the venerated head, stolen from Byzantium and held in high esteem by the knight-betrayers of this Christian realm.

A new dawn would come and bring together the region's disparate peoples. Blaise contemplated the damages of the past and the promise of the future, with himself providing the balance. He need only find his throne and ensure that those who refused to own their sins received their judgments. Somewhere in the depths, the thief's final cry gurgled into silence.

CHAPTER NINE

The client stiffened as if he held a gun to her head, then her fingers glided over the keys seeking safety in the familiar. "That's more absurd than my mother's stories, Mr. Casey. What would make you suggest such a thing?"

Grant sank down a little, bringing his head below hers, taking an angled view that let him watch her and the screen at the same time. "If you wanted to steal the manuscript and pin the blame on me, you needed a distraction. Shoot Vivek, send me on a wild goose chase, leave Nick to clean up the mess. Decry the situation, fire those responsible, meet up with your thief the next day and walk off with the codex. Nobody the wiser. How close am I, Ms. Akbulut?"

"Not very." She gestured toward the screen, her nails short, but perfectly manicured, striking a fine balance between the feminine and the practical. "Most of these people are just the usual academics and local leaders. The software can pull their profiles from the University or their own publications. They are hardly spies or assassins."

"Makes me wonder why you're indulging me, Ms. Akbulut. Oh, right. 'Somebody's been shot. Some kind of dart. Not by me.'"

Her fingers froze as he quoted her own text conversation, the one she'd been conducting when Nick confiscated her phone and forced her to save a man's life. Her chest rose and fell with faster breaths, and she flashed him a look.

"You didn't mean to hire an assassin. I don't know what the hell your plan is—" though her mother's monologue gave him some ideas— "but it's pretty clear, I think to both of us, it didn't go the way it was meant to."

Slowly, she turned her head and met his eye. She wet her lips, but still didn't speak.

Grant dropped a knee. "You had no intention of needing us, Ms. Akbulut, but someone who's willing to shoot me, with two of my men looking on, would be more than willing to shoot you, too."

She swallowed, then raised her finger, and Adem dropped in on her other side. "Take the car to the hotel. Norton and Donahue need their things. Ask Amita to prepare two guest rooms. Mr. Donahue will let you know which rooms they prefer. They'll need system access at the sub-admin level."

"Yes, ma'am." Adem set off. On the other side of the room, Nick kept Irene chatting amiably about Byzantine legends and Kyra's life, and the elements that joined the two. Excellent.

Grant ran his eyes over the faces on Kyra's screen, most now paired with profile shots from various sources, including the servers who had carried and poured the champagne, and Haldan Brunelle, the Varangian guard. "Where are the rest?"

"This is everything. The program has already eliminated photos with only duplicates of the faces here: mostly mine, Destry's, the lead archivist, and those with no faces at all."

He scanned them again. A few were unidentified, mostly Muslim female scholars who probably would've objected to their photos being taken to begin with. At least two missing entirely. One was no surprise: the photographer himself would hardly appear unless he was into selfies. The other, a phantom once again.

"I need to see the empties. The negative results."

She scowled but did as he asked, bringing up twenty-three images of the archives from various angles, or shots where someone moved, obscured or turned at the last moment. "What are we looking for?"

"The thief or the theft." One of the obscured photos showed an arm extended, a cane raised across the oblique light from the lanterns. Interesting. The photographer caught glimpses of the shooter, and flipping back through the photos revealed him in a few other shots, entering with the crowd, working his way toward the back raising the weapon. As if it didn't matter that the shooter had been captured in digital, but the phantom appeared only as a sleeve here or a turning of the head there, her body alert with a familiar tension. The omission of her image had to be deliberate. She had an ally, one who tried to prevent Grant from pursuing the thief on the motorcycle. Was she his adversary, once again? Then why had she moved to stop the man who targeted him at the archive? "Can we get all the official photos as well? And we need to reach out to Brunelle, figure out who this guy was, the photographer."

"What about the shooter?" She tapped the image and it zoomed in, a three-quarter view of the shooter's face, a skullcap, thick-framed glasses, beard he'd probably already shaved.

"If we track who wants the book, we'll find his boss. By now, the shooter has changed his appearance and probably gotten out of the country. Send over the pictures and let the police do what they can—they'll have eyes on the airports and ferry terminals." But given the strategic position of the city between the Mediterranean and the Black Sea, on the cusp of either Europe or Asia, the shooter was long gone. "What was your plan?"

Her fingers slid over the keyboard, saving photos, sending a message to the police, slowing at last when she had run out of work. "To have it for myself, not merely for study. If it doesn't contain what they say, it is found again, and I give it back." Her shoulders shrugged a little, more an adjustment of her creamy suit than an admission of any kind.

"And if it does?"

The pale light of the computer screen cast a bluish glow over her features as a slow smile spread. "Then my mother must apologize on my father's grave because she never believed."

"Who did you hire, and how?"

"Through a website, someone with principles who promised a careful job and did not share details."

Preserving the client's deniability. "You knew it would be stolen, but you didn't know how. Set up a meeting, let's get it back—but this time, I need in, for your safety as much as anything else." He held her eye until she gave a nod, and he didn't trust her for a moment.

"Chief?"

Grant pushed up and turned at Nick's summons. "Our man Brunelle's got a record back in France. Assault and battery, armed robbery. Somebody died, but not at his hand. Seems like he was an addict who went straight. Scared straight, maybe. He turned over on his buddies for a plea deal, got out three years ago, and moved here on a special pass."

"How does a guy like that get into security?"

"Maybe the Knights Penitents have something to do with it?" Nick displayed his phone. "That tattoo, it's for a new order of Templars, or so D.A. tells me."

"Sounds like the Viking and I have some things to talk about, after I do some more research. We need to be at the hospital when Vivek wakes up, to know if the box was already empty." The shooter ran off empty-handed, the phantom's photographer-pal had delayed him, the biker had the box, and the phantom herself hadn't left the archive before he did. Could be all four of them were on the same team, but he had the distinct impression the phantom preferred to keep things tight.

"Surely the thief removed the codex from the box after they seized it at the archive." Kyra started a gesture as if to pick something up, and frowned, glancing about, then shook back her sleeve and slid her finger over a blank watch face. The bot at her mother's feet woke up and turned, extending a gripper. "Mr. Norton, my coffee, if you wouldn't mind?"

Nick grinned as he placed the cup of coffee in the robot's gripper, and the bot hummed softly over to its maker.

Maybe they should get one of those for the Bone Guard office, to carry their game controllers and keep Nick in chai when he needed it. Meantime, Grant said, "They may've given it to someone outside, but the moment's getting complicated already. No serious operator likes that many moving parts. Every new part of the machine is another chance for a breakdown.

Besides, Shutterbug's photos show the box pretty far from Vivek's side when he fell. It didn't drop straight—"

"Ergo, it might have been empty already." Akbulut regarded him with a hint more respect, while her mother clapped her hands.

"It's like an Agatha Christie story. I love it," Irene announced. "I'll go fix my hair." She swanned off in the same direction she'd emerged from, now that she had thoroughly disrupted her daughter's control. Grant would have to keep an eye on that relationship lest it erupt into open warfare.

"Let's split up and look for clues." Nick stood up, making a subtle sign with his hand. "In the meantime, I believe Ms. Akbulut said we should pick our rooms."

"I'll buzz the housekeeper," she said, turning back to her computer—the place she felt most comfortable, Grant suspected.

He met up with Nick, returning to his apparent perusal of the bookshelf. "Sitrep?"

"Client we can't trust, and her loose-lipped mother, house full of bugs, three different hostiles, you. And me," Nick muttered.

"At least we've got each other."

Nick gave a breath of laughter. "You got that right, Chief. But I have to tell you. Vivek. He reminds me of Jamal."

Oh, shit. With that name, Grant's tension level shot upward. "You okay with that?"

"Doesn't help that the guy thought he was shooting you, and for a minute there, I believed it."

Shooting Grant and Jamal in one: a little surprising Nick hadn't gone full sniper. "I'm still here. You okay?"

Nick tipped his head one way, then the other. "At least this time I could save him."

Softly, Grant said, "We don't know that Jamal's dead."

"Educated, queer, Afghani and working with the enemy. What're the odds the Taliban let him live?"

He could apologize again for the idiots in command, the bastards who left all their allies behind while he and Nick were on medical evac, but it wouldn't help. In the end, nothing did. "You were bomber at the archive, Nick, but if you're in trouble, I need to know it."

"I hear you, Chief." Nick ran a hand over his smooth scalp and scanned the room. "The meds are working, the skills are sharp. I'm A-and-O times three. I just thought you should know."

"As your CO, or as your friend?"

"As my comrade." Nick showed a glint of teeth. "Where you go, I follow. I let you know the first sign of danger, out there, or up here." He tapped his temple. "Speaking of, why so squirrely about the pictures?"

"The Phantom was there. Odds are, she's our perp."

Nick's face continued to smile, and maybe only Grant would recognize its sudden stillness. "So," Nick said, "you got proof this time. Gonna show me the photo?"

Grant shook his head. "No photos. She doesn't appear in any of them. She's gotta be working with the shutterbug."

"During the de-brief, you said the shutterbug was blocking the biker— she was the biker?"

"Negative. Not sure where she went, but she went after the shooter at the same time I did."

"Then she vanished."

Grant's throat constricted as if the tattooed lion there flexed its claws. "That's part of the job, mine and hers."

Nick spanned his forehead with one big hand, rubbing his temples. "Look, Chief, I still see Jamal everywhere I go, everyone I want him to be. It ain't true. You're an optimist, I get it. You think this woman's got something special, something other folks don't. This woman that nobody's ever seen but you." Combat ready, alright. Nick seemed ready to go to war with his own side. "You ever thought maybe this is just another way to amp up your adrenaline? Make it an op—not just an op, make it a fucking adventure story, some beautiful thief on the other side. Save the day, get the girl—"

His voice dropped to a low thrum, and he said, "Bone Guard's got the best mental health coverage in the Commonwealth, man, you ever thought of using it?"

She was no hallucination, for all that he had nothing to prove her existence. What, a single text a year ago? No reason for anyone but him to connect that with Afghanistan, Russia, Mongolia. Jesus—during the aftermath of that operation, the first time they'd had this conversation, Grant half believed it himself, that the Phantom was all in his head. Tension coiled in his gut. "Don't gaslight me. You, of all people."

A spasm of pain crossed Nick's eyes, then he squared his shoulders. "Chief. You just watched yourself get shot. That's gotta be making some ripples. I told you, first sign of danger." He reached out and gently tapped Grant's temple. "We look out for each other." His hand fell to Grant's shoulder, a gesture meant as a comfort. Didn't feel that way.

"Message received." Given their history, every one of them walked the line with madness, even him. Paranoia was one of the symptoms, didn't mean it was the only one. "Thanks for doing your job."

"I'm being. Your friend," he said, two hard, solid phrases, like the bolt being drawn on a weapon Grant hadn't meant to prime.

CHAPTER TEN

W hile the men were claiming parts of her mansion for their own, Kyra gave those chambers priority in her surveillance feeds. She couldn't be too careful with her trade secrets, a fact that now came in handy with these mercenaries moving in. Her phone buzzed gently and she brought up the app on her laptop.

Her last message hovered at the top. *>given to understand you prefer to work with me. Willing to pay additional 20%*

> *>prefer to be paid and depart the city with no further trouble*

Excellent: her contact might be wary, but wasn't really the sort to take her merchandise out to auction. *>When and where?*

> *>plaza outside Topkapi Palace 8 pm. Send next installment as agreed*

>I will be there With a few keystrokes, Kyra authorized the next payment. Her plans may have experienced a setback, but she would readily bring them back on target, once she had the Latin codex in hand.

Casey flicked across her tiny monitors in the corner, Norton at his side, and she closed that tab as they re-entered the room. "Ms. Akbulut. Brunelle reached out and suggested we meet at a Turkish bath."

Kyra blinked at him. "Well. It makes sense—you can have relative privacy and at the same time, nothing to hide." Her cheeks warmed.

Norton gave a theatrical groan, drawing his employer's eyes over to him. Away from Kyra's embarrassment perhaps? Interesting. "Jeez, Chief, you get to have all the fun."

"He assures me that full nudity is not required." Casey's dark eyes revealed little, but Norton sighed, shaking his head. "You'll need to go to the hospital without me, Nick. Ms. Akbulut, I'd like to ask you to go along. Nick may need translation, and we need to play this close to our chest."

"Not adding any moving parts. I understand. Let me call the car—"

"Not the limousine, something less conspicuous. Part of the reason I want you two together is to watch your back, Ms. Akbulut. You okay with this, Nick?" Something passed between them in the slightest widening of the eyes, a slender nod in reply. Kyra tracked these things for her own work, but she could not puzzle out their meaning.

"Battle ready," Norton had changed into fresh clothing, somewhat more casual than before, but still with the Bone Guard logo and the dark tones that made him appear to absorb all light.

"Keep an eye out for the shooter or the thief—you should have their pictures."

"What about the shutterbug?"

"Short—" Casey held a hand up to his chin to demonstrate— "lean, but athletic build. Narrow chin, flare to his nose. Age..." He paused, the hand that had been tracking his description hovering in mid-air, his own gaze captured by it. "He presents as young, maybe twenty, but his hands were not. He's another operator. Gotta be. Had a cap on, so likely short hair, but hard to say. He's good. An infiltrator. Skin tone somewhere between yours and mine, scar across the back of his left hand."

Kyra wanted to pull out her pad and start making notes on the kind of things Casey observed. Facial recognition had nothing to compare with this sort of skill. How long had he even been looking at the man? Yet he talked as if he could pick him out of a crowd. Perhaps, if she maintained good relations, they would consent to some interviews, or monitoring to better map identity algorithms.

"We talk at eighteen hundred, unless I hear from you before then?" Casey flicked a salute and set out.

Apparently he expected to be free again by six o'clock, but she could use the moment of their connection to make her own departure and rendezvous with the contractor who had taken the codex. These men need be none the wiser. They might be smart and capable, but they were still in a foreign city that was Kyra's hometown. Let them solve whatever mysteries they perceived while she got on with her own affairs. At least she had a solid team back in Silicon Valley to handle the daily business.

"Ma'am?" Adem approached carefully.

She was already out of her seat, preparing to depart. "What is it?"

"Your invitation from the World Affairs Bureau, the Davos-ME conference. If we're taking the yacht, it needs to be re-stocked." He held his hands lightly together as if ready to spring into action on her behalf. As, indeed, he was.

"Davos? Sounds fancy," Norton commented.

"ME. Middle East. Half the leadership of the Levant will be there, promoting cordial relations. Fancy, but likely ineffectual. Adem, handle the re-stock—hopefully we can wrap this little problem and I can still attend personally." When she received the invitation some time back, she declined, then the manuscript turned up and she reversed that earlier decision because the conference dovetailed nicely with her plans. Now her plans felt...precarious. "I presume you've already made the goodwill shipment and had our display items shipped?"

"Yes, ma'am. They sent a fruit basket with their thanks." He almost smiled. "I believe your mother may have already claimed it."

Kyra snorted. Of course she had. "Tell her I may not be home for dinner, thank you. I hope she has enough fruit to hold her over."

Within half an hour, she and Norton stepped out of the car in front of the hospital, where she used the fact of her wealth and her facility with the language to gain access to a waiting room not far from Destry's recovery room. No doubt the rather large black presence at her back aided in delivering the right impression. Perhaps she should always travel with a bodyguard. Now, he stood in the hall outside while she used her tablet to respond to emails from the States. Yes, there had been a shooting at the archive. Yes, she was fine. Yes, she expected to be back in the office in three days time. A man crept by in a wheelchair, using his heels to pull himself along, slumping to one side, the wheels softly squeaking. Kyra winced, looking away as Norton straightened up, perhaps made conscious again of his own disabilities.

One of her engineers sent a mock-up of a drone propeller assembly Kyra had proposed, and she lost herself in the dimensional modeling, seeking out flaws—a blaring whoop cut into her concentration and Kyra jerked, the tablet falling from her hands. Norton popped open the door. "Fire alarm. Betting it's false. Our perp's trying to get us away from the door."

Retrieving her tablet, Kyra pulled her bag closer. "Isn't it just as likely that the—perpetrator?—has moved on by now? Isn't that what Mr.—your associate said?"

Norton parted his lips, then his brow furrowed and he turned away, glancing down the hall. The air grew hazy, thickening with smoke as she watched. She stuffed the tablet into her bag and yanked the strap over her shoulder. "That is no false alarm." She marched past him into the smoke-filled hall. An announcement came over a crackly speaker and Kyra translated, "All guests and ambulatory patients are evacuating to the west. Let's go."

Down the hall, away from the smoke, patients called out and nurses coordinated their efforts, shouting back and forth, managing the retreat. A pair of gowned patients shuffled past from the direction of the smoke. Doors flew open and slammed, causing billows of smoke. "Let's go," Kyra repeated.

Norton stared into the smoke, head slightly turned, then said, "That's right, Ms. Akbulut. Time to go. Your safety is paramount." He enunciated strangely, then caught her arm and propelled her into Destry's room. The actor lay under sheets, connected to machines, in the private room Casey had insisted on.

"We cannot evacuate him, Mr. Norton, the hospital will take care of him." Kyra tried to pull away from Norton, but he tugged her down to the floor.

"There's no fire—no heat, just smoke. Some kind of—" He broke off and pushed her behind the bed by the outside wall. She watched his polished black shoes take two strides into the curtained corner by the head of the bed, utterly silent.

The door swung open. "I will bring Mr. Casey—you go on," a voice said in Turkish.

Kyra aimed her glare at Norton's legs. No heat? She'd let him feel some heat. Then the new arrival's feet came into view. Brown shoes, worn and practical, and marked with dark, irregular stains. About to open her mouth to rebuke her bodyguard, Kyra kept silent.

Norton took a half-step and shouted, "Freeze! Keep your hands up!"

Brown shoes pivoted and Norton shouted, "Shit!" turning hard away. Blood spattered the ground between them. Whose? A black-handled knife tumbled across the floor. Norton's. Fear clutched her and every instinct urged her to stay down. But it was decision not instinct that had gotten her where she was.

Kyra swept her bag off the ground and leapt to her feet with a yell.

Both men startled, the attacker with a slim knife held back-hand, Norton arms wide, the attacker streaming blood across his hospital gown, overlaying an older stain. The attacker elbowed Norton hard in the gut and plunged his blade toward Destry's exposed throat.

Kyra swung her bag, slamming it into the attacker's arm and throwing him off balance. His blade tore into the mattress near Destry's head.

Norton bear-hugged him from behind and lifted him away from the patient. The attacker grappled with his knife, preparing to strike even as he struggled. Kyra leaned across the actor's legs, grabbing the attacker's fist, keeping the blade from Norton's side. Norton squeezed harder and something cracked. The attacker grunted, but gave no other sign of pain. Blood streamed from his wounds now. He slammed his head backward, flailing and kicking, forcing Norton into the door.

It shattered and both men fell into the roiling smoke outside, crashing to the floor. "Norton!" Kyra lay for an instant, then hauled herself up, stumbling to the other side of the bed.

Smoke rolled and men grunted, hitting each other, hitting the floor, then an American voice, "Shit!" louder this time. The attacker would leave, wouldn't he? He'd been foiled—wouldn't he run?

A shape moved from the smoke, leaping through the door, low toward her legs. Kyra grabbed the cart full of medical gear at Destry's bedside and swung it around. The locked wheels protested, and the cart toppled over on the attacker. He kicked back away from it, hands slapping the ground to pry him free. Dark eyes met hers. His surgical mask hung from one ear, exposing the determined set of his teeth, like a demon from an ancient manuscript.

He knocked the cart back into her, and she had no place to go. She stumbled backward, tangling into medical tubing and electrical cords, knocking the IV stand into the wall. He scrambled onto the bed like an over-sized cat, claw like hands reaching. Kyra grabbed the IV pole and jabbed it toward him, the bags swinging. One of them slapped his face, and the pole gouged into his cheek. He snatched it from her grip, twisting it aside and tossing it down.

In the bed, Destry's eyes blinked, then peeled open too wide and he screamed. The attacker, forced back by Kyra's assault, reached again.

Norton's fist slammed into the side of the attacker's head, then his arm wrapped the attacker's throat, hauling him backward. Norton dragged the attacker off the bed, the two men filling the space at its foot, then the attacker collapsed, sagging, his head pitched sideways. Norton went down with him, not falling, but easing the other man's descent—and keeping hold of him all the way down. Kyra stepped that way, ready for what? Her hands shook.

The attacker's arm flailed back to life and his hand came up from the blood-streaked floor with Norton's knife in his grip.

"Norton—the knife!"

The attacker carved a gash through his own stomach, up to the ribcage, violently down toward his beltline.

Norton grabbed the attacker's hand and yanked it away, but too late. Blood gushed. Blood, and worse. Kyra reeled and staggered. Her stomach churned. She turned away, but even the smoke couldn't stop the coppery slick odor of the blood from reaching her, and the sight—the sight—

Sirens wailed outside, the fire alarm blared inside adding fuel to the fire within. She couldn't breathe, couldn't think. She covered her face with both hands, gulping for breaths that didn't come.

A gentle grip found her elbow and she slumped onto the edge of the bed. "This. Take this. You need. More than me."

Kyra twitched and glanced at the thing being pushed against her hands. A clear plastic mask, with a connected tube. From his hospital bed, Destry's smile looked wan, perhaps twenty-five watts of the hundreds he could muster. He pushed the mask at her again, and she took it, breathing in the rich oxygen.

"Ms. Akbulut. How are you?" Norton stood close at her back, and his hand settled lightly on her shoulder.

"I am," she took another breath of the oxygen, her chest hitching and mind beginning to clear. "I am awful. Thank you." She shook all over and wanted to run, to get out of this room, away from these men, most especially from the dead man sprawling somewhere close, in a pool of—she hunched forward, clutching the mask, tears threatening, so out of control, such a girl.

"Great job," Norton told her. "Thanks for the back-up." He crossed the room and opened the window, pulling it inward, drawing in a fresh breeze that dissipated smoke and pushed away the scent of blood. "By the way, the name's Nick. Easier to shout next time you need to warn me of impending doom."

God willing, the first time would be the last, but Kyra placed that probability on a steadily falling curve toward nightmare.

CHAPTER ELEVEN

From the outside, the Bath of Solomon didn't look like much. An Ottoman-style peaked arch over the kind of push-bar door you'd find at a strip mall coffee shop. Grant pushed inside and found himself on a foyer of terracotta and painted tiles. Haldan Brunelle rose from a carved bench and held out his hand. "I'm glad you could join me. Seemed we both might need a break after that, eh?"

Grant shook his hand, still looking around like a rube. Partially true. "I've never been to one of these places. Do we strip?"

The male attendant behind the counter clearly spoke English, but turned his smile away to busy himself with other work.

"There are changing rooms. They give a wrap, like a towel. Then we get massage, scrub and bath. It's all men." Haldan's grin widened in his ruddy beard. "I hope you're not expecting more. There are other baths with the ladies..."

"No, thanks. Still got work to do, y'know?" He imagined the Phantom, the brightness of her eyes, that coy smile as if she always had some joke he might not be a party to. Grant set aside the image and brought his attention to the moment at hand, acting the American newbie, eager, curious, no agenda but some bonding over a shared experience of a very different kind than the one they had that morning. A double-door at the back of the reception room opened, and two men stood there, barefoot, each with a cloth bundle over an arm and a pair of slippers in the opposite hand.

"I asked for attendants who do not speak English, is this alright? Harder to talk with them a little, but maybe easier for us." Brunelle shrugged, looking to Grant for approval.

Grant nodded. "Good thinking. Lead on."

Brunelle addressed their attendants, and Grant showed careful inattention, as if he didn't understand a word. He'd been cramming Turkish since they got the job, and had picked up a few useful things. They followed their attendants through the doors into the central chamber.

One major entrance, stairs to an upper level, large many-sided room with lots of small chambers lining it, pierced dark woodwork, deeply incised with the thoughtful craftsmanship of centuries past. A fountain in the center rippled softly from below, no noisy splashing to echo off the marble. Numerous pendant lights in Turkish style with contemporary energy-efficient bulbs. Soft voices through one of several open archways. An attendant dressed similarly to theirs carried a large bag of something like soap bubbles. The whole place smelled damp. One of the most unusual places he'd ever been for a mission: bright, clean, and soon-to-be very exposed. Few places to take cover, no weapon of his own to hand.

"It's not the oldest in Istanbul, but close, established around 1500." Brunelle chuckled at Grant's surprise. "You know of the Varangian guard, so I think this history is something you will also appreciate."

The stockier of the two attendants, opened one of the carved doors and gestured for Grant to enter, while the other man did the same for Brunelle. The attendant put down the bath clothes and shut the door, his shadow moving away outside.

Within the changing room, he found a cubby for clothing, and a small keyed safe for valuables. Not very secure, but a nice gesture. He deliberately brought little with him inside, stashing his cell phone on the way over. He had a wallet full of fake cards covering the gamut from Visa to shop rewards, each with his assumed name, and some business card with the same. Enough cash to make it seem legit. That went into the safe along with his knife. If need be, he still had plenty of ways to fight.

Now for the fun part. Grant stripped and hung his pants and shirt on the provided hangers, the rest into the cubby along with his shoes. He felt no shame for his body: it had, so far, done pretty much everything he asked of it, and sometimes more. Run a marathon, dive a submarine, climb a tower...dip a dance partner. No shame either for the scars or the ink that overlaid them, covering half his back, wrapping his throat from behind, then down his right arm to a little short of his wrist. He stood at ease in his own skin, fully aware of the discomfort it caused in others. Could be useful, could be distracting. Key dangling at his wrist, he pulled on the wrap he'd been given, stepped into the slippers and emerged into the central space.

Another man, a stranger, lounged on the rim of the fountain, and Grant gave him a nod, even as the stranger jerked a little upright, scanning over Grant's marked skin. Could be an operator who knew enough to act surprised, or just some local businessman not expecting the Illustrated Man to enter his bath house. Grant took a spot of his own, studying the Ottoman architecture, with its interlocking stars and diamonds, arrowheads of brass inlaid in the walls with slices of malachite and lapis as a band around the floor.

Brunelle emerged from his changing room, his brawny physique revealed, his tawny chest hair parted by a few slender scars. Knife wounds? The pucker of a bullet scar at his lower leg. Only the one tattoo, that small cross at his wrist.

"That's a lot of tattoos," Brunelle remarked, making no secret of his examination. "Lot of styles."

Grant lifted one shoulder, a shrug that looked defensive, as if he didn't want to talk about it. "I had an interesting youth. I'm lucky Casey was willing to take a chance on somebody like me."

"Second chance? Me, too." He rolled his wrist outward, displaying the ink.

Grant stood up, and their attendants materialized from one of the arches to beckon them onward, into a marble room with a pair of massage tables placed at a distance and angle that allowed, but might not encourage conversation. Each man lay down on his stomach.

"What do you do now your boss is in the hospital?"

The attendant started with some oil and a gentle touch, starting at his shoulders—trying to put him at ease. Hard to lie easy with another man's hands that close to his throat. Grant forced himself to relax. With maybe thirty-seven per cent success.

"Dunno. There's really no succession plan. Hard to say if the company holds together without him." As he improvised, Grant made a mental note to look into that. Not that he planned on dying any time soon. Couldn't always think like an operator, sometimes, he had to play CEO. Later.

Grant groaned under the increased pressure as the masseuse ground his aches and tension between strong hands and a hard surface. "Even if it does, no telling if I'm asked to stay. This thing in the archives isn't gonna work in my favor."

Brunelle sighed under his own massage, turning his head to look at Grant while the attendant moved toward his lower back. "I'll put in a good word, if that helps. You did your best and stopped more violence at least."

Grant made a noise of negation. "I lost the objective, and the boss is the one paying for it. Most of the core Bone Guard members, they're his old war buddies. Took a lot for them to trust somebody like me."

For a moment, blue eyes met his, then Brunelle asked softly, "Criminal record?"

Grant hesitated, dropping the gaze. He swallowed and brought his eyes back. "Nothing I'm proud of, but there's a lot of folks who don't believe a guy can change. That doing the time could make you better, not worse."

Brunelle regarded him across the gap. "Repentance is real."

His voice had thickened, his expression shifted away from the buddy-buddy, to something more. Maybe it was the near-nudity, the vulnerability of their scars laid bare. Whatever order this guy signed onto, it went way past the skin.

"You, too?" Grant asked, matching his tone.

Brunelle chuckled in a breathy, nervous way. "I found it in the knighthood. I know, sounds ridiculous, eh? But think: code of conduct, noble behavior, discipline. Lotta that stuff Casey probably got in the army, right? But with a cause you could really believe in."

Grant laughed as well. "Knighthood? I thought the Varangian thing was more of a joke, but what do I know? You still in service to the emperor?"

The other man's brow furrowed, and Grant hurried on, "But seriously, you said a cause. Higher than the army. This Bone Guard stuff. I mean, I'm all in with protecting historical artifacts, but it's mostly about the money. If they cut me loose, maybe it's time to look for something deeper."

"How about peace in the Middle East? A peace that goes beyond borders."

Grant raised his eyebrows as the masseuse worked down the left side of his spine. "That's pretty deep alright. Peace without a bigger war?"

"This region used to be called the holy land, not for one religion, but for many, a place when so many peoples come together." His attendant was pushing and shifting his whole body from the core, distorting his words, and Brunelle waved the man back for a moment. "Armies haven't helped. We need symbols, ways to speak to those different peoples, things they will understand and respect."

"Like the knighthood."

"It's one. Think of the emperor with his Varangians, dealing with the Seljuk Turks during their expansion and trading with Venice, welcoming embassies. Even in the waning days, it was the greatness that drew them close, the symbols of leadership that went beyond borders."

"You guys have that kind of symbol?"

"We're working on it. More important, we have that kind of leader, the kind who inspires, who makes great plans and strong connections." Brunelle smiled. "If you happen to need a third chance, I think he'd like to meet you."

CHAPTER TWELVE

Feeling clean and fresh, his body pounded, scrubbed and rinsed to the point he wondered if he still wore as much ink as when he entered, Grant retrieved the bundle he had concealed in a damaged wall a few blocks from the bathhouse. He peeled off the waterproof stuff sack and slipped it into a pocket, sliding the gun into his waistband at the back. Kyra objected to weapons, but not so strongly she hadn't helped to procure them. They needed to be careful—no discharge without cause, but sometimes mere possession could be enough. He felt conspicuous without a go-bag, his kit for concealment and disguise. A trip to the souk might be in order. Still a few minutes to six, when Nick was scheduled to check in with him.

On opening, his phone displayed a series of message indicators from about half the apps available. Yikes—what did he miss?

Nick, brief and to the point: *shooter came for Vivek. Shooter neutralized. No ID, no identifying marks. With cops now. Client anxious re time. Vivek sez box felt light.*

Interesting. And on another app, one he rarely opened but religiously transferred from device to device whenever he had to ditch one, the single word: *hello.*

Twenty-one minutes earlier. His heart leapt. He wanted to sprint for the hospital and shove the phone in Nick's face. Except, from Nick's perspective, it could from be anyone. A single word. A single word shouldn't electrify his spine and make his every hair tingle. Twenty-one minutes ago.

In nine minutes, the app would delete the message completely. Grant kept moving, timing his withdrawal from the hidden redoubt so he wouldn't be noticed emerging from the shrubbery. He became just another strolling business man, enjoying the evening sun. *>hi there.*

Had to be too late. She would be long gone. Some of the relaxation of the bath slipped away, replaced by a jittery sensation he didn't care for. Just another way to get his adrenaline pumping. Nick was half-right, anyway. Grant walked faster. Take the train from the nearest station, walk from there to the client's place, get back to—the phone shivered in his hand. Tension gripped him, his muscles itching to run, flat out, anywhere, just so he could get there fast and burn off whatever the hell this was. He made himself slow down, pausing by an elaborate fountain with its own dome. Finally, looked at the phone.

>you safe?

She was real. He had seen her. It shouldn't be such a goddamn relief not to be nuts. He read and re-read the words. Why ask? Why had she taken action in the archive? Grant forcefully compartmentalized. *> yes, you?*

>meet me

No punctuation—a question, a demand? Reading too much into it. His thumbs slid across the keyboard almost before he could think about it. *>where?*

Both safe, for now. If they met, would that change? Safe from what: a whole other matter. They were operators, two of the best. The last thing either of them needed was a personal entanglement. The last thing she was after, certainly. She wanted intel, like Brunelle did, but with Grant, she was a recognized, if not known, quantity. They had a certain level of...Trust would be too strong a word. Whatever else this was, it wasn't personal.

Two dozen tourists flooded in front of the fountain, squeezing in close together, grinning for a guide who held a few more devices than there were people. Grant stepped away and faded back. At last, a reply *>by the Sofia, there's a strip of trees. Walk toward the old city.*

>on it

Neither of them asked when. How scared did she have to be to make this happen?

He walked briskly, not so fast as to attract attention, though it felt good walking in a place where just the darker shade of his skin wasn't enough to draw notice if he started moving fast. The suit helped, too, parting crowds almost subconsciously, as if he sent a wave out ahead that his business was urgent. Was it? The Hagia Sofia was close, towering over the parkland where he walked, its domes clustered like eggs, defended by minarets that pierced the sky. The first day they landed in Istanbul, two days early for the assignment, he and Nick had toured the sights. Not long enough for him, but what kind of history major came to Istanbul and didn't go to the Sofia?

Grant turned aside, walking north for a bit, checking reflections, noting the people around him, the cars and cycles on the streets. Horns blared, and the cursing here was in a few different languages. His wallet had been examined at the hammam, as he expected, and he'd picked up a tail for a little while, one he ditched with a few tricks. These guys were eager, but not pro, not really. He wondered if Brunelle noticed his own tail: the shutterbug. Grant wanted to take up that chase, but Brunelle had taken a car, and the shutterbug quickly made himself scarce. Given that Grant already had company, he kept to his own course, looking casual, tamping down the frustration of the missed opportunity. Now, nobody. He crossed traffic—drawing more honks and curses—slipped into the line at a coffee kiosk, and out the other side, just in case. A young couple—she in white, he in a tux, stood outside the ancient wall while a photographer snapped their picture smiling, embracing, kissing. Grant ducked his head.

A double line of trees, crowded with tourists, occupied a strip along the defensive wall of the enormous church-turned-mosque. From this close, most of the structure vanished, the interesting parts, anyhow. Grant slowed his pace. Still deliberate, but no rush. Definitely not meeting anyone. Crowds of tourists and locals strolled the area. Many women wore the hijab, and even the western women mostly covered their hair, out of respect as they toured the religious buildings in the area. Some men wore tunics, others suits not so different from his own, though without the hidden pockets.

The shop on the corner held a multicultural battleground of artifacts, among them a mounted archer, the horse rearing, the rider in a pose that suggested action—rather than what would really happen, the guy sliding off on his ass, the arrow loosed somewhere above him, just as likely raining death down on himself or his companions—or, God forbid—his own horse. Stirrups, man. Use 'em. A case of estate jewelry glinted from the gloom of the dirt-smeared window, slender golden bands with single gems, chunky bracelets, a silver diadem of ancient style that drew his gaze with dangling semi-precious stones unevenly cut. The rest was contemporary, real gold, sure, but lacking in artistry. This last piece looked to be several hundred years old at least, the kind of piece that a nomadic culture might use to carry their wealth from place to place, the marker of a tribal princess or a great lady of the Golden Horde.

"See something you like?" a voice inquired at his elbow. "I will get it for you."

Grant hesitated, expecting a shopkeeper, but the door remained shut and the glass before him gave a ghostly reflection of her face, the hijab covering her hair, the green of her eyes lost in the dark shadows. Her smile flickered like a fox through the trees.

His throat felt tight, as if his scars constricted, and he made himself relax. "Planning to pay for it, this time?"

"We'll see." She moved away, and he followed two steps, pleased to see she showed no evidence of last year's encounter in the forest on the Russian border—their tacit agreement not to kill each other. To prevent her allies from taking vengeance, she shot herself in the leg, a glancing wound, but it must've burned, even as it justified her own failure to kill. If she carried that scar, she gave no sign.

A kid jostled against him, trying for his wallet, and Grant sidestepped, the tail of his jacket swinging out. The kid's eyes flared at the sight of the gun and he fled into the crowds, looking for an easier mark.

"You shouldn't scare them." Her voice, suddenly beside him, her clothes tourist-bright, concealing her form, and whatever else she wished to hide.

"Can't help it," he said.

"You could if you wished." She held up a map. "Can you direct me to the Binbirdirek Cistern? I hear the coffee shop is very nice." She drew out the name, stumbling over the syllables, and he suppressed his laughter, certain beyond doubt that her Turkish was perfect, unlike his own.

He pulled out his phone as if to help with directions, letting the screen stay dark, reflecting her face. "I'm walking that way—"

"Maybe later." Swift, quiet.

"You took the package. On behalf of my client. This morning, before we arrived."

He caught the slender glow of her smile, and the slight nod, as if conceding a challenge. "Just business. One woman to another."

Except both of those women must've known the trouble it would cause the Bone Guard. "Sure." Letting the single word have an edge.

"I tried to convince her not to hire you." She turned, frowning at the map, then pointing and looking to him as if for his advice. The map now covered his phone. No accident.

"Then I wouldn't have seen you again." Grant's mouth felt dry. Why did he say that?

She gave the slightest laugh. "I might not have tried very hard."

Oh, shit. "Why ask to meet?"

"Your man, he's alive?"

"Killer tried again at the hospital. We nailed him. Who else wants it?"

"I wish I knew. I could get more money for it." The words too flippant. Bingo.

"How about your photographer? Does he know?"

She started walking, following whatever directions their personae had worked out while they spoke of other things. He paced her and she scowled. "Not mine."

"But not unknown to you."

"Nizari Isma'ili looking for the king. Bad news. Means somebody's going to die." She stopped and shooed him away. "I hope it's not you. Get lost, Bone Guard."

He stopped, sighing dejectedly and put his hands up as if accepting her rejection, as if she had him at gunpoint and he gave in to her demands. "Not you either." His heart thundered.

Her lips softened. She turned on her heel and walked away.

CHAPTER THIRTEEN

Minutes ticked by, the police asking the same questions, everyone distracted by the—the state of the body. Kyra sat in the waiting room, answering with increasing impatience and making sure they knew about it. Nick stood at her side, a solid presence, bringing her water or coffee, answering his own set of questions with clear, direct responses. Easy to translate, nothing to hide.

"Well," said the investigator at last. "Well, I guess we won't know why this man wished to kill Mr. Casey, but at least there's no public danger."

Nick's eyebrow rose when she translated that, but he said nothing.

"Thank you for your time, Ms. Akbulut. We will call with any further questions."

"And when you ID the body," Nick prompted. He glanced at Kyra. "We need to know who this guy was, who he worked for."

She didn't translate all of that, but stood up. "Thank you, officer. Please let me know when you find out his identity. I should like to be sure that I and my staff are in no further danger."

"Of course, of course." He almost bowed as she swept from the room, clutching her tablet without the shoulder bag. The bag she had used to help clobber and kill a man.

Her entire core from her throat to her belly tightened. Had she ever thanked Destry for sharing his oxygen? Should she? Probably. The real Casey would be on her about that, certainly. "I've already called the car," she said as she walked out, Nick holding the door for her, Nick taking on the part of her personal bodyguard—but only after he confirmed that two officers would remain in the hall outside Destry's room.

When they got downstairs, the limo was waiting. Kyra held out her hand to him, palm down, and Nick took it lightly on his own. "Nick Norton. Thank you for standing by. I had... a difficult time back there. It is only the second time I have seen someone die, and the first time—" she tried on a smile, tight as the rest of her— "I have told you about the first time."

"Yes, ma'am. Chief wants me to look out for you, I take that job serious."

"Would you mind taking the front seat on the ride home? I should very much like to be alone. I don't like—" she glanced away, not sure how much to say. How much of the truth did he need to know in order to comply with her wish?

"Of course. You take your time. It's always rough if you're not prepared." He smiled, taking her hand over his arm to escort her to the limo and help her inside. The door closed behind her, and a moment later, he got in next to the driver.

"Carry on, Kostas," she said.

The driver met her eye in the rear-view mirror with a nod, and she smiled back as she held the button to close the window between them. If she were to be honest, she did, indeed, wish for time alone, perhaps a tricky programming issue to solve or an advertising campaign to approve, something to take her mind from what she had seen. Twenty-four hours and this could be left behind. The mercenaries sent back to America, another check sent to the archives to cover damages, the book safely available for her personal study, and proving her father's dream within her grasp. She could relax on her yacht toward Cyprus to dress in magnificent clothes, display dazzling inventions and win some interesting contracts.

This wasn't a large limousine, as befit the city streets, but luxurious enough for her visits here. Kostas drove her mother around as well, but in a simple car; her mother disdained most signs of Kyra's success. Kyra slid from the center to the driver's side door, her hand on the handle. The sleek vehicle cut into traffic, working its way through the crowds. It paused at an intersection. She popped the door part way and slid out to the back, keeping low and trying to hurry. She had only a little time to get back to the old city, and hoped her contact would wait for her if she ran late. She'd gotten no response to her last two messages and refused to send again. Cross the street and jump into the nondescript gray car idling there. As it jumped forward with sharp acceleration, she glanced back and saw Nick leap from the limo even as it started away. He spun about, and she didn't need to hear his voice to recognize the curses on his lips as traffic closed around her. So. That hadn't been so bad. Kyra settled back and called out, "I'm late—make it quick!"

"Yes, ma'am." Adem replied from the front seat. He rocketed the car into gear and took off. The cramped buildings and busy hive of citizens fell behind, giving way in a few blocks to tourist hordes and opulent carpet shops for the export trade. At this hour, people were choosing wine bars and waiting at restaurants, or admiring the lights that shone along the sides of every old building, turning minarets into rocket ships ready to launch for the face of God.

They lurched to a halt behind an idling tour bus, and Kyra glanced at her phone. 8:07. "I'll walk from here."

"Are you sure? The mercenaries—"

"They worry over anything. The shooter from this morning is dead and I have no reason to fear. I'll meet my friend and see you again in half an hour." She slammed the door and set out fast, diagonally. At least her own people still accepted her orders. Her shoes, comfortable enough for office work and a hospital waiting room, began to rub after a little while, but she could see the meeting place up ahead. How would she even know her contact when she got there? No matter: the woman was a professional. Kyra would count on her to make the first move. Unless she had already gone. Kyra looked around. Above, the sky remained a little blue, with the depth of growing twilight. Down here, light pooled in artificial domes, leaving dark spaces between. The Four Seasons Hotel presided over an area of ruins her father had been involved in preserving. It was likely in this area where the

Throne had been placed, where it had been hidden for a hundred years before the Crusader assault had devastated the city. A series of stone arches and vaults, blocked off by plywood or rubble, formed a partial rectangle showing where the buildings had been, with rough gravel and patchy grass filling the gaps. Her phone buzzed.

>*keep walking, toward the old wall*

The message tightened her grip. Twenty-four hours and her life in espionage could be done. She could return to her own work, work where nobody died and one could simply meet for coffee without all of this nonsense. She followed the instructions. Given that a man had died earlier today, it was perhaps not as much nonsense as she had hoped, but still. As the police had said, a closed loop. In a matter of moments, it no longer mattered who else wanted the manuscript. She would have it. She would celebrate at the Davos-ME. Kyra rounded the corner, leaving most of the lights of the Hagia Sofia behind. The Topkapi palace wall rose to her left a block away, with the usual mix of shops, cafes and hammams in between. She scanned the crowd, remembering Casey's quick assessments of everyone around him. What must it be like to suspect that tall woman? That man with the cane? The harried woman with the pram? How about the van on the corner delivering flatbread? She found it curiously relaxing, this little make-believe. The woman with the pram started across the street, but the wheels jammed in the gap between the sidewalk and street.

"Miss? Help me, miss?" The mother waved Kyra over.

Glowering and glancing around, Kyra went. She hadn't time for this, but what could it hurt? Her contact would show herself—or not-in the next few minutes. Then she realized the woman had called out in English, despite her head scarf and all the trappings of Turkish womanhood.

Their eyes met over the pram, covered, but suspiciously quiet. Kyra picked up the front of it, to help maneuver. "Is it in there?" she whispered.

"Keep helping me," the mother replied, at the same time she gestured toward the broken wheel.

Kyra sighed. "Can we just—"

Across the pram, her woman's jerked up, eyes flaring. "Run!"

"What?" Kyra stood there, stupidly holding the side of the pram as the other woman bolted, diving sidelong.

The man with the cane grabbed the top of the pram, his cane pointed directly at her. Kyra flashed to Destry, lying on the floor in the archive, pumping out blood, and she screamed.

CHAPTER FOURTEEN

B laise shifted the van into gear as Darius intervened with the carriage. Akbulut didn't let go. Blaise scowled at her in the reflection. The less damage they caused, the fewer people involved, the easier this would be. Why wouldn't the woman simply give up?

"The other one?" Chloe's voice in his ear.

"If she's leaving, let her—"

But she wasn't fleeing the scene. She had run, yes, but she reappeared, circling behind Darius and now leaping onto his back, toppling him onto the carriage. "Stop her—get the carriage!"

Akbulut lay stunned a moment, then grappled with the pram while Darius fought off his attacker. He didn't draw, not yet. Good man. She fought back, using hands and feet, roundhouse kicks, dodging the cane as if she had been training for this.

Chloe ran over to Akbulut. "Miss, are you hurt? We must get you out of here." She offered a hand, readily accepted, and turned Akbulut away from the fight. "Take a seat, I'll see to—"

"No!" Akbulut shook off Chloe's help and righted the pram.

"Of course, of course, the baby!" Chloe moved to help, both of them with hands on the pram, dragging it toward the back of the van. Excellent. In the mirror on that side, he saw Akbulut pull back.

"Thank you. No really." She tugged harder.

The pram spilled, its blanket covering flung aside a few pillows

75

tumbling out. Where was the codex? Blaise gripped the wheel. People began to gather, some to flee the scene, others to gape. So much for keeping this quiet. "Chloe, get her away!"

He need say no more. She caught Akbulut's arm above the elbow. "Come on."

"Darius, we need that one."

"Yes, my lord." Darius's fight grew serious, not merely defensive, he grappled with the woman.

Akbulut struggled, frantic to reach the pillows, the pram, anything. Clearly, she still believed it contained a clue though just as clearly, the manuscript wasn't there.

A man in a black suit punched through the crowd. A Bone Guard. Just what Blaise did not need. The Bone Guard grabbed Chloe's arm and did something that made her cry out and release her target. "Go!" the man shouted.

He swung Chloe off-balance like a dancer, landing her full-length on the ground where she gasped for breath. His head rose, focused on Darius's fight twenty feet away at the front of the van. He reached around to his back, as if for a weapon, cursed, and sprang forward, still empty handed.

"Knights! To Chloe," Blaise barked.

Timing his entrance, Blaise popped his door. The Bone Guard spun out of the way, barely in time. The gun appeared in his hand as if by magic. Their eyes met for an instant, then Blaise dropped behind the van door. The van shuddered as two more knights, clad in baker's uniforms, sprang out.

Akbulut screamed.

For a moment, the Bone Guard hesitated. "Shit." He turned hard, gun extended. "Let her go!" he shouted in passable Turkish. Blaise reached back for his sword. He swept the blade under the door, catching no more than a pant leg.

One shot, one of the knights howled. The Bone Guard ran a half-circle, clearing the van door with room to spare from another cut. Akbulut staggered toward him, and he caught her, pulling her behind him, retreating, and covering his client. Good man.

The knights sprang after him, one of them bleeding across his white apron.

At the front, Darius let out a grunt, and Blaise left the safety of his door, sprinting to his knight's aid. The woman had him pinned and was already leaving. Blaise let his sword swing wild. She dodged easily, but into his arm's length. She turned aside again, swift and graceful as he punched out. A glancing blow across her lower jaw, his ring making a shallow slice.

She ran, gathering speed. The crowd, scattering from the gunshot, parted around her. Across by the ruins, the Bone Guard glanced back, then kept moving, his client tight alongside. Two knights rushed after. Blaise dropped his sword at Darius's side, and strode forward, hands open. The woman, the thief, ran a few more steps, then swayed as the drug hit her bloodstream. She shook her head, her hijab coming loose. She kept moving, stumbling.

"Darling," Blaise called after her in Turkish. "Darling, you must come home. Please. I cannot run the bakery without you, you know this!" He held his arms out, pursuing her slowly, with the desperation of love.

She never looked back, but kept running, her feet growing less coordinated, until she sprawled into the sidewalk. Blaise was with her in an instant. "Darling, darling, are you alright? These drugs, these things you do, they must stop. Imagine if our baby were injured?" He gathered her into his arms, careful to touch her gently, to do nothing untoward. "My friends and I, we just need you to come home." He cradled her against him, all the way back to the van where Chloe had already stored the pram and gone to assist Darius. Blaise carried his prize to the van as if he treasured her, and indeed, he did. The codex might have vanished, but the thief belonged to him.

CHAPTER FIFTEEN

Casey's arm was too tight around Kyra, his urgency transmitted through her body. How had he even come there? Should she be grateful for his arrival, getting her away from those people, or furious for how he must have tracked her? Had he saved her life, or lost her the manuscript—or both?

They dodged into the shadowy ruins—these ones not so sexy as to be lit up like a carnival. A gunshot pinged off the stone arch nearby, and he shoved her under it, turning back, not firing. Together, they plunged deeper into the darkness. Arches that had once supported the palace rose around them, crumbling to the outside, to the inside, still solid, and among them, a single building that rose from the ruins. Some of the arches had been blocked off with wooden doors. Casey scanned the area, then dodged abruptly toward an archway.

"Stay down and stay quiet," he ordered her, one hand for his gun, the other guiding her under a broken door. The while, he never looked at her, but kept scanning, his eyes ahead in the direction their assailant would come from.

"I didn't hire you to push me around and tell me what to do," Kyra said.

He cast her a dark-eyed look, sharper than before. "You hired me to cover up your secrets, but if you want to take point for an assassin, be my guest."

Casey spun the gun in his hand and offered the grip to her. For a moment, their eyes locked. She'd have to apologize sooner or later. Assuming they both survived.

Kyra sank into a crouch and sidled through the gap, watching out for shards of old wood and rusty nails. Not avoiding his gaze. Certainly not. Americans. Insubordinate asses. She emerged into another room, narrow and lit only by gaps in the restoration woodwork that allowed slices of light to catch the dust disturbed by their arrival. Outside, his shadow vanished, nearly silent in pursuit. People were shooting at her. They hadn't, until he arrived, waving his own gun. What idiocy had compelled her to comply with that request? They wanted the codex, that was all. She should have given them the pram once she thought it, too, was empty. Back off and see what her contact would do. What had become of the other woman, the woman who had intervened to give Kyra the chance to escape? She had been ungrateful to reject it. Last she saw, the thief fought with someone near the van. Kyra hoped the other woman had gotten away. Honestly, the villains, whoever they were, had no reason to come after Kyra. She had seen little enough, and she still did not have what they wanted. She fidgeted in the gloom, wishing again for the quiet space of a technical problem, anything where she wasn't so far out of her areas of expertise. Maybe she shouldn't have engaged in espionage to begin with.

Well. She heard no sign of pursuit or gunfire now. She had wanted to visit the ruin in any case, the place where her father had spent so much time, and she hadn't expected to be inside of it. The place reeked, making her gag and cover her nose and mouth with one hand. She thought about leaving, but the gunmen were still out there, both of them.

Kyra turned on her phone's flashlight function, careful not to shine it toward the door. A tumble of blankets and refuse occupied the far end of the arch. She started to rise, but the glitter of gold caught her eye. She waited, but the blankets didn't move, and shining her light over them produced no sign of current habitation. The gold drew her hand downward instead. She moved a torn drop cloth, then pinched her nose to stifle a sneeze as plaster dust assaulted her. A mosaic section lay on the floor, partially embedded in plaster and clearly belonging someplace else—likely it had been removed from a wall during the reconstruction, and now awaited its own fate. Like her. Kyra inched forward, peeling back the cloth as she went. Peeling back the layers of history, drawn in by the tantalizing gleam. The floor creaked a little, but the men and their guns would be far from here. It creaked more, almost a groan as she shifted her weight further into the gloomy chamber. A closet? A bath?

Under the cloth, another dark-eyed stare, this one formed by painted tiles but still aimed at her, accusing. Kyra glared back and stuck the phone in her pocket to free both hands. She stripped the rest of the cloth with a dramatic movement.

Wood snapped and she plunged out of time. A rush of water stopped the shriek in her throat and she came up choking. She flailed, gasping for breath, reaching for anything to save her. Her fingers stroked slime and she jerked back.

She forced herself to reach again, her hands sliding along the stone, her nails scraping at the algae. She kicked hard, propelling herself closer, searching along the edge for anything she could get hold of.

Her face bobbed beneath the surface again, water sweeping her eyes and mouth. She kicked stone and pain shot through her foot.

Her searching hand found an edge at last, a lump she could grapple. She added both hands, clinging and hauling her face from the water, leaning into the stone. A face stared back at her sideways, a pale, moaning mouth and vacant orbs for eyes. Kyra held back her scream. A sculpture, only that. A sculpture of a tortured face crushed beneath the weight of stone overhead, calling out for help that never came. Kyra's fingers wrapped coils of the statue's hair. No, they were snakes, writhing around that hideous face. The sight of Medusa struck her to stone, and Casey had won. She could get no more low or silent than this, shivering in a pit beneath the floor, barely hanging onto the past, the remnants of her own culture stolen away and buried in a watery grave.

CHAPTER SIXTEEN

Grant raced back in the direction they had come. If one of the assailants got in his way, they'd go down. He bolted from arch to arch, pausing, listening, running again, his palm sweaty as if he once more raced in the desert against the past he couldn't escape. Reaching the outermost, he froze again, longer this time. Someone retreated, not trying hard to conceal their steps, hasty but not hurried. He risked a look and saw one of the two who had pursued them loping back toward the scene. Knots of people shifted uneasily, but already shifting back toward calm. He'd missed something, something that eased the usual panic of hearing gunshots. A siren in the distance, a police car that would have to fight its way through the Hagia Sofia crowds even to get close.

Grant slipped from cover to the next patch of darkness, the scraggly brush that edged the ruined complex and fronted on the street. The shooter ducked into the back of the van. Different driver—the woman he'd taken down earlier. Should've taken her down harder than that. So much for trying to avoid excess force, especially in public. Where was the Phantom? He'd seen the blow—glancing at best—seen her escape, then caught a glimpse of her slow-mo collapse. What the hell had they done to her? What did they hit her with? No doubt where she was now, as the back of the van closed, the van already squealing to life and accelerating down the road. Grant took a few shots, with the sinking feeling the vehicle was either stolen, or would be ditched before the night was through. Fuck.

The moment replayed in his head, meeting the driver's eye, forced to choose between his client and his—what? Nothing. He slipped the gun away and called Nick as he walked back toward the ruin, keeping to the shadows but less concerned about getting shot.

"Chief, did you find the client?"

"D.A. did. When I find her again, I'll—" he broke off, working toward control. "I interrupted assault and theft. Got the client to safety."

A moment of silence, then Nick, soft and urgent. "Chief. Talk to me."

"They got the Phantom. You were right about the meet. I got in two minutes too late."

"Condition?"

He swallowed hard, his gaze drawn toward the gleaming minaret, then back to the darkness, the illuminated spear hovering as an afterimage in his vision. "Unknown."

"Dang."

"Damn straight. Inbound to the client. Will keep you apprised. Oh— and I need the hours of the coffee shop at the Binbirdirek Cistern."

"Maybe it's time for something stronger." Nick rang off.

Grant returned to the arch where he had stashed the client and called softly, "Ms. Akbulut?" Nothing. He crouched and slipped under the broken door, hit by the smell of somebody's flop space, urine, sweat and vomit. Between him and the rumpled bedding, a jagged hole in the floor. "Ms. Akbulut?" He pulled out a Maglite and clicked it on, shining it down into the hole.

"It's about time you got here!" Bedraggled, she cling to the pillar of a column at least twenty feet below, shivering.

Grant lay down on the stone parts of the floor and stretched his arm over the gap, shining the light in all directions to get a sense for the space. More columns, dry ground to one side, and a scatter of leaves.

"Well? Get me out!"

He drew the light back toward her. "If you follow the edge for three columns, it'll bring you to a platform of some kind. I can't see far, but there are leaves—there's an opening somewhere close."

She stared back at him, then lowered her eyes, sullen as a teenager. She crept her hands along the rim, and he kept the light moving just ahead of her, lighting her path. When she reached the dry span, she tried to scramble up, cried out and fell back again with a shriek. He twitched forward, not breathing until she broke the surface again, floundering and finding the rim, struggling for purchase.

"It's too slick. I can't." Her hands shook and her lips compressed. Terrified.

Man shot this morning at her own shindig, another one gutted in a hospital while she helped, and now this. Yep, cause for terror, for sure. "Hang on." Grant withdrew his hand, and she gave a stifled cry. He flicked out the compact drybag and slipped his gun and phone inside, securing it to his belt. Flashlight between his teeth, Grant shifted to sitting, letting his legs dangle into the hole, broken wood jabbing at him through his pants. Mental note to thank Nick for his choice of materials. Looked like fine suiting, wore like tactical cloth. He pulled his shoes off, tied them together and stuffed his socks inside, then tossed them across the cistern to land on the dry ground. That done, Grant turned and swung himself down, holding onto the edge of stone past the broken wood. He dropped into the water.

It rushed up over him, flooding his mouth. He found bottom, absorbed the impact and pushed back for the surface, not far. Flashlight in hand, he spit out the water and shook back his hair, then swam over toward her, the waves of his entrance subsiding, one of the last slapping her face. Grant hooked one arm around the nearest column and beckoned to her. She crept back toward him, and he drew her in closer, leaning back from the column and bracing his feet against the slimy wall beneath the surface. "Hold the column, pull yourself up as far as you can, then lie onto the ground. I'll give you a boost."

Silent and accepting, as if the defiance had finally been wrung from her, she did as he asked. He set his hand at her tailbone. "One, two, three, go." She grappled with the column, scrambled higher and flopped partway onto the pavement while he pushed, then lifted from behind. While she crawled further from the water, he tossed the light after her, got both hands on the column and walked his feet up. He gave her a moment to collect whatever dignity remained to her, and replaced his socks and shoes, sweeping the light over the surfaces around them, and finding the passage where the leaves tumbled in.

"How did you even get here?" she muttered.

Grant turned back, liberating the gun from his dry bag, keeping the phone inside it while he tucked it in a pocket. "Still got your phone?"

She produced it. "Even if it survived the water, I don't think we'll get a signal." She started to poke at it, and he snagged it from her hands. How had he gotten here? Tracked the goddamned phone he had told her to ditch. How had they? They hadn't tracked Akilah, she was too good. Condition? Unknown.

He gripped the phone as if he could throttle it, then hurled it in the air over the cistern its flight tracking through the flashlight's beam. He whipped out the gun and fired, shattering the screen into a mosaic of high-tech garbage. The sound echoed around them, covering the splash as the phone hit the surface and sank from view.

The gun weighed down his hand. Could he have shot her assailant? Not without risking her, not without endangering all those civilians. He slipped the gun back to its place and collected the flashlight, aiming it down the corridor. "I assume you have a ride?"

Silence. She sat in the same place, her knees drawn up and arms pressed over her ears. Her eyes gleamed white as she looked at him.

"Don't worry. I'm all done shooting." For now.

She brought down her arms. Nick would've offered her a hand up. Nick was the better man. Kyra Akbulut crawled onto her knees and finally rose, starting to clean herself off, her hands drooping as she abandoned the effort. Her crisp, white shirt looked as if she'd slept in it. At the bottom of a swamp. "I have a ride. Adem is to meet me."

"Let's go." He indicated the slanting corridor.

"Home?" she asked with a tremor of hope.

"Negative." He glanced back at her. "I know where she stashed the codex. Let's go see what she might have died for."

CHAPTER SEVENTEEN

During the quiet ride to the coffee shop, the well-scrubbed sensations of the hammam transformed into stiff clothes and strange odors, not to mention the algae-slick feeling on the bottoms of Grant's feet. He mustered up something like good cheer to confront the disbelief on the barista's face as he handed over the package to a guy who literally looked, and smelled, like he had crawled out of the sewer. The rest of the way back to Kyra's mansion, Grant stared at the label. Plain brown wrapper, tied with string. Clear, slanting script. *"Grant Casey, care of the Bone Guard."* He had never seen her handwriting before. Maybe never would again. He could count on one hand the number of times they'd ever spoken—the fact of her absence shouldn't scrape at him, like a fresh scab. What had he ever known but her absence?

To the app: >*you okay?*

Expecting no answer, maybe ever. The phone gripped in his hand. Needed a plan. What else did he have? He pulled up Brunelle's number and opened a message. *Third chance may be needed. Boss Lady pissed, and it's on my head. Screwed up bigtime. Again.*

Third chance. Maybe Akilah's only chance—and he didn't know enough about the enemy to know what he wanted, how to find her, how to stop him.

Kyra glanced toward his phone, but he'd already put it away, and she didn't raise her eyes to his face.

Only two sets of boots on the ground, no allies in sight. No knowing what they were up against. The situation stank worse than he did.

On her side of the car, wrapped in a thick blanket Adem had retrieved from the trunk, Kyra stared out the window and said nothing. Just as well. This time, they pulled up around the back where Kostas, the limo driver, waited to close the gate behind them. Nick pounced on the car as it halted. Grant got out and shut the door. He and Nick shared a glance, and Grant gave the slightest nod.

Pre-empting Kostas, Nick went to Kyra's side and opened the door, offering a hand. "You must be exhausted, ma'am. There's already a bath running for you."

She gazed up at him, smiling as if at her guardian angel. "Thank you, Nick." Adem hustled after her while Kostas stowed the car.

"You retrieved the objective and kept the client safe," Nick said. Grant walked over and placed the package in Nick's hands.

"She doesn't open that without me. She doesn't take a goddamn step without me."

"Chief..." Nick flashed a smile. "How was the bath?"

Grant spun at him, fist flying, then slammed it into his own palm just short of Nick's face. "Fuck you, Norton."

"Next time, send me to lounge with the guys in towels—you stick with the boss lady." Nick shrugged. "Irene and I got some tea brewing you want some after you clean up. I'll take charge of this." He pulled the bundle to his chest and offered the stairs.

"I met the Phantom—she made me her back-up, told me where to find it."

"The Phantom? Not just the thief?"

"Gimme a break, Nick, it was the same woman. And before you ask, no I have no proof." The app would've deleted their message string, and nothing connected the package today with a woman he met a year ago, the single word she had given him then: her name.

"You're toeing the line, Chief. I don't wanna think what you think that I'm thinking."

"I know and I'm sorry." He took a pause on the stair, briefing Nick on what had happened since that meeting, and getting Nick's report about the shooter's death. He scanned his friend as he listened, looking for the jiggle of nervous movement, the icy stare, the way he held his right hand vertical as if he already held a gun, the two missing fingers only emphasizing that shape. Nothing.

Nick tipped his head. "Dosed up when we got back. Thought I might blow it when the boss lady ditched me." He turned his right hand vertical, back to horizontal. "I'm okay."

"Glad to hear it."

Nick gave a little salute at the door to his room.

The shower didn't help much, not the sluicing of the clear water between his toes, nor the pounding of full pressure against his neck and shoulders. At least he smelled better when he stepped out. He pulled on a tactical shirt and pants, no logos, slipping into the pockets a few things that might come in handy. Grasping for the edge of a plan.

In the salon, Irene sat with her feet tucked up in a big soft chair, Nick regaling her with a story from their Mongolian adventure. The parcel sat in his lap, and Kyra sat across from him, her hair draped long over her toweled shoulders, her eyes on the package.

Adem stepped forward to pour a glass of tea for Grant, then set down the pot and hovered uncertainly.

"That's all for now. Thank you, Adem." She took a very deep breath, and let it out in a measured way, then finally looked at him. "I owe you an apology, Mr. Casey. I dismissed your concerns for my safety and that of others."

He sipped the tea and decided whether to forgive her. Every minute he spent here, Akilah lost time.

When he didn't speak, she looked to Nick, and back. "Well? We shall open it, yes?"

Grant flicked a knife out of his pocket and offered it to Nick, hilt first. Kyra drew back a little, her lips pinching.

"You shouldn't scare them," she had said. *"Can't help it." "You could*

if you wanted to."

Nick cut the string and peeled back the paper, as carefully as if he wanted to save it for next Christmas. Or as if he knew what it meant to his boss. Underneath, in a layer of archival cloth, lay a thick sheaf of parchment, irregular in size and color, bound along one edge with careful stitches that ended in ragged threads where covers had been removed, possibly re-used in a bygone day. In spite of himself, Grant held his breath and finally sat. Nick placed the codex, still on its cloth, on the round table between them, and all four leaned in. Partially obscured by the graying of time and mildew, spidery Latin text scrawled the front of the book.

"*Being the observation,*'" Irene muttered, translating. "Then some words are obscured, then, '*one Aleume de Clari*'. Robert's brother!" She sat back a little, fingers to her lips. "Aleume was a fighting priest, the first through the wall into the treasury." She patted Nick's knee and explained, "Robert's account of the invasion is known the world over."

"The invasion—the Crusade, 1204, right?"

"Indeed." She beamed at him. "Let's see what we've got." She reached out, but Kyra turned the manuscript to face her, covering it with a possessive hand.

"What we have, is what I've paid for." She aimed a hard stare at Grant. "That means your job here is over. When I transfer the funds, I shall ensure a generous bonus for your troubles. Of course you may stay the night. Adem can book your flight home in the morning."

Kyra had just made his message to Brunelle plain facts, no ruse. Take her up on it. Grant stared at her through the steam off his cup, acutely aware of the phone in his pocket, and how it failed to buzz. He still needed Kyra. Needed the book, and whatever it held. "You don't seriously think this is over." He set the cup down with deliberate care. "A man died today because he was trying to kill me—again. You and I were shot at when I broke up an abduction attempt. The codex is now the least of your worries."

She stiffened.

"Wait a minute—what happened?" her mother said, but Kyra ignored her.

"How did you know where to find it?" When he gave no immediate reply, she went on, "The thief said nothing in my presence, left no clues in that carriage. You claimed you would be straight with me, Mr. Casey. The woman, the thief, how do you know her and how long did you intend to keep your relationship quiet?"

CHAPTER EIGHTEEN

Mother tried again to interrupt, but Kyra waved her to silence. Kyra held his gaze, and his preternatural stillness suggested much was passing behind those eyes.

Finally, he said, "She's another operator. Our work intersected in Mongolia. I made her—recognized her—at the archives when she put out the flames on the burn victim. She made contact earlier today to exchange information. She didn't tell me in so many words where to find the manuscript, but she said enough to make me her back up, in case something went wrong with delivery—to you, as it turns out."

As he spoke, his fist clenched, then slowly released again. "She was scared, and it takes a lot to rattle someone like that. She's now in enemy hands. Because of you."

"She's a thief, a risk-taker, not unlike yourself. Presumably, this is an occupational hazard, and one she is prepared for." Kyra pulled the manuscript into her lap. Part of what he wanted, she knew, was to be among the first to view it. "How can you be sure it wasn't your own earlier meeting that called attention to her, and not my phone at all? With the phone gone, there is hardly a chain of evidence, is there?"

Mother clapped her hands together, as if she were getting the attention of an unruly class. "You can't just shush me—someone shot at you?" Mother said. "You didn't mention that! And who's died?"

"Not now, Mother." Kyra tossed back her hair. "Perhaps there was danger, but it's done now: whoever they are, those people don't know we have the manuscript, unless you think your friend the thief will tell them? She swore discretion when I hired her, do you think she would betray that now?"

"That may depend on what kind of pressure they apply."

She very much wanted to misunderstand him, and couldn't think how to reply.

Casey unfolded himself from the couch. "Ask Adem to bring up the contract on your tablet. If our obligation here is over, you need to sign off on it. Whatever happens next is not our problem and not our fault." He put up his hands. "There's a hotel by the airport. Nick—I'm calling a ride."

He stalked toward the stairs, and she fought not to look after him. Her fingers tightened on the manuscript. Was he really planning to leave? She merely wanted to force his hand, to show that he was as complicit as she was —but she had severely misjudged the situation.

"'Not now, Mother?'" Mother's voice rose. "Did I not hear this? Did he save your life? What on earth is going on, Kyra?"

With a pat on her hand, Nick said, "There's an order of knights with a messianic leader who claims he can unite the peoples of the Mediterranean, and isn't afraid to use violence to do it. Right so far, Chief? He's looking for the symbols to draw those peoples together and make them believe in him. Your daughter and this guy both believe the clues are in this book. Your daughter thinks he'll stop now he doesn't know where the book is, thinks he'll leave her alone. Meantime, the thief—" he stopped abruptly, looking after his boss. Nick worked his jaw, then said, "It was a genuine pleasure, Irene. I need to go."

Mother grabbed his arm as he rose, sliding her hands down to grip his. "No, please don't leave. He won't give up, he won't stop."

Kyra dropped into Turkish. "You're acting crazy, Mother. Just let them go. I can hire some local thugs if I need protection." Someone easier to control. Someone who took orders from her instead of the other way around.

"No, no, no! Kyra." Mother's head shook as if with a palsy, tears streaking her face. She'd always been dramatic—part of teaching literature,

Kyra supposed—but this was going too far.

"Mother! Calm down. There's no need for this, certainly not while there are strangers present."

Casey's voice, low and clear. "Mrs. Akbulut. Would you tell us what you know?"

"She doesn't know anything," Kyra shot back, hugging the manuscript now. "This was my father's work, his love. She's just overprotective of me, and won't see that I'm an adult, and I make my own way."

Mother's mouth screwed up as if she were about to start yelling. Nick stroked her hand, squatting down before her with some effort on his part. "I think she knows that, Kyra. More to the point, I think the chief's onto something. It's okay, Irene. If you know more about this, I'd love to hear it."

Her mother's troubled eyes shifted from Kyra, to the man before her. "He wants the Throne of Solomon."

"Which you have always insisted either does not exist, or was destroyed a thousand years ago," Kyra snapped. "Besides, how would you know what he wants, this mystery person? Maybe he is the one who doesn't exist."

Mother blinked at her as if astonished. "Because he claims to be the king of Jerusalem. What else could he possibly want but the throne?"

CHAPTER NINETEEN

A camera carefully hidden in a whorl of stone enabled Blaise to keep an eye on the woman chained to the wall. The knights had transferred her from a cell to the wall in anticipation of her waking. This one had not received a full dose, so he came to the office a little early hoping to catch the moment she realized her predicament. She hung a foot or so off the ground, her wrists in padded cuffs fixed to a chain that rose another two feet above her head to an iron loop below one of the boarded-up windows. When he first arrived, finishing off an after-dinner drink, she hung limp, her hair in her face, stripped of the loose gown she'd been wearing earlier to reveal practical dark pants and tunic underneath. She carried nothing. No wallet, jewelry, cash, phone. She must have stashed them someplace before the meet. The pram had been similarly empty, not only of a baby, but of any sign to who she was, what she wanted, or what she had done with the book. She intrigued him. She possessed the spirit of a warrior, but none of the upstanding moral quality a true knight required.

Her extended arms tightened almost imperceptibly, and Blaise zoomed in on her. Her eyes stilled beneath their lids, but did not open and her cheeks twitched slightly. She woke, but wished to pretend to be unconscious. Interesting. For a long moment, she remained as she had been, then her head lifted, her hair flung back and shaken down her shoulders as she swept the room with her gaze. Three dim bulbs lit the space, leaving the area behind the pillars in shadow. After that first quick sweep, she targeted each of those areas in turn, twisting against the wall to look to either side. Apparently, whatever she saw satisfied her because she began moving more, her fingers groping the opposite wrist, exploring her bonds. The angle and the strapping mechanism prevented someone from working free—Blaise felt confident in that. How long should he let her hang? What would it take, for this particular witness, to convince her she was utterly in his control?

She kicked off from the wall with one foot, pushed, and turned herself to face the stone. Blaise set down his glass and leaned in.

She pushed her feet into the wall and walked them up until she looked to be sitting in mid-air. Then she grabbed the chain above her hands and walked further, slow, deliberate progress, working her hands up the chain, her feet up the wall until she got to the bolt below the windowsill. Hanging on tight, she inched one leg higher, then hooked her knee over the bolt, locking herself there, bringing her hands up to grab the window. She bent her body forward, the toe of her other shoe still dug into the gap between stones. For a moment, she kept her hands up, working her fingers, probably trying to relieve the pressure from hanging down. She reached again, and found something to grasp with her fingertips, working her feet again and angling herself sideways into the narrow window, her feet braced opposite. The chain wouldn't reach high at that point, but she bent her head down, biting for the straps at her wrists.

Good Lord, she might even succeed. Tempting, almost, to let her try.

What then? How far could she get from this chamber before the knights brought her once more to heel? Last time, she had nearly brought them to heel. Blaise pushed back and donned his silver mask. One staircase down through the centuries, two knights at the door outside her chamber. He unlocked the door and slammed it open to the inside.

The woman's precarious balance slipped. For a moment, she tried to grab something, but her awkward position and the sloping windowsill conspired. She tumbled from the perch scraping the wall. The chain stopped her descent with a jerk and she swallowed her cry, her gaze immediately directed to him. One end of the wrist strap stuck out from the buckle, halfway undone. Very impressive.

"Welcome," he said in Turkish. "Please pardon the accommodations. Security is an important concern as I'm sure you'll agree. If you prove cooperative, conditions can improve rapidly. How should I address you during your stay?" He strolled closer to her, his hands kept low and inviting, every gesture and tone non-threatening, his smile gentle and concerned rather than pointed.

"I should like the return of my hijab."

She spoke the language well, but with a Syrian accent. Interesting. Blaise nodded gravely. "I'll see what I can do." He summoned one of the knights by the door. "Would you please find a suitable head covering for our guest? Thank you."

"Of course, my lord." The knight bowed out of his presence and hurried away.

"'My lord?'" she asked, her eyes a piercing green as they flicked over him, taking in his mask, his cape, his suit. Her gaze lingered at the signet ring. A bruise marked her cheek with a slight scrape showing where the ring had marked her. Her gaze returned to his face as if to memorize him. What little she could see of him.

"My sworn knights use this honorific to show their respect for my leadership."

"The book is already sold. I have no more information for you."

"So it is only money for you? What if I offered you more money to get it back?"

She made no reply.

"What do you believe is more important than money?"

She frowned.

"It's alright." He strolled closer to her, their eyes almost on a level. "There are no wrong answers. Just as there are no wrong religions, no wrong peoples."

"If this is so, why am I chained?"

He raised a finger. "No wrong peoples. Wrong individuals, certainly. People who have taken their priorities to an extreme that makes them a danger to others, yes. Even then, they are mostly misguided. Given the chance to repent of their misdeeds, they may redeem themselves. Even you. So. Is family more important than money?" He watched her closely, keen to see what she believed, what lever he might use to draw her back. A minute sadness pinched her lips. "Is love more important?" A cynical eyebrow. "Justice?" Interest, suspicion. "Peace?"

"Peace without justice is tyranny," a whisper.

Blaise smiled, letting it ring in his voice. "Precisely. So you can see how important it is to achieve both peace and justice, in order to bring peace to our troubled times."

"Another man who speaks of peace to a woman in chains. What is this, if not tyranny?"

He slapped the wall beside her. "Of course there will be struggle—it will not be easy to create the peace that we need, and those who cannot repent of their misdeeds and move forward, they will suffer. But those who can embrace their wrongs and accept the pain, they will together forge a new order and bring peace to all. It will take leaders both strong and inspiring to make this so."

She flinched a little at the slap of his hand against stone, then said, "My abductor wishes me to repent of my theft?"

"Would you have listened to reason if we tried to speak? I think not. I've dealt with your kind before."

"You know nothing of my kind."

"Thieves who hire out for money? Who offer illegal services to anyone who can pay?" He taunted her, opening the rift. "What about the money? Do you hide your treasure like a pirate until you can retire to the tropics and reap the sweat of others' work?"

She almost laughed—not the reaction he anticipated. "It is already spent. To smuggle a hundred women and children to a place where they can breathe free. That is the kind of treasure I keep. What is more important than money? Almost anything."

A thief with a cause. Interesting. "Then we are in agreement. Tell me where to find the codex and you may carry on with your work."

"You say there will be suffering. Why must it always be the weak who suffer?" She hung in chains, bruised and defiant.

"So you see nothing wrong in what you do? Nothing at all?"

"I have skills. I use them for the weak."

Blaise frowned over this. "You have no other skills, nothing that would provide you an honest living?"

"I used to. This pays more." She offered a smile that did not reach her eyes. "I don't repent of what I must do in service to others. Do you?"

"I do, in fact. Even when the cause is worthy, and that is the difference between you and I." Blaise straightened away from the wall as if the interview were over. Let her relax, just for a moment. The knight returned to the doorway, a scarf across his hands, but Blaise held up one hand to stop him.

Blaise turned sharply, wrapping his palm over her forehead, pinning her to the wall and prying open her left eye with his thumb. He slipped the ring from his finger and held it up. A carved lion with ruby eyes, it concealed a small reservoir. With slight pressure, the sharp ears could deliver twin thrusts of the powerful tranquilizer he had topped off after their earlier encounter. He brought the ring up to her eye, the open white reflecting dull gold as she squirmed. "Are you Nizari? Are you here to kill me? Tell me the truth or I take your eye."

For a moment, she hung still, breath held, then she jack-knifed, pulling up her knees and knocking him back. Her feet lashed out at him, driving him off. The ring flew away, tumbling on the ground.

Blaise staggered and regained his balance. His hand curled into a fist, and he launched back toward her, then stopped short. Anger gained him nothing. Should he test again the Lion of Truth? He already knew she was a skilled dissembler. It would merely be punishment without effect. Better to preserve her, such as she was. She had no value for him, but she would for others.

One of the knights knelt and retrieved his ring, offering it up for him, and Blaise accepted, sliding it back onto his right hand.

He walked to the door where the other knight remained with the scarf. "Prepare her for our allies. I don't think there's any more to be learned.

Perhaps they can reach her while I cannot."

He glanced at the scarf in the man's hands and added, "Do what you must to subdue her, but keep her intact if you're able. Bind her tightly." He glanced back at the woman. "After all, she has skills."

CHAPTER TWENTY

Kyra's mother swept from the room, and they all trailed after, as faithful as one of the daughter's bots. Grant exchanged a look with Nick. "Every minute counts," he whispered.

"I know, Chief. But the more we learn more about the enemy, the more ammo we have to defeat him. You got a plan? A direction?"

Still nothing. Irene led them to a door on the courtyard side of the building.

"That's his office," Kyra said, her arms folded over the book.

Irene set her hand on the handle, the other palm flat on the center of the door, as if over its heartbeat. She opened the door, and Nick stepped through. Grant moved to follow and Kyra cut him off, gliding inside as her mother turned on the lights. Floor-to-ceiling shelves heaped equally with books, boxes, and artifacts. A model of the Antikythera mechanism, replicated from the first century, stood ready to predict the next eclipse while a fragment of mosaic looked on with a single open eye. Fragments of sculptures in bronze and marble held down stacks of papers, and a stand magnifier occupied the center of the desk. Irene started opening drawers, rifling papers, closing them again.

"Mother, stop." Kyra approached the other side of the desk. "Stop it! What are you even looking for?"

And how would she ever find it, in all of this? The knowledge and resources gathered here filled Grant with a hunger he'd nearly forgotten.

How many mysteries had this man uncovered? How many had he solved, and how many remained obscure through the passage of time? If he had a few hours—if he had had another lifetime. He scanned the shelves, then frowned.

"King of Jerusalem, you say?" He pointed, and she turned at the sound of his voice. On a crowded bulletin board, a folded sheet with a wax seal peeked between memos dated from years ago. The wax seal showed a simple mask, a long rectangle with eyes and a strong nose, but no mouth. "One of the kings wore a mask to conceal his leprosy."

She pounced. "I like you, Mr. Grant, I do." Eager fingers pulled the letter free and held it up, triumphant. Kyra snatched it, placing the codex on the desk and opening the letter on top of it, but her mother said, "He sends his condolences, and asks if my husband's papers will be deposited at the archive or if he may come view the collection here. He says he has a historical as well as personal interest because a relative of his was—!" she broke off, her hand in the air as if reaching for the answer.

"The king of Jerusalem," Nick supplied.

"Precisely!" She beamed as at a star pupil.

"At least you didn't let him in." Kyra scanned the letter, then dropped it on the desk.

Irene's mobile face folded in concern. "Certainly I did. Despite what you may think, I don't wish your father's legacy, however strange, to be lost." She shrugged and plowed on, oblivious to Kyra's horrified expression. "He found nothing of interest. If he sought the throne, he would find nothing. Your father's notes on the throne, his speculations, are among the papers you took away. The most important things, he published before his death. Otherwise, there is nothing to know." Another shrug, but halfway to a sigh this time. "Because it no longer exists, if it ever did. There is no record of the throne after the tenth century."

Kyra bowed her head over the codex, and Irene's gaze stroked over her daughter's hair. Grant walked softly over.

"So," Nick said, "this delusional king thinks it does, and he'll kill to find it. Don't know if that's any better than looking for the real thing. If a thing's real, you find it, the op is done. It doesn't exist, you could go mad with the searching."

"Like my husband did," Irene murmured. She turned away toward the window, rubbing her elbows.

At the desk, Kyra opened the codex, flipping a few pages. "You're wrong, Mother. You always have been."

She flipped a few more pages, then her hand hesitated. She glanced back to Grant, then straightened, permitting him to see what she did. A drawing emerged from the medieval paper, an ink sketch that showed a seat with seven steps, lions on some, birds on others—eagles? The back of the throne formed a circle at the top, with a six-pointed star framed by smaller circles: the Seal of Solomon. From behind an artificial tree rose up. "You are so very wrong. Aleume de Clari saw it in 1204." Her fingers shook as she traced over lines of text. Latin. Her brow furrowed.

"'...and beneath the chamber,'" Grant murmured, taking a knee to get closer to the page, "'another with treasure...more remarkable, a kingly seat clad in gold and open to see—'" he frowned. After the adventure in Mongolia, he'd taken up the study of Latin during his down time. Too many ancient texts and academic works relied on a dead language he hadn't looked at since high school.

Irene flicked on a desk lamp and bent its neck toward the manuscript, while Nick leaned over him.

Grant continued translating, "'The mechanics?' Screws?" He chose a more generic word. "'The workings of Solomon that only his—sophia, his wisdom, could bring about.'"

A drop of water struck the opposite page. Kyra wiped the tears from her eyes. "It is real. It was here. My father was right." Nick pulled an armload of books from a chair and placed the chair behind her. She sat heavily, dazed.

Grant dabbed away the tear from the book, and turned the page. Staining confused some of the drawings: a griffin with rods for a neck, a lion with a bellows at its back, a bird constructed of small plates like scaled armor. Here and there, the narrative picked up, Aleume noting the contents of this hidden room, vowing to keep it silent, even from his fellow Crusaders. "*For so many would strip this gold for booty and not for the treasure it is in faith. To Jerusalem it must...and there to glorify the seat of Solomon's heirs...to our refuge... Until again the holy land is in our grasp.*" He looked up from the page. "It sounds like this Aleume hid the contents and smuggled them out of Istanbul, to some kind of refuge where he thought they'd be safe until they controlled Jerusalem again."

"But they never did," Irene pointed out. She waved a hand at an antique map framed on the wall. "It was only a few years before that the King of Jerusalem was slain by assassins."

"Nizari Isma'ili." Grant sat back on his heels. According to Akilah, they were trying again, searching for the man who would be king. Let them, if it would save her life. Could be already too late while he worshiped at the altar of history. This, right here, was the kind of thing for which the Bone Guard was born, both as a business, and as a man. How much would he risk for a virtual stranger? Would he turn over the throne if he knew its location, if he knew how the king would employ it?

Akilah had called him. She made him her back-up. She had, so far as he knew, nobody else. The king's letter lay on the desk and Grant picked it up, not following much of the Turkish script save that he'd recognize the handwriting if he ever needed to. The date, seven years ago. But the address...

"Irene. Hagia Dynamis. You said it was never built." He held up the letter. "But our man used it in his return address."

CHAPTER TWENTY-ONE

Kyra blinked to clear her eyes. The moment Casey's attention shifted to interrogating her mother, she turned reverently back to the image of the throne. A stronghold of the Latins. Where would they have taken it? Where might it lie hidden for centuries? Why had her father not lived long enough to know this? Then a name caught her attention and she returned to the conversation. "What was that?"

"Doctor Paleologos. He would have the best maps and the most information on where to find the Dynamis." Mother pressed her hands together.

"Would he tell us?"

"It's the middle of the night," Nick pointed out.

Casey's hands rested on the shelf as if studying the Antikythera model consumed him. "It has to be. We don't have time." He pivoted abruptly to face them. "What do we have to do to get information from this man? You both agree he's the most likely to know. What will it take?"

"Show him the codex?" Nick suggested.

Both women immediately shook their heads. "I would believe a text," Mother said. "Him? Never. He is the head of archeology, my husband's boss, if you will, and he thinks he was crazy for believing. Doesn't matter if the text is the *Book of Ceremonies*, or the narrative of an Islamic captive of the reign. The stories of that time are stories only, as likely to be fiction as fact, their drawings as fanciful as a child's. Text is nothing to this man."

"For Paleologos?" Casey almost smiled. "Ironic, wouldn't you say?"

Nick gave a gesture of confusion. "You're the history geek, not me."

With a chuckle, Mother explained, "The professor's name means 'old words.'"

Kyra shied away from anything to do with the old donkey, as her father used to call him. "Why even pursue that? We have the book, we have the lead: we look for the refuge. We read the book more closely. Fit up the yacht, and we go."

"We?" Casey folded his arms. His expression had gone still and dark again, the way it had when he shot her phone out of the sky.

She traced the throne with one cautious finger. The book required proper conservation, but her heart already raced. Where would the journey take them? Sidon? Acre? She had imagined this mad king would give up when he couldn't get the book, only to discover he'd been on the quest even longer than she had. If seven years of nothing had not swayed him, a single day's setback would certainly not. He seemed as determined as she was, but for utterly different reasons. She wove her fingers in her lap. "Mr. Casey. I have many resources, as you know, but you and Nick have others. Complimentary skills." Shooting a moving object in the darkness. Fending off armed assailants. Stopping a killer with one's bare hands. Stabilizing a life-threatening injury. Not to mention reading Latin. "I hope I don't need that kind of skill on this journey, but it may be that I do."

"It's a new contract. A new mission. I'll get D.A. to write it up and we'll have it to you in an hour."

"That's acceptable."

"Paleologos. How do we get to him?"

"We don't need to, do we?"

Nick stepped in. "If he's got the intel to understand the enemy, yeah, we do."

Casey squatted in front of her, touching the codex. "Ma'am. There's a woman's life in the balance. And you put her there. If you can't see that, I am through." Low, even, precise. Almost, she wanted to say, mechanical. Save that machines were so much easier than people. People lied and betrayed. They got confused, concerned, upset. They got in trouble, got hurt, got hemorrhagic fever and died just when you needed them most.

"I know what he wants. Paleologos. Wait here."

He shifted back to let her pass. Kyra found the narrow stairs to the next floor, unsurprised to glance back and find Nick following her a few paces back. He spread his hands in apology, but did not stop until they got to her childhood room, then he waited at the door. Her meticulous arrangement remained from her youth, in a clear and organized contrast to her father. Sometimes, it was a wonder they'd gotten on as well as they did. Furniture with clean, Scandinavian lines, drawers without knobs or handles, shelves of books in alphabetical order. Neatly labeled boxes of clothes and memorabilia, including one labeled, "Spolia." A word she learned from her father to describe the so many things stolen between nations throughout history, treasures taken by one culture after another, stripped of their context and displayed like trophies, until another conqueror. This box used to live with her in California, until her father's illness when she brought it back to share with him one last time. She imagined she might bury it with him, like the grave goods of an emperor, but in the end, she could not bear to do so. Enough, then, to be parted from it by continents and oceans. She slipped the box from its place and carried it back, Nick escorting her in silent procession, aside from the slightest squeak of his prosthetic as he took the stairs.

Back in the office, Casey sat in the chair she had vacated, and her mother beside him, both of them examining the Latin manuscript. Kyra placed the box on the desk across from the codex. "I was about eight when my father first showed me this. He made me put on gloves to hold it. It was when I took my first engineering degree he gave it to me. I brought it back when he died. I thought it should be close to home again." She opened the lid, all three of the others getting closer with a gratifying excitement. That changed to disappointment when she removed the smaller box inside, an ornate tin that once held Turkish Delight. "My father's idea of a joke. We spoke all the time of how cultures would steal from others, like the bronze horses of San Marco in Venice that used to be in the hippodrome of Constantinople."

She wiggled loose the lid of the tin and unfolded the linen to reveal her father's delight: a fragment he should never have taken, more proof, Paleologos would say, that her father had been unfit for his job.

"Oh," her mother said. "I wondered where that had gone."

On the antique linen lay a partial arm, elbow to wrist, part of the hand with two fingers remaining, but the structure of the arm was wooden, its casing of gold-worked bronze, a special mix the ancients called "orichalcum." The elbow showed a broken joint, of wood and metal. The wrist and fingers, too, were carefully jointed to emulate natural posture. The sight of the arm lying on its little pillow sent her straight back to childhood, to the first time her father had opened that box, when she was maybe eight years old, and her own arm about the same size as the artifact.

She and her father gazed into the box, both wearing gloves. He had cleaned the arm of any debris from the rubbish fill where he had found it, and now revealed it for her inspection.

"But Bapi, who broke the girl made of gears? Why would they hurt her?"

"I wish I knew that, Tatli. She's made of strong things, and must have been beautiful—like you." Her father squeezed her shoulders. "Very clever people made her—also like you. Sometimes, angry people are jealous of those who are clever and strong and beautiful—"

"Like Ibrahim. Just because I beat him at maths. Because I always beat him at maths." She lay her arm alongside the broken one, and imagined the girl made of gears being whole and beautiful again. "Should I let him beat me, so he won't be angry?"

"Tatli. Don't ever let anyone beat you. Give them something to be jealous of. If they are smart, you will inspire them. And if they are not, don't let them hold you back."

Kyra ran a gloved finger over the broken arm. "Maybe I can fix her one day."

"We can't fix the past, Tatli. We can study it. We learn from it. Maybe you learn to make a better one." He folded the cloth back over his treasure. "I shall study the gifts of the past, but you are my gift to the future." He kissed the top of her head.

The memory almost brought back the tears, but Kyra refused them.

"Are you sure?" Casey asked her, his voice warmer now, almost gentle.

How much of herself had she revealed? "Paleologos would love to get his hands on this." Kyra put the lid back on the box. "If you are right, the technology of today condemned your friend. Perhaps the technology of yesterday can save her."

CHAPTER TWENTY-TWO

B laise woke instantly when the phone rang. He'd been asleep only a few hours, and it had been rather a long and frustrating day already. Technically, it was the next day now. "Hello?"

"My lord. I suggest you look at the external monitors. The carpet store entrance." Haldan, succinct and unapologetic.

"Give me a moment." Blaise switched on a light and opened his laptop, calling up the surveillance for the building. He clicked through a few silent views of empty streets and alleys—empty except for his own people. The carpet shop occupied a narrow store front beside a cafe on the side of the block they allowed to molder like most of the city. Outside the carpet shop, a man stood as if in thought. Dark hair, dark suit, controlled movements as he walked a few steps past, glanced up at the facade, then a few steps the other direction. He leaned in close, putting a hand against the glass to look into the shop.

"It's him. Donahue. The Bone Guard who contacted me."

"How on earth did he find the carpet shop?"

"I don't know, my lord. How should we handle this?"

Blaise watched the man study the area. "You thought he was a good prospect, a likely penitent."

Haldan hesitated. "From what you said of the incident last night, and what he said in his text, I think so."

"And yet, you pause."

"My lord." Haldan remained silent a moment longer. "In the

bathhouse, as we spoke. He wants me to think those tattoos are prison work, but they mean more to him that that, I'd swear on it. He's careful, cagey."

Haldan's voice held a note Blaise rarely heard. "You respect him."

"His attempts to address the archives situation impressed me. If we could win him over, he could be one of the greatest knights we've ever had."

"And if we cannot, he's dangerous." Blaise smiled grimly in the darkness. "He's outside our door at three in the morning. Unless you gave him the address—which I don't believe you did," Blaise hastened to add, "he is already dangerous."

Another pause. "Yes, my lord. I'll have the night watch take care of him."

"No, Haldan, not yet. Invite him in. See what he does. We can always choose to stop him, to end his incursion, if that's what this is. And if it is a defection, the fact that he's found us only suggests what level of talent he brings to our service."

Haldan rang off while Blaise brought up the rest of his monitors and turned on the listening devices. In a moment, when the Bone Guard seemed about to leave, the lights in the carpet shop came on, and Qassim shuffled across the shop in his slippers and Persian robe. "What do you want? It's three am?" Qassim shouted out the door.

The Bone Guard turned back, his eyes looking haunted in the yellow light, his faint smile contrite. In halting Turkish he said, "Apology. I look for Haldan Brunelle. I am late. More apologies." Then he rolled back his left sleeve and displayed his wrist. It was hard to make out on the monitor, but he wore a small cross inked over his pulse, an apparent match to the tattoos of the other knights. The man had gone to some length for whatever he was trying to achieve. Blaise's curiosity grew.

Qassim startled and looked at him more closely, then bowed back from the door. "Sir, forgive me. Let me see if I can reach him."

The Bone Guard entered and hovered between the heaps of carpets on low tables while Qassim made himself look busy on the phone, scowling at his unexpected visitor. "Mr. Brunelle. So sorry to disturb you. Yes, someone to see you—your name?"

"Michael Donahue," the Bone Guard supplied.

"A Mr. Donahue." Qassim exaggerated the name, listened, said, "Yes, alright, alright." He hung up. "Mr. Brunelle can be here soon."

"Thank you." Donahue rubbed his neck, glanced around, fidgeted with his cuffs. Finally, footsteps echoed on metal stairs, the curtain at the back of the shop ruffled, then Haldan ducked through, wearing a t-shirt and sweatpants. He rubbed his eyes as if he hadn't been awake.

"Michael. Sorry I didn't get back to you."

"It's okay, it's fine." Donahue shook his head. "Sorry. I probably shouldn't have come." He gave a hopeless gesture toward the door, as if he should go, but couldn't bring himself to leave. "I wasn't sure what else to do."

"It's alright. Come on up. Thanks, Qassim." Haldan gave a wave and Qassim relocked the door. Haldan led their guest through the curtain at the back, up the narrow stairs to the apartment over the shop. "You want a drink?"

"I don't. No alcohol."

Haldan nodded, but poured a little for himself. "We get a lot of that around here. What's the trouble?" He leaned against the counter while Donahue sat heavily at the small table.

"Our client did an end run around the Bone Guard, says she can't trust us. She had a meet with someone who claimed to have the book. I showed up a little late and a fight had already broken out. Now, she's holding me responsible, threatening to sue and cut the whole contract. This is on top of the mess at the archive." He rested his elbows on his knees, head in his hands. "That black guy, remember him? He's Casey's second, and they're both looking for somebody to blame. They're looking at me." He paused, massaging his temples. "I'm not saying I haven't screwed some things up, I have, I know that. But this—they're gonna hang me out to dry, and it's not fair."

"There's no justice in the western world."

Donahue snorted. "Got that right. I took this job for the history, y'know? The chance to maybe use some of the bad shit—sorry—the skill that I have to do the right thing, for once, but it's just more of the same. Money, fame, fancy houses. No loyalty."

Haldan made noncommittal noises, sipping from his glass. Amber-colored water, but Donahue couldn't know that.

"It got me thinking back to the bath, talking to you." Donahue looked up, his hands clasped together. "Knighthood. I mean, it sounds crazy, but… Nobility, chivalry, honor. Maybe that's the kind of crazy I need."

"The kind the world needs." Haldan drained the glass and folded his arms. "How did you find me?"

"I couldn't sleep at the client's house. I was—" he looked away. "I wasn't casing the place, it wasn't about finding valuables, just about the information, trying to figure out what's going on, what I could do to stop things getting worse."

"I understand."

"I found a letter. I think from the leader you were talking about, the one who could bring peace. Figured I'd have to convince somebody to let me in, to even get to talk to you." He ran his fingers over his wrist and the fake tattoo. "I hope that's okay."

That letter. Blaise recalled the hours he spent in Professor Akbulut's office, hoping to find some clue to the location of the throne. Akbulut believed it had survived the centuries, but his papers provided nothing of use. What else had Blaise put in that letter? He'd been more open back then, believing he could draw people together—and he drew the attention of the Nizari instead. They sent him a dagger, a warning to their intended target to change his ways. At the time, he had few knights and little other support. He backed off, seething, but submitting. So far as they knew, he obeyed the threat and stopped trying to organize and mobilize.

"I'll let it pass, this time—you haven't been inducted yet." Haldan grinned. "If it happens again, though, I might have to kill you."

CHAPTER TWENTY-THREE

Kyra returned from the Paleologos residence, smothering a yawn as she stepped from the car and found the lights still blazing in the salon. Kostas moved about the house, checking cameras and locks, looking self-conscious without Adem there to direct. Nick, playing body guard, trailed Kyra up the stairs. He had let Casey go on without him, but his body revealed the strain, holding himself back as his boss, his friend, walked into danger. How much? Who could say.

Mother curled like a cat into one corner of a sofa, the manuscript held in front of her, though her eyes barely remained open.

"You should go to bed, Mother."

"We should all go to bed," Nick announced, "But I got a call to make, little more research."

"Yes, of course." Mother didn't take her eyes from the page. "Perhaps its because I'm so tired." She sighed, pushing the manuscript aside, but Kyra came alert in an instant.

"Have you found something?" She crossed the room and lifted the book from her mother's aged hands. Nick followed, though his phone was already out of his pocket.

The Throne of Solomon took up most of the page. Her hands sagged. "Or were you thinking of Bapi?"

"Wait." Nick caught the manuscript's top edge, guiding it back up again, her hands drawn along, reluctant to let it go. "Did you see that?"

"The Throne?" She stopped herself from saying something harsh, and looked back at the page. A series of lines framed the throne, outside of its structure, and barely visible. They indented the surface lightly, as if Aleume employed them to lay out his drawing and erased them later. "It's an underlay." She frowned.

"But it's—pointy," Mother said, gesturing wearily. "Not round."

Kyra carried the manuscript over to the dining table. "Cari, lights, full on the table."

"Lights full," a mechanical voice purred. Her in-home personal assistant complied promptly, spreading brilliance over the surface, and Kyra recoiled a bit from the sudden brightness.

"Kostas—bring me a sheet of trace—from the study!"

Kostas broke off what he was doing and hurried away, returning in a moment with a stack of her fine paper. For most things, she relied on digital, but some things still felt better by hand. She swept a sheet off the pile and lay it over the image, finding a soft lead pencil in the sideboard drawer. She gently stroked the lead over the paper surface. The shape emerged, a simple pyramid, topping a longer structure. Not quite an underlay, then.

"That's an obelisk," Nick muttered. "We saw one when we toured the city on the first day. Egyptian, right, not Byzantine."

"They made hundreds, maybe more, and the Romans brought one back with them." Spolia again.. "There's one in town that used to be in the center of the hippodrome." Kyra frowned at the drawing. nothing out of the ordinary, except when paired with the Throne of Solomon.

"So...the Throne's in Egypt? Or it's underneath that thing?"

Mother joined them, rubbing her arms. "I'm glad it wasn't just my eyes, or in my head."

"No, ma'am," Nick told her, his voice gentle.

Kyra flicked aside the tracing and carefully turned pages past drawings of Roman and Byzantine monuments, to a series of sketches she'd barely noted when they first examined the manuscript, flat and boring compared with the technical drawings, they showed outlines of birds, hands, wavy lines, a throned figure that first excited her—save that it was a Pharoah, predating the Throne of Solomon by centuries, if not more. Hieroglypics.

"The clue is here—it has to be."

"Thutmose the third," Mother said, resting her hands heavily on the table. "The honoree of this particular stone. It tells of his various victories over all kinds of enemies."

"That's not a hieroglyphic." Kyra jabbed her finger at a small cross drawn among the Egyptian symbols. "And the pattern. They are in two rows, but some are missing."

"So, the clue isn't here—it's there. The Hippodrome." Nick grinned. "Guess we know where we're heading in the morning."

"Some of us," Kyra said, raising her eyebrows at her mother.

"Perhaps," said Mother grandly, "we should sleep on it."

CHAPTER TWENTY-FOUR

A genuine death threat, disguised as a joke. Wasn't the first time. Grant kept his hands together, not quite a prayer. "What do I need to do, to be inducted?"

Brunelle pushed off from the counter. "Foil, saber, or epee?"

"There's fencing involved?" Grant rose, recalling the sword the driver had swept at him from the van. "I'm not Olympic, but I can give it a try."

"That's not the only test. Wait here." Brunelle walked into the next room and closed the door, beyond the door, drawers opened and closed, clothes rustled, and water ran—no doubt to cover a quiet conversation with whoever watched over them. Grant could practically feel the surveillance. He glanced around just enough, the way a man would in an unfamiliar room. He stared at the bottle left on the counter as if he hungered for it, forced himself to look away, slumping back in his seat. Acoustic tiles, old, could hide any number of mikes or cameras. The place as a whole looked vintage 70's, but careful, like a stage set, a performance as precise as his own. What the hell was he getting himself into? He burned to ask the only questions that mattered, keenly aware he had placed himself in their hands.

Brunelle emerged dressed in dark clothes that allowed easy movement. "Michael, what's your martial arts background?"

"Strong hand to hand, expert marksman." No need to conceal a skill he'd already shown. He'd chosen the alias in part because of how common the name was, but if they googled the name, plus the ink—his more distinctive tattoos—they'd find a disgraced soldier, bounced from the Rangers for a borderline offense, someone with firsthand knowledge of the strife in the area, who might well have reason to want it to stop.

"Follow me." Brunelle escorted him out the door. "Comfortable fighting in those clothes?"

"Could be." Part of the job, back in the Unit, was to be comfortable fighting in whatever, and with whatever, the moment required. They walked back down the narrow metal stairs, then followed a hallway that bent, circumnavigating something, like Kyra's courtyard.

"I'm a little surprised you found this place. I don't think it's a usual return address."

Grant gave a nervous chuckle, playing it vulnerable, cards on the table. "Hagia Dynamis. You know I'm into history. Military, mostly, but some other stuff. On the plane over, I read up on the empire, hoping to see the sights, y'know? Three churches they meant to build, but not all of them were meant to be found. The Akbulut's, their place is like a treasure-trove, including some great maps with unexcavated ruins. Seems like he really wanted to find this place, but it got built over, what, four times? Four different regimes? Never got permission to access the block." Grant paused, indicating a boarded over arch that came up from the floor to about the level of his knee. "Do I get to see it?"

"Pass the tests."

He grinned. "Bring 'em on."

They reached a lower level, the air slightly moist, reminding him of the cistern. Brunelle said, "Point only or flat, not to injure."

"No waiver to sign?"

Brunelle's beard quirked. "Little late for that."

"Anything off limits?"

"No, but here's a piece of advice. I'm a knight. I believe in honor, and also in justice." Brunelle rolled his wrists as they walked, to limber up. "Don't hit anyplace you don't want to be hit back." They walked through a series of brick vaults, maybe nineteenth century, to a wooden door. Brunelle popped it open and charged through.

Grant's heart raced. Brunelle knew the room, what it held and where. Grant didn't. Where would Brunelle set his ambush? How would he arm himself? Grant dropped low. A light came on, but dimly in the room ahead. Slip inside, drop and roll.

"Ha!" Brunelle's first swing went completely over him.

Grant found his feet, taking in the chamber. Square, anteroom of some kind, old stone, older than Byzantium. Two doors out, both closed. Hooks on the walls, and a lamp center ceiling. Rack of swords.

Brunelle moved that direction, a sword already in hand, trying to block Grant's access. Knight, perhaps, but not above playing dirty. Had to be prepared for what your opponent might do, and knights had failed in the past for holding their code higher than the need for success. At times that was the right choice. Now wasn't one of them.

Grant bolted across the room and slapped the light switch, plunging them into darkness. Sprint along the wall, kick the rack from behind. Brunelle yelped and jumped away as the rack crashed and clattered to the ground.

Grant swept a sword from the floor, a curved Middle Eastern blade. Brunelle turned about, dropping into a fighting stance just in time to block Grant's thrust. Dim light slanted in from the corridor they had left behind, making their shadows long and ghostly.

Grant slid to the side, getting away from the wall that inhibited movement. Brunelle followed, taking advantage of his long reach. Parry, block, watch his opponent's core. Grant kept low in his knees, mobile, making Brunelle overreach. He dodged a good slice, sucking in his core, then turning hard to follow through, landing a point at Brunelle's lower back.

"Point!" Brunelle cried, slightly breathless. They parted, turning a circle. "So far so good."

"Should I mention I'm not left-handed?"

Brunelle laughed, and lunged. He was aggressive, solid and quick. A worthy opponent, but his training was Olympic, and even now, he had a hard time breaking from the forward-and-back of the tournament lanes. Grant vaulted the tumbled swords, skidded on the landing, and Brunelle jabbed at his arm and hit. "Point!"

Again, they separated. "How many points?" Grant asked. "Or a killing blow?"

"Five. Or one of those, yes."

He thrilled to the movement, the chase and retreat, both of them more wary now that each had landed a blow. Dang, but he was having a good time. Sucked that he had to get serious. Grant sprang in with a flurry of blows, driving Brunelle toward the entrance.

Brunelle fought back hard, turning, breathing faster now, getting close. Grant let him, measuring the distance. Brunelle's tip stroked along Grant's leg, gentle enough the guy might not have noticed. Be the knight, be the penitent striving for virtue. Grant called, "Point!" and indicated the area of impact as he stepped away.

Brunelle's eyes flared, and he gave a slight nod. He withdrew his blade, but not his advance, already preparing his next move. A breath followed by a flurry of blows.

Grant parried, as if in desperation. He pressed and retreated. Three steps, two, one.

He slipped back to the fallen rack and stumbled over the blades. Brunelle grinned, going for it. He slammed his blade to Grant's. Grant let the saber fly, twisting down and away, with a stifled curse. He debated just for an instant if it might be better to lose and decided he didn't care.

Left hand swipe low, a slender foil. He brought it up and in as Brunelle pressed his advantage, his blade thrusting for Grant's side.

Grant pivoted away and slashed. His sword lay across Brunelle's chest, point just above his shoulder. One sharp move, and his opponent's throat would be cut.

For a moment, their breathing was the only sound, then Brunelle stepped back from the blade, and swept up his weapon in a swordsman's salute. "Well done."

"Desperate more like. Good bout." Grant skirted the scattered blades to turn the lights back on. "Sorry about this. Should we clean up?"

Together, they righted the stand and began placing the swords back, all quality weapons, but a little battered. Sparring blades, not anyone's prized collection.

"You improvise well. That's a good skill."

"Yeah. Wish I could've done it better out there." Grant replaced his off-hand weapon on the rack, and retrieved his saber from the ground. "Boss lady, Kyra Akbulut? She's livid about what happened to that other woman, the one she was trying to meet." He used his sleeve to wipe down the hilt and blade, treating it with respect. "I thought one of the assailants was a knight as well."

Brunelle watched him sidelong, then shrugged. "I heard they were trying to catch the person who stole that manuscript. It was a woman?"

Grant nodded. Brunelle knew something, and the way his eyes dropped for the shrug suggested what he knew made him uncomfortable. Interesting. "Crazy, right? My best guess is, she was disguised as a server for the champagne, and smuggled the book out in one of those cases." On going back through the photos, he had recognized her hand with a champagne bottle, her sleeve in a random shot of the secure room door.

"Huh." Brunelle took that in. "Clever."

"What do you guys—" Grant offered a slight smile and a shrug, "maybe what do we do, with somebody like that?"

Finding a cloth on a hook, Brunelle wiped down the blade he had used. "Everyone is given a chance to repent, to take responsibility for their past and to pledge for a better future. Our leader takes a dim view of addiction, people who can't control their own impulses, but still they can choose to change. Those who do are welcomed. Those who do not…well, it depends upon their infraction."

"Not their gender? Does the knighthood include women?"

Brunelle nodded, setting his blade in place. "If she repents, this thief, she could be offered that chance." Brunelle swallowed, and gave that little sidelong glance again. Did he know he was doing it? Grant didn't rate him that highly as an operator, no matter how fine a swordsman he might be. Again, his training had been in other areas. "If not, she'll be exiled."

Repents. The present tense swept him like a benediction. Would she repent? The tenor of Brunelle's voice had shifted, and Grant didn't want to press his luck. "What now?" He assumed a posture like parade rest.

"You have passed a test of strength and resourcefulness, that's good. What comes next is character."

Grant's core tightened. So far, he was acing the interview. What the hell kind of test would this be? "How so?"

Brunelle squared his shoulders. "You asked about seeing the Hagia Dynamis. I can give you a glimpse. We must be certain of your loyalty, your willpower, and your truthfulness."

A chuckle. "You're making me nervous."

"If you are as committed as you say, there's no need to be." Brunelle assessed him silently, then said, "If you pass this next test, you'll be given a task, something to demonstrate our mutual trust. Oh—and our leader would prefer if you can maintain ties with your client. It may be useful to us to have someone close to her and to the Bone Guard."

Grant wet his lips, then nodded. "Do my best. I can't guarantee I haven't already been fired, but I'm okay with groveling if that helps the cause."

Brunelle produced an old-fashioned key and inserted it into the lock on the left-hand door, the one that would lead into that hidden space at the heart of the block. They stepped back in time, to a perfectly restored sanctuary with a layout that might date back to Emperor Constantine. Smooth columns in groups supported the dome above, separating a central chamber from four vestibules joined by aisles. They entered one of these, and Brunelle powered on the perimeter lights, but nothing at the center. Or at the right-hand aisle. Grant swept the room with his gaze, taking a little longer in appreciation. Listening. A few dark spots on the floor in the other direction. Blood. What else formed droplets like that? Some dried, some still slightly glossy, suggesting someone bleeding had passed this way twice, hours separated from each other. The second time, only a little while ago. No sounds beyond the doors.

"It's fantastic—thank you." Leaning into the space, suggesting eagerness, but not violating any boundaries—he hoped—Grant let his voice echo. Was she close? Could she hear him?

"You're welcome. This way."

Again, Grant followed. No response to the sound of his voice, no scuffle or moan. He stalked behind Brunelle. If he heard the slightest reason for hope, a mouse's whisper, he'd catch Brunelle by the throat, choke him or slam him headfirst into a column. Snatch the keyring, right door first, then around in that direction. Couldn't see the whole chamber. How long after an attack before the spycam sent help? The lack of any other visible people suggested Brunelle's total confidence in his safety. How many knights could be hidden in this warren of a place? A building like a Russian doll, and he wasn't sure they were even at the heart.

Grant still had two knives concealed—hadn't been sure if there'd be a search, so he stashed the gun and the larger blade. Pity: he kinda liked Brunelle. The man took his knighthood seriously, and Grant could honor that. But if Akilah were here, he'd crack the man like a watermelon.

On a low stone altar, with its own spotlight, sat a sculpted bronze lion with an open mouth and lolling tongue. The style looked Byzantine, with a far east influence.

"The Lion of Truth," Brunelle announced. "You place your hand in his mouth. I ask a question, and you answer truthfully." He activated a lever Grant hadn't noticed, and a shield slid up and into place bearing an inscription. "The honest man has nothing to fear." Brunelle tilted his head toward the beast.

"What about the rest of us?" Grant said, half-serious. He recalled the images from the codex, various machines activated by simple things. How could a machine determine the truth? Contemporary lie detectors used variations in the pulse or in eye movements, but the Byzantines had nothing so subtle. His palms itched. And what was the penalty for lying? A blade, a bite, a burst of poison? Shit. Had they done this to her—and how had she fared?

He expelled a long breath and took another, then met Brunelle's gaze. "Can you tell me what this is about?"

Brunelle matched his serious tone. "Our leader has an assignment for you, one for which you are particularly suited. The rewards for joining us can be great. You will have comrades and a cause. You will be part of an order as ancient as the Holy Land itself, given new life for people like us, the ones so often cast aside or imprisoned, never again allowed their dignity. But you will be asked to confront a great challenge, one that will risk your own life and demand that you abandon old loyalties. And if you succeed, you may find your calling. Michael, will you take this challenge?"

If the Bone Guard were going down tonight, slain by a bronze automaton had to be a good way to go. Other options: refuse and be killed outright. Take on Brunelle and summon unknown legions in an unfamiliar space. And she might not even be here any more. Grant swallowed and nodded.

He placed his hand between the lion's jaws. It couldn't be pressure activated. The tongue bifurcated toward the back, providing a broad space, but forcing his hand flat. Two projections of metal pushed into his palm. Grant held himself still and calm, counting back from twenty. Sweat-based activation, had to be. *The honest man had nothing to fear.*

If it stabbed him, he tore free and went for Brunelle. If poison gas, he'd hold his breath. If teeth locked his wrist—

"Michael Donahue. Yesterday morning, a supplicant like you, a penitent who wished to join our order, tried to kill an apostate, a man who stepped beyond the warrior's code and took service for money against the needs of our leader. Our supplicant's attempt failed, and a later attempt was stopped. It will be harder now to get close, to make the chance." Brunelle regarded him like a judge administering an oath. "If you would become a Knight Penitent, in service to the risen King of Jerusalem, you must kill your former boss and give us your full allegiance. Will you do it?"

Grant kept his face clear, his heart steady in spite of his incredulity. He met Brunelle's gaze and spoke as clearly and firmly as he could. "Sir, Grant Casey will die if it's the last thing I do."

CHAPTER TWENTY-FIVE

The image of Paleologos' gloating face lingered in Kyra's memory as she changed into more comfortable clothes. She had given up her father's treasure, her own treasure, for an educated guess. Mired in the past, the words of a man dead for centuries, drawings of things made centuries before that, the ruins of empires long dead as well. And the woman —Kyra stared at herself in the mirror. The woman, the thief. Muslim, like her, but living in the shadows. Or dying in them. Kyra glared at herself, her dark brows pulling together over the stormy eyes that made her engineers jump to whatever task she set them. She helped to kill a man today, a murderer himself. It made her ill, but also victorious. Together, she and Nick had stopped a killer and saved a man's life. Two days ago, she would not have imagined it. Had she killed the woman also, because of her own aversion to taking orders, especially from a man? She was not adept at walking through worlds, not into the past of her father's obsessions, nor into the words of her mother's. Somehow, she walked from her own world of smooth, precise technology, easily controlled or altered, into Casey's world of subterfuge, distrust and danger. Anything could be a clue, anything could be a trigger.

She slapped off the light switch and moved into her adjoining bedroom. What she told him was true: the thief lived in that world, too, and knew the risks she had assumed. Kyra gave up the bronze arm. What more could be expected of her? Leave it in Casey's hands and go to bed. She slid between silk sheets. "Cari, nightlight."

The lights dimmed to a faint, warm glow.

"Cari, alarm for seven am."

"Alarm set," answered the soft voice of her embedded personal assistant. Her mother didn't care for that either, so Kyra refrained from using it in the public spaces.

She curled onto her side, snuggling in to the best money could buy. If they had captured the thief, was she dead already? Was she locked in a dungeon? Don't be ridiculous. In spite of the talk of knights and kings, people didn't use dungeons any more. Did they? "Cari, wake me when the unlock code is entered."

"Yes, Miss Kyra."

She would know when Casey got back and find out then what he had learned. Kyra settled her breathing. She should have done her stretches, a little yoga, even though it was the middle of the night. By anyone's metrics, even the Bone Guard's, she suspected, it had been a difficult day. Theft from the archives, attack at the hospital, near-drowning in the cistern, the execution of her traitorous cell phone. No wonder she couldn't sleep. No amount of technology—Kyra's eyes flew open. Ridiculous, indeed. Simply entering his world was no reason to abandon her own. In an instant, she knew what to do, how to track the stolen woman. She pushed out of bed and stuffed her feet into shearling slippers. From its hook by the bathroom, she grabbed her robe and stalked down to the salon where she had left her tablet.

She heard voices as she approached, and hesitated.

"Okay, Ruad, what else?" Nick spoke aloud.

A tinny woman's voice answered. "That's it, the last one. It fell in 1302, and the king had to retreat back to Europe."

"Thanks, D.A."

"Thanks for getting me involved—he wasn't going to."

"This thing with the Phantom is messing with his head. He's totally convinced that it's her, and maybe it is, maybe I'm the one who fucked up for doubting him." Nick paused, then added. "And it's gotta be kinda freaky watching yourself get shot. Sure as hell freaked me out. Either way, Chief's not on a very even keel right now."

Not on an even keel. What form might that even take for a man like Casey? She'd already seen the medicine bottles in Nick's room—antidepressants, and a low-dose anti-psychotic. What sort of men had she brought into her home? Powerful, capable—certainly people she'd rather have on her own side, but she preferred to keep their intensity pointed away. Away from herself, and certainly away from her mother, whose Agatha Christie adventure began to look more like Stephen King every moment.

"No doubt," said the voice on the other end of the line. "I'm trusting you guys to keep an eye on each other. Let me know what else you need, okay?"

"Yes, ma'am." He rang off what was obviously a trans-Atlantic call, apparently on speaker phone.

Kyra swept into the room and found Nick in shirt-sleeves, leaning over a large map that crossed one end of the table. He wore a pencil behind his ear and his phone lay in the middle of the Mediterranean. Without looking up, he said, "Good evening, Ms. Akbulut. I certainly hope I didn't keep you awake."

"Looking for the Templars?"

"Yes, ma'am." He traced his finger across the map. "Big question is, did they move it more than once, and/or has anybody taken it off their hands? These marks are the most likely targets, these ones less likely: they're too well explored. If it were there, it's been gone a long time. Either way, we need more intel to mount a proper search."

"Mother spent more time with the book before bed, she may have some details." Kyra cleared her throat, and he faced her. "I'm glad you're awake, Nick. I'd like your help."

"Absolutely." He smiled, though his eyes looked troubled. He and Casey had had one of their wordless conversations about going together, and the result had been him staying here, protecting her, while a man he clearly cared deeply about walked into the enclave of their enemy.

"You men have extreme powers of observation, and I do not, but I need to re-create the scene from this evening, the van. If they took this woman, that is how. If we find the van, we might learn what happened next."

"Oh-kay." He trailed her to her office, a sleek chamber unlike the rest of the house. Built into a windowless room, it had cabinets and panels almost floor to ceiling. "Nice digs."

"Cari, lights, and full station."

Panels opened, her monitors sliding into place as she dropped into a chair and started the system. "Cari, grant access, limited data entry, name: Nick." She gestured for him to take the seat in front of the keyboard. "Place your hands on the keyboard. It will scan your fingerprints and let you type."

"Man, D.A. would love to see all this." He did as she told him. "What's the brief? What are we doing here?"

"Programming a drone for a search function and perhaps hacking some cameras. My company does not merely do home assistance, we parcel and sell the components of our hardware and software to various corporations and entities that can make use of them. Perhaps a quarter of the cameras in the city use my tech, and some of those also use our secure cloud to store and overwrite the recordings. Theres a very good chance at least one of those cameras caught the crime."

He whistled softly. "Nice. What do you need me to do?"

"Help me find an image of the van. Ask me questions. I am your witness, but I am not a good one. It was a large white van, a baker's van."

The tapping of keys. "Logo on the side?"

"Yes, but...minarets and domes. A building."

"Close your eyes, sometimes that helps. So, white van, with a logo on the side. Familiar building?"

She frowned into her memory. "The Sofia, of course. Half of the businesses here use it."

"Words? Name of the business?"

"Something peeling. About the same length as the image, but nothing legible."

"White van. Taller than you or shorter?"

She hesitated, recalling the walk past it. "Taller? But partially on the curb, so not a lot taller."

"Flat front?"

Kyra's hand waved over her own face. "Not flat, protruding, but sloping.

The hood was dented." She slapped her armrests. "I remember that!"

"Single or double-door at the back? Any doors along the side?"

"Not on the side." She envisioned walking past, the two men unloading racks of something, a half-door open, blocking— "two doors at the back."

"I think you're looking at a Ford Otosan transit variation. Here." He showed her a series of images. "You're right, though, about the logo. Everyone uses the Hagia Sofia." Another screen showed dozens of thumbnail images of business logos.

Kyra swung the keyboard toward her. "Let us see what we find." She grabbed the image of the van, and the logo that most closely captured her memory, fusing them together.

A soft chime sounded. "Your requested alert," said the voice of Cari.

Casey? She switched to the entrance camera as Adem entered the courtyard and closed the door behind him. Ah, well. Nick glanced at the time on the corner of the monitor. "Gone for two and a half hours. He do that often?"

"Adem?" Kyra shrugged, already working on re-routing programs and communications protocols. "He often does his errands late at night when I am less likely to have need of him."

"You just pay him 24/7, like he's on call? Must be nice."

On the larger monitor in front of his seat, an angled view of an urban street appeared, looking down from above, a few spotlights shining back, streetlights and security lights around some of the buildings. Kyra leaned in, then triggered another command. A small box appeared on the screen, then another. She peered at them and clicked them away, one after another, but a few she left, marking their targets. Nick leaned in with her, and murmured, "You're looking for cameras."

"Only three have the right tag. We'll have to scroll through a few hours to—"

"Eight seventeen. Twenty-seventeen military style. Chief's cellphone has a shot detector on it. That's when he fired his weapon for the last time." He glanced at her sidelong and the blue light of the screens let him an air of menace she had not seen before. "Ma'am, I do not appreciate being ditched when my CO finds himself in a situation needing shots fired. Am I clear?"

Another view of the same street, blinking through frames, but the camera focused on the area right in front of the shop. Nick placed his phone in front of them, a map of the area on screen. He pointed back to the original screen, from one of the security cameras on the Topkapi Palace wall. "This view's too steep and narrow. This is the area of the attack, right?" He zoomed on the cell phone. "Can you get us a view over here, or do some kind of proximity search? The ruins are here—but there's a few hotels, probably one of them—"

"Yes, yes." Her fingers slid and searched. Four cameras this time, one on a loop already erased. Two with partial views—

"White van, minarets." Nick indicated an area of the screen, a shop front across from the hotel.

Kyra cocked her head, then zoomed in. Against a confusing background of leather goods and handbags, the reflection in the window showed the back end of a van, the minaret logo distinguished by the negative impression on the glass. Shadowy figures moved to and from the van, then someone loaded the pram into it. A moment later, a figure carrying another, someone who looked asleep. They climbed inside. The doors were closed, and the van drove away. Kyra scrolled back and froze just after the doors closed. She enhanced the image a few times until a partial license plate could be seen. Copy that, create an algorithm with multiple parameters: the vehicle type and color, the plate number, the hours—

"Search back as well as forward," Nick suggested, then settled back. "Ma'am, I am in awe of your programming prowess."

"I am principally an engineer, mechanical, that is, but I do maintain familiarity with other aspects of the products."

The chime repeated, and Cari's voice announced, "Your requested alert."

On the local monitor, Casey let himself in to the courtyard and walked up the stairs. "Oh, shit," Nick muttered, and was already out of his chair, out the door, back down the hall. It did not surprise her that he had no need of a guide despite not having been to this part of the house before. Casey looked the same as ever to her, but Nick clearly saw things differently. The search function would take a while in any case. Kyra pushed back and followed, finding the men in the sprawling kitchen, Casey getting himself a glass of water.

"Ma'am." He squared his shoulders and faced her, and she caught a glimpse of what Nick had seen: resignation? Nothing so strong as defeat, no. What would Grant Casey look like when truly defeated? The moment she framed the question, Kyra knew she did not want to be there to see the answer.

"Nick tells me you've got a search on. Thank you."

"What else can I do?" She meant the question rhetorically, the kind of offer of generosity that is meant to be refused.

Casey set down his glass and said, "We need five more actors: two police, a doctor, two nurses. And a private ambulance, or maybe a hearse with a real nurse inside."

Faintly, she said, "I'll ask Adem to—"

"No, way," Nick interjected. "Don't trust him. Don't trust anyone who cuts out when his boss is in trouble." His own head fell, and Casey swayed an elbow, gently bumping Nick's elbow, but the big man shook it off. "Just. Don't."

"Will you at least trust me?" Kyra asked, chastened.

"What say you, Chief?"

"We'll need some bribes to pull this off, Ms. Akbulut, and a lot of things going our way."

"My mother was right, earlier. You saved my life. I have not even thanked you."

"You're welcome." Casey's dark eyes settled on her, then he smiled just a little. "First thing in the morning, I have to kill myself."

CHAPTER TWENTY-SIX

In a crowded parking lot across from the hospital entrance, Blaise sat in an unremarkable mud-brown car, sipping unremarkable coffee. The car made sense. Only logical to choose something unlike his true tastes. The coffee, on the other hand, had no need of subterfuge. He should have waited for a proper brew. A cluster of nurses and aids breezed up to the doorway, adjusting their hijab. An indigent man slumbered on a bench not far from the entrance. From the direction of the train station, the Bone Guard Michael Donahue strolled up. Just a few minutes before visiting hours began. Donahue glanced back when he reached the top step, then walked through the automatic doors, as if he'd been distracted by the indigent.

Blaise flicked his device. "He's on the way."

When Blaise began his rule, he would take care of this problem of indigence. Most people would prefer to work, he knew. Most people preferred to live in virtue and strive for improvement. Those who refused such work ranked among the unrepentant.

Haldan replied, "I'm in position. The police changed officers a little while ago. No trouble for me, they bought the story about archive security sending me over."

"Good."

Donahue walked like any ordinary man, without the pride of the soldier, or the roll of the athlete. "You let him beat you last night."

Haldan chuckled. "You want him with us, yes? No good if I beat him too quickly. The Samurai would say he should not lose face."

"He's no samurai, and neither are you."

"If necessary, I'll beat him next time. He's undisciplined. Fast and clever, not very powerful. I could overcome his defenses, I think."

"Sounds as if you'd like to." A few more people came and went from the hospital. The indigent man who'd been lounging on a bench got rousted, maybe by the same police who just came off duty at Casey's room.

"Here he is."

The connection went silent, and Blaise opened up the file on his passenger seat. He reached for the coffee, scowled, and set it down again. This new case involved a divorce with a prenuptial agreement—unusual in the city, from his experience. Interesting. He grew absorbed in the list of assets, the things these spouses wished to hold back from one another, plus the list now in dispute, the items they bought together which they fought over dividing. One of those items caught his eye: a tandem bicycle, very high-end. Each of them wanted it. Why? From the filing, it seemed that neither had an affair, a lover on the side with whom they wished to share such a thing. To even ride such a bicycle required so much balance, cooperation, communication. If he could convince them to ride it again, together, might they not find a way out of this trouble? How irreconcilable were those differences, truly? Blaise made some notes.

His phone rang. Blaise glanced over, and the number gave him pause. It rang again, and he set down his pen, closing the folder, then took the call. "Yes?"

"Do you have it now? Whatever you needed?" Brusque, angry men, every one of them. Farouk was no different, but he had always been true to his calling.

"It's on the way, my friend. I believe it will—"

"You believe? We're tired of what you believe. It is well to say we take common cause, but not if it means we delay our own plans for years while you play at knighthood."

Blaise glared at the hospital entrance. "Farouk, this is not a battle to be

131

won merely by slaughtering the other side. It is our vision, and our symbols that will show us who the other side is. Until we can raise up—"

"We're thinking of going ahead with the bomb. No throne, no king, nothing. Just the bomb. Boom. Done."

Blaise could picture the man's infantile gesture, his pinched fingers blossoming open like an explosion. "And if you do, in a matter of days or weeks, your entire cell will be the same. Boom. Done. Is that what you wish? Is that what your people have been waiting for, the quick deaths of martyrs who will never be remembered?"

Farouk made a harsh sound in his throat as if he would spit. "Of course they wish to be martyrs—why else do they get their reward?"

"Boom will not mean done, not at all. Boom, in this case, is only the beginning. If I am not there to take up the mantle, you will instead have chaos, worse, even, than what you have now. You joined in the cause, you brought along your people, Farouk, because you know how vital it is to have permanent, peaceable change."

For a moment, nothing but the man's rough breathing. From the hospital entrance, Donahue emerged, descended a few steps, almost meditatively, and brought out his mobile. He walked aside, turning as if to reduce the glare on the screen.

"Also, I have another delivery for you, have you heard? I shipped this morning, along with a few other things you'll need."

A feisty one. I heard. That type is less popular now there's a bit of a surplus. We've picked up on recruiting, though."

"That's good to hear." Blaise smiled, projecting the warmth. "I know the operation is in good hands with you and your crew, Farouk. I look forward to shaking your hand one day very soon."

A text shivered his phone, and briefly materialized above. "*Code just called. Casey is dead.*"

Blaise's warmth grew. Apparently, he had a new recruit himself. "What else do we need to discuss?"

"I have some concern about bringing the Israelis on board," Farouk began, and Blaise listened to a milder form of the anti-Semitic rants that so many in the region were subject to. Haldan stepped out of the hospital door, pausing to don sunglasses against the brightening day. He started down the steps toward the left, his mission there achieved. He moved from the sunny plaza to the shade of the buildings. From the gloom, a darker shadow rose up swinging. With a crack of bone that Blaise could hear in his car, Haldan collapsed onto the sidewalk, crumpled like a refugee against the night.

CHAPTER TWENTY-SEVEN

When Brunelle walked down the steps, Grant started moving. They were meant to text each other, to keep apart until his handler reeled him in for the next stage of his induction, but that homeless guy, the one with the scarred hand, still bugged him. From the portico, he couldn't ID the shutterbug definitively, but the man's presence lingered at the back of his neck, an extra weight he carried into the hospital, through the moment he shared with Destry. Grant had leaned in to the hospital bed and whispered, "I need you to play the greatest scene of your life. Consider this your exit interview from the Bone Guard. You up for it?" The way Destry's eyes lit, he hardly had to listen for the answer. Plant a device that counted down to a flatline, pass the time, be seen leaving long before the moment hit—then, instead of heading back to meet up with Nick and the client, he lingered, every sense on high alert even though the homeless guy was nowhere to be seen.

Grant kept himself from the hospital's line of view, loath to give Brunelle any reason to suspect him. Ironic, that, given he'd just "killed" his own boss. When Brunelle's gaze skipped over the patch of shadows where Grant lingered—a knight, not an operator—Grant performed another scan of his own. Shadows shifted on the far side. Brunelle was about to pick up a tail, another lead, and hopefully the one who'd know more about Akilah. All Grant had to do was—

The shadow lunged, swinging nunchuks in a wide arc that intersected perfectly, horribly, with the back of Brunelle's skull. He went down hard and tumbled onto the sidewalk.

Grant was already running.

The shutterbug popped open a car door, grabbing Haldan's limp arm and hauling him up with the ease of a weight-lifter bench pressing a guy half again his size.

"Hey!" No gun this time, not in the hospital. No fucking distance weapon. The shutterbug froze, encumbered by Brunelle's body. He executed a half turn, flinging Brunelle into the street. From down the block, the sound of a truck. No way the driver saw Brunelle as anything but darkness across the pavement. Shit.

Grant dodged and leapt into the road, putting up his hands, waving as he moved toward the fallen man. Making himself a beacon. "Stop!"

The delivery vehicle roared toward him. The driver's eyes flared as he finally saw Grant—Grant calculating how fast he could get out of the way and leave Brunelle to his death.

Brakes screamed then a car shot out from the parking lot across the street. It sheered against the front end of the truck, knocking it off target and slamming to a halt as the truck crashed into the shutterbug's car at the curb. The open door snapped off, and Grant spun away, ducking like a vulture to cover his head and protect Brunelle. The door struck him a glancing blow across the shoulders and scraped into the street.

The smell of burnt rubber singed Grant's nostrils. Brunelle groaned, and a businessman slid from the rescue vehicle, his face clouded with concern. His dark eyes familiar.

No time for that. "Sir—take care of him!" Grant barked—then added, in Turkish, "Please." He backed a step, making sure the guy was on board with the job he'd volunteered for.

Turning on his heel, Grant vaulted onto the crumpled car by the sidewalk and slid across it, scanning quickly. A woman stood on the sidewalk ahead, half-turned away from the accident, distracted by something that had just passed.

Grant dropped to the pavement, already running. He dodged by her, skidded, listening. Nothing ahead. To one side, an alley. A street opposite, and the arched entryway to a mosque, a pre-recorded call to prayer ringing out overhead in the wail of faith. A number of men shuffled through the gate, and Grant slid between them, earning a startled cry. A courtyard opened beyond, with the ritual bath under its shade. A squat contemporary mosque stood ahead of him, more like a high school gymnasium than the richly embellished holy buildings that filled the older parts of Istanbul. A small minaret rose to one side, the door just closing. Closing, but the call was a recording, and nobody was leaving the vicinity.

Grant slowed as he approached the door, letting the rest of the congregation file out of the courtyard. The slight echo of movement within the structure ebbed as the call died away. He visualized the interior of the narrow tower. Three stories tall, but only large enough for a spiral staircase to the balcony at the top where the loudspeakers pointed over the neighborhood. Two choices for ambush: go higher, or wait just inside. Trouble with higher was, if the enemy got behind you, you ran out of choices real fast. The wall at the gate reached halfway up the tower, but landing on the spikes meant to keep off birds would hurt like hell, and the drop to the street was a likely injury. Second choice: wait behind the door. Enemy goes up, you get out or you get the drop on him. When the last of the meager group of worshippers had shed their shoes and entered the mosque, Grant approached the minaret carefully. A quick glance showed the courtyard empty.

He slammed his foot into the door, snapping it backward and earning a muffled grunt. Before the door could rebound fully, Grant pressed his advantage—literally—shoving the door hard inside, hoping to pin the shutterbug. Instead of meeting resistance, the door flew backward again, and Grant stumbled.

The shutterbug dropped from above, whipping the nunchuks as if to wrap Grant's throat.

Grant dropped to his knees, slipping the trap. Right hand caught the flailing end of one metal rod, still slick with Brunelle's blood. He clung, and the assailant let the other end fall, smacking Grant's arm.

Grant spun the nunchuks, but the guy dodged. He sprinted up the stairs. Was he really? Yes, yes, he was.

Grant bounded after him, taking them two at a time, leaning into the run. The guy yanked open the door at the top, but Grant seized the back of his belt. He kicked and twisted, nearly tossing himself over the balcony wall.

Grant's grip brought him down hard. He dropped the nunchuks and tackled him with both hands. The guy tried to drop as Grant had done, knees buckling, but Grant slid a half-step forward, knee to the other man's back, his chest pinned to the wall.

Grant caught his head before he struck the spikes, gripping the back of his skull. Buzz-cut, just as he'd suspected, harder to get hold of. He turned the man's head, getting a good look at him, and lining up his eye with one of the six-inch wires that sprouted along the wall. "The woman you protected at the archive. She's a friend. Stop trying to kill me and I won't kill you."

The guy breathed heavily, his glance rolling up toward Grant, down toward the spike. He got his free hand up against the wall, adding that pressure. "I fear no death." He spoke English with a thick accent. Syrian. Like hers. He lurched as if to skewer his own brain, but Grant denied him, gripping his head like a basketball, straining against the man's own will.

"Fuck that. Kill yourself if you want to, after you tell me how to find her."

The guy dropped into Arabic. "Ignorant fool. There was no woman. A man on a motorcycle, nothing more."

"I saw your pictures, dog," Grant replied in the same language. "I know who's missing. You were protecting her, even then."

The man's breath hissed, his upper eye staring, then he gave something like a chuckle. "She has no friends. Never has."

For a fleeting instant, Grant was tempted to let go and drop the man's face to be skewered like a tomato kebab. His voice sank low. "She has now."

The guy's glance rolled downward again. "You wear the mark of the devil. At your wrist."

Sh'tan: the devil, but this time embodied by a cross. Good eye. "I wear the mask I require," Grant answered, the language another mask. "What's your choice—talk or die?"

"You'd kill me? You saved him."

"He's not like us. He's got a conscience."

"Says the man who is here for a woman."

"What was she after? Not the money." His palm sweated against the other man's wrist, but he did not let up.

"Not the money," the guy agreed. His breath jerked, squeezed between Grant's knee and the concrete wall now smeared with his blood. "A friend. She needs one." He gasped another breath. "If it's not too late."

CHAPTER TWENTY-EIGHT

Grant shifted his grip. He eased back, and guided the shutterbug a little back from the wall to find his balance. He didn't let go, but let the man's arm subside to a slightly more comfortable angle. He stood almost a foot taller than the shutterbug, but he'd already seen, and felt, what the man was capable of. Grant focused on the shutterbug's movement and balance, the level of tension in his wiry muscles. The guy was good, maybe he could fool Grant—but all indicators were he didn't plan to jump.

The guy put up his off hand in a placating gesture, and Grant finally released him, stepping back to cover the door. He could easily span the balcony with his outstretched arms. Unlikely the guy could get past him. The guy was quick, but also not very tall: clearing the balcony wall would take serious, and visible, effort.

The guy turned sharply to face Grant and they sized each other up for a long moment, then he sank down to one knee, a curious posture between readiness and relaxation. Grant squatted down opposite, each man with his back to the curved balcony wall, their knees nearly touching.

"That man in the hospital, he's not the boss—you are,"

"I know who I am. Question is, who are you?" Now that he was still, the bruises on his back and arm ached. He shifted one pantleg and wiped the blood from his hand to his sock, slipping his pantleg back down again.

The other man's lips curved. "So they won't notice blood." He regarded his own scraped hands, then pulled a kerchief from one of his layers of clothes and wiped his face where he'd had a rough encounter with the door frame. How many weapons could he conceal beneath those layers? Grant hadn't done homeless in a while. It was a look that hid a multitude of sins.

"You said it's already too late. Don't waste her time."

The guy briefly bowed his head, more than a nod, less than an obeisance. "These knights. Their king gives women to terrorists."

Shit. "How and why?"

"He has an ally, Farouk Djibar, in Syria, the head of a sleeper cell called Shifra. They give women to their soldiers. The madman wants these soldiers happy and loyal. He has two armies, but I don't know what for." He crumpled the cloth in his grip, and met Grant's eye, his head tipped sidelong. "You are both not the sort of man I could see befriending her, and also exactly the man."

Grant decided that was a compliment. "She said you were Nizari Isma'ili, aiming for the king."

"He's not a king, he's a madman."

"Figured. What does he want?"

"To rule." The other man looked away.

Fucking pointless reply. "So you are Nizari?"

Again, that slight curl of the lips. "If I were such a thing, I should have to kill you."

"Why haven't you? How many knives do you have in that outfit?"

A sharp look. "How many have you?"

Grant smiled. "At least one more than you think."

The other man smiled back and slipped into English. "Call me Bashir."

Grant offered his hand, open, empty. After a moment, the other man took it in a firm grasp, brief and utterly controlled.

"How do I get her back?"

"How do I get to the king?"

"Not by assaulting his buddy."

Bashir pursed his lips, tipped his hand one way, then the other. "Worth a try. There's a lot of people go in and out of their block. Even when I get in, I can't find the way." His dark eyes focused with a marksman's precision, his face suddenly very much at odds with his motley garb. "But you know the way."

"You're not getting in there, not if they've made you. They didn't take me into the sanctum, and I haven't met the king."

"Not yet. But you just saved his...buddy?" Bashir tried on the word.

And completed the task they asked of him, or so they would believe. King or madman, Grant wasn't sure he had enough on the guy to make him worthy of death. "I'm no assassin."

Bashir's face went blank. "I would not ask you to be. I would not judge if you are fit for it."

The word, applied so casually to any stealthy killer, carried very different expectations for Bashir. Noted. Grant shifted his position, settling in, also giving his conversant an apparent advantage. "I mean no disrespect, Bashir. I'm the stranger here."

"You want help to find Akilah. We have a plan together—no, no, not together." He made a gesture as between himself and another. "Rather, an agreement. She ensures the king does not get the book, we give support with her own mission."

"You didn't want the book?"

"It's meaningless, except to him. A bunch of pictures."

"What's he plan to do with it?"

Bashir flicked his fingers, dismissing that.

"She's done her part," Grant said. "And you haven't."

Bashir's jaw twitched. "We are not without honor. But my people..." Again, that side to side gesture with his hand, tipping the balance.

Grant's core tightened, holding himself back with a will. "You know where she is, who's got her, and you don't care."

"Do not say this." A knife appeared in his hand, ready for thrusting.

Grant imagined what would happen next. The sharp movement, his dodge aside—his relaxed pose making him ready for a quick turn—catch the man's arm as he moved and lock off his shoulder. Head first into the wall. Or over it.

Neither man moved.

"You care, but not enough to do anything about it."

The knife spun in his fingers, fast and flickering. "This is not the sort of thing we do, this...frontal assault. We are too few, our secrets too deep. A long time ago, we were allies, even with the Templars, but they betrayed us. They surrendered their last stronghold and were taken prisoner while my people were slaughtered. Since then, we are not warriors, not like that."

"Get in, kill, get out, don't get caught." Grant nodded. "Tell me where to find her."

"We do not make gifts in our business."

"You want to know if I can get to him. Or get him out to you." Grant weighed the options, one life against another, Akilah's against that of the man who assaulted and drugged her, then gave her into slavery. He lifted his chin. "Of course I can."

"Very good. I am very pleased." The blade vanished back into his sleeve. "If you do not, Mr. Casey, I will not rest until you die." He smiled thinly. "For the last time."

Chapter Twenty-Nine

Blaise slid the rest of the way from the passenger seat of his car. He shouldn't be here, not like this. Foolish to have been on watch for Haldan to begin with, except that now his vehicle had been his man's deliverance. A religious man would think this a miracle. To Blaise, it indicated that he'd been correct about offering back-up, and that Haldan's assessment of his recruit was accurate.

The truck driver scrambled out onto the sidewalk, hollering and insisting he hadn't hit anybody. "Of course you didn't. Now would you please go to the hospital and request a stretcher and a nurse," Blaise requested. He took a knee at Haldan's side. The knight moaned and his limbs twitched, then his hand jerked and his eyes flew open. Tears and distraction glazed his eyes for a moment.

"You've had a hard blow, my friend," Blaise murmured in French. "Be still."

Haldan didn't notice him at first, trying to sit, reaching a hand toward the blood at the back of his head.

Blaise caught that hand in his, gripping it tight. "Mon ami," he said again.

A woman on the sidewalk had her phone out, and Blaise turned slightly, putting his back toward her, hiding his face.

"My lord," a breath, no more. Haldan's expression shifted from gratitude to horror. "You can't be here—you shouldn't—the Nizari, they know me—"

"And have just tried to kill you. Be still, it's alright. Your man's gone after them."

"My—?" Haldan's brow furrowed, making his ruddy eyebrows jut all the more. "Donahue?"

"He may be the finest knight since you."

Haldan used the strength of their grip to pull himself to sitting and found the blood that matted his hair and seeped into his collar. "Sacre bleu."

"Indeed."

"Sir?" A voice called from behind them. "I'm a nurse—don't move."

Haldan shook off his hand and almost pushed him away. In Turkish, he said, "Thank you, sir. I don't know what happened. I hope your car isn't badly damaged."

"It's nothing, really." Blaise shifted back as a pair of women in medical scrubs arrived, the truck driver hovering behind them, making a call. From beyond the crash, horns blared, and the sound of a siren began. The call to prayer faded away. Blaise spotted Haldan's phone almost underneath his assailant's car. "Ah, my phone, there it's gone."

One of the assortment of on-lookers handed it over. "Convenient being so close to the hospital, eh?"

"Quite." Blaise slipped the phone away alongside his own. One of the nurses spoke softly to Haldan while the other woman, a doctor, examined the back of his head. Two orderlies arrived with a gurney, and Blaise took another step away, reassured that Haldan would be well-treated. Good, excellent. Haldan was too good a man to lose that way.

Blaise felt exposed there on the street, where an Assassin had been lurking only moments ago. His glance took in businesses and parked cars, the horns growing louder, the siren as well. He retreated toward his car, circling it with equal parts concern and interest. The front driver's side had been crushed with the glancing impact of the truck. Wait for the police. Wait. The assassin hadn't known he was there, couldn't have known. And Assassins used nothing so crude as car bombs. Even the attack on Haldan had been startlingly, well, blunt. Perhaps deliberately so, to send a message.

Blaise must maintain his impression, an important man, a professional man, his car in the wrong place, or, fortuitously in the right one, from the perspective of the man who would have died beneath the truck's tires, within sight of the hospital's front door. So close to dying.

Blaise's pocket vibrated. He tugged open the driver's side door and sat a little too heavily, frowning at his own phone, then pulling out Haldan's.

Donahue: *Got him. Are you alright?*

It vibrated again in his hand. Donahue: *That's not your phone.*

Blaise fought the urge to look up immediately. Instead, he settled against the seat, leaned his head against the rest. Donahue had gone behind the truck. Nothing to be seen in that direction, no. A man in a dark suit at the back of the crowd, the only one with no need to see what the medical team was doing. Just another tourist with a cellphone, not even seeming to glance toward the car. No, not a tourist, not with his coloring. He could be anyone. Another Blaise, even, a professional man caught up in a startling moment.

Donahue: *Thanks for your help. Knight?*

Blaise slid his thumb over the keypad. *Yes*

Two knights, one horse. Will he be alright?

Yes. Thanks to you.

Does this mean I'm in? Do I get to meet the king?

Americans. So impatient. *Soon, I'm sure.* Blaise started to type instructions, then hesitated. If he were not, himself, the king, but simply another knight, he wouldn't know what Donahue's other assignment might be. *Carry on. We'll be in touch. Yours, in service.*

Donahue tipped the phone to his forehead, a casual salute, and walked away.

Blaise breathed out. Call in to the office. Await the police. Tell them just enough of the truth—he reached for the files that had fallen from the passenger seat—and found a package on top, a folio similar to the ones he used at the office, but thicker, and bound with string to hold in the contents. His heart thundered, and he schooled himself not to look around to see who had delivered it: he had already circled the car and knew that no one lingered near—the gory parts of the accident were on the other side, Haldan's blood on the street, the door torn from the other car.

He pulled free the string that bound the packet and glanced at the pile of pages within. Photocopies of yellowed pages, the lines of text even more skewed than the ancient hand that wrote them. Not copies, then, but printouts of images, page after page. Someone had been working late in his service, and they had delivered him all he needed.

Blaise took up his phone and placed the call to Ozan. "So sorry, there's been an accident. I'm not hurt, but I won't be able to make it to the office today."

"It's the last full day before we head out to Cyprus, Blaise—are you sure?"

"I'll have to take care of too many details. Don't worry, I'll inform the clients so we can reschedule. And I look forward to seeing you at the conference."

Ozan chuckled. "I'll be there in style!"

In style. Maybe so, but nothing like Blaise would be. His knights had delivered him the path to his throne, and his allies would give him the boost he needed to attain it. Their latest shipment, dispatched by van in the early hours, included the woman, the guns, enough explosives to throw quite a party. Blaise let his smile warm his voice. "I'm sure it will be one for the ages."

CHAPTER THIRTY

Kyra translated carefully while Nick stood listening, head hung low, thumbing away an occasional tear as a doctor explained what had happened to his boss. Sudden cardiac incident. Two nurses and a doctor responded, but to no avail. "No death examinations," Nick told the doc. "He's Native American. It's against his beliefs."

"Of course, of course." The Turkish doctor looked from Kyra to Nick and back again.

"Of course," Kyra echoed, "if we have reason to believe there has been any dereliction of duty—"

"Not that I'm aware, ma'am," said one of the fake police officers, taking his job a little too seriously. "We were on duty the whole time, as ordered, and the response was immediate." The other officer just nodded. Well, Kyra couldn't expect first rate actors on such short notice.

"I have called for a private ambulance to transport him to a funeral home for embalming, officers. Would you please escort him? He deserves such dignity." Kyra held herself still and calm, letting Nick be the emotional one—just the right level of grief. How did he manage to counterfeit tears on such short notice? But then, imagining Casey's death, given how close they seemed, might be enough to shake him in truth.

His gestures this morning emphasized the missing fingers on his right hand, underscoring a sense of vulnerability that she suspected was not all for show. A local reporter who'd been hanging about since the incident yesterday where she and Nick had—anyhow, the reporter stood by, taking notes and snapping photos.

"Thank you, Ms. Akbulut. It would mean a lot," Nick said.

She slipped her hand over his elbow, and they made a small procession of it, taking Destry down in the elevator, out the back, into the ambulance—where the actual nurse immediately got to work unzipping the body bag and hooking him back up to all of the equipment she could muster. An officer shut one door, but before he could shut the second, Nick leaned in and whispered, "You hear that, Vivek? That's Oscar buzz. Very, very nice work." Nick gave him a salute, and earned a hundred-watt smile in return.

Nick shut the back door and leaned to wave. The vehicle started up and drove away, heading for a country hospital where Destry could recover in peace.

"Shall we go?" Kyra prompted.

"Not even a moment of silence for my boss and best friend?" He winked.

"Not when we have an obelisk to find."

She stalked through the hospital's emergency room from the ambulance entrance, dodging a patient who lay face down on a gurney, the back of his tawny-red hair matted with blood. "What's the plan with Casey?"

Nick caught her up and said, "You mean Donahue, ma'am—Casey's dead."

"Right, sorry."

The doctor attending the injured man scowled at her and tugged down his mask long enough to say, "If your patient is gone, you can't be back here."

"Sorry, sorry." She put up her hands and walked faster.

When they reached the public area, Nick finally said, "And we don't talk shop until we're in a secure location."

Kyra led the way back to the car where Muminah perked up immediately and started the engine. With Adem under suspicion—by the Bone Guard, if not by Kyra—and Kostas preparing the boat, Muminah filled in, a placid, capable woman who spoke no English. Mother turned from the passenger seat.

"Hello, darlings. I hope you don't mind my joining you."

Kyra froze, half in the car, while Nick climbed in on the other side. He beckoned her, and she finally sat all the way. "Mother, you know that someone's already died for this."

"Likely more than one," Nick rumbled.

"I am seventy-one, and never had such an adventure. By the way, you are taking me to the Davos party, aren't you? I've packed my gown and sent it off to the yacht."

"I've not even agreed to attend." To Muminah, she said, "Let's go."

Nick popped open a laptop and zoomed in on part of the image already on the screen, a page from Aleume's text with carefully made hieroglyphics. He reached into a pocket she didn't know he had and produced his mobile, frowning at whatever he saw there. "Chief'll join us by the hippodrome. Says he's okay, but his contact went down hard in an attack outside the hospital. Say, Irene..." He held the phone toward the front seat. "Do you recognize this guy?"

Mother took the phone and pushed her glasses to the top of her head to peer at the image, then she said, "Yes, of course. That's him. Older, but still quite distinguished, don't you agree? The King of Jerusalem."

She added an intonation as if she were reading aloud from Shakespeare and Everything Required Emphasis. She handed over the phone with an unnecessary flourish. She looked tired, after staying up late examining the manuscript and finally being coaxed to bed by Nick himself, or so Kyra understood. She couldn't survive on less than 7 hours and had already tucked in by that point.

"Mother, you need to go home."

"Because of the danger? Yet I should allow you to walk straight into it?"

"I'm an adult, Mother—"

"And so am I."

From his seat, Nick said, "I've got D.A.'s translation here, but it doesn't make much sense. Does either of you know an Egyptologist?"

"At the Topkapi, your father had a friend, a Doctor—"

Kyra leaned forward, gripping the back of her mother's seat, trying to interrupt the line of sight between Nick and her mother. "Home."

"Would you like me to turn around, Ms. Akbulut?" Muminah inquired, stopping at an intersection that would take them in one direction or the other. The car behind blared its horn as it blew past.

Mother seized her hand, and her cheeks sucked in as if she were about to explode, the volcano face Kyra well recalled from her childhood. "I know that you miss him. I know that you've been wounded by his loss, Kyra, but you seem to forget that it hurt me, too," a stream of rapid-fire Turkish. "I loved him for years before there was you. I loved him through his madness, through his illness, through the gouts of blood, Kyra, I was there! I loved him, too. You will not shut me out of his legacy as you have shut me out of your heart. If I have been wrong about him, about his obsession, you have commanded me to weep upon his grave, as if I wouldn't do so every birthday, every anniversary. Do not send me home."

She even pleaded like someone in an ancient drama.

Kyra blinked, turning her face aside. Out the window stood an ornate shop, ostentatiously Turkish, selling fancy tins of sweets for the tourists. Sickening. Even from here, the smell of the sugar nauseated her. Her mother's hand fell away from hers, and she took her hand back, folding it into her lap.

"Keep driving," said Nick softly, sternly, like a father himself.

Muminah's eyes sought Kyra's in the rear view mirror, and she gave a sharp nod. Muminah smoothly re-entered traffic, steering toward the Hippodrome.

Nick shifted in his seat, facing Kyra. "Your mother's got skin in this game. I don't know what she said to you. I don't know what you're wishing you could say in response, and I don't know that I want to be here when you work it out, but I do know this. She's the one who's been translating all this stuff for us, and she's got the kind of expertise and connections we need to solve this thing. If we're gonna stop more people dying, it's because we know more and we move faster than the competition. We need people like your mom in order to get that done. You two have a lifetime of stuff built up between you, more history than Istanbul. But I need you to focus on this. That stuff, that history, means the world to you—and this moment means our lives. If you can't focus, this ends now."

"Oh, it might in any case," Mother chirped from the front seat. "That's the king, right over there."

CHAPTER THIRTY-ONE

A rriving a little early to the rendezvous with Nick and the client, Grant weighed the options and decided to change his look. A quick walk through the nearest souk found him a cap, a windbreaker with the logo of a Turkish soccer team—football team, Grant corrected himself: time to drop into the local atmosphere—a string backpack for his Bone Guard suit, a pair of loose-fitting pants, sandals. With a slouch and a pair of shades, he could be any hustler or gig-worker in the local economy, scrolling through his messages as he cruised the tourist zone near the Hippodrome. Fifteen hundred years ago, this place had been the heart of Constantinople: a long oval racetrack, lined with stadium seating including a box for the emperor, capped by a structure to let loose the chariots for the races at one end, and at the other, a deadly curve where the cheap seats got a great view of catastrophes in motion as charioteers lost control and smashed up. Grant imagined the roar of the crowds, and the death of the horses. Blood sports, whether they were meant to be or not.

And down the center—one of the few features that remained from the Roman Days—a long dividing wall called the spina where the stolen treasures of a dozen cultures could be displayed. Robert de Clari, the crusader, described the ruin of the place, the bronze statues gathered or created over hundreds of years lying in pieces. The Crusade's Venetian sponsors carried off one grouping, a set of fine bronze horses who once led a chariot of their own, the horses now an international symbol of the city as they pranced over the entrance to the Cathedral San Marco. An international symbol of greed, of one culture stealing the prize of another. If Grant lived a thousand years ago, would he be a Crusading invader? A Varangian defender? One of the people trapped in the middle, trampled by each side and just praying the taxes of the new regime wouldn't be the death of him?

Up ahead, the sight that drew Grant in among the tourists now: an Egyptian obelisk hauled here by a long-dead emperor and erected along the spina for the admiration of the hippodrome crowds. The obelisk still towered over the smaller crowd today, an exotic monument to the layering of history. Aleume's drawings even reproduced the hieroglyphics, what must have been, to him, inexplicable pictures of stylized people and strange animals. According to Kyra's critical gaze and D.A.'s long-distance analysis, he had drawn them well, almost all of them. Somewhere among the symbols was the clue they needed to find the secret place Aleume had chosen to conceal the Throne.

Find the Throne, complete the mission, thwart the king, find a way to dodge the Assassin's threat if he didn't follow through and give up the madman. The king might be deluded, might have hired someone to take out Grant himself at the archives, but that attempt wasn't personal, just a tactic, a way to cover for the theft of the book. Then Grant saw again the moment of the blow. The king's fist. Akilah's cheek. Her swiftness and grace turned to a stumble, then a sprawl. And he thought about taking the bastard out himself. An unreasonable, irrational urgency.

His body felt electric, stinging with the need to go. He didn't know where she was, but he knew who to call, he knew what came next. All he had to do was throw over his client and his best friend and get the hell out of here.

She was hardly an innocent, definitely not a civilian, not since the first day he'd made that mistaken identity. The Phantom, they had called her, teasing him. She haunted him nonetheless.

His phone buzzed. Nick: *spotted the king, inbound to the zone.*

He shouldn't know where the zone was. Shit. *I'm there.* Grant slouched his way toward a stand of trees. *How did he know?*

Nick: ¯_(ツ)_/¯: *suspect Kazan. Midnight meetup Check it out.*

Grant lounged, waving to the tourists, sending gestures of smarmy invitation to any women who glanced his way. Being somebody else. He scanned the crowd, using his cover. Tall woman across the way had been part of the scene with the van when Akilah went down. Lanky young man not quite ready for ops. Two middle-aged men who made like tourists only they walked back again later, slowly, but with the coiled sense of former soldiers. Young woman at the back of a crowd of Italians who kept rubbing the band aid at her wrist, same place he'd made his own false mark. Five of them. The king was getting nervous, after that morning's encounter. But where was— Two of his agents quickened to his presence. Two confirmed by their lack of interest.

The king walked like one: tall, proud, level-headed, his ring in place. Hadn't been a couple hours back, when he intervened to save Brunelle at the risk of his own car, if not his life. A man for whom loyalty went both ways. Made it that much harder to hate him.

The king carried a large paper map, poorly folded, cover for the extra pages tucked inside. He paused a little way back, tracing the monument with his eyes. He had the kind of clear profile that made for good coinage: deep-set eyes, strong jawline. Grant pictured him mounting the steps to the Throne, his fingers stroking the heads of golden lions while bronze-worked birds proclaimed his presence and an artificial plane tree spread its fronds to defend him from the sun.

Dang. What Grant wouldn't give for a solid female accomplice right about now, someone he could meet with, ostentatiously, to the annoyance of the well-dressed businessman, getting a close-up look at whatever he was carrying.

Grant's thumbs slid over the screen. *Print out. OMW Negative. He knows you.*

He doesn't know shit, Grant thought, but he tapped, *Not like this.*

Grant picked a target, an older couple who had separated from their tour group. He waved and grinned, walking toward them, angling his path into the shadow of the obelisk. The woman noticed, frowning, then muttered to her husband.

"We don't want any," he called out, his mustache ruffling with distaste.

"Guide service?" Grant called, accenting his English with a hint of Arabic. "Yes? I take you, all the best ruins. Hammam, too, for the both of you! Discount for couples."

They were already retreating around the other side, forcing him to angle his approach, wrapping behind the king who stepped out of the way without looking up from the image he carried. Hieroglyphics laid out like the ones above, but missing a few. The drawing ended there, but the tower didn't. A Roman-era base supported the obelisk, embellished with the exploits of the emperor who had claimed the Egyptian king's own monument as his own. Under that, a more quotidian image of the obelisk being erected in the Hippodrome. In between, a narrow decorative stone, heavily scored with lines.

Grant kept moving, pursuing his would-be target to the other side, then tossing up his hands, turning away and brazenly seeking a new mark. Other tourists started shifting away from him, and a tour guide scowled. "That's not allowed. You can't do that—"

"Sorry, sorry." Grant retreated, hitching his backpack up a little higher and slogging across the green to blend in with the locals on the sidewalk.

Is the drone queen prepared? Need an image, lower SE side. Shoot them all

Ok. That you in the hat? Nick texted back.

Nope

Tall woman, your five

Grant trotted a few steps as the walk light came on. "Hey! Guide service!" He followed after his new mark, maintaining an easy patter until they turned the corner, shoulders hunched, trying to outpace him. He let them.

All clear.

Tall woman was pretty good. Noted.

Who else?

2 ex-mils w/ coffee, college student striped dress, skinny local guy

Got it

Over 2 U Grant signed off and kept moving, wishing he had D.A., Gooney, anybody. Bashir said the king had two armies—the knights, and the jihadis. Grant had an army of two. Hope it didn't come to a melee, or he and Nick were royally screwed.

Chapter Thirty-Two

Kyra's fingers slid deftly over her screen, establishing parameters as Nick, wearing a flowing tunic, an embroidered cap and a beard strolled over to the plaza, holding his phone sideways like a game controller. The camera drone followed along near his head, and he maintained an even patter in a language she didn't recognize. He gestured toward his surroundings, then came up to the obelisk, arms spread as if greeting an old friend. He even gave a little bow, then managed his phone more carefully. As Kyra flew the drone in a careful pattern, bottom to top, Nick mimed controlling the drone close up.

The other tourists—no, the actual tourists—glared and grumbled, some of them putting up their hands to block their faces. Nick called out apologies in a sing-song. Egyptian, wasn't it? Nick's extraordinary performance distracted her. He'd bought the clothes from a souk near her home, and apparently invented this character on the fly, an Egyptian tourist overjoyed to find something from the homeland.

"Kyra, I think there's a problem," Mother chimed from the front seat. She pointed to where a tour guide was talking with a policeman, drawing him back toward the restive crowd. The king, meanwhile, had been sketching, stepping out of the way when Nick and his drone cruised through, scowling, but not apparently concerned.

The policeman called out, and Nick freed a hand to wave. Kyra dipped the drone, and Nick immediately reacted, gaining control and "flying" his little craft away from the crowd. The policeman quickened his pace, shouting, "It's not legal. Sir! You must—"

Nick grabbed the drone out of the sky and made a show of turning it off, wafting his hands through the air in a placating gesture as the officer confronted him.

"Did we get the picture?" Mother asked.

"That is why we started at the bottom," Kyra slid her fingers again, completing transmission, shutting off the propeller blades so they didn't either injure Nick, or expose the fact that he wasn't actually driving it. Mother was halfway helpful, and half the same interfering drama queen she always had been.

The passenger side door opened and Kyra startled, the tablet tumbling from her lap as Casey climbed in. "Drive around the block. Two blocks north, one west."

"Ms.—" Muminah began

"Just do it." She turned in her seat, feeling safer when she was facing him. Like Nick, he had donned a disguise, which he had partially shed in favor of a long-sleeved t-shirt and a safari cap with a drape at the back of his neck.

"What about Nick?"

"He knows," Casey said. "What've we got?"

Muminah pulled out and drove. Retrieving the tablet, Kyra called up the footage and scrolled backward to the south-east side. She expanded the lower part of the marble plinth upholding the obelisk. Mother leaned over the seat.

"Oh, dear. It's not much is it? You don't think the hieroglyphics are the answer after all?"

"Could be." Casey peered at the screen where gray and white marble resolved into a series of gouges as if someone tried to deface the vacant stone.

Not truly vacant, she could make out vague figures, performing their role in the narrative of carrying the obelisk to set it here. She discerned their feet, in any case. "It's badly degraded. Possibly the years of bad weather have made it illegible."

He shook his head, his finger tracing over her screen, following the gouge marks. "These lines are too regular. You can see the weathering, sure, but they're clearly deliberate. I'm just not—

Kyra blinked, and the pattern came clear. "It's a map." She selected a tool and drew over the lines with black, solidifying the ghostly outline. Mostly straight, with a distinctive oval to the lower side. "This is—"

"The hippodrome," they said together.

With a tap and a slide, she saved the layer she had made and brought up an actual map of the city, working to overlay her drawing. She flipped back and forth between the original footage and the sketch, increasing the resolution to make sure she captured any important detail. Muminah pulled over by a cafe with outdoor seating where Nick lounged at a table, her drone nowhere in sight.

"I don't know where we're going to put him," Mother said, "He's rather large, isn't he?"

"Nice work," Casey said softly. To Mother, he said, "Don't worry, I'm getting out."

Kyra's concentration broke. "Where are you going?"

"At a guess, Syria." He faced her fully, hands at rest, as if they needed to be visible to reassure her. The sight of his hands rather did comfort her. Unlike her own hands, his never trembled. His looked ready to tackle the world while hers were more comfortable on the screen.

"Ms. Akbulut. Kyra." He took a deep breath. "I'm going after her. If this is a deal-breaker, I understand. I'd like Nick to stay with you, at least until you get your own security personnel." His dark eyes met hers, more serious than she'd ever seen him. "I hope you know I'm not doing this lightly."

"You expect us to do this without you?" She waved a hand at the screen.

"Ma'am, there's nothing I'd like more than to help you—nothing except knowing she's alive and she's safe."

"Oh, dear," Mother said, "That is serious."

"My hope is to rejoin you ASAP. The king has the images, he might work out the map. Do what you can to throw him off. If all else fails, get out of town and hide in a crowd."

Kyra nodded. She thought about fighting, putting on the imperious business woman she could be. And she thought about the thief, somewhere alone. She hired the woman because she admired her ethics and her cause, supporting embattled women who had nowhere else. Now that she was embattled, what would Kyra wish for her? No less than the most competent help she could find. Kyra touched his arm. "I understand," she murmured.

"Makes one of us." He nearly smiled. "Stay safe." He slipped out into the street and she wasn't sure when or if she would see him again.

CHAPTER THIRTY-THREE

S he's not part of our fucking mission, Chief."

"No, she isn't. But she's one of us. And I'm the only person she might trust." Grant met his friend's eye, finding it hard to breathe, as if the weight of that stone lion once more collapsed on top of him, pinning him in the rain of Nick's blood.

"Bullshit, Chief. She's got no reason to trust you." Nick leaned slightly, favoring his prosthetic, and Grant's own thigh ached a little. "Why are you doing this? Why really?"

He remembered the museum in flashes: the explosion, the smell of cordite and blood, stone dust rushing the air as Nick flung him out of the direct line; then the pain, feeling like his head was being torn from his body. Feeling Nick's hand stopping the blood at his throat, combat medic to the rescue, holding Grant's life in his hands. Nick could've been—should've been—saving his leg. Nick wasn't even supposed to be there. Unit rules: you don't go back, certainly not for the Chief who'd gotten them in trouble to begin with. Nick leaning over him, panting with his agony. *"Need you to hear me, Chief. Don't die on me, Chief. Don't you fucking die on me."* Maybe saving his life had saved Nick's own, giving the big guy something to focus on other than dying.

A thousand miles from that day, Grant stood on the sidewalk, the car idling half a block down the street, the client waiting for him to send Nick along, waiting for Grant himself to move on. He wrapped his fingers through his hair. Why the hell was he doing this? Why leave his friend, his client, his fucking mission, as Nick put it, for someone he barely knew? The answer clawed at the back of his neck, and he hated it. Hated even more that he was afraid of it. The last thing he wanted was to put a name to it. But this was Nick. Grant force his hands to unclench, noted Nick's hand turned half-way to making the gun. Oh, fucking shit.

Every word burned his throat. "She moved to save Vivek. She had nothing to do with him, or us." He swallowed, straining for some comfort beyond the heat, and reached for humor. "You think she was just a party crasher looking for some free champagne?"

"That was me, as I recall."

Grant gave a nod. "Doesn't change the fact that she had her own mission. She was willing to blow it all to save the man she thought was me."

"Seriously?" Nick looked away, his jaw muscles straining against his own scars. "Maybe she is like you, maybe too much so—running in where angels fear to tread. She saw the danger and ran to embrace it. Just like you. Don't make like I'm heartless, I'm not: I just resent the hell out of you dropping me and the client for some daredevil op in a combat zone for somebody who is—odds on—already out of reach. This isn't a lone wolf operation, Chief. We need you here." His fingers jabbed toward the ground, as if he were snapping back the slide on that invisible gun. "I need you here."

"I know," he whispered. "Jesus, Nick, I know."

Nick stood with his back to the sun, shadowy trees shaking their leaves behind him, his face in shadow, his shadow making Grant feel all the smaller. Nick said, "Y'know what this mission was supposed to be? You and me, like we were the first two days. You and me taking our coffee on a balcony on the Golden Horn, watching the sun set on the Mediterranean. Maybe I made believe we're an item, indulge that old crush of mine—and you let me—the fuck do we care what other people think?"

Nick's words conjured the scene so clearly Grant could taste the coffee on his lips and feel the burn at the back of his eyes. Those first two days, before somebody shot him in the archive, before he saw her, before he —that was bliss, a kind of quiet camaraderie neither of them had known for a long time. "Nick..."

"I almost lost you in Arizona, Chief." Nick's voice fell into a bass rumble, like the sound of thunder in the distance. "Had to count on fucking Gooney to get you safe. You got any idea what it felt like, sucking up to him as the conquering hero?"

Yeah, he did. Almost lost Gooney out there, too. Grant settled his hand on his friend's bicep, the muscle rock solid, the friend even more so. "Nick." Then, very carefully, "I need you to hear me."

Nick's eyes came back to his. His jaw worked, and he finally said, "I'm listening."

The words came slow, piecing together the truth as carefully as an archaeologist assembled any shattered thing. "It's not that she moved to save him, because she thought he was me. Vivek told you the box was light, right? By the time he got shot, it was already empty. Her mission was over, Nick. She'd already done what she came there to do. She could've picked up the champagne case with the codex inside and walked it out, then just kept on going, nobody the wiser. The only reason she stayed was that she thought he was me." He sucked in a breath. "It's not that she risked her own mission to save me. She didn't know, she couldn't know, that I was in danger until well after she had what she came for. Nick—" he'd been thinking it over, thinking too hard, digging too deep to lay bare what he feared. "She risked her own mission...just to see me again."

Nick's eyebrows rose slowly, his eyes sparkling in the patchy sunlight. "The hell."

"You told me you've been seeing Jamal, thinking about him. If you knew it was him, if you knew who to call—"

"Just go. Get out of here, Chief. You're gonna do it anyway." Nick walked toward the car, and Grant absorbed the impact like a blow, Nick's broad shoulders overlaid with the image of every friend he'd ever seen for the last time, not knowing which one of them wasn't coming home. "I'll be fine."

The words, the image, the attitude snapped Grant out of his own damn head. It wasn't just him Nick was worried about. The way he tensed, the way his hand twitched, those two pill bottles on the bedside table. Nick wasn't just his wingman, he was Nick's, watching out for trouble, not just around them, but within.

"Nick."

His friend paused.

"You don't trust yourself, Nick, but I do."

The hard line of his shoulders straightened, then he kept moving.

At the door of the car, he did a hard pivot, breaking the dangerous spell of memory, his expression furious. "Don't you fucking die out there." His finger aimed in Grant's direction. "You do not die out there alone, Chief. Not without me."

Nick's words shot the life back into him, like a geas laid upon a knight in an ancient tale. "No, sir."

He saluted, then he got moving, phone in hand, checking the number Bashir had given him, Farouk's response to his query, in Arabic: *Always seeking the faithful. When can you get to Hama*

Active war zone, serious no-go according to the State Department—and any other rational source. *Be there tonight, Insha'Allah.* Grant answered, then he started to run, burning off Nick's anger, Akilah's absence, his own coiled tension at being caught in between. Strike like an assassin: get in, get the prize, get out, and nobody knows you're there. Insha'Allah. God willing.

CHAPTER THIRTY-FOUR

Back at Chloe's car—a recent model, nicely kept, but inconspicuous, Blaise examined his sketch, the map revealed in the ancient markings. He thanked his predecessor, the warrior-priest whose careful work had brought him to this moment. Aleume gave him no more beyond this, but he trusted in his brother knight across the centuries. Aleume altered the monument to point the way. Blaise might, even now, be seated only a few hundred yards from the moment he had so long been waiting for. They parked in a busy lot down the street from the target block. No sign of the Nizari, but still he didn't want to expose himself without need. Two knights took another cup of coffee at a nearby table, a third faked a phone call across the way.

Chloe approached the vehicle with a shopping bag swinging from her hand, looking as relaxed as any woman out for the morning and thinking about where to go for lunch. She cut a striking figure, athletic and lean. Not classically beautiful, but for purposes like this, it was better thus.

"No sign, my lord." Chloe tossed her bag into the driver's seat. "I may have been mistaken. Perhaps he was just a hustler, hoping to make money off the tourists."

"You're sure you would recognize him?"

She hesitated. "If he did a full wardrobe change, it would be difficult, my lord. But his general type, yes."

It would have to do. Haldan needed, deserved, at least the day off, after his ordeal of that morning. Blaise would need him in Cyprus. Half the knights were there already, and the Shifra as well had begun their infiltration. He hoped, after what had happened, to bring Donahue into the fold as soon as possible, but had received only the most courteous of denials: *Deepest apologies, my lord. Sent to investigate possible lower obelisk section in museum storage. She's consulting Egyptologist @Topkapi. Not sure they trust me with whatever they're following. Means a lot to know that you do. Should be back in 24 hours.*

So Akbulut and her man knew it had something to do with the obelisk, but hadn't worked out what. In twenty-four hours, Blaise and most of his supporters would be far from here, poised to claim his place in the world. *Sorry to hear that, Michael. You have more than earned your sword. I stand ready to welcome you. Send word when ready.*

"In that case, let's go." He let himself out, clad more casually than was his wont, but with a felt hat that partially shaded his face. He worked hard for his local connections, but the last thing he wanted today was to be delayed by too many greetings. He offered his arm to Chloe, who accepted gracefully, her long strides a good match for his. She swung a little handbag by her side. Just an ordinary couple, perhaps thinking of where to go for lunch. They were a little early for the cafe in question, the medieval building that stood at the intersection marked so plainly on Aleume's map. But when they entered, Blaise heard a door shutting in the back and thought they might be right on time.

CHAPTER THIRTY-FIVE

Kyra couldn't stop glancing at Nick as they descended a stone staircase, the man with the lantern just ahead. "He'll be alright?" She wanted the words to be reassuring, but they came out as a question.

"All those tattoos?" Nick kept moving, kept his head down. "Each one is a time he almost died. Lazarus Club, he calls it."

She had caught only glimpses, at his wrist, his throat. "How many are there?"

"I don't even know. Hope to God he gets another one."

Kyra's brow furrowed briefly as she parsed, then understood what he was saying. Because it would mean that Casey lived.

"Will you be alright?" Mother asked from the back.

Nick glanced her way, and, to Kyra's relief, mustered some of the tenderness he had shown her before. "It's kind of you to ask, Irene. He and I, we've been through a lot together. Lot of times I thought it'd be the last time. Swear to God, he knew I was gay before I did. Pretty much introduced me to the love of my life." Nick stopped on a landing, and Kyra glanced back at him, her mother still on the step behind him.

"The three of us had some downtime during an op in Afghanistan, and he turns to Jamal and goes, 'What's the Arabic for homosexual? Not as a slur, but just the word.' Jamal looks surprised, scared almost, then says, 'Why do you need to know? Are you?' and laughs, making it a joke. 'Not me,' says the chief, 'but I know a coupla guys who are. Be a helluvalot easier if they weren't so scared of me that they wouldn't talk to each other.' Then he gets up and says, 'I'll go patrol. Back in two,' and takes off. Jamal and I are just...sitting there, not looking at each other, and he laughs again, but kinda shy this time. 'Wonder who he's talking about,' he says, and I do the bravest thing I've ever done. I say, 'I'm pretty sure I'm one of them.' And Jamal finally looks at me, the way I keep wanting him to..." Nick's fist beat softly in the air, as if holding on, and he continued, "then, real soft, he goes, 'Me, too.'

"Chief came back two hours later, and never mentioned it. Two and a half years, he just eased the way, kept us invisible. He gave me the time, and the space, not because I asked him, because he knew I what I needed, and he gave it to me, every chance he could. Have you ever had a friend like that?"

After a moment, he started walking again. Their footfalls echoed in the rough stairwell, then her mother's voice came faintly. "I did once, Mr. Norton." And with a breath of laughter. "I married him."

Kyra stumbled and Nick found her elbow, supported her briefly, then released her. "Then I am especially sorry for your loss," he said, but low, and forward, maybe not speaking to her mother at all. Kyra kept her chin up, and tried to recall when she had last had a friend, much less one with the intimacy his attachment implied.

"Here we are," said their guide, in Turkish, holding up the lantern. "Nobody comes here. It's not an important place, just old, so the archaeologists don't care, and the tourists won't pay." He shrugged, swinging the lantern side to side. A narrow, arched chamber stood at the base of the stairs, with low stone benches carved into the wall to either side. To one side, a stack of crates and boxes alongside a dry stone wall with a half-door. At the other end, a wall painting, made barely discernible by the passage of time.

"Fresco," said her mother, the know-it-all. "Byzantine art is almost exclusively mosaic. That makes this Latin at least. It could be older, pre-Constantinian, but the image itself suggests otherwise."

They walked closer, Kyra passing the guide, the young man who had inherited the restaurant from his family and now struggled to make it pay. "Is this all?"

He reluctantly shuffled closer, holding up the lantern, and Nick snapped photos of the image revealed: pale blue gown, golden circle at the back, the dark smudges of eyes and mouth. The Virgin Mary, based on iconography alone—little else would identify this vague shape as the Mother of God. Another pair of dark smudges hovered to one side and a pale shape with protrusions that might once have been arms occupied her lap, the remnants of a Baby Jesus.

"Well," said Mother, "Aleume was a priest and a warrior, not an artist."

From above, a bell jingled, and their guide perked up. "That's the front door, I have to check. Won't be a moment." He set down the lantern on what would be the altar and started up the stairs.

"Ask them to leave—whoever it is. Nobody comes in. We'll pay for the seating," Nick called after him. "Kyra, tell him, he's gotta lock the door."

She trotted partway up the stairs to relay the message in Turkish, and the young man hurried a little faster. Kyra returned quickly. "I don't know that he believes me, we'd best hurry."

"This type of image is often called the Hodegetria, 'the one who shows the way,'" Mother intoned.

"But to what?" Nick held up the light from his phone, scanning the image.

"It should be to the baby, the symbol of redemption for mankind, if you believe that sort of thing." She leaned in along with him.

"Yeah, but her hand's pointing down." They turned outward like a pair of doors opening.

Kyra paused on the stair. "The part of the floor you're standing on, it's a different shade than the rest."

She hurried back down and helped Nick to get a grip on the edge of the large square inset. Together they pried it up. From overhead, the sound of voices.

"Damn it—he didn't listen." Nick heaved the square out of the way, letting it pivot up, a trap door to the subflooring where another painting awaited.

"Casey, he said we should destroy the clue, prevent the king from following." She frowned down at the floor, trying to make out the image and the lettering, then realized she was viewing it upside down.

"Pictures—shoot it fast!" He held the slab while she took the camera from his coat pocket and started shooting.

"Oh, dear. We can't really destroy it, can we? How awful." Mother put her hands on her knees, peering down.

"What do we have? What can we use?" Kyra spun about, searching the chamber

"Acid?" Nick suggested.

"That would do," Mother sighed.

Upstairs, footsteps approached, and the voices grew louder. "What are they saying?" Nick asked, his own voice dropping low.

Kyra raced to the crates of restaurant supplies, and yanked out a bottle of balsamic vinegar, holding it aloft. He waved her over.

"They claim to be police, he says, 'She just wanted to see the basement, officer, that's all—she's really a criminal?'" Mother translated. "Then, 'Yes, she's very subtle.'"

Kyra doused the painting with vinegar, cringing as it dissolved in a sluice of dark liquid.

"Behind the boxes—try that other door," Nick whispered, urgent. The two women ran in that direction while he eased the block back down, wincing a little, his movement made awkward by the prosthetic. Footfalls echoed closer on the stair. Kyra got her nails into the edge of the wood and pulled it open.

"Come on!"

"Is there a way through?" Nick scrambled over as she used the camera flash to light up the space beyond.

"I don't know!" They hustled under the low door, and Nick swept the place with his cellphone light, then his other hand emerged with a sleek, black gun. Kyra clung to the rough stone wall. More crates along one side—storage, and no exit.

"Get in there," Nick said, "Both of you." His grip tightened on the gun, his face gone grim.

Moments ago, he said farewell to his friend, believing it was Casey who might not return. Was it worth it? Worth dying for her father's dream? Worth killing for? "Let's just give it to them. Let's just go."

"No," said her mother calmly. "I will. He said, 'she' wanted to see the place." Mother straightened and wiped the dirt from her harem pants. "You two hide. With any luck, there will be no dying today."

Nick flashed her a glance, then followed Kyra into the darkness.

CHAPTER THIRTY-SIX

T hey reached the basement, the young man clearly agitated, then surprised. "I'm sure, officer," he began to say, and Chloe raised her weapon, glancing at Blaise. The place reeked of vinegar and stone dust, a single lantern casting weird shadows on the wall where it sat. Blaise squinted at them, making out a painting of the Virgin and Child, but ghostly pale.

"Oh, oh dear! I do hope my little whim hasn't gotten you in trouble."

Blaise spun about, and Chloe's gun shifted hard to the wall beneath the stairs. An older woman rose from one of the benches at the back, where she had been sitting in the shadows. "Goodness. There is surely no need of violence."

"Uh, no, ma'am?" The restaurateur turned, and bleated, finding the muzzle Chloe's gun aiming over his shoulder.

"Madam, please, there's no need for alarm," Blaise stalked a little nearer to her, and she shifted away from him, her hands clasped at her chest.

The woman looked frail and slightly familiar, a scarf draped rakishly over her head and shoulders, another tied at her hips. "Who are you? You don't look like police officers? Oh!" She stumbled theatrically into one of the boxes and it slid across the rubble floor to thump against the wall.

An old woman's stumble, or the work of an actress? "We should as well ask who are you. You look familiar."

She startled, then smiled in an old woman's imitation of flirting. "You can't place me? Sir, I am so disappointed." She tried to straighten and strike a glamorous pose, leaning on an open box, only to have it tumble to the ground in a crash of bottles. The sound echoed, almost deafening, made worse by her efforts to trap some of the bottles so they only fell further and hit harder, cracking and spilling their contents across the floor.

Blaise leapt back from the spill, but vinegar had already splashed up onto his pantlegs and he frowned. That explained the odor, in any case. "What are you doing here?"

"Weren't you in that soap opera?" The restaurateur said, pointing at her. "That one about the heiress—"

"Darling, thank you! You have renewed my hope in humanity. I am so sorry for the mess. I did say I would pay? Of course I will, dear boy."

A soap opera actress. Wonderful. "Go—just, go."

"I've gotten so clumsy, officer." She reached out as if to put a hand on his arm, and he withdrew in a fencer's glide, his sense of chivalry at war now with his need to know more, to explore this place. He had expected to see Kyra Akbulut here, which would explain the young man's attempt to stop them at the door. Instead, he found this eccentric old woman slowing his progress.

"Oh, forgive me." She withdrew her hand, but took a few wobbly steps. "Bone cancer," she said in that whisper old people use for bad news. "It is my wish to see every church in the city before I die, but taking those stairs again may be the death of me." Her hand fluttered at her face.

"Sir, do you want me to escort her?" Chloe put her gun back in a holster under her jacket.

"I'll take her," The restaurateur hurried forward, offering his arm, and she accepted gratefully, snuggling into the young man's support.

Blaise almost laughed. A few moments ago, he'd been trying to convince the young man they were after a hardened criminal, a smuggler in search of a stash, someone subtle and sneaky. Her performance was peculiar at best, and she might still be connected with Akbulut. His beneficence extended to letting her go. All he really needed was the space to make his examination. The odd couple shuffled up the stairs, the old woman chattering about famous people she had met.

From her handbag, Chloe pulled a flashlight and flicked it on, allowing them to study the Virgin together. "Likely medieval," Blaise said, "but unremarkable." The Virgin's shadowy hand pointed down, instead of up. He cocked his head, then glanced to the floor, an ancient pattern of large and small flagstones, now damp with vinegar, the largest stone bubbling around the edges as he stepped on it. The only stone uneven in the floor. "Help me."

Together, they grabbed the corners and hauled the stone up, scraping it onto the floor and revealing—a thin slick of vinegar. He wiped at it, flicking the stuff of his hand, revealing a line of black paint that his own effort scrubbed away. Blaise jerked back, then his head shot up. "That woman! Get her back—both of them!" Chloe's gun was back in her hand as she raced up the stairs.

For a moment, he was alone, and the room throbbed closer to him. Did he hear something? Blaise stood up from the ruin of his discovery and turned carefully. He took up the lantern and held it aloft to see the rest of the room, the stack of boxes cast into dancing shadows. A sound from the corner? Blaise took a step closer, regretting that he had no sword at his side. Behind those crates, not another box, but a doorway. He stalked near, his shoes crunching the glass of the broken bottles. He reached for the edge of the door, certain now, that he could hear careful breathing. He grabbed the corner.

From the stairs, a man's voice called down, "My lord, what aid?" Footfalls clattered toward him. Two of his knights. The second said, "They've gone, the woman and that skinny man as well. A car picked them up and we lost them among the tour busses."

"Guns ready," Blaise snapped. He yanked open the half-door. To find a wall of boxes, a sack of flour on top. He coughed as the dust reached him, the sound echoing.

Blaise slammed the door, causing it to rebound and shiver, dust and flour spiraling through the lamplight around him. "When I find her, that old woman will beg for repentance like none since the Templars' trial." It had been a long time since anyone burned at the stake, but he found the image, in that moment, alarmingly satisfying.

He pulled out his own gun and fired, splintering wood and spraying flour in a puff that settled slowly to the ground.

CHAPTER THIRTY-SEVEN

Kyra's hands muffled her face, her hands and face both buried against Nick's strong arm and shoulder, his hand stroking the back of her head—his other hand holding that gun. She saw nothing in their mutual tomb, but she had felt the tension shoot through him as the king's footsteps approached. She felt his partial turn, readying his weapon even as he pulled her closer, clamping his arm over her ears, defending her even from this.

Shoot him, shoot the king and make the world safe again—only in an instant to have the king's men stomping to the rescue.

The door flew open and streaks of light sliced into the darkness.

Nick held her close, both of them frozen.

The king's fury echoed around them, the slamming door shuddered through her bones as he issued his threat.

The gunshot made her jerk, a full-body spasm of terror, her muscles clenched, and Nick wrapped around her, his lips sealed. Powder settled over her, tickling her ears. She stifled her sneezing, curled up like a child, eyes watering with the effort of being silent. The first time one of these men forced her to shelter, she defied him, sulking like a child, exploring her prison, getting them both into more trouble, but she wasn't the one being shot at, until now.

The shot echoed through wood and stone, through her muffled ears. She had not been devout for years, but in that moment, she wished she had been. She wished she believed in that distant god in whose hands her fate would lie. Instead, she had this one: this dark-skinned stranger whose hands built the wall to protect her, whose arms cradled her now against fear and death, whose gun, if need be, would deal it. Whose own death, if need be, would follow.

She waited an eternity lest the shot be repeated. How had they not been hit?

Silence. And a warm trickle against her scalp. For a moment, she thought he was dead, knew he was dead, believed that even then, in the moment of dying, he kept his silence, saving her. She made herself breathe, made herself listen, and heard the steady beat of his heart.

Nick's grip on her eased a little, his hand once more soothing, and she wondered if the movement weren't as much for himself as for her. They waited an eternity underground, through shuffling, muttering, footfalls receding. Nick's arm gradually relaxed, but it did not withdraw until she lifted her head and pulled back from him. No light came through the slats of the door. The camera strap lay over her chest, the camera digging into her in ways she only now noticed. She fumbled for her cellphone in shaky hands, and brought up the screen alone, giving a pale blue glow.

"You're bleeding." She illuminated his head, where he had ducked over her, and found a few shards of wood piercing his skin at the side of his neck and across his shoulder, among the scrapes left by others as the door broke behind them. His shoulder must have been exposed. If he hadn't been wearing his black suit, or if the king had been more persistent than he was furious, Nick would have been spotted. Perhaps, indeed, there was a god.

"It doesn't look bad." She searched his face. Flour transformed him with his scalp suddenly pale, his face still dark.

"Scale of ten, this is nothing." He touched the area, and grimaced. "Need some tweezers, though."

"Is my mother alright?" she breathed.

"Sounded like yes. You ready to be sure?"

She nodded. He shifted away from her in the gloom, stretching out his leg with a wince, then grabbing the hurriedly piled cases and sacks and shoving them out of the way. The sound and the scrape paralyzed her for a long moment, braced for another shot. Flour trailed from the burst sack. Nick pushed the door open with his left hand, his right clasping the gun, making his hand seem whole again. "Clear," he murmured. He gestured her back and stood slowly outside, then waved her up, a series of gestures clipped and efficient, like the way he and Casey could have a whole conversation without saying a word.

Kyra rose stiffly beside him, and brought up the flashlight instead, giving more light to the spilled vinegar, the shattered bottles of her mother's mad ruse. She had warned them, she who had been a lifelong dancer, claiming clumsiness and making enough noise to cover any manner of construction projects, more than enough to move a few boxes. For a big man, Nick could move with startling silence and precision. The gun waved her forward, and he took the lead up the stairs. Walking, listening, walking again, finally at the door into the empty, unlit cafe. They walked between the empty tables, shedding flour, bits of wood, shards of glass from their shoes. He stopped her again, looking, this time, then gestured toward the kitchen. They walked through the swinging door, along a tiled floor and he checked through the back door, propped open with a brick. Finally, they emerged into a back alley, into the blinding sunlight of a day that didn't know anything had happened at all. She felt an urge to laugh until she collapsed, and realized that Nick's hand was supporting her lower back, light but strong.

"Noises on?" he said, tipping his head.

She startled to find her phone still in her hand. "You must think me such a fool." She turned her ringer on and dialed her mother's number.

"No, ma'am. Civilian, for sure. But the vinegar was a nice touch. You think fast, here and at the hospital." His eyes didn't stop moving, sweeping both ends of the alley, lingering where another alley joined theirs. "These people. They're angry and they're armed, but they're not operators. They like things above board, face to face."

"Kyra!" Her mother's voice leapt from the phone in a stream of Turkish. "Oh, my, oh my. I was so sure you would be dead. I was so afraid to go back, to make things worse."

Tears streaked Kyra's face for the second time in as many days. Nick's hand returned, a solid, human warmth as he said, "She's okay, Irene, just a little rattled. Very nice work back there."

"We're at the harbor, I wasn't sure what else to do—I paid off that nice young man and suggested he take a vacation." Mother carried on a little more calmly, still in Turkish, but Nick had told her what she needed, after all. HumInt, Human Intelligence, they called it. Kyra could use some for herself.

"I think a vacation is an excellent idea," she said. "Do you still want to go to Cyprus?"

"Oh, darling, more than ever! I cannot leave this town too soon! What about Nick?" Her voice took on a plaintive tone.

"We'll talk about it. See you soon." She rang off.

Kyra found Nick's eyes back to her after another sweep of the area. "This has to end," she told him. "It's not worth more blood. I have the proof the throne was here—that will have to be enough. Perhaps later, when the king has gone off to whatever mad house will have him. Maybe then we can keep looking." She swept the flour from her shoulders and shook out her clothes as best she could. Nick did the same, plucking the largest slivers, leaving the smaller ones for later.

"You pulling the plug on this?" He looked a little smaller, no longer the powerful deity he had been in the dark.

Kyra ventured, "You don't think Mr. Casey would approve."

Nick gave a shrug, though his uncertainty remained. "Chief knows better than to pursue an op after it's gone bad—besides, you're the client. Let me see you safely to Cyprus. We re-evaluate the risk factors, get a call-in and sign-off from the chief if I think you're in the clear." He slipped the gun away at last, and said, "Which way to the harbor?"

She pointed, taking the lead again, if not so confidently this time. "This has been quite an adventure. Not one I should wish to repeat."

"I hear you."

"And yet, you are..." She studied him, then guessed, "disappointed." They strolled onto the sidewalks, back into the daytime crowds, and she knew enough by now to recognize his relaxation as another costume.

"On a scale of one to ten. It's nothing."

"You don't trust me." This should be no surprise, no disappointment. She had hardly shown herself worthy of trust.

"That's not it." He held her back from crossing the street as a bus roared into gear and passed their corner. The smell of its diesel disintegrated into the salty freshness of the sea. They kept walking, his knee emitting a soft squeak with each step. "You're the client. It's nothing personal."

She arched an eyebrow. "I fear I already know too much. You are aware of the surveillance in my house?" At his nod, she said gently, "And I am aware of the pill bottles you packed along. I'm sorry. I shouldn't—"

"I didn't break," he said suddenly, his voice clear and melodious. "All that shit we've been through, me on my own. He told me he trusted me and I treated him like crap, but he was right."

He beamed into the sunshine, hands spread, and did a turn in front of her, the sea wall behind him, and the masts of ships dancing in a slow wave. "I'm a charity case, I know it. I got skills sure, so maybe this is the only job where I don't think it's just pity that got me in the door. But this—it's the first time I'm flying solo, and I didn't break!"

She had been worried. She should be worried, especially given this admission on his part, and yet...She cocked her head, regarding him. "I have a very hard time, Nick Norton, imagining you as a charity case, regardless of your disability. I have found you to be remarkably effective."

He took two, swaying steps back from her, losing his smile. "And you are the last person I should be saying this to. Apologies, Ms. Akbulut. If you'd prefer I not accompany you to Cyprus, I would be happy to advise you on the hiring of a proper body guard."

"On the contrary, I cannot imagine going without you, if only because my mother would be heartbroken."

He shifted, standing tall, a dark monolith against a clear, blue sea. "I heard what he said about your mother. If he lays a hand on her, Ms. Akbulut, I will empty him like a sack of flour."

Maybe, indeed, she should be worried all over again.

CHAPTER THIRTY-EIGHT

I t had been a few years since Grant went full Muslim, bare feet, forehead to the ground, the whole thing, but his body remembered. The insults, too, were familiar. Beardless boy, Farouk had called him when they met. Cast him back fifteen years to his first tour, his first mission, self-selected, to rescue a woman in need. Not unlike this one. The murmur of men's voices surrounded him, the chant of prayer, accompanied by the shifting of bodies against prayer rugs. Twenty-eight men packed the room, part of a former warehouse on the outskirts of Hama, in a makeshift prayer room clearly made to two or three times as many—was the set-up optimistic of more recruits, or reflective of a number of people already on assignment elsewhere?

The light outside grew long, the prayer likewise. Farouk watched him intently, an automatic rifle propped on one knee, an unlit cigarette between his teeth. He rolled it from side to side, in a way that made Grant anticipate the slide pulled back, the gun taking aim. He knelt in the middle of these men, clad in old fatigues, a scarf at his throat, marking his status, hiding his ink.

Each of the other men had a gun as well, lying alongside their rugs. Three in a quick reach. Even with an automatic gun, even with reflex on his side, the only way out was through. If things went south, how many could he take down? Farouk had placed him in the middle of the group, ensuring he'd have to pass through a line of armed men on any side if he tried to flee. And it wouldn't get him any closer to her. He bent his back, he bruised his knees, he whispered his prayers—a little louder than the other men to prove his creds—and his thoughts were anything but godly.

If he had to take the truth-test now, to place his hand between the lion's jaws, whatever fate the lion held would bite him for sure. The heat of the metal building pressed down on him, the smell of other men's sweat hovered in the air. What the hell was he doing? He had no back-up, knew nobody around except the woman he'd come to find and the man who had told him who to call, and even then Grant had to listen between the words to know the Nizari had their own base somewhere close. The king said he had earned his sword, and he wished he had it now. Wouldn't last long against three dozen men with semi-automatics, but still.

Stay cool, stay cool. Wasn't his first rodeo. Nothing to do but ride this mustang to the finish.

They reached the end of the prayer cycle, and rose, some with the stiffness of old injuries, others with the vigor of youthful enthusiasm. Three dozen men willing to die for whatever Farouk said next.

"My brothers, there is one more transport in the morning. I believe you all know your tasks. Tomorrow night will be a great victory for Shifra, and also bring in a new regime, one that will support our goal of a pure land for Islam."

The men cheered, and Grant cheered with them, fist pumping. Clearly, he'd arrived in the middle of a major op—good news, if it meant most of these people would be out of the way for whatever it took to get Akilah to safety. Bad news was, without knowing what they had planned, he had no way to stop it or alert the right authorities. Nothing like calling US Army intel from the middle of a terrorist camp to get somebody's attention and get himself dead. As usual, he had concealed his own cell phone and gun outside of town, and carried only the drop phone he used with Farouk, plus a few knives, some obvious, others not.

"But first, we have a new soldier in our holy war! Welcome, Yusef Al Numan!" He gestured toward Grant, who offered a measured grin, equal parts excitement and nerves, presenting as younger.

182

Then Farouk turned his sharp gaze on Grant, the gun laid across his lap as he sat on a barrel. "All the complicated work is done already, my friend. The plans made, the steps taken, but maybe we have some work for you. Tell me, Yusef, what brought you to us? And why so late in coming?"

"I was training for a mission in the North when we were raided by the Kurds. I spent seven months in their camps before the Americans ran away," Grant told his audience, the men now ringed around him. "The Kurds can't stop us alone, not without their mother America to hold their hand, so I ran along with some others."

The crowd hooted and roared approval at this story.

He gave a slight shrug. "I had to dodge the American retreat, the Turkish incursion. It's too much, too much! All these foreigners, and most of them not even Muslim. I heard about Shifra from one who thought to be a sleeper is lazy, one who doesn't understand strategy."

Some faces looked grim, their beards pinched and guns twitchy, so Grant plunged ahead, drawing them in. "People say the lion is lazy until he strikes, and then, he tears off your head at a blow. That's why I came to you." He nodded to Farouk. "Thank you, brother, for letting me join in your prayers."

The tension he had conjured broke into renewed cheering, and someone slapped him on the back.

"And not just because we have women?" said one of the younger men.

Grant laughed and ducked his head. "Maybe that, too. It's been a while."

The young man and a few companions shouted at this, but Farouk gestured for silence. "So, do we give him a gun?"

Most of the men called their approval, though a few still looked doubtful.

"More important, do we give him a bride?"

"Give him a bride," hollered one of the others, "for tomorrow we die!"

CHAPTER THIRTY-NINE

Aboard her 88-foot power yacht *Altin Hayal*, with Kostas at the helm, Kyra made good time across the Sea of Marmara to the Aegean. She sat on the back deck, her feet curled under her, sipping a glass of ice wine and watching the sun set over the isle of Crete. Now that they were past the thousand tiny islands of the Aegean Sea with their complex shipping ways and no-wake zones, *Altin Hayal* could open up her speed and make it to Cyprus in just a couple more hours.

She had taken some time to arrange her cabin and frown over the clothing she had chosen two days ago, in more innocent times. Clothes to impress the millionaires of the Mediterranean with her bold style and sense of vision. Clothes to display confidence and demand respect as she demonstrated the capabilities of her technology. She had even changed into a silk lounge suit that kissed her skin like the warm, rosy rays from the dying sun. It made no difference.

In the past twenty-four hours, she had become a person capable of violence, a person against whom it might be directed. She had employed her technology to track a baker's van to the Turkish border, and to take HD images of an ancient monument. She had hired actors to play a live scene of a man's death, and grown to trust another man who seemed exactly the wrong sort of person. She had even grown fiercely protective of her mother. She had gone so far as to reject her father's legacy if it meant her mother might be hurt in the searching.

Every hour revealed new layers, reshaping her as if a 3D printer shot light into the murky resin of her soul and crafted a whole new person. A quitter.

Kyra recoiled from that thought, setting down her glass and sharply shaking her head. She had made the right choice, even Nick agreed, albeit reluctantly. A few steps away, beyond the glass doors to the lounge, lay the items she counted on: her tablet and laptop, cellphone, a bottle of sparkling water. One thing stood out: the compact HD camera they had carried into the cafe basement. Nick ignored it, moving on to take charge of his own cabin and, as he put it, "Deal with some things."

She was no quitter. Even her father surely wouldn't wish his family hurt in trying to prove his research. *"He gave me the time, and the space, not because I asked him, because he knew I what I needed, and he gave it to me. Have you ever had a friend like that?"* Nick had said of Casey, and her mother replied, *"I had one. I married him."*

Her father had been that man. When she gave up the bronze arm to know the location of the Hagia Dynamis, Kyra did so with the assumption that there would be more of his work to discover, that she would continue searching.

And so she could. Later, after the king had moved on and given up, or gone back to lurk in his temple. But would he?

She rose and stalked to the lounge, taking up camera and laptop.

"Something you need, Miss?" Muminah asked, looking up from a novel.

"Not just yet, thank you." She settled inside, not wanting to give up the light, but knowing the glare would make it harder. She wasn't actually going after the clue, not now, just replicating the evidence, perhaps giving herself a chance to work it out. Next month, or even later. Her father's legacy had waited this long, it would hold a little longer. It had waited since the Days of the Templars. *"That old woman will beg for repentance—"* Not the words of a patient man. A man who sold women to terrorists, who trained knights—who—

Enough, enough. Her fingers shivered as she uploaded the handful of photos. What she had taken, with her own eyes, for another degraded fresco resolved into smears of ancient dirt, and a handful of markings that could be letters. She flicked through the images, enhanced, and rotated, and finally had something that might make sense to anyone but her. Where was Casey when they needed him? Syria.

Her mother might do. Kyra cradled the laptop against her hip and descended toward the bow and the cabins

She heard her mother's voice as she walked past the galley and lower lounge, and stopped in front of her door, only to realize the voice came from a different direction. Kyra turned, puzzled, to find Nick's door standing open, her mother's voice scrolling out in... Greek? She reached a crescendo and stopped, to light applause.

"Dang, but that is beautiful. Thank you, Irene."

"It's no trouble, really. I've no students anymore and no one to share these things with."

Kyra stepped up to the door and knocked. "Am I intruding?"

"Come on in," Nick called back to her.

The cabin held two berths, with an aisle between them, a table at the far end under the window. Mother sat on the left, an open book in her hands. Nick reclined on one the right-hand berth, his right pant leg flat and empty from the middle of his thigh. "Hope this doesn't offend you. My prosthetic needed some clean up and oiling."

"On the contrary. Let me know if you need any tools or supplies. I keep a workshop here for my air and sea projects."

He pushed up onto his elbows, then scooted to lean his back against the wall by the window. "Like submarines?"

"ROVs. Remotely operated vehicles. I've always had a fondness for them. Mine is just a prototype, a pet project, but fun for exploring wrecks and reefs, that sort of thing. It can't go very deep." A few years back, personal submarines had been the new accessory for the real super yachts—those twice as large as hers—and she had felt a little envious.

"The longer I know you, the more fascinating you become, Ms. Akbulut. Please, have a seat."

She walked the aisle and knelt between them, setting the laptop on the table.

"You said we were done." Mother slammed her book and rapped it on the edge of the table. "Done with men with guns—no offense, Mr. Norton—and with untimely deaths, both real and feigned."

Mother didn't know what the king had said of her, or she would likely be all the more adamant. Kyra nodded. "It seemed prudent to at least duplicate the photos and take a look." She traced her finger over the screen. "We took it for an image, an icon, because of this old water staining. Perhaps there was an image at one time, but nothing the camera could discern."

"And now there is nothing to discern. The trail is broken."

"You must be curious at least." Nick shifted to see the screen better, his foot on the ground, his empty pantleg fluttering.

Kyra expanded the top of the image, the markings: IOB XVIII XXXVIII XVI

"Roman numerals," Nick muttered. "Eighteen, thirty-eight, sixteen, but I don't know the first one. Romans didn't have zero."

"That's what I thought," Kyra said. "But if it's actually Roman it's long before the Crusades, or even the Byzantines."

"There's reasons your history calls them 'Latins,'" Nick pointed out.

At his soft voice, Mother grudgingly turned to the screen. "It's Christian," she snapped. "They had no zero, but no letter 'J' either."

"The Book of Job," Nick said. "Chapter and verse. Do you all have a Bible on this ship?"

"Not that kind." Job. That was ominous. She remembered little of the religious education or iconography her mother tried to impress upon her at an early age, but she dimly recalled that Job had been visited by all sorts of catastrophes. "Well. No problem." She accessed ship's signal and did a search. It was tediously slow compared with her land-based systems, and she asked, "What were you reading, Mother?"

"Sappho, if you must know. I like to read the Greeks when we pass through the islands," Mother said.

Kyra's screen started to populate with references. "Does it matter which translation?"

"Of course it matters." Mother twitched toward the wall, and finally leaned in along with them. "What have you got?"

Kyra tapped one, King James, but they all looked fairly similar in content. "'*Hast thou entered into the springs of the sea? or hast thou walked in the search of the depth?*' The springs of the sea? What does this mean?"

Nick chuckled. "Means we know where to look, assuming we were planning to, which, I am aware, we're not." He spread his large hands displaying his palms. "Ruad. Known as Arwad. It's a dry island off the coast of Syria, the last retreat of the Templars and the King of Jerusalem in the Levant. Story goes, the Templars and their Syrian allies defended the island, but they were losing hope and running out of supplies. The Seljuks made a deal: submit yourselves, and we'll ransom the knights while the Syrians go free. Only they didn't release the Syrians. Seljuks killed 'em all, and half the knights died in Egyptian prisons."

"What a dreadful tale. But I don't understand," Mother said. "How can an island be dry?"

"That means it has no natively occurring fresh water," Kyra cut in, excitement rising. "The only spring at Arwad is under the sea."

CHAPTER FORTY

An hour after prayer, now fully equipped with a rifle of his own, Grant guided his motorcycle along the river, through the heart of town. People froze at his presence, instinctively ducking their heads and protecting their children. He wanted to apologize for his disguise, and knew that a friendly wave would be taken as anything but. Men stared in defiance or perhaps solidarity. He wasn't Syrian Defense, that much was clear, but which of the other factions he might represent they could not know. He wasn't sure he knew anymore. Did he earn a tattoo by apparently killing himself at the hospital? Would he fulfill the Nizari's geas to bring out the king—or the oath he made to Shifra that he die for their cause? At the end of all this, would he even know who he was anymore? Assuming he did to begin with. The layers of his guises stifled him, and he tried to focus on the mission at hand.

Hama showed a little damage from shelling and street fighting, with crumbled buildings in some areas and pitted sidewalks, though not nearly as bad as some places he'd been. The famous water wheels still towered along the river, like Medieval Ferris wheels that once carried water onto the aqueducts running over head and into the city's fields, palaces and baths. Mosques emerged from the city blocks on a regular basis, alongside shops, homes and markets, subdued, but occupied. The city held itself together like a beauty once assaulted who still dared to rise.

Not far outside of town, where buildings gave way to agricultural land, the address he'd been given brought him to a farm house, two-story with stucco walls and a few ramshackle outbuildings. Two men guarded the drive, men whose failure to shoot him suggested Farouk had, indeed, called ahead on his behalf. Another man lounged in the shade of a scraggly tree by the door. He straightened up and plucked the cigarette from his lips. "What do you want?" he demanded.

"I'm going on the mission tomorrow, but I want to be a married man before I go," Grant told him, echoing his accent, just in case the guy could recognize an American. So far, his "brother Muslims" seemed more than pleased to welcome additional cannon fodder for whatever the mission was. "Farouk sent me."

The guy's cigarette wavered in the air as he looked Grant over, then said, "Aright, go in. Leave the gun." Shouldering his own weapon, he reached over and banged on the door. "We got a volunteer in need of a wife!"

Laughter from inside, some of it feminine, then the door opened, and a woman beckoned him through. "We have a number of righteous girls who are eager to serve as well."

He nodded his thanks as he ducked through. Seventeen young women waited inside, and he scanned them, keeping his face noncommittal. Some women did, indeed, offer themselves as brides to the soldiers, but more often than not, they'd been given no choice. Even when they had agreed to this life, it meant they had few other options. The average age here looked to be close to eighteen—at least they weren't children—but many of the girls clung together, their eyes hollow and postures hunched.

Two more men sat in the room, one with his arm around a young woman and his other hand on the grip of his rifle as if he couldn't decide which one he'd rather be touching. Grant met his eye, and the man smiled broadly, pulling the woman in for a kiss. The other man stood with his back to the opposite wall, gun resting in his arms. Not the time to go all liberator and get these women out of here. If he tried, how many would die?

A few of the women examined him in turn, some of them bored, some meek, three with bold interest. Apparently, they liked what they saw.

Wonderful. Two doors led out of the room, to the back and west.

One woman, her hair cut in a bob and her makeup smeared, dropped to her knees from the couch where she sat. "Please, get me out. Take me, please." Turkish. Her eyes searched his face, her hands trembling as she reached toward him.

"Shut up, you brazen whore." One of the armed men jabbed his gun toward the pleading woman, and she shrank away.

Grant's nausea roiled. Fury tightened his shoulders. At least six guards outside, two more here—who knew how many past the door or up the stairs? Where the hell was she? Or was he really, as Bashir implied, already too late?

"I feel in me the power of conversion," he told the woman by the door. "Do you have any brides who are in need?"

She pursed her lips, brow furrowed. "A few." She shrugged one shoulder. "You are welcome to try. Some of them may have been tried already. They are impure. Infidels and Western whores."

He mastered himself with a will, keeping the rising anger from his face. What of the Phantom? Had she been 'tried?' What happened if he didn't find her? Take the Turkish woman and hope she knew more? Or just shoot as many of these men as he could before they took him down?

He forced his heartbeat even. Would a man in his position reject an impure bride? "This need, it's like a fire." He gripped a fist by his chest, fixing her with his stare, making himself a zealot, a martyr-in-training.

"Come, then." She picked her way across the room, and a few of the women on the floor shifted their feet to let him pass. The guard on the other side banged on the door, then opened the lock and shoved it open. He fired a volley across the room beyond at about chest height. In the main room, some of the women flinched, and a pair barely in their teens clung tighter as the gunshot echoed through the space. Inside second room, someone coughed, a small, choked sound.

The woman guiding him—the Madam, he wanted to say—leaned inside, then gestured him forward. "This one has resisted conversion. And everything else." She made a rough sound in her throat and shook her head.

"She defies the Lord in all things. Look at her."

Grant stepped up and did as she bid him. Clad in Western-style pants and a man's shirt, the Phantom crouched against the far wall, eyes narrowed over the gag at her mouth. Her bound hands rested on her knees, her body swaying a little, perhaps in reaction to the gunfire. Dried blood marked the corners of her lips and her fingers, tracing her knuckles. Some of her injuries looked defensive, some clearly not. Her hair hung in dirty waves over her shoulders, and her breathing hitched in spite of herself: he could see the clenching in her body as she worked for control.

"Eh, she's not worth it. You deserve better for your service." The madam turned back. "Here, let me—"

"This is the bride for me," Grant said. "She will yet know the truth."

At his voice, the Phantom looked up, glaring, the slightest flinch marking the corners of her eyes.

The madam sighed. "Very well. Take her and may you bring her to the fold." She turned to the guard. "The ceremony?"

Grant crossed the small, dark room, and took his new bride by the elbow. She pushed up beside him, overbalanced, and nearly fell, but for his hand at her upper arm. Tension shot through her, her muscle like iron in his grip. How many times had she been grabbed by a man? If only she had her hands: he'd knock down their escort, getting that gun, she could roll underneath and sweep the legs out from under the second armed man. Together, they could rout the place. Instead he became just another oppressor.

"Come," he ordered, and she stumbled alongside him. The sound of her labored breathing throbbed in his ears, hating her dependence maybe as much as she did. No, probably not. She kicked his ankle, but her bare foot made little impact, whether by design or not, he couldn't tell.

He brought her up to stand before the guard who mumbled a few garbled verses from the Koran. Grant half-heard. "'...he created for you mates from among yourselves, that you may dwell in tranquility with them, and He has put love and mercy between your hearts...'" tranquility, love, mercy. A man armed with a machine gun was marrying Grant to a woman bound and gagged, beaten into submission. Maybe worse. Did the man understand what he was saying? Or did he just not care?

Step up, grab the gun, swing the barrel up to the man's chin, spray the man's brains all over the wall behind him. And get taken down along with Akilah by the guards outside. Grant restrained himself. He accepted the man's blessing, shifted his grip on his "bride" toward her shoulder, pulling her closer to him, supporting more of her weight. She growled and twisted in his grasp.

"Talib! You and the others escort them to the suite!" The madam called, and the man on the sofa groaned as he released the woman in favor of having both hands on his gun.

"No need," Grant said. "If you tell me the way."

Talib squinted at him. "We must be ready to take care of your bride when you go." He jutted his chin toward the Phantom.

The others turned out to be a half-dozen men on motorcycles very much like his, forming a cordon around his own bike like a police detail for a celebrity couple. Grant mounted up and tugged her behind him, then pulled her arms up over his head.

"Be careful—I wouldn't let her get too close to your throat," Talib warned, and the others laughed. "Liable to rip your head right off, that one."

"He's not wrong," said another man. "That black eye? That was from the last man who tried to marry her. He threw her back for something more pleasant—but she's not kicking you. Maybe he softened her up for you."

"I'll judge that," Grant told them. He wrapped his hand around her arm just above the rope, only as firm as he needed to be, steadying her. All hope of an easy getaway faded with the roar of the engines around them. There was no softness in her, her arms hung stiff over his shoulders, her muscles corded beneath his touch, her body arching away from him though the hiss of her breath betrayed her pain. It felt like an accusation, as if the injuries to her body were those of every woman ever subjugated to a man. As if he stood in for every man who had ever taken a woman's body or her freedom as his right.

A few miles of turns down the winding streets brought them to a low apartment building. Grant cut the engine, ducking free of her bound hands, drawing his arm across her back to pull her close. She tensed like a bow about to fire, and Grant had the sick feeling that she—like everything else around here—was aimed directly at his head.

CHAPTER FORTY-ONE

O ffering Grant and the Phantom the open archway, Talib showed them inside. He adopted the manner of a gallant doorman taking the bridal couple for the nuptial night. They mounted a few flights of creaking stairs. No way to sneak out on the stairs, and she hardly seemed ready for a rooftop escape.

"And here you go, second floor!" He unlocked a door and ushered them in. "You just let me know you need pillows or towels... or whips." He grinned at the bride. She lunged toward him, and Grant restrained her, swinging her like a Dance partner in through the door.

He matched Talib's grin. "Thank you."

Talib waved him inside, and locked the door again behind them. Shit.

The moment the door ground shut, she jerked away from him, staggering, and he caught her elbow before she fell. "For God's sake," he whispered, "Let me help you."

She pulled again, her pale-green eyes tracing his face. He followed, letting her sink onto the stained couch. "One minute," he said, then, louder, in Arabic, "Be still, and stay quiet!"

He moved swiftly through the small apartment: living room that gave onto a kitchen, table with two chairs in the space between, shuttered window over the kitchen counter that would look out to the street. One bedroom, no windows: it backed up to the second apartment on this floor, though they had probably been a single unit at some point. Bathroom with a raised tub, a gray curtain dangling from the ceiling overhead. Chipped plaster revealing a hole. Closing the door, Grant made a show of using the facility, then exited, closing the door again behind him. Might not be the only eyes on the place, but he saw no sign of tech, nor had his impression at the warehouse been of a tech-forward organization. At least he had that.

In the two minutes he was gone, she slumped on the couch, her hair flicking first one direction, then the other as she watched him. At last he returned, sinking to his knees before her. A stale, meaty odor rose off the cushions. Stained with blood and worse.

She drew back from him and Grant bowed his head. "I'm sorry."

She made an angry sound, her hands already working at her gag, though her fingers looked puffy and off-colored.

He pried a slim blade from the sole of his shoe and held it up on the palm of his hand. "Please. Let me help."

She tried to snatch the blade from his hand, and it fumbled to the floor. She caught her breath, her eyes glazing with a rush of moisture. Grant searched the floorboards and retrieved the knife. This time, when he held it up, she met his eye, and lowered her hands. He shifted toward her, indicating her mouth. "You need to breathe."

She gave a nod.

Touching her as little as possible, he pinched the leather strap and slid the blade underneath toward the back of her jaw. Her pulse jumped at her throat, marked by a scar as of some other blade cruelly wielded. With a turn of the knife and exacting pressure, Grant sliced through and peeled away the gag, tossing it aside onto the cushion. Were they listening? Would he have to perform the sounds of rape and abuse, the crack of flesh on flesh? Christ. He'd rather take on the whole fucking lot of them with the thumb-sized blade in his hand than pretend to be hurting her. He barely breathed. Her lips parted and her head tipped back as she drew down a breath, deep and shaky.

Grant bent his attention to her wrists, a mess of knotted rope toughened by blood, thickened by dirt. How long had she been bound?

"You have claimed me. Will you take me now? As a man takes his

196

bride?" A thick murmur.

His head shot up. "That's not who I am." He stripped off the scarf at his throat and tossed it aside. "I will take you—out of here. Anywhere you say."

"I am not leaving those women," she answered in a low, harsh tone. She needed water and rest, medical treatment.

He let out a breath. "I know."

He scraped at the rope and finally was able to work the blade in, carving up and out, always away from her battered wrists. The first layer tufted free and he put the knife away, peeling back the rope. Her breath hissed as the strands tugged her skin and he held up a finger to pause, then moved to the kitchen, filled a bowl with water and found a cup to pour it from. He set his basin down at her feet and poured a thin stream of water over her wrists, softening the dried blood before he got back to work. Rescuing those women wasn't his mission. Didn't matter. Leaving them behind was not an option. "We'll find a way."

"I don't know this word 'we,'" she told the back of his head.

"Time to learn it." He unwound the rope, dropping that, too, onto the floor, still cradling both of her hands in one of his.

"That is not what you said you would teach me."

The whole conversation set him on edge. Nothing he could say seemed adequate to the situation. He poured another stream of water over her wrists, then set the cup down, and searched for any fibers that remained embedded in her skin. "I said what it took to get you out of there without anybody getting hurt. More hurt. That's what they expect between men and women."

"Yet it is not what you plan."

"Absolutely not."

"I am not a maiden in need of rescue and you are no knight." Sharp words, edged with fear.

"Actually..." Grant peeled back his own sleeve and displayed the tiny cross still inked on his wrist. He flicked a glance up, but she dodged his gaze. "Most days, you are the knight, the warrior for justice." He resumed his work. "Even warriors need rescue some times." He flashed back to a night in the desert, a gag biting his own mouth, gravel biting his knees, his hands numb, a gun to his head and the only thing that could save him was the man on the other side of the weapon.

Finished with her wrists to the best of his ability under present circumstances, he started to gently rub each finger, encouraging her circulation. She flinched as sensation returned, but she didn't stop him.

"You do find me attractive." Her voice came low and hesitant.

His own circulation felt uncertain. The bowl turned pink with her blood, flecks of dust floating at the top. His fingers wrinkled a little with the moisture. She flexed and moved her fingers through a pattern of exercises, as if playing an instrument. What had she been before she came to this life? He released even the tenuous clasp of his hand on hers, but she kept her palm over his for a long moment. Her hand warmed his—warmed a lot more than that, if he were being ruthlessly honest.

"Do you?" she repeated, a question this time.

Her hand hovered over his, both of them scarred, the marks of his last bonds faded against his coppery skin, her own shade a little more olive, the two of them warm browns in the midrange of the human spectrum. Their hands bore dozens of scars, marked pale by the lives they chose to lead, those same hands attacking and defending against other hands, against blades, against stone, metal, flesh, bone. Each of them had fought a thousand demons. This shouldn't be so damned hard.

"What do you want me to say?" This time when he spoke, she met his gaze, her eyes clear, pale green, the left one reddened and puffy at the outside edge where the mark of a man's hand bruised her. He drew back, sat away from her on his heels. A strategic retreat. Some kind of bullshit.

"Are you a beautiful woman? Yes. Are you intelligent, fascinating, challenging, dangerous: yes." The words came fast, his heartbeat faster and he made himself slow, deliberate. She took back her hands from the space between them, curling them to rest in her lap. Hands with the strength and the will to kill a man.

Grant picked up the bowl of water stained with life and thought of walking away, taking it back to the kitchen, breaking off whatever it was they had begun. She made a small, thoughtful sound. Was his inability to read her expression because he didn't know her that well? Because she was that good at concealment? Or was he losing his objectivity. Over a woman? Wouldn't Gooney get a laugh out of that.

"Would I ever touch you in anger? No." He set the bowl aside, suddenly afraid it would reveal the tension in his hand. He swallowed hard.

"Would I ever hurt you out of lust?" he continued, "No, I would not. Is that what you need to hear? Unless we can trust each other, we're not getting out of this alive. What oath can I make to get you to trust me?"

For a long moment, she studied him, her gaze flicking across his face, his shoulders, down to his hands, back up again to his throat. Her hand rose, and he forced himself still. She touched his jawline and he twitched away from her on instinct, baring that part of his throat. "This..." Her fingers didn't quite trail over his skin as she traced the design. Didn't matter. He felt it anyway. "This is the lamassu, from the museum in Mazar-i-Sharif."

The winged lion that saved his life. The first time he ever met her. "Yes."

"All of the Americans were leaving. You returned because of me. No —" she interrupted herself just as he was about to deny it— "you returned because you knew someone remained inside. You went back in to save me, not because I am any of those things you say, but because you would have done that for anyone, and you almost died for it."

"I wouldn't have done this for anyone." With a gesture toward the room around them, Grant managed a smile. "For one thing, they wouldn't have let me marry Nick. Not that I'm really married to you, of course," he added.

Her face remained serious. "We stood before an imam and he spoke the words of the Koran over us. By the ways of my people, we are married."

Grant's hand curled into a fist. "You were bound and gagged, and he had a gun. Where I come from, you're not married unless you freely speak your vows."

"And then the wife follows behind her husband, supports him in all things, loses her own voice and her own life."

He shook his head slowly, thinking of his own parents. "Not if they're doing it right. They become partners, supporting each other. Like the Templars. Two knights on one horse."

At that, she smiled faintly, a turning of her lips, a gradual brightening of her eyes, like the clear steel veins in a Damascus blade turned toward the light. "Very well then, I accept your vow. And I promise that I will not hurt you in anger nor from fear."

"So if you decide to kill me, it'll be cold-blooded and deliberate."

Her smile grew.

Wait—she accepted his vow? Grant gave a little shake. "You—in the archive, you moved to save him, thinking the assassin was shooting me."

She rested her fingers at his throat, where the pulse leapt beneath the scars he earned in that museum.

"Perhaps you are also intelligent—" she traced the wings of the tattooed lion—

"fascinating"—tracing down toward his collarbone toward his other illustrated deaths—

"challenging"—moving along the back of his neck, her fingers in his hair—

"dangerous."

She leaned in and kissed him.

CHAPTER FORTY-TWO

G rant made no move to undress, some combination of their precarious environment, and a sort of reticence he wasn't sure he'd ever felt before. He hadn't been shy about his body in the bath house; hadn't cared any number of times he stripped in front of the people he served with, male, female, queer, straight, or anyone in between; wasn't concerned about changing in public place or performing the pretense of seduction with any number of partners. This was nothing like any of that. For the first time, he wondered if the ink was too much, if his scars were disfiguring, if his athletic build were exciting or frightening.

He knelt before her as she touched his face, his throat, his hair. She kissed him softly on his lips, his temple, the corner of his eye.

"This is in the way," she whispered, tugging at the bottom of his shirt until his hands joined hers and freed it from his belt, his hands parting as hers slid along his ribs, skin to skin, her hands sending fire through him.

"Can I touch you like this?" he asked her, and she nodded as he slipped his hand beneath her shirt, feeling the sudden tension at her core, following her sternum, resting lightly as her breathing caught, then flowed.

"How about this?" He shifted his hand a little to the side, and she whispered, "Yes," guiding his hand to cup her breast, drawing a soft moan as he touched her. She nudged off the couch, kneeling between his thighs. Her hair tumbled over his face, their cheeks together, and her breath in his ear. She tipped her head and kissed the pulse at his throat.

He stroked along her ribcage to the small of her back, suggesting she move closer, and she leaned into him.

"Your belt?" she asked.

Absolutely. How's this?

Their voices murmured, overlapped and mingled as they drew breath from each other. Their hands stroked, held, cradled, lingered. Their kisses grew deeper, longer, stronger

May I touch you here?

Yes.

Kiss me there.

Yes.

Will you take me?

Yes.

Do you want me—yes and yes and yes and oh, god, yes.

CHAPTER FORTY-THREE

G rant lay on his side on the bed, his head propped on his hand, studying her face, afraid to close his eyes lest she turn once more phantom and vanish. Moonlight seeped between the slats of the window blind, along with the flickering yellow light of a street lamp nearly as old as the waterwheels along the river. They were curiously safe here, the men who prevented their escape keeping vigil as much on their behalf as against it. So damned indulgent, just lying here beside her, waiting an uneasy dawn. He needed the sleep, but in the darkness beside her, he dared consider that he needed this, too.

She lay still, her eyes shut. A little too still, as if she tried not to disturb him, and, after a moment, a tear seeped along the edge of her lashes, and silently slipped down her cheek. He reached out to stroke it away, but before he could touch her, her eyes flew open and she rolled sharply to face him, one hand up.

He froze. "Did I hurt you?" he whispered.

For a long moment, she simply stared as if she had forgotten who he was, or how they came to be there. "No," she breathed. Her hand slowly relaxed to the sheet between them, pinching it and curling until it she wrung a handful of the cloth even more dry than the desert around them.

"Then...What?"

"In the van, when they carried me here, the man told them you were dead. I knew that I was dead already, or I would be. To see you there, in that place," she broke off, gripping the sheet. "It was beyond a prayer, beyond a hope. I would have to find my own way, or I would die. And there was no way, not with all of those men and their guns. I would not have imagined that you should come for me, much less that you should come back from the dead to do so."

"They don't know my name. They still think the man in the hospital was me, but he's not dead either, not really." He crept his hand up to hers, his thumb tracing her knuckles.

"You have not married before. Why not?"

A shake of his head. "We're not married," he reminded her softly.

"This is not what I asked you."

Who would willingly marry his scars? "My lifestyle's not conducive."

"When you were a soldier, but now? You are well-off, yes? With a good business."

"You weren't married either," he pointed out.

Her gaze went distant, looking through him. "Akilah. You—"

"I was," she said abruptly. "Those things you swore you would not do? He made me no such vows," her voice had gone hard, her lips pressed together. "Nor did I to him." She shot him a look, fierce, framed by the bruise at her eye. "I spent five years in prison," she whispered. "Five of what was meant to be a lifetime before I found my escape."

"You would." He smiled faintly, cupping his hand over hers. She was no damsel in need of rescue, for all that he might have saved her this time.

"I am impure. A whore, a killer. After we free those women, denounce me, and any imam would release the bond."

Fuck that. "Because you killed your abuser? You're not a whore, you're a hero."

She sank her face to the sheet and muttered, "Americans."

"Spoiled, privileged, bullying rich boy, that's me."

She quivered, then peered at him, her lips pursed, then parted, openly laughing. "Of course. It is so obvious, now that you say so. I am lucky to have a wealthy American husband who shall give me television and manticores, and all of such decadent things."

"Manticores?"

She freed her hand to wiggle her fingers. "For the nails?"

"Manicure." He tried to imagine her sitting in the salon chair, a manicurist bent over her hand, staring in disbelief at the short nails, the rims of grime—probably blood—the tracery of scars across her skin. "Manticores are completely different. It's a mythological beast, smart and dangerous. Like you. But if you want one, I'll do my best."

"I believe that you would."

"What else did you hear?"

"Not much. They moved me to the trunk of a car, the van, the rest of the contents went another way. To a boat, I think. I smelled the ocean and the diesel fuel."

"The rest of the contents?"

"Wait." She rolled to her back, closed her eyes, and her hands moved slightly, as if she were pointing to things around her. "Air tanks, like SCUBA, yes? Lots of gray bricks in a carton. The lid falls off, they put it back on, they are mad, but they should not pack so much. Boxes of other parts, other things that rattle, but no markings."

"Gray bricks: C4 explosive?"

A nod. "Could be, yes."

"They're blowing something up, underwater. Any idea about the target?"

"They don't speak of this, the knights. When they give me to the Shifra—" her eyes opened, staring at the ceiling— "those men don't speak at all."

"How big a carton?" He indicated with his hands. "Case of paper? Steamer trunk?"

"Big," she said. "Between those. If we get the women out of the farmhouse, if we can take on the guards, then the Nizari will get them away —this is our arrangement. The way they got me from prison. I planned to get those women out; I did not think it would entail me becoming one of them."

"The Shifra take off tomorrow morning for their target, they'll be on a skeleton crew at the house. I'm meant to go with them." He hesitated, then added, "You're meant to go back. Can we get the Nizari to be there, to back us up? Can we take on the remaining guards if we get you a weapon?"

"Many of the women will help us. Some of them are like me, they are widows, they know guns."

Grant saw the way her eyes lit like copper in flames, never so beautiful as when she was working for justice. She was wrong: there was nobody like her. "We need to know what the Shifra and the knights are planning to hit. They don't trust me enough to tell me. Another day or two, I'd get it, but this is too soon." Something the king wanted? Had to be.

"I'll ask the women what they've heard. A few of them are already brides." She grimaced, then said, "But they were not so lucky as to win a rich American husband."

"I don't know about you, but I make my own luck."

CHAPTER FORTY-FOUR

Swords rang. Chloe's breath hissed as she darted and dodged. She spun away from Blaise's weapon, but he lunged, landing a slash across her lower back that dented the padding of her fencer's jacket. "Five!" she cried as she stepped back on shaky legs. She held up a hand for a pause, and gulped from a water bottle placed on a nearby bench. She tipped her bottle toward Blaise's own, which sat untouched despite the sweat that glued his hair to his forehead.

She was his knight, sworn to defend him, perhaps even from his own neglect. He snatched up the bottle and took a long swallow then slammed it down.

"Again!" Blaise roared. It had been four bouts already. He had won three.

Chloe straightened and stepped away from the bench, but her sword took a long time to rise. "My lord, if you wish to punish me for what happened today, for losing that woman—"

He slashed his blade through the air and she flinched. "That man from the Akbulut household, you've called him?"

She gave a nod. "He doesn't answer, my lord. I'm sorry."

"That a man doesn't pick up his phone is not your fault. That a frail old woman fools us with a lie, is also not your fault. I was there with you, I should have known better."

Chloe swept stray hairs back toward her ponytail. "My lord, she appealed to your chivalry. Your sense of honor and your duty to protect the weak."

Blaise had been ready to sink into his stance, but he paused, bringing back his sword to rest upon his shoulder as he considered what she had said. "My chivalry. On purpose, do you think? Was it more than the fact she knew we were not police as we claimed? Do you think she knew me?" He had been trying so hard the last few years to keep his private life separate from his public or professional sphere. Most of the knights did not know his real name—they knew him only from his mask. But he had believed the old woman's story, her fragility, her tale of being a soap opera star, and that was why—

"Mother of God!" With a sharp pivot away from Chloe, he hurled his sword across the room. It cracked against the wall and fell to the floor in two pieces, winking in the dim light of the practice room. He stared at the pieces, watching them rock, trying to master his fury. For so many years, he had been master, his past whims and angers subsumed to his dream of balance and guidance for himself and for all. His breath burned through his nostrils for five breaths, seven, ten. He worked his jaw, loosening the tension, and finally turned back.

Chloe knelt, sword at her side, head lifted, alert for his next desire.

"Chloe, you are correct. If I had been more centered, I should have seen it. She took advantage of my nature, my desire for noble deeds. That old woman was no actress—she was Kyra Akbulut's mother." He shook back his hair, and took up his water again for another, longer swallow. "I met her once, years ago, when she was so generous as to allow me access to her deceased husband's papers. I found hints there, but nothing more. She is a scholar of later Byzantine history, into the Crusades." He studied the dark mouth of the bottle. Water, only. Long ago, he'd fallen down the mouth of a bottle and into such debauchery as to put the Latin invaders to shame. "I admit myself disappointed in Kyra Akbulut. I had thought her above involving her mother in such an escapade."

Chloe nodded. "What do you wish me to do, lord?"

"I need to know where they are, what they're doing. Go to their house

208

if you must. Search for any sign of them. They must have taken the clue or photographed it before they destroyed it: that damage was not just an old woman's clumsiness. Send two of the knights back to the cafe to have another look. If they clean up the mess, perhaps they can find some sign of what's missing—or they can find the owner and convince him to reveal it, one way or another."

She rose smoothly, and swept her blade up into a salute. "My lord," she said, then compressed her lips, until he gave a nod of assent. "Tomorrow night. Will this delay your revelation?"

Blaise sighed. Not with his Syrian allies getting so restless. He would make the best of it. "It would have been better to have the throne, but the plans were lain before we conceived of possessing it. No, the revelation will go on as planned." But how could he expect to be the savior this realm required if he could no longer control his temper? "Go on, Chloe. I need some time for contemplation."

She bowed and let herself out the room. Blaise unbuckled his own padded jacket and tugged it off, hanging it on a peg to be cleaned later. He retrieved the broken sword, regretting his impulse. In the early days of learning about the knighthood, in the basement of the library where he fled to escape the gangs that stalked the city, Blaise grew to admire the sword. He loved the discipline of it, not only the act of fighting so close to an opponent, but the grace of the movements, the way a man must truly see his opponent in order to strike effectively. A swordsman could not afford to crack and allow anger to overcome him. Blaise left the broken sword on the bench and moved into the sanctuary, lighting the chapels and lowering himself to kneel by the head of Baphomet. The chill reached him through his sweaty pants and light-weight shirt. It snuck through his damp hair as he bowed his head, his hands to his sides, shoulders down. His faith rose beyond religion, and his meditation beyond prayer. Such things enabled the weak of will to focus in the way that he could, and such things would be the trappings of his realm: the cross, the crescent, the star of David. He, himself, must rise above those things, to become as Solomon, a king admired by all nations for his wisdom and justice.

Someone approached from the practice room, and Blaise frowned. He should have left word not to be disturbed. "What is it?"

"Forgive me, my lord."

Haldan. Blaise burst from the floor and bounded across the room to where his lieutenant stood, head bandaged, and shoulders weary. Blaise clasped his arms, then pulled him into an embrace. "Haldan, I have feared the worst." Haldan returned the embrace with a brief, perhaps embarrassed warmth, and Blaise took a step back, still gripping Haldan's bicep. "But how are you out of the hospital? Come, come, sit down."

Haldan twitched as if to nod, then stopped himself. "Thank you, my lord." He allowed himself to be led to the bench and sat stiffly. "They would have kept me overnight, my lord, but I had to see you."

Blaise wiped this away with a sharp gesture. "I need you hale and healthy. If you need the rest, Haldan, then you must take it."

"My lord, I cannot rest until you know the truth."

That stopped him. Blaise eased his shoulders back, fearing some foul admission, some breech in Haldan's penitence. "What is it?"

"It's about the man who saved me, whom I commended to you."

"Donahue? I was frankly astonished by the lengths he stood willing to go in your defense, on top of what he'd already done at the hospital. I have offered his sword, and I hope he'll take it."

Again, Haldan's head and neck twitched as if he wanted to indicate something and held himself back. "I overhead his associates at the hospital. He's not Michael Donahue, my lord. That man is Grant Casey."

CHAPTER FORTY-FIVE

When Talib first started banging on the door, Grant ignored it, wasting time, hoping to clear out more of the welcoming committee on the other end. He showered long after the hot water ran out, after filling the kitchen sink so she could wash out of view from the bathroom peep-hole. His claiming the proper facilities served to lord his status over that of his wife—and to defend her. Newlyweds for a day, and they had yet to see each other naked. Maybe they never would.

Talib banged again, and Akilah let out a theatrical shriek as a door slammed open. Grant pulled on his pants, wrapped a towel over his shoulders to hide his ink and flung open the bathroom door.

Talib stood in the kitchenette with a grip in Akilah's hair. He shook her. "It's not time for washing, woman!"

"What's the time?" Grant asked, then scowled at Talib. "If my wife is to be punished, I should take care of it."

Talib shoved her away, and she stumbled, sinking to her knees not far from Grant's bare, wet feet. "We said eight o'clock. We were to be gone at eight, and already it is half-past—why didn't you answer your phone?"

Grant looked confused, patting down his pockets with his left hand.

"The bedroom," Akilah stage-whispered. "Please, my husband, no more. Please."

He hauled her up by her arm, or at least, made it look that way, and propelled her toward the bedroom. "Go find my phone. We're late." When she had stumbled into the other room, he hung his head. "Forgive me, I got— carried away. And I don't think she should wear the blood outside. A thousand apologies." He snugged the towel around his shoulders. "Five minutes—less."

Talib glared as Grant sprinted to the bedroom and shut the door between them. "Did you turn the ringer off?" he shouted, and slapped his hands together hard enough to sting. Akilah yelped in fear.

"There's no time for that," Talib shouted. "Five minutes! No more." The outside door opened and shut again.

Akilah reached for him, and he pressed her close. "You get the guards, I go for the women," she whispered, and he kissed her: his one-night wife, about to become his partner in one of the riskiest ops he'd ever run. Take out the guards, count on an ally whose spokesman had already told him they lived for secrecy—whose only response to the message they sent was an enigmatic thumbs up—get him and his partner out of there safe. Oh: and identify the target of a major terrorist attack in time to convince some authority to take it seriously.

They dressed quickly, Akilah taking a long, flowered dress from the closet and a headscarf that gave her the illusion of being a freshly subdued and proper wife. He squeezed her hand and led her into battle.

Once at the door, he shifted his grip to her wrist and she stumbled behind him, utterly speechless. *The wife follows behind her husband, supports him in all things, loses her own voice and her own life.* Just as she said. Was she thinking the same thing?

He mounted his bike, tugging her behind him, settling his gun across his lap. She pressed against him, compact and demure, her hand over his heart, holding him with the strength of a gymnast. Their escort was reduced to two: his compulsive analysis suggesting how easy it would be to lose the tail and ensure their own safety—but not at the expense of those other women. No way. Her fight had become his own. They took the roads a little too fast, Grant indicating his contrition with renewed eagerness, and the sensation of her pressed up against him warming him against the breeze. Phantom no more. But for how much longer?

One guard at the end of the driveway, another down the way, in the shadow of a crumbling outbuilding. One by the door. Anticipate two or more inside that were about to be Akilah's concern. On the way down the drive, he spotted an open shed being used to repair a jeep, two men still working over it. Minimum four outside, plus the two he brought with him. His job: take care of the guards. Hers: get the women out of there, and pray that Bashir would come through.

"Say good bye. Allah willing, you'll meet again tomorrow," Talib commanded, turning his bike, glancing back at Grant.

Akilah slid from behind him. At the door, the man pushed it open, beckoning with his gun. Grant turned his face, placing his back to the house, giving her a glance inside as he brought down his face to kiss her. His hand between them palmed a knife from beneath his shirt.

For a moment, their eyes met, then she grabbed his gun and vaulted the bike, running for the house.

"Careful, she's armed!" Grant sprang after her, grabbing the guard as if to drag him from the line of fire. He snagged the strap of the man's gun, slicing through it and yanking the weapon away.

With a hard step in, he shoved the man against the side of the house and stabbed hard and low, then backhand into his throat as he started to fall.

Grant spun about, flipped the gun to automatic and started firing. Talib, his gun half-raised, his face furious, went down in a spray of blood. Grant pivoted to the other cyclist, ducking his first shots and firing dead on. The man staggered back and crumpled.

Inside, Akilah shouted, "Women get down or get their guns!" A more restrained series of gunshots followed.

From the north end of the road, an engine rumbled, a panel truck chugging slow along the street. The driver flashed a thumbs-up.

A second Shifra emerged from the barn at that side, two of them now running, firing at him. How long before they realized the truck was in on it? The man at the top of the drive tipped the bucket he'd been sitting on, tumbling a load of spikes like sharpened tacks the size of a fist. No getting the truck any closer.

"Caltrops on the drive," Grant shouted over his shoulder. "Take the grass!"

At the back, his eight o'clock, he heard sudden shouting and running feet. Grant hunched low, sprinting to meet them. The house had at least one back door—last thing he wanted was these guys getting the drop on Akilah. He burst around the corner and brought up the gun, already firing.

"Clear six-to-eight!" He shouted. "Taking eleven o'clock!" Hard turn, dash partway up the drive. One of the two Shifra on that side took a knee, steadying his gun. Grant hit the ground between the gunman and the driveway, taking advantage of the old furrows as some kind of cover. Lying on his side, he fired low and heard shrieks and cursing. Bullets whizzed overhead from the enemy position. Someone returned fire from the direction of the house.

"Eleven o'clock, clear!" Akilah called back to him. Grant popped back to his feet, scanning. Behind him, women streamed from the house. Two of them had weapons now, running with the rest, firing at random, and he hit the dirt again, rolling. He got to his elbows. If they had two guards north— they had to have at least one south. Sighting through the sparse grass. Another tumble-down structure, some kind of tall manger. Movement. He fired, and the hay tufted in all directions, then someone fired back, but poorly aimed.

"Twelve o'clock clear! Come on, soldier!"

He fired again, scrambled to his feet, running along the driveway. Akilah stood at the back of the truck, helping an injured woman inside.

The sound of a jeep rumbled from their five o'clock. Grant swung about. The jeep from the shed bounced toward them, a mounted machine gun in the back and a gunner scrambling into place. Oh, shit.

"Go!" he shouted. The truck lurched into motion, surging past.

Grant skidded to the top of the drive. The guard lay still on the ground, his emptied barrel alongside, his motorcycle a little further back. Grant took a knee by the barrel. Feeble cover, but something. He brought up his weapon to the raspy sound of dirt in the breech. Shit. Extra helping. Grant tossed his gun and reached for the fallen man, lying on top of his own weapon. He grabbed the man's gun—and the man grabbed back with one hand, rolling to his side.

"Infidel traitor!" His other hand was already pulling the trigger.

CHAPTER FORTY-SIX

Grant bent back, using his grip to deflect the weapon, his hand burning against the barrel of the gun as the bullets sprayed. Grant with the weapon, but the man had both hands on his gun. He wrenched it away.

Grant knocked the barrel hard into his assailant. The gun flew upward in a new hail of gunfire. Grant caught the strap this time. He swung it into his control as he found his footing.

A long blade in his hand, the guard sliced toward Grant's legs.

Jumping from the path of the swing, Grant landed hard. He jerked as pain stabbed into the sole of his left foot. He managed the gun and kept running, hitting the ground on his toes, lurching and stabbed anew with every step. Another house across the street, some kind of cover, buy time for the women's escape. How long could he go on? Twenty paces? Not even. Christ. Every step burned, then he staggered and barely remained on his feet. Honeymoon's over. Time to make it count.

Let him be the magnet to draw their fire. Grant raised his weapon, turning back. He could run no longer, but he did not fall.

The jeep bounced over a furrow, and the bigger gun pounded rounds into the street ahead of him, trying to recalibrate in a shifting landscape—not anticipating his halt.

The sudden roar of a motorcycle called for his attention. He swayed. Enemies on both sides. Bone Guard's last stand. Just as he had sworn when he asked for his bride: he would be married at night, and buried in the morning. Whole new meaning to the phrase "shotgun wedding."

"Get on! Hurry!" Akilah's voice, sharp and commanding. The bike spit gravel as she spun up beside him. She steadied the bike with one foot, reaching toward him. He found her hand, let himself be pulled, had to step down—pain spiked through his foot—to get his leg over the bike. It sprang into motion, and her grip kept him falling off. She tugged at his arm, then let him go, needing both hands to manage their getaway. Gun still in his right, he shifted his left hand, sliding his arm about her waist. Too loosely. Nearly lost it at the next turn.

Gunfire spit behind them. He tightened his grip. His arm wrapped her, his hand settling near her hip. The bike wobbled on gravel. He drew himself closer to her, making of them a single unit, feeling how she leaned and when she turned. He moved with her, twisting back to return fire as they pulled slowly—too slowly—out of range. Finding his breath, Grant cupped her body with his own as if he could draw strength from her body, courage from her heart.

His head tucked close to hers, the wind whipping her hair against his throat and shoulder. "Thanks," he breathed, when he was able, his lips close to her ear.

For a moment, she brought her hand down to his arm and held him in turn. The wind carried her words straight through him. "Two knights," she answered. "One horse."

She drove like a barrel racer, dodging the jeep in a series of alleys and streaking back onto the road near the edge of town, the sound of gunfire fading at last. His vigilance slipped to secondary, and the pain intensified as he let himself relax.

"We need to take care of your foot or they'll track us by blood alone," she said, slowing to a more rational pace.

"There's a field, a brick shrine on the D35, outside Tzin. Left my kit there."

"Bandages? Antiseptic?"

"Negative," he sighed against her back. "Thought you were going with them."

"I will be—they'll need me." Her chest rose and fell with a deeper breath, and she said, "So did you."

For a time, they drove in silence, traffic picking up around them, the city falling away. In the smaller town of Tzin, she pulled the bike behind a dumpster, and slung her own gun over his back, letting her hand linger. "You have some money?"

He gave her what he had, and she vanished among the other shoppers, returning with a bundle a little while later. They set off again, pulling up in a stand of trees by the stream that ran past the shrine where he'd hidden his stash. Grant stumbled off the bike and limped into the shade while she followed his instructions to locate the waterproof bag.

"We need to ditch the guns. I've already seen us getting a few looks. Might be less conspicuous if I drive." The caltrop had knocked loose somewhere, leaving an oozing hole through the bottom of his shoe. Grant worked on the laces. Sucking in a breath, he tried to pull off his shoe and pain flared.

Akilah grabbed his shoe, tugged the laces out completely and drew it off in a quick movement that sent waves of agony. "I've hired a car and driver, the druggist's son—he has no English. He'll take you to the coast, but you'll have to pay him."

"Negative. I can—" His voice was ragged, words lost in an effort to control his breathing.

"Don't be an ass, Soldier. You can't drive in this condition." She tossed his dry bag at him and settled near his foot with the supplies she had purchased earlier. "Lie down and shut up." She pulled out a bottle of ibuprofen and another of water and opened both, staring at him until he took a few pills and washed them down.

"Keep drinking. In twenty minutes, you'll feel better." She peeled off his sock and threw it away. "I'm not leaving the guns. I'll need them. At the least, I can sell them. The Nizari won't use them." Her back toward him, she took a firm hold of his ankle and poured something over his sole.

Grant's core clenched. He grit his teeth and lay back, unwrapping his pistol, wallet and cell phone. They fumbled from his hands as she worked, pain streaking at every touch. Her words, too, fractured like an ancient mosaic. He had all the pieces, and he didn't like the picture they formed. The image of her leaving. "Akilah—"

"Can you just be still for a moment? I'm trying to save your foot, if not your leg."

"'Still' is not my strong suit." He made an effort not to jerk away from her aid, then gulped a breath. "You know what I do for fun?"

"Oh, so now we get to know each other?"

"Long distance running." How long would it be before he could eat up the miles with an easy stride?

"Oh," she said again, quieter, her hand briefly cradling his heel without prodding the wound. "I used to play the oud, you know what this is?"

So he had guessed right about the finger exercises. "Like a lute." She nodded, and got back to work, shining a flashlight at his sole to check for any foreign material. "Damn," he whispered.

"Sorry," she said, but she didn't stop probing.

"Not you—the other women. Didn't get to ask what they knew."

"I did, while we waited for your all-clear. We had only moments." She applied something to the wound and starting to wrap, tight and firm.

"Were you gonna tell me?"

"When I feel certain you won't run into trouble on this foot without even a band aid. The first layer is a hemostatic dressing. It should help."

That fast, it was like they'd been married for years, like she saw right through him. He wanted to laugh. Instead, he wiped a hand across his face, feeling the grit and sting, like he hadn't showered an hour ago. And in the hour since, killed a half-dozen men, lost a half-pint of blood. No wonder he felt so exhausted. "What did you learn?"

"There's a big party, some of the men had to get uniforms to pretend to be employees. They're not used to this, acting like Nizari, instead of jihadi."

"Infiltrating."

Her hair tossed as she nodded. Her head scarf had gone in the fighting and her flowered shirt bloomed with spatters of blood. Not her own, thank God. "The Turkish woman, the one who spoke to you, it was the knights who brought her. She says they were excited to see a castle, a place they say belongs to them. Limassol."

"Cyprus. Oh, hell." He knotted his hands through his hair. "Davos-ME. Kicks off tonight. I need to warn them—we've got ten fucking hours." Fighting inertia, he started to sit up, groping for his phone. Akilah gently pressed him back, then picked up the phone and wrapped his hand around it. He caught his breath. "Thanks." She didn't let go.

"That's why I got you a driver with no English. You make the calls on the way."

He nodded, still trying to assemble the meaning.

"The women had a question for you, too." She smiled at him, her bruises fading as if action dispelled any sense of her own vulnerability. Her beauty grew more present at every moment, at every movement. "They want to know do you have any brothers."

He managed a laugh, breathy and light-headed. "No brothers. A few cousins."

She settled their hands, phone and all against his chest. "Soldier." His eyes opened. "You've been a hero for the last twenty-four hours, it's alright if you are human for twenty minutes."

"I copy."

She leaned down and lightly kissed him. When his eyes opened again, nineteen minutes later, she was gone.

CHAPTER FORTY-SEVEN

Kyra always slept better at sea, something in the waves and the rocking of the ship. She had the forward most cabin, a triangular private room with lush cushions on a separate couch and a larger bed, all in pale blue. When her American employees spoke of "going to their happy place," she imagined this, her quiet bedchamber at one end of her ship, her small workshop at the other. Waves made for excellent sleeping, less so for mechanical work, but the seclusion of the place made her work feel once more like play. Mother called it her "lair," as if Kyra were a mad scientist. Kyra dressed more practically today and entered the galley where Muminah set hot plates of eggs and toast in front of Nick and Mother. Those two. Kyra wasn't sure what to make of it.

Pasting on a smile, she went to prepare her coffee. She thought about Nick's medication, the things he was capable of. On the one hand, his most dangerous threat had been made in defense of her mother. On the other hand, she fully believed he would do it. Empty the king like a sack of flour.

She turned back. "That image—the picture of the king that Casey took, can you forward it?"

Whenever Casey's name came up, Nick's eyes flinched a little. "Yes, ma'am." He slipped out the ever-present phone and tapped a few commands, regarding it with a lingering glance before he finally put it away, and she didn't need to ask if they'd heard anything.

She triggered her facial search algorithm, sent an order to Kostas on the bridge, and put the phone away.

The engines came on a moment later, rumbling up to half-speed. Mother interrupted herself in the middle of a proclamation about the toast to say, "Aren't we already at Cyprus?"

Kyra sat next to Nick, opposite her mother, and took a sip, the bitter-sweet aroma filling her nostrils then her mouth. Heaven. Finally, she said, "We passed it in the night and anchored further out."

"So we're circling back." Her mother toyed with the toast point she had been using to sop up runny yolks.

"We are going to Arwad. We don't have to be in Cyprus until late this afternoon, or even tomorrow if we don't want to go to the—"

"We are not!" Mother pushed her plate away. "Nick, did you know about this? Was this your idea?"

He put up both hands. "Not my idea. Not my fight." He slipped off the bench at his end and took a moment to adjust to the movement of the deck, then walked away. His frame making her grand lounge look smaller. "I'll be topside if you need me." He vanished up the stairs.

"Kyra! Kyra, these men want to kill you."

"Mother, these men don't know what we know." She leaned forward, pressing her fingertips together. "You raised me to fight. To stand up to the bullies, to stand up for myself, like someone from your old stories."

"Most of them are tragedies." Her mother looked away, her face crumpled, suddenly older than her years. She whispered, "I don't want you to become a tragedy."

"You have said for years my father was a madman."

"It wasn't an insult, Kyra, it's how I teased him, every time he got so excited about some obscure reference, half of which I found for him." Her mother shrank into herself and looked as if she might be about to cry.

Kyra's hand parted, but she didn't know what to do with them next. She thought of her mother's reply to Nick's rhetorical question back in the cafe where they might all have died. "I know, Mother. I don't think I knew until these last few days. It made me so angry for so long, thinking you dismissed his passion, and now I see that I was wrong."

Mother's brows rose a little, but she blinked fiercely, and Kyra saw the tears at her eyes. "Mama," she whispered. "I know now what a madman really is. What will this king do with the throne? I don't know, but I cannot bear the thought of him taking it—not when we could get there first. My father's insanity was kind and generous. It was a madness that believed in us, in the greatness of our people and what we achieved together. This king, he thinks he can draw people together, but all we have seen of him is violence."

Mother continued to stare at her hands. "So many people would be inspired by the throne."

"And not all of them in a good way."

She lifted her chin. "If we do this, Kyra, we do it together. I don't want you in danger, and I'm afraid that you might—" she swallowed— "I don't want to live alone, not anymore."

Finally, Kyra knew what to do with her hands. She slipped from her place onto the bench at her mother's side, and opened her arms. They came together awkwardly, then melted into each other, in the embrace that had been years in coming. Her phone chimed in her pocket, and Kyra ignored it. Nothing could be more important right now than this.

CHAPTER FORTY-EIGHT

The motorcycle and long guns were gone as well—no surprise—and she had left Grant a stash of snack items and medical supplies, including two small syringes of lidocaine to manage the pain. Damn, but he was growing fonder of her by the minute. He administered one shot to the muscle not far from his injury, then finally stuffed his foot back into the damaged shoe. Get to Tartus. Get a boat. Get hold of Nick. Bottom line: get moving.

Stand up. Every muscle going rigid as he put weight on his left foot. He limped heavily from the copse of trees to find a grubby Kia sedan idling near the monument. The driver, a young man about the same age as his car, peered around, half a set of earbuds dangling from its wire by his head, the other end still plugged into his ear. He lit up when he spotted Grant and waved eagerly. "Your wife says you need a ride?" he called in Arabic.

"That's right. I hurt my foot. Thanks." He hobbled over, starting to feel the numbness of the lidocaine taking hold. Straight-faced, he switched to English and said, "I find you very attractive."

The driver shrugged and shook his head. "Sorry, only Arabic."

Good. "That's fine, no problem," Grant told him in his own tongue. "I need to get to Tartus. You can take me?"

"That's like two hours' drive, and that again for me to get home. You can pay?"

"Absolutely. She gave you some up front, right? I'll get more when we arrive, okay? I'm meeting a friend at the harbor." Insha'Allah. Rule number one of driving with strangers: never admit to having the cash. Kid probably didn't have any job aside from running errands for the pharmacy.

Grant opened the passenger door, which groaned on dry hinges, and the young man hastily swiped a pile of books and papers into the back seat to make room, shifting the phone at the end of his earbuds into his lap, then waving Grant into the seat. "I am Amal."

"Yusef. Pleased to meet you." First thing, move the seat back as far as he could and prop his left foot over his right.

"You're good?" Amal gave him a thumbs up.

Grant heaved the door shut. He settled in, the chunky foam and old vinyl cradling him like memory foam and Egyptian cotton. Be lucky not to fall right back asleep—but no way was he sleeping in this guy's car. "I'm good. I have to make some phone calls, okay?"

The young man bobbed his agreement, tapped a button on his phone and pulled out into the road while the dangling earbud whispered in the voice of Taylor Swift as it swung to and fro.

Autodial Nick's number. Let it ring once, twice. Hang up, dial again.

"Jesus, Chief—you're alive?"

Grant rested his head back, relief flooding him at the sound of Nick's voice. "Damn straight. You, too?"

Nick laughed. "You kidding me? I got the kind of digs that would make Gooney sign on immediately. Boss lady's got a super yacht out here, tooling around the Mediterranean, currently dropping anchor off Arwad."

"Syrian coast, right? Can I get a lift?"

The laughter deepened. "Where are you?"

"I'll be in Tartus in two hours."

"Arwad's only a couple miles from there—you could swim on over."

Not with a hole the size of a nickel in his foot. "Not today, Nick."

"Jesus, man, it's good to hear your voice." Nick paused. "What about the Phantom? Did you find her?"

Grant's throat felt dry, and he took a swig from his water bottle, then said, "I have to make another call, to regional command. Tell you everything when we meet up, okay?"

"Army command? That's bad. You think they'll even talk to you?"

"They don't, people are gonna die."

"Be safe, Chief."

"Do my best." He rang off, stared at the phone, then took another swallow before trying the next call. His left foot seemed completely numb, a blissful absence that might let him focus on what came next.

Grant dialed from memory, a number he'd never thought he would need again. One he couldn't even be sure would pick up.

"Magic Transit, your leader in just-in-time delivery," answered a chipper female voice on the other end, in Arabic.

An instant disappointment slipped his memory, imagining that it could once again be D.A.'s voice he was hearing, but that was years ago. He answered in the same language, hoping the same protocols applied, or, if not, that whoever he was talking to at least knew what they had been. "Hello, yes, I need to send a package to Mr. Davis."

A long pause, then the voice said, slowly, "Mr. Davis is no longer with the company."

"Then can you get me to his replacement. This package is signature required."

"I'm sorry, sir, I'll have to look up that information. Can you please give me a callback number? When my supervisor comes in—"

"Look," he said, "you've got two possibilities. One is, I'm a scammer and I have an old call list. The other is, I'm legit, and I've been out of the office long enough I haven't been updated. If this call is legit, every minute you spend waiting for your goddamn supervisor could jeopardize a critical delivery. That's gonna lead to some very unhappy customers."

"There's no need to take that tone, sir," she snapped back. "Please hold and I'll see if I can find someone for you to talk to."

Minutes passed, then a man's voice came on the line, in serviceable Arabic. "My receptionist tells me you're asking for Mr. Davis."

The voice sounded familiar, but one he hadn't heard for a couple of years. "May I ask who I'm speaking to?"

"That's a question you should answer before you ask it. How are you acquainted with Mr. Davis?"

The guy gave him the right challenge. Maybe he was getting somewhere. "I met him at the conference in Dubai." A claim that gave Grant's intel the highest priority.

"Dubai," the man echoed doubtfully.

Don't hang up. Don't fucking hang up. Grant held the phone to his ear, praying for a countersign.

"Was that the one where we shared a hotel with the football team?"

Breathed a sigh of relief. "Yes, sir," he said in English, the last question confirming they had a secure line. At least, to the best of his abilities under present circumstances.

"What the hell is this about? Who is this?"

He flicked a glance to Amal, who was, at that moment, gently trying to "Shake it off" to Ms. Swift's singing. "Lieutenant Grant Casey, US Army, retired."

"Holy Moly, that's a good one. According to the international news, Casey died yesterday in a hospital in Istanbul. Maybe you think we don't monitor our—"

"The reports are inaccurate. As part of the contract with my client, I had a publicity stand-in. He feigned death as part of the operation."

"Rumors of his death have been greatly exaggerated, huh? You really think I'll swallow that line?"

Shit. "You must have access to Casey's record, right? I left the service after a stint in Walter Reed, following injuries sustained during the clearance of a museum in Mazar-i-Sharif."

The voice on the other end didn't reply for a long moment—the voice he felt sure he knew. Finally, the man said, "The hell're you doing calling this number? You got a problem at the VA, Casey, you call your representative, you don't call—"

"Commander Wilson?" Grant beat his head against the rest and fought the urge to fling his phone straight out the window.

"Major Wilson. Cut the shit, Casey, why are you doing this? I could have you brought up on charges—"

Wilson was the guy whose obstinacy had forced Casey to take his people into the museum to begin with, the action that ended with him and Nick in critical condition, and out of the service, all because Wilson was a conservative commander who'd rather wait and see, even if civilians were dying and their heritage being destroyed. "Major. I wouldn't be calling if it wasn't justified." Words that most anyone else would at least consider, but with Wilson, he didn't place much stock in that. "I have solid intel there's going to be an action in Cyprus tonight, against some or all of the Davos-ME conference."

"Oh, really." The sound of a swiveling office chair came through loud and clear, as if Wilson were kicking back, bored already. "Solid intel. From where?"

"Major, I'm on the ground in Syria, wrapping a mission with a private local agency that works to combat sex trafficking. I embedded briefly with a group called Shifra—you've heard of them?"

"Sheee-fra." Wilson sighed. "They're the sleepiest of sleeper cells ever. Been hearing the name for five years or more, but they haven't claimed a single action. You're telling me they finally woke up?"

Everything the man said sent Grant's blood pressure a little higher. "They're working with a secret organization out of Turkey, a cult that thinks they can bring peace to the Middle East—but their idea of peace involves a lot of C4 and a SCUBA kit."

"What's the target?" Something scratched quietly. Grant hoped it was a pen on paper, not a bamboo rod with fingers at the end to scratch the major's back while he sat on his ass.

"Uncertain. I wasn't embedded long enough for full disclosure."

"You always have been an arrogant bastard, Casey. You think we don't have intel all over this thing? You think we haven't worked all the angles, ears on? I told you, Shifra's a no-go. It's like the frat house boys at Jihadi U—the guys who talk a lot and do nothing. Bring 'em in with the promise of girls and put guns in their hands so they can shoot off at rallies. It's the org for those who wanna look like tough shit, but they can't even hold their liquor.

Maybe I'm not surprised they took you on."

Grant swallowed his fury with a vengeance. "Believe you me, Major Wilson, if I didn't think the intel was good, I would've hung up the minute I knew it was you."

Something dropped on a desk with a clatter like bamboo, and Wilson said, "Tell you what, I'm heading over there myself, in a couple hours, to meet up with the VP and do some goodwill crap. If I see something, I'll say something. Meantime, I hope at least you got a good fuck out if it."

"Major, would you please just set aside—" The connection broke, leaving Grant with nothing but a headache and a bomb to find.

CHAPTER FORTY-NINE

K yra stood on the dive platform, her pants rolled up to her ankles while Nick braced the ROV, a yellow torpedo shape about three feet long. Mother leaned over the top rail above them, monitoring their progress.

The *Altin Hayal* bobbed gently in the gulf between Arwad and the Syrian coast. The island looked to be entirely man-made, its strategic location making it a target for seizure by everyone from the Phoenicians to Pharaoh Thutmose III—the same one commemorated by that obelisk in the hippodrome—to the crusaders and onward, or so her mother reported, diving into the research with the relish of a first year graduate student. To the East, dry mountains loomed over a rugged coastline that gradually eased into a plain, like the island, completely consumed by buildings. On the left, a medieval fortress and ancient Turkish walls eaten away by the sea, on the right, the modern city of Tartus, just as crowed and not nearly as attractive.

In between, a swath of blue Mediterranean dotted by sails and slashed by the wakes of motorboats. "Almost there, Nick?"

"Three green lights! Got it." He closed the access panel and twisted the latches to seal the compartment. He wore a pair of rubber boots, defending his high-tech prosthetic, and let her do the down-low.

Kyra looked to her tablet screen, wearing it in a plastic case around her shoulder. On screen, a sidebar showed the ROV controls, and two splits showed her own ankles and sloshing water at the back, and Nick's grinning face and thumbs-up at the front. "Got it. Cameras on, and we're a go." She slung the tablet onto her back and they rolled the ROV into the water.

"You got a name for this thing?" Nick pointed to the ROV as it vented air to sink slowly below them. The spring lay about six meters down, just far enough that she wasn't comfortable free-diving, besides, the less erratic movements of the ROV stirred up less silt than a diver's fins would, and they had launched from a little ways to one side of the spring, coming up on it carefully so as not to disturb the search site.

"Not yet." She watched the readouts from the various sensors scrolling on her sidebar. "To be honest, Nick, I don't get that attached to these things."

"Oh, that hurts. Pretty little piece of tech like this deserves a name."

She cocked her head. "Does your prosthetic have a name?"

"Sporting Jenny."

Overhead, Mother burst into laughter. "Nick, that is delightful. I do hope it treats you better than that."

Nick kept his focus on Kyra. "It's from an Irish song. Chief named it, actually. Jenny's the love interest, but she's not so reliable—actually turns the hero in to the authorities. Of course, the name first applied to the one the VA made for me, which was...adequate. We've made a bunch of upgrades since then."

The ROV reached a level one meter above the ocean floor, relaying a rough surface between ten centimeters and 50 centimeters below its hull. Once there, it initiated a search pattern, laying out a grid with the spring at the center. At such a relatively shallow depth, they did not need external illumination: sunlight penetrated, creating a murky blue-green atmosphere flecked with tiny things and the occasional fish that flitted past the cameras. The spring itself showed up as a wafting vertical current disturbing the spotted water and roiling out.

"Imagine them even finding this," Nick murmured. He had shifted to stand by her shoulder, watching the scroll of the camera.

"We don't give ancient peoples enough credit for innovation and discovery. It's hard to say how they found it, but Mother found some descriptions of how they actually gathered the fresh water using a tube and funnel system lowered down from small boats."

"I can see why it couldn't withstand a siege though."

On screen, a line of rectangular stones emerged, pointing between the island and the mainland. Nick's finger traced over it. "Signs of the causeway built by the Seljuks?"

She appreciated his use of the term "Seljuk" instead of calling them "Turks" as most people would. Her people didn't need to be seen as the enemy, these many years later—current politics notwithstanding. "Probably. It would help to know what we're looking for, to tell what we're looking at." She raised her voice and called up, "Anything new, Mother?"

"Much of it is a travelogue about saintly shrines and legendary elements like the castle without doors. I can't even tell what he means to be real. Of course, our Aleume was in the area a hundred years before the Battle of Ruad, so things may have changed, and the causeway or the siege itself might have ruined the clue he meant to leave us." Mother had been perusing the codex more closely, in search of hints. "How does it look?"

"Blue and blocky," Nick reported with a frown.

"Anything valuable or historically interesting would've been taken by divers or fishermen in any case." Mother sounded disappointed.

Nick said, "Can you interrupt the program, Kyra, go back a little?"

Kyra's hands slid over the tablet, stopping and confirming. "I've asked it to repeat the last two sections, but at half speed."

"Something behind the rocks there—there!"

She jabbed the interface, hovering the ROV over the gap between two of the rectangular stones, then moving it slowly out of the pattern. Another worked stone embedded into the ocean floor, made soft by growth and age, but distinctly round at the bottom and about as tall as the other stones. When she brought the ROV closer, making the weeds wave as if in greeting, she made out scalloped edges peeling off from the stone and a cross-like pattern on the top, the grooves marked by a deeper pattern of green.

"Acanthus leaves. Looks like part of a column they used as fill for the causeway. Probably stole it from a church." Nick sighed and glanced at his watch. "Chief should be in town pretty soon."

"Let's finish the search pattern."

Kyra removed the over-ride and the little ROV buzzed back to resume its pattern. Several other worked stones emerged from the sea floor around the spring, bits of masonry re-used or cast away. Nick sat on the bench at the stern, his rubber-booted feet sticking out in front of him, letting the roll of the waves move it gently back and forth. After a moment, Kyra sat as well, staring at the screen, her eyes beginning to glaze from peering at it, hoping for something more, anything. "We might need to dive it, perhaps a metal detector. Or I could fit a new sensor." Anything heavy would require additional thrust—her little pet project wasn't built for extreme duty.

"Maybe so," he said, "but not today." He rubbed the back of his neck. "Let's face it, Kyra. Even-odds there's nothing left to find. The trail's not just broken, its drowned."

CHAPTER FIFTY

Grant sat on a bench near the harbor, watching a zodiac bound over the waves from a jumbo yacht that lay a little off shore. He centered himself, prepared to put on a show of "not so bad" so his condition wouldn't freak out the client or her people. He needed about twelve hours sleep, and another few shots of lidocaine, and he was a hundred miles or more from the nearest Twinkies. But as the boat approached, Grant let himself relax. He didn't need binoculars to recognize the driver. As the boat pulled alongside a guest pier, Grant rose stiffly and hobbled down the ramp to meet it.

Nick tossed a rope around one of the cleats, then climbed out onto the pier and hustled its length to meet Grant in the middle and seize him in a bear hug. "What the hell happened to you? What happened to your foot?" He slipped his arm low, offering support, and Grant accepted, hooking his hand over Nick's shoulder.

"Caltrops on a driveway." The foot remained numb from the earlier shot, but it helped getting the weight off. "Do they have a three-legged race at the Paralympics?"

Nick gripped him a little tighter. "Hope to God in a week or two you wouldn't qualify."

"Sitrep?"

Nick got him to the boat where Grant sat on the edge, then slid into the Zodiac and Nick followed, casting off the line and starting up the motor.

"We got squat at Arwad. Boss lady's got a mini-sub she used to have a look-around—I'll show you the footage. Oh—and she got a hit on that photo you took. The King of Jerusalem is a professional mediator who works on contract with half the law firms in Istanbul. Very high in demand, great reputation. Guy by the name of Blaise Lebreque, son of minor nobility back in France."

French, like Brunelle. The accent fit, faint, but still present.

"D.A. says he's got a juvenile record, but nothing since. He was implicated in a fire at a library, of all things—seems to have scared him straight. Seems like him and the Viking crossed paths back then. How about you?"

Grant regarded him across the boat and shook his head. "Buddy, I don't know if you'll even believe me."

"Try me."

"Coffee, and a couch—and another look at Aleume's codex."

"Coffee and a couch, but you don't get your hands on that book until you level with me. You found her?"

"I married her."

Nick cut the engine. "Bullshit."

Grant threw up his hands. "Told you."

Propping his elbows on his knees, Nick stared at him. "Not moving til you spill the beans."

"Much as I'm inclined to indulge you, my friend, we've got a bomb to find and regional's not helping."

Nick pulled the cord and turned them back for the yacht as Grant briefed him on the last twenty-four hours, leaving out the more intimate details. Didn't matter, Nick still regarded him softly.

"So she insists she's married to you, then she takes off while you're unconscious by the side of the road."

"She got me a driver," Grant pointed out.

"That is one fucked up marriage."

"You know me, Nick—what other kind could I have?"

Nick pulled up and threw a line to Muminah belowdecks. "You

earned your coffee, man. Big time. Maybe even get you that book to read as we get back to Cyprus."

Grant let the wave that pushed the zodiac onto the platform help him to standing. Making like he was unsteady because of the footing, not the foot. Who was he fooling? Idiot. He caught the rail and pulled himself up to the back deck.

Kyra appeared at the hatch as the crewmen raised the zodiac back into position. "Welcome aboard, Mr. Casey."

"Nice place you've got here."

She glanced between the two men and stepped out of the way. "Meet me in the upstairs lounge when you're ready?"

"Affirmative." He straightened. "I need a change of clothes at least."

She gave a quick nod. "The showers are warm, but preferably brief."

"Copy that. Where are my things?"

"Follow me, Chief." Nick brought him along the corridor two a room with two berths. "I put your stuff here." He gestured. "The head's through there."

The shower was brief indeed, complicated by the fact that he had to keep his injury dry. At least the bleed-through was minimal. Cyprus would have more supplies. The engines started up somewhere toward the stern and he balanced with his hand against the doorframe, his foot elevated. He had another hour of numbness, give or take, then his balance would improve and his pain threshold would drop. Shit. Find the bomb. Stop it going off. Get back to the mainland for some serious medical care. Right.

He pulled on his dark suit pants and a wicking shirt, no logo. His phone lay on the little table between the berths, two messages.

Grant's heart rose and he scooped it up, dropping onto the bed. Not the right app. Damn.

9:01 >*Have you returned to service?*

10:15 >*Will your client be coming to Cyprus? Special knighthood ceremony awaits.*

Two hours ago. Hadn't answered yet, no harm waiting a little longer. He stuffed it in his pocket and braced himself to put on shoes. At least the ruined one had been part of his costume, so he had spares. A twinge of pain from the center of his foot. Wearing off. Better save the second dose for when he needed it. Grant spanned both walls with his hands, avoiding setting down his foot until he reached the narrow stairs heading up, then he found an expression of determination not too grim, and entered the lounge where the little party awaited. On a television screen, blue-green footage streamed, a careful search pattern covering an area of the ocean floor with curious fish, shy shrimp, lotta the most boring stones he'd ever seen. Wouldn't have been worth the tanks to dive it. The footage paused, backed up, and hovered over part of a column, then continued.

The smell of coffee lured him to the table where Kyra, Nick, and Irene occupied one bench shoulder to shoulder, looking up at him as if he were a doctoral candidate about to defend his thesis. Kyra slipped her glasses back on her head. "It's got to be the dinner, right? On the Arab's yacht?" She turned her screen to show him a schedule of events for the Davos-ME.

Nick added, "The presidents of Turkey and Syria will be there, the American vice-president, the Israeli premier, half a dozen sheiks. Take out the boat, and half the leadership of the region goes down."

"And into the void, rides the King." Grant slid his phone across the way, displaying the message. He sank onto the couch at the end of the table and Irene nudged a china cup his way. "US Army intelligence regional office won't help us, but they've been alerted—if anything suspicious comes up, they'll probably do something about it."

"Probably," Nick echoed, and their eyes met. Grant could almost see the reflection of fire and blood from the last time Regional let them down. He was sure he looked the same. At least the coffee was excellent.

Kyra fidgeted her tablet on the table between them. "I have tried to call the Turkish delegation, but they won't let me through to anyone important."

"How are we supposed to stop a bomb?" Irene said. The codex sat beside her and she ran her fingers over the cover. "I know this is vital, but I rather wish Arwad had shown us something—and we might have..."

237

"Let the bomb be someone else's problem?" Nick asked softly.

"It should be, shouldn't it? You gentlemen are certainly very capable, but there's only two of you, and you're retired, not to mention, well—it's not your job is it? It certainly isn't ours."

Grant set down his cup. "Irene. My grandfather has a saying, that we honor the dead, but we work for the living. We do what we can to stop this thing."

"If we fail to find the throne, so what? It's an artifact, a thing lost a few hundred years—it's important, but nobody will die. If we fail at this, if this bomb goes off..."

"Then at least we'll know we went down trying."

She recoiled. "That's rather final, isn't it?"

Nick gave the slightest nod, and Grant said, "I have no expectation that you should risk your life for this, and no doubt that once I start trying, somebody's going to die. I hope it's not any of us. I hope to keep the dying to a minimum, and I will do my utmost to ensure that." He hesitated, trying to find the words, and said, "You're right, Irene, it's not my job. It's my calling."

CHAPTER FIFTY-ONE

Mother looked so inspired, just then, as if she were once more in the classroom, envisioning the effect of some great speech from a thousand years ago. Inspired and afraid.

Kyra tapped the intercom on the wall. "Kostas, we need full speed for Cyprus."

"Yes, ma'am."

After a moment, the throb of the engines grew and the boat picked up speed.

"How long?" Casey asked.

"About five hours. We should be there for dinner."

His brows rose, and she smiled. "We made some modifications to the engine compliment. We get almost sixty knots if there's not too much traffic." Kyra pulled her tablet back. "This explosive, this C4, can be used underwater? So, if I can deploy my ROV, I can perhaps locate the bomb on the outside of the boat. I cannot defuse it, of course, but if we have witnesses, we have proof—we can get them to clear the boat."

Nick was already shaking his head. "Negative. This party boards at eighteen hundred." He tabbed the screen back to an image of the superyacht. "How many people you figure they can fit on the yacht? Hundred, maybe one fifty? I'm only seeing two gangways, assuming this thing can even dock, otherwise, they'll be loading with tenders, and there's no way you get everybody off. Best case scenario, nobody ever gets on."

"Call in a threat," Irene suggested. "Make sure they never board."

"We effectively already have, me to the Americans, Kyra to the Turks," Grant said. "What's left: the Arabs, the Israelis or Cyprus local."

"How much does the enemy know that we know?" Nick asked.

Casey appeared to consider this question. "Almost nothing. Depends if they connect me with Yusef, the guy who went rogue at Hama. The king and company still think I'm their recruit, and that I killed Grant Casey."

"This is why you don't allow photographs." The connections leapt across Kyra's mind. "A bomb threat tips our hand, shows them that we have information they'd rather we didn't."

"And, more importantly, it gives them the chance to change their plans," Nick supplied. "They've got boots on the ground, divers in the water, and a big payload waiting to blow. I don't see these guys calling it off—"

"No way. Farouk and the others were irritated they had to wait this long. My take is, the king's been hoping he could get his hands on the throne to make for a more impressive reveal. Shifra is already considered the lazy jihad. If they think it won't work, they'll find another way, even more destructive."

Kyra whistled sharply, and the men stopped, even her mother staring at her, lips parted. "I know how to do this. As it is, we arrive barely in time, we make an entrance, like at a party. This ROV, I don't think you understand the level of innovation it represents. The Arabs and the others, they'd love to know about it. So. I send a press-release. I invite them all to join me on the dock before the party—if they're on the boat, it's too late. I will offer an exclusive pre-release demonstration of this new technology. I use it to show the hull of the party ship, talk about taking a tour of the harbor."

"Would they accept this?" Mother asked, dubious.

The men shared a glance, then Nick pointed toward the screen. "Top quality images with a craft that has both a drone mode and a remote control facility that operates underwater without a tether? They'll want to know all right. They'll want to weaponize it."

Mother absorbed this with some dismay. "You've always said you wouldn't make weapons, Kyra."

Her dark concern matched Kyra's own. "It may be more useful defensively, as we'll be doing." Whether or not there was something to see, she would have exposed her personal project to international scrutiny and be hounded by warlords. Casey's words still echoed in her head: *not a job, but a calling.* "Most of what I make are toys, tricks for the wealthy to enjoy, or systems for business. This is a chance to use what I know for something more important."

Casey gave a nod. "Big audience, nobody boards the ship. Nick can make sure of that. Don't specify the variety of tech you'll demo—we don't want them to get anxious, maybe just announce an innovation in drone technology? Make like you'll do a fly-over of the crowd."

Nick's brow furrowed. "Wait, if I'm managing access to the ship, what will you be doing?"

Casey pulled back his phone, with its invitation of knighthood. "Keeping the king busy—maybe stopping the bomb from blowing at all. If he's going to trigger it, I can get to him first. Take him, or just disrupt his communications. I'm accepting his invite."

"What if he does know it's you? What if he knows what you did in Syria?"

Elbows propped on the table, Casey's eyes slid shut, his head bowed in mute acknowledgment, resting on the tips of his thumbs. Finally he said, "What if he blows up the entire leadership of the Eastern Mediterranean?"

CHAPTER FIFTY-TWO

I f it's alright, I'd like to call Adem, to have him coordinate," Kyra said, and Grant let her words wash over him. He was in crappy condition: A&O times four; physically and, if he had to admit it, emotionally at maybe 4 out of 10. No fucking state to be running an op, much less one with so many lives—so much fallout—in the balance.

"What do you need from him?"

"Press releases, international contacts, the guest list for the summit, and a large-format screen on the dock to share the view. It's a lot to manage in only a few hours." Her fingers already tapped and slid, organizing as if they were heading for a big-splash marketing release.

Big splash indeed. "Do it." The whole point of her side of the op was to make it public, no reason to shut out her PA because he might overshare.

"I'll work from the lab below decks. Buzz me if you have anything to add." Indicating the intercom, Kyra unfolded from the bench, gathered her electronics and departed down the stairs.

"I'll oversee lunch, shall I?" Irene asked. She picked up the codex and lay it down next to his arm, reached out almost as if she would pat him on the shoulder, then took back the gesture. "We'll all need the energy, and it sounds as if our dinnertime might be quite sensational. If you'll excuse me." Nick rose to get out of her way. She scooted off the bench and glided away, her silk caftan fluttering in her wake.

Grant tipped his cheek onto his hand. "Lunch sounds excellent, thank you." What had he eaten for breakfast? Whatever he and Akilah found in the cabinets a thousand years ago. One fucked-up marriage.

"Are you sure you're up to this?" Nick asked.

"I'm sure I'm doing it. Tell me the options."

"Feel like that's right up there with, 'Never tell me the odds.' In the meantime, couch, coffee, codex—" he pointed to each in turn— "Knock yourself out, Chief. You could use the rest. I'm gonna head to the bridge and learn how to drive this thing." Nick grinned. He never could resist a vehicle. He flicked a salute and cross the salon and galley to the bridge.

On the phone, Grant tapped out a brief message: >TY for your message. I am ready.

Then he added >Haldan okay? OMW to Cyprus with client >she plans to show off. So ready to serve a higher cause

Left on his own, Grant eased back to get his left leg onto the couch and prop his back. He finished the coffee and set the cup aside before taking up the book. Should be wearing gloves, especially with all his hands had been through the last twenty-four hours. He settled in to frown over the structures of Medieval Latin, and pretended for a little while that he really was just some hapless grad student on a deep dive into obscure history. Aleume gave succinct accounts of various battles, lamented the loss of Christian lives even as he justified the Crusaders' diversion to Constantinople as perfectly Christian: after all, they had among them a young man who claimed the throne.

His phone vibrated. >Haldan well, thanks to you. Meet at harborside, 5 pm? Haldan will greet you

>Glad to hear it. CU then

He claimed readiness. He knew himself well enough to say, by that time, he would be.

In the meantime, back to Aleume. After the battles came his sketches of the treasury items, his worries about what would become of them, his little tour of the shrines of the Levant—visiting the obscure homes, hermitages and martyrdom sites: Saint Maron of Syria, Saint Simeon Stylites, the repetitively named Saint Sabbas the Sanctified of Turkey. In the midst of his study, Irene and Muminah emerged from the galley, delivering plates of hummus and stuffed grape leaves, something minty to drink, and more coffee. Grant thanked them as they went on their rounds.

Irene returned with her own lunch a little later and took a seat at the mirror-image of his table across the aisle. She took a book from the shelf beneath her bench and propped it against the edge of the table to read.

As he worked through the text, Grant paused from time to time, looking up and considering various translations. Once in a while, he called out to Irene, who supplied her interpretation—seemed about to plunge into a lecture, then interrupted herself and primly returned to her own book. On the large screen above the door to the outside deck, the ROV footage spooled in an endless loop. Outside, the same ocean, seen from above, unspooled rapidly. They slowed around other, smaller boats, sped up again afterward. Kyra's oversized yacht passed many of its peers, and a few even larger.

Aleume had inscribed an Egyptian obelisk—a pagan artifact, from his perspective—and painted on the floor of a church. What had he meant for them to find at Arwad? What evidence of this medieval traveler had been swept away by time or swiped by an opportunist visiting the spring? Grant's gaze unfocused, the blue-green view of undersea stones washing through him, there, again, the column that had caught Nick's eye. "Irene! The remote! Do you know how to pause this?" Grant pushed away from his couch, setting his foot down too soon and wincing as pain raced up his leg. Yep, lidocaine worn off for sure.

Irene snatched the remote and froze the screen, then looked at him with horror. "Are you alright?"

Failure in his filters—should've tamped down his reaction sooner. "Saint Simeon Stylites—" He limped to the screen, tracing the outline of the cross on top of the column.

"Saint Simeon!" Irene rippled over to join. "Mr. Casey, that's brilliant!" She clutched his arm. "Stylites, from the Greek for pillar. Because Simeon sat atop a pillar in Syria for thirty-seven years! The trail isn't broken, not at all."

They knew where to go. All they had to do was live long enough to make the journey.

CHAPTER FIFTY-THREE

Blaise strolled the gathering crowd near the marina center at Limassol, a small cluster of buildings on a large wharf in the midst of the marina itself, close to the gap in the stone jetties so the super yacht didn't have to maneuver very far. It had berthed there last night, backed in to the dock, ready to receive passengers, but currently off-limits to the attendees. Pity Blaise wouldn't be aboard the vessel. His own destination in a little while stood a few blocks away, in the Old Port, where the city's modest castle rose above later construction. A square keep with a hall and yard, now a museum, the castle could not compare with other Crusader properties on the island, but as a meditation center and gathering place, it would do.

Long, golden light overlaid the late afternoon. A perfect time of day, a perfect day to rise up. He thought he might feel jitters or tension. Instead, he welled with the excitement of a task on the horizon. A hard job, but a vital one.

He nodded and spoke softly to various heads of state, lawyers he knew, men in uniform and others in their national garb. The American vice president moved with two men in stiff military uniforms, and a small cadre of people in black suits. She shook hands, posed for selfies with a few men in skullcaps. Stirring to see so many different people, for a moment without fighting. It wouldn't last, he knew it wouldn't: both because these people were not capable of seeing beyond their own petty problems, and because he had already laid plans in motion to fracture the pretense of the occasion. A few of his knights moved among the gathering, and Farouk's men showed themselves able to improvise better than he thought: delivering cocktails along the dock and hardly spilling anything.

The message from the false knight about Akbulut showing off had prepared him for the flurry of messages from the conference organizers, breathlessly prattling on about the Turkish entrepreneur's exciting new invention, which she wanted to share here first, in a stunning demonstration of local achievement—and so forth. Blaise had his own considerations. He even felt thankful for the false knight's insight. Akbulut had yet to appear, though her assistant hovered about barking orders at a technical crew like the little dog he was.

Baris Ozan sidled up. "Lebreque! When do we get to the party, eh?"

"It's hard to say, Baris."

"What's even the point? The conference has their own drones to take our picture." Ozan waved his hand at the pair of drones buzzing around the crowd, presumably snapping photos and collecting video. Hopefully they would capture nothing of interest.

"She's a Turkish phenomenon at a time we wish to be known for something other than the pig-headedness of our leadership. It seems a good thing to celebrate." Blaise schooled himself to patience, and imagined a day without this boorish man at the helm of the law firm. Tomorrow, in fact. And every day after that. Not that Blaise took pleasure in what he must do, it was simply the most efficient way to sweep clear the chessboard and bring the region into a brighter future.

"Sorry you didn't get an invite—I did try for you, but even a ship that size can only take so many. I'm sure you understand." Ozan gloated with the glee of the over-privileged.

"It's alright, I have my own gathering tonight. We're planning something special."

"Always so magnanimous. I guess that's why you're good at your job. Hai! Waiter." Ozan waved someone over, utterly unaware that the man might be a terrorist-in-waiting.

The PA's head jerked up suddenly, and he scampered to the side of the jetty where a zodiac tender approached. The Turkish delegation hustled over to greet their favored child. First up the ladder was a man in a black suit, dark haired, eyes keen as he scanned the crowd, then he stepped aside. Grant Casey. The false knight right on time. He put his hand out to assist Akbulut herself as she climbed the ladder. She disdained his hand, instead offering a bright smile and waving to the gathering.

People clapped around Blaise, the crowd tightening toward the end of the dock where the yacht awaited to one side, and the giant screen to the other. Blaise allowed the crowd to shift beyond him, staying at the fringe.

Someone down below handed up a leather case, which Akbulut accepted, then stepped out of the way herself, immediately falling into conversation with her PA. Next up, the unmistakable figure of the woman who was no soap opera star, Akbulut's mother. Blaise's gratitude for the woman's graciousness years before had soured with her recent betrayal. No matter. He had seen her name on the guest list, the exclusive few allowed onto the boat. A suited black man followed her up, sharing a nod with Casey at the top of the ladder, then escorting the elder Akbulut toward the podium to join her daughter.

Blaise raised his hand to signal a waiter. And to signal someone else entirely.

"Sir, may I take your order?" A gruff male voice.

"No, thank you. I've changed my mind." Blaise turned away and left the crowd to be awed by whatever technical marvel Akbulut would uncover. Shadows moved on one of the docked boats where a few more of Farouk's men waited. In less than an hour, the yacht would depart the dock, and shortly after, the people on it would depart the world. The hundreds left behind—the hangers on, the security force, the undersecretaries, lesser partners, and all of the functionaries who actually made their nations run would be left behind, in a panic, as the mad terrorists rose up among and around them. Blaise, mask in place and sword held high would be there, leading his knights to gallantly rescue the survivors.

CHAPTER FIFTY-FOUR

G rant scanned the crowd, spotted the king, kept scanning, so far, so good. Tall woman, two others he recognized from Akilah's abduction. And among the servers, the dock workers, the security personnel, a few faces he recognized from the Shifra's makeshift mosque. He prayed the suit, the sunglasses, and the change in demeanor would be enough to conceal him for at least a little while.

The crowd tracked Kyra's movement, clustering up around where she would address them. For an instant, he caught sight of Major Wilson himself, at the Veep's side, looking glum and murderous, as usual. Grant debated if he wanted to be seen, maybe put the asshole on alert as he should be. Of course, then he'd be alertly watching Grant, who might well have to behave suspiciously the next little while.

King on the move, letting the crowd shift past him. A few others filtered out down the dock. Not staying to see Kyra's show—but also not staying for the fireworks. For a moment Grant wondered if he had drastically misjudged the whole situation. That wouldn't explain the Shifra infiltrators, or what Akilah told him she had seen. Any possibility she'd been lying? The moment he thought it, Grant foot itched. He'd taken the second shot of lidocaine before boarding the launch. Drugs she provided when she got his ass out of the line of fire. Trust issues, man. Someday be the death of him.

Someone came up along his other side, and Grant glanced over to find

Haldan approaching, his hair trimmed, his pace maybe a little slow.

"Michael. Good to see you." Haldan put out his hand.

Grant gripped his hand. "You've got no idea. You really alright? That looked like a helluva blow."

Haldan's smile spread genuine pleasure, but his eyes betrayed that twinge of regret. "I wouldn't be here, if not for you. Well do I know it." He kept Grant's hand a moment longer. "Thank you." He seemed about to say something else, his glance slipping aside, back toward the zodiac where Kostas kept the ROV at the ready. A flicker of recognition, then—what? The slightest crease of worry.

"Don't mention it. What happens now?" Grant kept scanning, as if his assignment tonight were to guard whatever Kostas was doing down below.

"We take a walk." Haldan indicated the dock with a curl of his hand.

"We're not joining the party."

Haldan started to shake his head, stopped himself with a slight groan and a hand at the back of his head. "No. It's very exclusive. We have our own gathering. Come. They're waiting." He turned and walked away, leaving Grant to choose.

What was the king up to? Not here for the party, not the Arabs' party or his own—at least, not matching Grant's model of what would happen. What if his model was totally fucked? Go along, track the king, try to stop the bomb from blowing. And leave Nick to deal with whatever came up at the dock, each of them flying solo. Shit. What would Haldan do if he tried to stay behind? Time to drink the martini.

Grant strode after him. His rest on the boat, and a fresh dressing on his wound, had done wonders. He just hoped they weren't walking far. "I hope you won't be sparring tonight, seems like you're not quite ready for active duty."

Haldan's shoulders hunched a little. "Not for me. But I—" he almost shook his head again.

"I hope you didn't come all this way for my sake. But I appreciate it if you did." Grant's own neck and shoulders felt tight.

"The king commands." His voice warmed, and he said, "Though he, too, thought I should stay in hospital."

Grant had been there, recovering from a head injury when the brass wanted you on deck.

"Besides," said Haldan, "looks like you've picked up a bit of a limp yourself."

Not an operator, also not an idiot. "Twisted my ankle on that stupid side trip—side trip. Ha." They shared a smirk about that.

Marina security nodded and waved them past, looking bored, as they reached the land. They followed a curved road between short waterfront cafes and shops, a few of them American brands. The street widened, and a small distinctly European castle came into view, a low square tower and connected hall, all fenced in and posted with opening hours that just ended. A few other people strolled the plaza between the castle and the modern buildings, stopping to take photos in the warm light. A man and a woman stood by the open gate, capes rippling from their shoulders, swords resting tip down between their feet, their hands relaxed upon the hilt. They stood taller as Grant and Haldan passed inside. The guards pivoted within and shut the gate behind them. Wrought iron fence, five feet high, though the gate was lower, atop a stone base that tracked around the courtyard. The keep stood flush against that lower wall. An excavated mosaic floor showed where the castle had been larger at one time, and a rose garden softly scented the evening air. It would be idyllic, save for the creeping tension that reminded him of the thorns if he had to run that way, of the spikes topping the fence if he had to vault over, of the impossibility of escape through the small stained-glass windows.

They walked him beneath a stone arch where another pair of guards waited, again closing the door behind him, a solid wooden one this time, in a stone wall a foot or more over his head.

Stop thinking of them as guards or wardens, and think of them as brother knights. This was his ceremony, these were his comrades. Grant walked taller as well, taking on the mantle of solemn duty. The chamber they entered, a high square of medieval stone would be the gift shop and entry to the museum the castle had become. A velvet cloth covered the glass display case, with a few phones, wallets, two handguns, and other pocket contents.

"If you would place anything of the world you carry with you," said the woman in careful English.

Grant emptied his obvious pockets, leaving his handgun, burner phone, Michael Donahue's wallet. He smoothed his hands over his jacket and upper pants as if to be sure he forgot nothing.

"Tradition holds that a knight candidate shall mediate prior to their ceremony, but this night is special. We hope you will not suffer for this lack."

"Me, too," Grant said.

Two knights and Haldan preceded him up a set of stairs and into the upper hall. The ceiling here had been replaced with a modern one, with clerestory windows letting in the light. One corner with a little interior balcony and a door back to the tower. A few dark beams spanned the sides of the room between older barred windows. A few broken statues stuck out from the beige stone of the walls, and a tall column stood alongside the stairs, not quite reaching the lofty ceiling. A pair of tall cases held full suits of armor, one with a poleax, the other with a sword. Smaller cases had been moved aside and draped with velvet to make space for the twelve people assembled there, ranked to either side of the long narrow space. Spiral staircase blocked off at the far end. Four more doors: small chambers lined with displays of dishes and other household items of bygone days. A nice little museum.

Haldan stopped just inside the larger room, and the other two knights remained in the shop.

From the darkened end of the hall, a tall figure in a gray suit strode. He wore a deep purple cape—royal purple—and a silver mask of medieval design that concealed all the gleam of his eyes. Ring on his right hand. Don't forget about that. "Welcome, candidate. Please, come forward."

A square carpet occupied that part of the room. On top of it, a few feet in front of the king a velvet pillow lay on the ground, and a second one with a sword atop it. Classic Crusader style with a cruciform hilt, but of modern make and similar to those worn or carried by the knights all around him. Four guards at the doors, twelve knights inside, Haldan and the king. Very, very poor odds if it came to a fight.

Grant walked forward, focusing on landing each step evenly. The carpet felt a little strange under his foot, a slight slip as if plastic underlay it. The king gestured, and Grant sank to his knees on the cushion.

"In this hallowed chamber of our former brethren, we welcome the pure and the true candidate."

The mask gave the king's voice a slightly hollow echo, but his natural timbre was rich and appealing. Very impressive. The king took another step forward and lifted the sword from its place. "We are the Knights Penitent. Repentance comes when a man sees the gulf between who he believes himself to be, and what his actions reveal about him. For most men, this gap is not in their favor. We overwhelmingly believe ourselves to be good, righteous, noble and true, we all too often act in ways that show us to be venial, narcissistic, and cruel, and we spend our lives justifying the gap."

His words echoed in the chamber. "I hope you have truly meditated upon what it means to repent, to reconcile what you have done with who you believe yourself to be, and to strive to become that person, noble in word and deed, a model of integrity, a standard-bearer for what man can be."

Lot to ask a guy, and he'd just gotten here. Grant set aside the inner voice, the rumble of nerves. Plastic under the carpet: great way to make sure they didn't have to clean his blood off the stone.

"Have you come before me in the spirit of true repentance, ready to leave behind the life of sin and enter upon the path of virtue?"

Grant came there to find out what the hell the king was up to and put an end to it, not to play at chivalry. "Yes, my lord."

"In that case," the king said, laying the tip of the sword on Grant's left shoulder, "Tell me your name."

CHAPTER FIFTY-FIVE

Blaise stared down the blade at the false knight. The other man stared right back, his features so composed, his gaze so direct that Blaise felt it was Casey who wore the mask while Blaise stood naked before him. Vulnerable. Blaise controlled the sword with extreme care in spite of the buzz that built beneath his skin as the moment stretched. Go on, apostate. Lie again and justify the blade.

"My lord. I am Grant Casey."

A murmur rushed the knights and Blaise, poised to sweep the blade through Casey's throat froze. He expected the lie, braced for it, for the moment Haldan presented his evidence, and the false knight was stripped of all honor, deserving of his punishment. "That is not the name you wore when you met with Haldan, nor when you passed your first trial. Why did you lie?"

"I have dwelt in darkness, my lord, far from the light of chivalry. When I came to Istanbul, it was necessary to conceal my truth. Men have died for my lie, my lord, and I will bear that regret for the rest of my days."

Blaise's off-hand twitched toward a fist. Casey seized the voice of repentance and claimed it for his own. Blaise must get it back before his knights felt any doubt. Casey had to die. Had to. Whether he pledged tonight or not, whether he lied through his teeth or told the truth, this could not be allowed. "Every word you have spoken to us has been a lie—why should we now trust what you say? Even to the Lion of Truth, you lied. Or are you merely so expert at deception that even the mechanisms of truth could not tell the difference?"

Casey breathed calmly under the blade, his hands spread to either side, almost as if he invited the blow. "My lord, when I faced the trial of the lion, I spoke nothing but truth. I stated, and I have faith that Haldan will confirm, that Grant Casey would die if it was the last thing I did."

Did he dare to smile? Even the slightest crinkle of those shark-black eyes? At the far end of the chamber, Haldan made a soft noise of surprise. Blaise allowed himself an edge of righteous anger. "This order is neither game nor jest. Such a deed is daring and dangerous. Impious at best, insolent at worst. That bodes ill for your future as a knight."

Chloe, who stood to the right, tapped her wrist, only once, in mute reminder. They had other business tonight, and could not afford to fall behind.

Casey said, "I was torn, my lord, between the deceptions of my past, and the urgency of my present need. I choose the middle way, and if that has caused you to waver in your trust of me, then I understand. I wish only for the chance to prove my truth. I wish, as you have said, to reconcile my spirit with my deeds."

Thus making Blaise look like the king of hypocrites if he took action now. Casey's words were traps, a circling ring of teeth ready to bite. Blaise should have swept Casey's head from his shoulders the moment he knelt and explained it later. Another penance on his soul, to be rid of the false knight. He would risk it. After all, he had come tonight for blood.

CHAPTER FIFTY-SIX

Kyra took the microphone and placed her tablet on the podium. Her palms sweated like no presentation she'd done since the national math competition when she was twelve. All she had to do was hold their attention, guide her ROV, give Nick enough time to secure the vessel. She half-hoped they were wrong about the bombs. She would reveal her tech, win some applause, wave and smile and fend off a half-dozen warlords as she and her mother sipped cocktails on a yacht of enviable magnitude. The alternatives set chills along her spine and churned in her stomach. They were right, and they succeeded. They were right, and people died.

She plastered on a smile, which appeared on the huge screen to her right, thanks to the camera on her tablet. Good, it was communicating well. She would ordinarily take time over every stage of the technology, but had no way of knowing how much time they had. "Thank you, everyone, for indulging me." She spoke in English, the chosen language of the conference, and a few translators murmured in areas around the gathering. The American VP and her military sidekick pushed into the front row. "I know you have been expecting to see my latest in drones." She gestured toward the two drones already circling the area, their controllers down below in small fenced-off areas to keep them getting trampled by attendees while they focused on the sky.

"But today, I'd like to dive a little deeper." She shifted her gesture toward the enormous yacht behind her, and tapped the feed to live on her screen. The forward ROV camera showed blue-green shadows and the long forest of pillars that supported the platform where they all stood. Several people gasped, and a few applauded, excited to see something new—or just slightly tipsy already before they even boarded. A few of the waiters and crowd management personnel began frowning, sharing furtive glances.

The Saudi delegation, who had provided the yacht and planned the evening, stood sourly to one side, waiting for her to be through upstaging them. Nick spoke with their security man near the boat, and gained access while Mother hovered about, hands clasped as if begging the world to stop now, a phone clasped between them, the line already open.

"We can all see the magnificence that is the *Falcon*—from above. Let's take a quick tour of the vessel from below." She keyed the programmed sequence, allowing the internal computer to guide the ROV through the forest of pillars toward the pre-set target. The word now made her cringe. Fish flitted out of the way to the delight of her audience. Algae and mollusks crusted the lower parts of the pillars, making an underwater zoo full of crabs and shrimp. "We are all familiar, I think with the idea of the remotely operated vehicle, but most such have only two options: independent, programmed sequences of movement, like this one. And tethered guidance from a nearby vessel.

"You must either sacrifice flexible missions where you can reconfigure movement on the go, or you sacrifice that very mobility we demand of a remote intervention. Magnan Industries is developing an approach where we can do both, using a revolutionary communications approach." She started to veer toward commercial, and shifted her own direction, midstream. "Just as we hope that this conference will result in an upgrade of communications around the Mediterranean basin." Scattered applause.

The dark bulk of the *Falcon* emerged in the ROV's view, and she keyed a new sequence, taking control. Three large propellers came into view as the ROV drew closer. "Prop inspection for all sorts of vessels is a key use for vehicles like this one." She moved her little craft closer and skimmed to the side, scanning the image, no longer bothering to look at the crowd. A small light shone in the gloom beneath the hull where it notched inward for the propeller mounts. Kyra zoomed in and clarified. Adem cleared his throat next to her, and she forced another smile. "As you can see, I have the ability to request new information from the cameras, to choose a new angle or level of clarity. I can even—"

It was a rounded rectangle attached to the underside of the vessel, with a small panel encased in plastic and softly lit.

"What is this?" one of the Arabs demanded, striding closer. He waved one of the others to follow him and they conversed in a flurry of Arabic.

She tapped screen captures, and steered the ROV out of the shadow of the boat. "Nick, it's a go!" Kyra wrapped the microphone with her hand. To the Arab, she said, "Sir, do I take it you don't expect to see this object on your vessel?"

He shot her a furious look, and gave a tiny shake of his head. "We need to clear the deck—and move the boat. Get it away from the city," he muttered.

On the mic, Kyra said, "My Saudi associate has requested a security review. Perhaps while we complete that, I can ask the rest of the delegates to please proceed back toward the conference center."

The mayor of Limassol, who had introduced her a moment earlier, now turned on her, his back to the crowd. "Ms. Akbulut, you can't just—"

The ROV, continuing on its program, puttered slowly down the side of the vessel, drawing closer to an identical package fixed amidships. Oh, no. They were right. They were right. Kyra's stomach threatened to revolt.

On the boat, Nick's voice emerged from a loudspeaker, first in Arabic, then English. "All hands report to the upper deck for evacuation. I repeat, all hands to the upper deck."

"Who is this?" the Arab demanded, then waved that away. His PA handed him a phone and he fired off commands to the vessel himself. The engines started up, and a wash of bubbles roared past the ROV's cameras. On the second device, the LED light blinked cheerfully faster.

"Go, go, go!" the Arab shouted. He ran toward the ramp where his security man was already struggling to cast off the heavy lines.

On the deck, servers, maids and cabin crew emerged, looking puzzled, and Nick rushed out behind them. "Go! Run—get the hell out of here!" He channeled them to the stern, along the ramp. A few ran and stumbled onto the deck, a few stepped across the gap while others jumped, landing on the deck or in the water. Toward the bow someone called out. Nick spun about and ran in that direction.

On the dock, Mother helped a maid to her feet. "There's a dear, run along now." She put out her hand to steady a young crewman.

The huge vessel maneuvered around the stone arm that defended the marina, at every moment, pulling further away from the heart of the city and the hundreds gathered to see it. Nick appeared on deck again, propelling people into one of the lifeboats and slapping the button that dropped it into the sea. When was he going to get in himself?

Into the phone, Mother said, "Nick, it's time to go. Please get in the next boat, would you? Please?"

He flashed a thumbs up, then raced back inside. He tossed someone overboard into the water, the man bobbing up again in a life tube of the sort all the dock crew were wearing. A moment later, another crewman tumbled after. Kyra found her mother backing slowly up until they stood together, her mother's side pressed against her. The ROV gamely sped up, keeping pace with that awful blinking eye. The light steadied, and Kyra cried out.

Mother shouted into the phone, "Nicholas! Get off of that boat, this minute!" as if he were a child at play.

Under water, the device shivered, then exploded, expelling a rush of water. A wave ripped through the center of the boat, for an instant, utterly silent. The yacht bucked hard, tossing a few more people overboard.

"Nick!" Mother wailed. But the phone remained silent as the air shook with explosions.

CHAPTER FIFTY-SEVEN

The king's leg tensed, his foot shifted, just a little, and the blade hissed across Grant's shoulder. Grant twisted aside. Left foot to the floor. Left hand snatch up the empty pillow before him. Low lunge.

He twitched the cushion upward as the sword swung down. It sliced deep through fabric and into the foam, driving for Grant's throat. Deflect over his shoulder, shoving the blade outward and behind. Forward lunge, right hand to the sword at the king's hip.

Lebreque felt his movement and tried to recover from the swing. Too late. The king's sword slid free into Grant's hand. It swung back as he drove to his feet, and blocked Lebreque's backswing with a clang of metal. The sword was light and lively, a measure above the rest, and just as well maintained as Grant would expect. He turned, keeping low, the king and all his knights arrayed before him now, and the only way out at the far end. Shit.

Lebreque sprang forward, easy on his feet, his cape rippling and mask forbidding, like the goddamn Phantom of the Opera. Grant parried, sliced. He dove in, and danced back.

"My lord! What aid?" the tall woman demanded. Along the hall, swords swished free. Eighteen people against one. Haldan was unarmed and injured. Four knights no longer visible. Still.

"Chloe, on me!" Lebreque shouted. The king plunged toward Grant in a flurry of blows, one-sided, like an amateur. Or like a man who wanted to get Grant's back to the rest of the posse.

Grant backed up, refusing the easy way out. Sword: not his strong point. His left foot edged off the carpet. He stepped back on the right, and kicked up the carpet, fouling the enemy's advance.

The mask snarled. A break in the king's powerfully smooth demeanor. Good news or bad. Either way, Grant couldn't last long against all of them. Make it last, keep their focus—and maybe their own plans would die along with him. The tall woman had feinted left to take advantage of king's tactic. As Lebreque faltered over the rug, she launched an offensive of her own.

Backhand parry, forehand thrust. Suck in his core as the knight's blade sliced his shirt over his kidney. Too damn close. Grant swept his blade in an arc, taking the momentum like a dancer's turn, his back to the wall. One of the display cases stretched out alongside, full of the trinkets of the past. How many belonged to the siege, to the Templars embattled here who would die for their cause? Would his own relics one day be encased in glass, a curiosity of a man long dead?

When the king lunged for him, Grant leapt up, sliding a little on the sloping surface of the waist-high display case. Glass cracked underfoot—thin ice, for sure. One wrong step and his escape route became a bear trap. He tucked the sword through his belt, two running steps along the wooden edge, then he launched himself upward off his right foot. His hands wrapped the wooden beam overhead, the grain digging in. He worked his feet against the wall like a little kid climbing a tree by catching the lowest limb. A sword bit his calf as he got his legs up, wrapped the beam and shimmied his way onto the top, poised, for an instant: treed like a cougar by a ring of hounds. Still at the far end from the exits, but also out of reach.

Barred windows pierced the stone wall between the beams, modern windows set in a long row above, beckoning like a side-mounted ladder. He could do this easy. If he weren't straddling a pit full of fury with blades. No way he could lead this traverse with his left, not with the lidocaine still in effect.

"Guns!" shouted the king. "Get the guns!"

Shit. Swords, he could rise above, bullets, not so much.

Haldan started in that direction. "Aye, my lord!"

Two of the other knights outpaced him.

The king stared up at him, that silver mask reflecting his own image warped by the contours of an empty face. "Give up, Casey—there is no escape. At least take your moment like a man instead of a coward."

Grant flashed him a smile. "I will, my lord—when it comes."

He dashed across the beam, counting on speed for balance when his bad foot hit. At the far end, grab the upper window ledge, a narrow frame, unlike the foot-thick wall below that made an easy step. Grant bridged the gap, brought his left foot to follow, reached again, and stepped to the next beam. One to go, then the balcony. Fifteen feet, like a long jump back in high school, combined with a life-or-death game of "the floor is lava." The chamber below him boiled with knights. He scrambled the next gap, his left foot slipping so that he dug in with his fingers. World's worst chin up bar. He flung himself forward.

A bullet shattered the window behind his head as he wobbled, then he reached the final beam. He tumbled forward, to a cheer from the knights. Another bullet, then two, trying to keep up with his erratic movement. He jumped to the next glass case, a tall one containing a suit of armor. Grab the railing and kick off as a bullet sizzled across his thigh. The case wobbled and crashed to the floor. Glass shattered and armor clattered to the floor. The bulk of the case blocked the tower entrance below.

Grant pulled himself up to the balcony and dove through the door as bullets skittered from the metal roof and light fixtures. Down and out? The clamor of knights in the gift shop already running up to meet him. He sprinted the chamber and flung himself up the stair, bursting into dazzling sunlight. Feet pounded behind. Grant scanned in a rapid circle, bringing up what he'd seen on the way in. Two-story drop to a cobbled street at the back or side. Jump the wall to the roof of the hall he'd just escaped. And in the rose garden, a few cedar trees that peaked above the level of the low wall surrounding him.

Two knights dashed onto the rooftop, one of them arms extended.

Grant took a running leap and launched himself into the air.

CHAPTER FIFTY-EIGHT

Blaise pounded down the hall and leapt the fallen suit of armor. Two of his knights had gone ahead, the others followed as he reached the stairs and ran up. At the door to the next chamber, Haldan leaned against the wall at the base of the stairs, awkwardly holding a poleaxe with one hand, and the back of his head with the other, utterly blocking the way.

"Haldan!"

"What?" Clutching his injury, then swaying, first more into the way, forcing Blaise to stop, then back toward the wall. Blaise caught him with one hand and eased him into the room.

"Sorry, my lord, I'm sorry." He slumped against the wall.

Blaise quashed his frustration and ran, the capes of his knights vanishing up to the rooftop. The king smiled behind his mask. The only escape from there would involve a dangerous leap to a rocky landing. The coward would have to fight them. He must stand and face what he had done. Blaise bounded up the steps to the sound of gunshots. Had his knights already taken down the enemy?

Sunlight poured over him, golden and warm like a benediction from the heavens. Two knights at the far side, one of them firing—into a tree? The tree shook, the knight aimed at a new spot, and clicked onto an empty chamber. "Guns above! Come on!" Blaise roared, tempted to hurl his sword at the false knight. Two more, then a third crowded up the stairs.

"My lord, let us handle it," Chloe said. "Go to the rendezvous and prepare—there could be only moments before they—"

He glanced beyond her, beyond the tree with its fugitive to the specter of the super yacht already pulling out of the harbor. As if Casey had meant to delay him all along, but he could not possibly know the plan. "They have started the engines already."

"But it's not even six." She glanced to her watch.

"We've only moments," he murmured, but the scene looked wrong, utterly wrong for how he had envisioned it, how he and Farouk had laid it all out. Why? Because only a handful of people occupied the large upper deck of the boat, and most of them were jumping off of it. Because a lifeboat dropped into the bay on one side. Because the hundred people meant to be dying were already making their way back toward the shore. "No!" he howled. "No!"

The walkie talkie in his pocket chirped, the one which was his direct line to Farouk and his men. They'd want to know what to do, they were all expecting him to lead them. Just at that moment, Blaise had no answers. Nothing but a growing fury and a single target: Grant Casey.

CHAPTER FIFTY-NINE

Grant scrambled to the back of the tree, spiraling a little downward as he went. Branches slapped his face and scraped his hands. The tree shuddered with his own movement and the bullets that pounded into the—thankfully thick, old—trunk. On the other side, knights shouted, the king and his female lieutenant spoke in Turkish—then he broke off abruptly.

Into that silence, an explosion. No, not one, four. One after another after another after another.

Grant turned his head, his eyes now on a level with the rooftops that sloped down toward the sea. The arm of the jetty flexed into the Mediterranean as if it defended the marina from the floating fireball that roiled just beyond. Waves rushed from the yacht, swooped up the jetty and crashed back again, flinging aside a dozen smaller craft. Two sections of the white hull rocked, topped with flames and billowing smoke. Smaller explosions followed: gas for cooking, reserves, anything flammable, bursting with deadly power. Half the yacht had been disintegrated, raining debris down into the ocean, the jetty, the heads of the bobbing survivors. The king hadn't ordered anything: the bomb went off without him.

Grant let himself drop, crashing through branches, arms protecting his head, knees tucked. The branches slowed him, tossed him side to side and spilled him onto the ground where one of the rosebushes stopped his roll. The sword's hilt dug into his spine as it shifted with his movement.

He tore free of the bushes and ran.

Overhead, someone started firing again.

Grant kept to the garden, following the line of trees. He reached the fence, grabbed the top rail, his hands sticky with pitch and stinging from a thousand tiny scrapes. He pulled hard, got one foot up and was over, dropping to the other side into a roll, collecting bruises over scrapes over bullet trails. And none of it mattered.

Some long ago yogini, during his recovery period, spoke of moving energy through your body with each breath. He sucked at the air and sent the energy to his left foot. Let it sustain him. Let it not fail him now. He fled down the curved road, the first scent of smoke seizing him, hot with the memory of everything in his life that had ever blown sky high.

Everything. And everyone.

Sirens started up somewhere beyond. People gathered in the street, calling out to one another in fear and wonder.

Nick hadn't been on the ship. He would've gotten off by then. He was good. Solid. Nimble in spite of his leg.

Last time a boat blew up, Grant had been on a coral atoll in the Caribbean, and the men shooting at him had been on board. D.A. rigged their own destructive cell phones against them. Nick held a grudge about the fact he hadn't been there as back-up. Lot of things Nick could do, but pretend to be a white supremacist wasn't one of them.

And one time, they had blown up together.

"Sir!" A uniformed woman addressed him in Arabic, her hands raised in front of him, dozens of people streaming past her away from the marina, guided by other officers. "You can't go this way. We need you to stay back."

He sidestepped, not getting into her space. He was one block short of the marina now. Dodge down the street alongside a Pizza Hut. The beginnings of a sunset competed with the ball of fire to cast its glow across the deep blue sea. The trail around the harbor was already thick with gawkers, civilians and conference delegates, tourists having a show. Fucking dinner theater. But who'd been barbecued?

"Out of the way!" Grant shouted in Arabic.

He slid between them. People stumbled at his advance, crying out at the sight of the sword at his back— "Shifra!"

At the edge of the path, he stripped off his jacket. Three more steps and he dove, arcing long over the stones that supported the trail, his hands sweeping ahead of him to break the water. Deep breath and the plunge. He kicked hard, streaming through the water and broke the surface, stroking now past the boats tied at their slips, heedless of shouting, bullhorns, and the flotsam that plied these protected waters. Crazy man swimming past the police cordon with a sword in his belt: terrorist for sure. Either go ahead and shoot or shut the fuck up.

Grant swam to the t-shaped end of the pier and found a ladder, dragging himself from the water, gasping for breath. Dockhands and a few boat dwellers stood here, transfixed by the tower of smoke that poured from beyond. He staggered past them. Saltwater stung his skin at every scrape and injury.

Someone else tried to get in his way, and he strong-armed them aside, passing the back of the screen, ducking the cordons around the conference gathering area.

"Sir! You can't be here—" someone shouted behind him.

Too late. He already was.

"Security! He's got a sword!" or words to that effect. Fear sounded the same no matter the language. He almost dared them to tackle him.

A long dark braid hung against a woman's back near the podium, one of a handful of civilians remaining on the pier: target acquired. Heads turned as the warning rang out, security already inbound to his location, their path eased by the tiny knots of people remaining.

Almost there. His breath hitched. His power drained as if his battered skin could no longer hold it.

Kyra spun about as he approached. "Casey!" She and her mother ran to him, intercepting the guards.

"He's with me," Kyra shouted, waving back the guards.

"Nick," he gasped, braced his hands on his knees. "Was he on the boat?"

The women grabbed hands in reflexive comfort.

"Yes, I think so, yes," Irene said.

Kyra clarified, "He was on the deck, moving people along, getting everyone else to safety."

He raised his head.

Tears streamed down Irene's face and her voice trembled. She clutched a cell phone like a relic to her chest. "He doesn't answer."

The numbness of lidocaine spread through his body, every nerve, every muscle, numbing his skin, his heart, his mind, and he hadn't even needed the shot.

"Grant Casey, I presume."

He wanted to fall back into the water, to dive the wreck over and over and not emerge without Nick in his arms. The definition of futile. Grant hauled himself to vertical, his feet planted, most of his weight on his right, his left leg trembling.

Major Wilson wore his full dress uniform, his puffed-up chest covered with ribbons and medals. A step behind him, with her chorus line of Secret Service agents, stood the vice president.

The sword at Grant's back nudged his hip as he stood. He imagined the draw, the slice of that beautiful length of metal shearing the air. A clean sweep of the blade would open the Major's throat and rain down blood to stain Grant's face and freshly salt his wounds. "Major Wilson, you are absolutely the last person on the face of the planet who should be arm's length from me right now."

"Come on now, Casey." Wilson waved a hand toward the inferno. "You were right, don't you want to lord that over me?" Then he glanced in that direction, and his eyebrows rose. "Unless you think your buddy out there maybe hit a speed bump?"

Grant drew a breath, and channeled every ounce of power remaining to him into six square inches. His fist slammed into the major's face.

CHAPTER SIXTY

Something cracked when Casey punched the major. Major Wilson staggered, his hand rising to his face, his face flaming nearly as red as —Kyra shook off her stupor, Insha'Allah it was Wilson's jaw that broke not Casey's hand. The Secret Service started forward, converging on Casey. Kyra intervened, stalking between them. "Back off."

To Casey, she said, "I've ordered Kostas and the zodiac out there, as close as they can safely get. The police and fire have boats on the way as well. The ROV was kicked back by the explosion, but it re-targeted. It's recording, but I took it off the screen." It had shown footage of the hull torn open, machinery and deck chairs flung about, legs flailing into the water. The churning stuff of nightmares.

Casey made no reply. He sank to one knee, his left leg curled under him, fingers braced on the ground, head bowed. He had a sword tucked through his belt, and the blade chimed against the decking, as if it sighed in mourning. Blood seeped from scrapes across his skin and a little faster from a few larger cuts, one across his bicep, carving into his tattoos. His hair dripped over his face, his shoulders hitching with every breath. The sight of him like that horrified her.

"Honestly, Major, if he chose to throttle you, right here and now," the vice president drawled, "I'd call it justifiable homicide."

"He needs a hospital," Mother volunteered. She caught Kyra's arm and pulled her closer, whispering in Turkish, "His foot. Something's very wrong, and he'd rather you didn't know."

Kyra closed her hand over her mother's arm. To their audience, Kyra snapped, "You heard the woman."

"We've got ambulances on the way, for those the rescue boats are bringing in," the mayor said. He paced from the Americans to the edge of the pier where the Arabs and the security supervisors clustered over the images Kyra had captured. Adem hovered with them, answering questions and sending screen shots. Most of the delegates had been herded out of the way, draining back toward the bars and hotels past a checkpoint meant to confirm who had lived and who had died.

"Mr. Mayor." Kyra walked after the mayor halting him in his tracks. "If not for Mr. Casey, over one hundred people would have been on that boat, and you would need more than a few dinghies to collect them, you would need fishing nets and body bags. You will get him an ambulance immediately."

"But he wasn't even—" the mayor began, a poor little man caught in circumstance much larger than himself.

"She's right," Wilson mumbled, still cradling his jaw. "He's the one who raised the alarm. I need medical attention, too, but definitely not in the same ride."

"I have a diplomatic limousine just down the way," the vice president said. "Let's go." Then cut her eyes to Wilson. "Him, not you."

"Mr. Casey?" Mother said, reaching out for him, as she had been reaching out to the victims since Nick began the evacuation.

Casey rose unsteadily, and pinned Kyra with his gaze. "Will you hold this for me? Might need it later." He reached behind him and drew forth the blade, holding it close to his chest carefully point down, to appear nonthreatening. Standing like that, he looked eerily like an effigy for a knight's tomb.

Kyra reached out to accept it, and the sword hung heavy in her hands. "What of the king?"

Casey's gaze shifted back toward land. "Ceremony at the castle, but they were in a hurry to get back here, before the explosion. Must've been on a timer—he didn't make the call. He got a signal on a walkie talkie as I was leaving. Guessing they called off whatever they had in mind."

"Good work," she said.

He seemed about to speak, then simply gave a nod, and a brief salute. Dismissing himself from duty. Mother didn't actually touch him, but her hands hovered near. She glanced back at Kyra, then handed her the phone. "I'm going with him." As if the two mercenaries were her personal charges and she refused to lose another one. She joined in as the vice president's phalanx led the way. Casey limped among them, defeated.

Sword in one hand, phone in the other, there had to be something else for Kyra to do. Handing off the sword to Adem and sliding the phone into a pocket, she stalked over to where the two drone pilots had stood in their little cordon. One of the stanchions lay on its side, the pilots gone. One transmitter still lay there, like an oversized game controller with a small monitor in the center showing a slanted view of a few boats. In the absence of commands, the drone had landed in a clear zone, awaiting orders. Kyra scooped up the transmitter and tapped the home button. After a moment, the drone appeared from the direction of the buildings and landed at her feet. She launched again immediately.

"We need to clear the area, ma'am," someone told her.

"My people are the reason you're not dead." She watched the drone soar away toward the smoke. "I move for no one."

The smoke stung her eyes and nostrils as the drone's propellers swirled it around, then the wind shifted a bit. She lifted the transmitter to where she could see the monitor and glance up to see the target zone. It was hard to miss the plume of smoke. Even from here, the wind felt warmer than it had just a few minutes before. Two small boats worked the inner edge of the marina, fishing people out of the water. The lifeboats Nick had filled bobbed toward the piers, the people inside huddling, sometimes weeping, covering their ears. From so close, it must have been deafening. No sign of Kostas and her own zodiac.

Beyond the jetty, larger, less maneuverable boats shifted away, clearing the area near the yacht both to save their own vessels and to allow rescue and fire boats to close in. The fire suddenly roared higher, reaching some stash of flammable materials, and Kyra jolted the drone out of the way.

Another small boat plied the waters there, containing a few men dressed as dock workers and waiters. Survivors or terrorists? Smoke washed over her view, then the drone skewed sideways and dropped, the angle tumbling and ending with a splashdown and darkness. As if it had been shot from the sky.

CHAPTER SIXTY-ONE

After the debacle at the castle, Blaise doffed his mask and cape, and tried very, very hard, to doff his fury. He put in an appearance at the checkpoint and made sure he was marked safe and accounted for in the chaos of the aftermath. Ozan seized his hand and went on about how Allah had defended them all, and he should return to his prayer schedule—but first, he required a stiff drink, and wouldn't Blaise like to come along.

"No, thank you, Baris." Blaise smiled and tipped his head toward the door where Chloe lingered, clad in touristy capri pants and a broad hat. "I came to this young lady's aid during the...difficulties earlier, and I have promised to return her safely to her hotel."

"Oh, ho!" The lawyer grinned and winked, slapping his meaty hand against Blaise's shoulder. "If I didn't have a wife back home—well. Maybe this once, she'd understand, eh?"

Once? A moment earlier, Ozan proclaimed himself returning to the fold of the faithful, now he drank and philandered as if Mohamed had been a rock idol instead of a prophet. Among Blaise's many regrets, the fact that Ozan still lived should be lower on the list. It should be. Blaise needed a proper seclusion, and wished he had brought the head of Baphomet along with them to focus his mind as it should be. Instead, he responded as graciously as he could, and, under the cover of the mayor's placating speech, strolled over to meet Chloe. He settled his hand at her back, precisely as if they were what Ozan believed, lovers made by the shared experience of fear.

"What is it?" he said as they moved beyond the checkpoint. He slipped his hand away when they were beyond the view of those within.

"My lord, I had a call from my contact. It began with an apology."

As well it should.

"He's on Akbulut's vessel. The manuscript is there and he wants to know if there's anything else you need from it or were the pictures enough."

"He's on the vessel, but she isn't—" Blaise pulled out his walkie talkie and triggered it.

After a moment, Farouk came on. "I wondered if you ever would get back to me. We need to talk."

"Akbulut. She's still on the pier?"

A growl, a holler to someone else, then, "Still there," then "Allah! He's here, Yusef. I swear it's him. Gimme the gun, the rifle, give it to me."

"Don't shoot anyone now!" Blaise commanded. "How many police are out there? Do you want to get caught?"

"My men came here ready for martyrdom, your highness, and now we've seen the man who betrayed us."

Blaise stopped short. To Chloe, he muttered, "We'll call him right back, okay?" She nodded and stepped a little apart. They stood in the gloom of an empty street halfway between the castle and the convention center, a few blocks off the harbor where the giant lights over the wreck site made a glow in the sky almost as bright as the inferno. "You know the man who gave up our plan?"

"New recruit came to us, asking for a wife, willing to die. This was yesterday. I don't trust him, I'm not a fool, but I give him a wife—the one he wants, it's that one you sent, the thieving bitch.

"This man, this Yusef, he and his wife stole all these women and took them away. They must have planned this. They must have known each other before and worked it all out. You sent us a spy."

"I did nothing of the kind. I sent you a thief, a woman who refused to return to virtue and thus would benefit from your instruction, nothing more. So far as I know, the woman was a free agent, unaffiliated." Unless she was part of the Nizari. It was perhaps best to if Farouk did not know the Nizari had Blaise on their list. Unless... Blaise closed his eyes, remembering the day he captured her, the baker's van, the Bone Guard who hesitated torn for a moment between covering his client, and defending a woman who was, theoretically, a stranger. "This Yusef, what does he look like?"

Farouk shrugged expansively. "Like you. Like me. Coppery skin, dark hair, dark eyes, skinny. My men thought they'd got him because he hit a caltrop on his way out—they found it in the road, covered in blood, but it doesn't seem to have slowed him down in his getaway. Now what am I going to do for my men? No martyrdom. No wives to offer, and half of those women she stole were already married. What if they're carrying Shifra babies?"

Hit a caltrop... *twisted his ankle, he said.* Haldan's words. No, it hadn't slowed him down. Casey had stolen the wives of the Shifra and learned enough to evacuate the ship, then run again from Blaise himself. The rage he'd been suppressing exploded in a white-heat.

"Damn it! He's getting in a car—he's leaving!" Farouk let out a string of inventive curses describing exactly what should be done to various parts of Casey's anatomy. Crude, but agreeable.

"Farouk, you have a tender? Good." He turned to Chloe. "Your friend. Tell him we're coming to the boat. There's a lot of money for him if he lets us in."

CHAPTER SIXTY-TWO

G rant endured an hour or more of surgery under local anesthetic. Didn't matter where he looked, the day's events ran on an endless loop before his eyes: a last salute from Nick, spotting the king, following Haldan, running for his life, arriving way too late to stop the blazing inferno. Nick's last salute.

His hand ached from punching Major Wilson. So unprofessional, with his client right there. With the goddamn vice president right there. His skin had so many scratches and bruises he felt flayed from head to toe. Scrapes from stone; cuts from broken glass—hadn't even noticed when that happened; the shallow puncture of a sword's point; two gouges from near-thing bullets, one of which carved his ink to hell; scratched by tree bark and branches; skewered by the rosebushes. For nothing. For no intel, for a bomb he didn't stop, for a friend he couldn't save.

They finally wheeled him into a recovery room, his arm and thigh wrapped in bandages, his foot propped up and thoroughly swaddled. Irene reappeared, recovered from her nerves, and ready to mother him. Might as well let her, it made one of them feel better.

The doctor arrived a few minutes later, speaking in rapid Greek. Irene stopped her with an imperious hand, and Grant caught a glimpse of where Kyra got it from. "Doctor, I can translate, but please be patient," she told him, repeating her words in English and Greek.

With Irene translating, the doctor said, "Whoever took care of your foot did quite well under the circumstances, but your recent activities have worsened the situation, as I'm sure you are aware. If there is no sign of infection in the morning, I may be able to discharge you, but I would urge you to put no pressure on it for at least a couple of weeks. You must give yourself time to heal."

Honestly, that last part might have been strictly Irene. He met the doctor's eye. "What can you give me so I can walk on it tomorrow?"

Irene glowered at him, and spoke.

The doctor glowered as well. "That's a very bad idea, Mr. Casey. Very, very bad," she said in decent English, then let fly with a tirade in Greek, which Irene summarized as, "She's got many, many reasons why you shouldn't walk tomorrow." She raised her hands with a helpless smile, the sort of fond sadness of the grown-up who knows she won't be obeyed.

Grant looked down at his hands, the hospital wristband tracking over a ring of scars. He wished he could go back to his field medic, either one of them. Akilah knew he needed to move. She worried, she shrugged, she gave him the shots. And Nick would've busted his ass for not sitting still, then given him a hand up to get back on his feet. Same time, he could be making it worse. How bad? No bone damage, just muscle and nerve. He'd recover. Someday. Unless Grant Casey was slated to die again, this time in a hospital in Cyprus.

"The men who did this are still out there, both sides." He shot Irene a look. "Me, out of commission, is not an option. I need the doctor to give me another choice, or I will get out of this bed and go find one."

A brisk hand knocked on the wall that separated his alcove from the next. The Veep stood there, just past the curtain, with only two Secret Service agents this time.

"I'm glad to see you on the mend. May I come in?" She was an angular woman, ex-lawyer. Hair in a fashionable cut, blouse carefully chosen to feminize without making her look girly.

"No visitor," the doctor said. "He need rest."

"Please do, ma'am," Grant replied. "How's Major Asshole?"

"His jaw is cracked, but not badly. I'll have to put up with his small talk for a few more days at least. He'll be trying to ingratiate himself before his likely demotion." She took a few steps toward him in the narrow aisle between the bed and the wall. "Under other circumstances, I'd love to make this a photo op. Headline story about two American veterans thwarting a terrorist action and saving the lives of hundreds. America's armed forces could use that kind of publicity."

Before he could protest, she folded her arms. "However, I know this is not the time nor the place. My boss feels otherwise, but he wasn't here." She flashed him her big politician grin. "There's two officers outside, one Turkish, one of ours, who'd like to ask you some questions and get a start on tracking the evil doers. After that, you need some rest, no matter what you have in mind. Your security detail is fully covered, and they answer to you—you tell them you don't like the look of somebody, they're gone."

"Thank you, ma'am."

To the other side, the doctor flipped pages on a clipboard as if she could tear them to bits right then.

"Anything else you need, Lieutenant Casey, you say the word. I will give you my direct line." She gave him a salute and stepped back. "I know it sounds especially inane right now, but truly, thank you for your service." She turned to go.

"Actually," Grant called, stopping her at the curtain. "Two things. I need a cell phone, smart phone, full service. ASAP."

She pointed to one of the agents, who gave a nod and strode away. "Done. What else?"

"A helicopter. On the roof at oh-seven hundred, with permission to enter Syrian airspace."

CHAPTER SIXTY-THREE

Farouk brought his tender to the back of the Akbulut yacht, anchored outside the marina. In retrospect—as what wouldn't be now—Blaise should have suspected their mode of arrival, keeping their own expensive vessel far from the target zone. He should have known they knew too much. Casey now lay in the local hospital with Secret Service men to protect him while Kyra Akbulut herself was likely holed up with the Saudis and the anti-terrorism experts sharing everything her little trick had discovered. He should give her to Farouk as a special present. They had passed quietly from the outer marina where Farouk had been smart enough to berth after he and his crew became part of the rescue effort—scooping a few more Shifra members from the water where the Black man had cast them.

Blaise had waited until those men piled out before leaving the shadows to accept his ride, with Chloe and Darius a step behind him. Haldan wanted to resume his duties, but he looked exhausted, as worn out by the castle scene as Blaise had felt, and he insisted his lieutenant retire to the hotel for the night. Haldan suffered the moral angst and remorse of having brought the false knight into their midst. When the chance arose, they would speak of penance, but Blaise was inclined toward lenience. He, too, had found "Michael Donahue" to be a worthy candidate.

Most of Shifra still believed their only objective had been death and destruction. Even from Farouk he would prefer to stay distant, but he did admit to certain obligations. The wreck lay bathed in light, partially thrusting from the shallows and surrounded by police, army, and gawkers like buzzards at a predator's kill. He had expected less to remain of the vessel, but that wasn't his department.

Akbulut's ship, though substantial for a private yacht, looked like a toy after the Arab's *Falcon*. He contemplated torching it when they were done, and felt slightly ashamed at this vindictive streak he thought he had suffocated decades ago. On the dive platform, a man paced in short strides, turning about fast at the sound of their motor.

"I thought you would be faster. She could get here at any moment." He had a thick Greek accent to go along with his mustache.

"Have you spoken with her since the accident?" Blaise accepted the hand up to the deck, letting Farouk tie off the boat.

The man shook his head. "Not since she sent me with the rescue parties, but I should be calling in soon. It has been two hours or more. She —" a tip of the head toward Chloe— "told me not to talk with anyone else about anything. I—never mind. What are you looking for?"

Blaise walked past him, making room for the other three. The man offered a quick, nervous smile to Chloe, who graciously smiled in return. "Where did you pick up Casey?"

"I'd rather. I just." The man gulped and glanced again at Chloe. "Look, I don't want to make trouble, I just need a little extra, that's all. If you tell me what you're looking for, then I can help you."

Blaise faced him, employing a stern, but kindly expression. "I am looking for information. The faster we have it, the sooner we shall leave and let you carry on with what you must. Agreed?"

The man's mustache ruffled, then he nodded. "We picked up the other man at Tartus. It wasn't me, his friend went to get him."

Blaise nodded. "And between? Where else have you gone?" He prowled down the corridor into the living quarters, stopping first at what should have been a bedroom but instead held a fully fitted workshop with a hundred tiny drawers all secured against spillage at sea, and a number of tools neatly arranged. Some electronic components filled the bins, but only parts, nothing ready for her use. "Well?'

"Arwad. We anchored for a while off the coast, and she ran her little submarine, taking a lot of pictures."

"Wonderful, that's very good to know, thank you." The clue from the cafe had led them to Arwad—another Templar fortress. "See? Just information." Blaise gestured toward the doors to either side, narrowly spaced from the next ones.

"Crew berths, mine and Muminah's."

"No need to violate your privacy." Blaise kept smiling, as if he were a cheerful harbormaster eager to get the ship inspected and underway. "This?"

"Irene. Ms. Akbulut's mother."

Blaise popped the door, and scanned, but did not enter. "The codex?"

"It's in his room. Their room." The man glanced upward, then offered that nervous smile again. "Really, we can't take much time."

Blaise was beginning to wonder if he had a woman upstairs waiting for him. Or a man—in any case, a liaison he'd rather not have discovered. "This?"

"Empty. The two men share a cabin." He reached forward, not able to pass Blaise in the narrow hall and pointed toward the next door. "Ms. Akbulut is at the end."

Opening the door to the men's room, Blaise entered, gesturing for Darius to accompany him while Chloe remained in the hall, looking pretty for their uncomfortable host.

"What are we doing here?" Farouk demanded in Arabic.

"Finding information, as I said."

Farouk snorted and stalked back the way they had come. The pilot called, "Sir, please don't! Sir?"

Blaise directed Darius to take up the manuscript, wrapped in linen, from the table. In a drawer, he found a phone and a few other things, presumably the true contents of Casey's pockets. He tapped at the phone, not expecting much. Worth taking? Not if it might lead the Bone Guard to him. He replaced it. On the other side of the room, a few pill bottles, a kit full of tools for some specialized work. Both sides cleanly organized, few possessions, nothing of a personal nature.

"Your majesty!" Farouk shouted from above—knowing how much that title annoyed Blaise— "You'll want to see this."

"Oh?" Blaise gave up the search and Chloe, who stood blocking their host into the bow section of the hallway, stepped further to let her ruler pass.

"Please!" the man squeaked.

Blaise mounted the outside stairs and came up to a back deck with a patio table and chairs, then entered the glassed-in lounge where Farouk spread his arms in grand presentation. When he saw the gift he was offered, just like when the bombs burst on the ocean, Blaise felt as if the darkness had once more turned to day.

CHAPTER SIXTY-FOUR

A bsolutely not." Kyra planted her palms on the table and stood up, leaning in. In the police department's cramped conference room— the more cramped by the dozen people now crammed inside of it —she was conspicuously the only female, and none of these people had given her their names. Half of the men twitched when she spoke and would not look at her naked face. They spoke obliquely, addressing the walls or the light fixtures.

"Madam, this is a major terrorist incident. It is hardly up to you," said the Arab with the pointiest beard. His two companions barely spoke at all.

"Of course we are very grateful for all of you help, all of it," said the Cypriot captain, his lips stretched into something meant to be cheerful. With his fringe of stiff, brown hair, he resembled a badly carved coconut.

"Sir. It was my team that uncovered the plot—one of them is in the hospital and one—after evacuating your people from the boat—remains missing, as does the man I sent with my own zodiac to aid in the rescue efforts."

They had known that Nick was in trouble, of course: he'd been right there at the flashpoint. Strange, not to have heard from Kostas for so long, but it was possible his phone became waterlogged during the rescue efforts. He had brought a few people to the jetty, then returned to the wreck site, but the smoke kept shifting, the chaos growing, and nobody had seen him since. Adem murmured on his phone in the corner, then rang off of another call. The sword lay wrapped in Casey's recovered jacket across Adem's lap, and he defended it as a sacred charge. He caught her eye and gave a shake of his head. Still no sign of Nick. Or of his body.

Kyra returned her focus to the matter at hand. "It was my technology that revealed any of this and captured the proof, the rest of the proof is now floating or sinking on the waves outside." She slashed her hand through the air toward the harbor beyond the walls. "I have given you every assistance, and your men are badgering Mr. Casey in his hospital room as we speak. I am not entrusting a unique prototype to your security, nor am I leaving a tablet full of my confidential information in your care."

"This will be an international effort, Ms. Akbulut," said the Turkish intelligence representative, his fingers steepled on the table, giving him something to look at other than her. "I can assure you that security will be at the utmost."

"Like it was four hours ago?"

The Turk gazed at his hands, the Arab at the wall, the Cypriot's grimace twisted at the corners as if his coffee cup pained him.

"Perhaps you can understand why I might place no trust in local security." Kyra slapped the table and the Turk flinched, his gaze darting up toward her. "Check your office phone records. Confiscate those why don't you? I called your office ten hours ago. Ten. Hours. And you would not even take my call," she spat, the words loathsome on her tongue. "Sergeant, what is the record of the dead?" She pointed to her right.

The military attaché flicked back through his notes. "As of now, we have confirmed five dead, four in critical condition, and an additional eight people still missing." He pushed his glasses up. "Including your men. And an uncertain number of minor injuries."

"How many people were on the guest list for that party? How many crew were on that vessel?" She focused on the Arab, but nothing would make him look at her.

"We understand your point," he told the wall opposite. "Indeed we owe you a great debt. Indeed, if some of our intelligence services had received your messages earlier, even this loss of life could have been averted.

There will be a separate investigation to determine our intelligence failures in this regard. None of this alters the fact that your devices are evidence. I assure you the greatest caution will be taken with any personal data, and your prototype will be returned to you as promptly as may be."

The Cypriot police captain nudged a piece of paper toward her across the table. A receipt, taking responsibility for her ROV and her tablet. Kyra's braid slapped her back as she shook her head. Loose hairs frayed across her forehead. "It's unacceptable. Absolutely." Trust the Arabs to keep her technology private? To secure her data? Just as well trust the falcon to watch the pigeons.

The American groaned and stretched in his seat. "It's very late," he said at last. "And it seems like this discussion is only going round in circles."

It wasn't the man Casey had punched, but perhaps another one who deserved a punch of his own. "Because I am not satisfied with this arrangement. Not at all."

"I believe you have made your concerns abundantly clear, Ms. Akbulut. It's now time for this commission to move on." He stared at her pointedly. "And for you to move on as well. We'll be in touch in the morning, I am sure."

A gentle, familiar voice. Adem said, "Ms. Akbulut, perhaps it's time to speak with the lawyers."

"Yes, I think it is." She pivoted, intending to stride right out of the room, then realized they had no way to return to the *Altin Hayal* with Kostas and the zodiac still missing. She unclenched her jaw and said, "I shall require a ride back to our boat. It has been a very long day, and it seems not to be over yet."

Four men immediately stood, chairs scraping, talking over each other to offer assistance. The Saudi representative merely put up his hands in a little shrug. "I wish I could, but I must find my own accommodations, since ours have..." Another little shrug.

The Cypriot coastal force had the closest tenders, so she followed a young officer toward their dock, Adem trailing along after her, the sword tucked under his arm, remembrance of their absent companions. "Thank you, Adem," she said softly, "For letting me know it was time to go." Past time, in truth. A sense of defeat cloaked her shoulders, and she recalled too vividly the image of Grant Casey's graceful collapse to the dock, his posture half runner-at-the-blocks, and half "The Dying Gaul." Desperate for action, and knowing with heavy certainty, that nothing could be done.

They stood in the darkness, watching city lights flicker on the water, deliberately not looking to the glow of the wreck. Now that the work was over and her hands were still, Kyra kept flashing back to the way the ship buckled, the hull rending, the roar of the explosion. Followed by screaming, shouts, sirens, the thrashing of legs in the water.

Something buzzed against her side and she jumped. Adem put a hand at her waist, preventing her from stumbling toward the water. The buzzing continued, and Kyra snatched her phone from her pocket. Kostas? The hospital or one of the makeshift clinics working with the survivors? Let it be Nick. Insha'Allah, let him be found! An unfamiliar number showed on her screen.

She wet her lips and answered, "Kyra Akbulut."

"Kyra. Grant Casey. Don't go to the boat—it's been compromised."

"What?" She blocked her other ear against the sound of the tender starting up. "Compromised?"

"I called home. D.A. got a notification of attempted tampering on my cell. The one I left in my cabin."

"Oh." All she wanted was her pleasant bed in the cradle of the sea. Kyra stared at the sky, the lights above in the blue-black night mirroring the lights below. "I am so tired," she breathed, not sure she had spoken aloud until he answered.

"Ma'am, I know just what you mean. I hope you don't have trouble finding a room. Thanks for helping me get to mine."

"You're sure about the boat? There's no other possibility?"

He drew a deep breath on his end of the line, then said, "Kyra, you and your technology delivered evidence of a terrorist attack, one in which the architects are still at large. It's better if they don't know where you sleep tonight."

Better if they didn't know where she slept. Because she had seen what they did to a boat much larger than her own.

"Your mother's here with me. Give this number a call when you know where you're staying so I can send her over."

"Sleep well."

"You, too."

She was about to ring off when he said, "Kyra, please accept my apologies about what happened on the dock. My behavior was highly unprofessional. I'll be back on the job tomorrow."

She actually laughed, recognizing the nervous response for what it was. "I agree with the vice president, Mr. Casey. Given all that has happened—" better to mention Nick? How much they all missed him? Perhaps not. "Given that you had a sword in your possession, merely punching him seemed to me a model of restraint."

She hung up, and the officer beckoned her down the ramp, but she turned to Adem. "We can't stay on the boat tonight."

He nodded. "I have a cousin in town I meant to stay with when you called me in. Let me see if she has room."

"Sorry—we'll stay on land!" she called to the officer, who duly turned off the engine. The stillness felt more calm, letting her shoulders sink back down when she hadn't noticed them rising. The way the yacht lurched and buckled, the flames surging above, the legs of the survivors kicking, desperate to flee—

Kyra spun about, leaving Adem where he stood, phone again pressed to his ear, sword tucked under his arm. "I'm going back in!" She ran for the door before he had a chance to respond, flinging herself, breathless, at the dividing wall that separated a small reception area from the inner offices. A bulletproof window allowed her to see the duty officer with his all-important buzzer to open the inner door. Kyra knocked on the glass and the officer looked at her quizzically, then poked an intercom button. "How can I help you?" he asked in Turkish.

"The task force, for the attack, I need to see them—to speak to them."

"I'm sorry, ma'am, but they're in a closed session. If you'd like to fill out an incident or witness report—"

"I am Kyra Akbulut. They will open for me."

The man tipped back his hat, scratching his head underneath. "I don't think so, ma'am." He pointed to the phone on his desk. "See that red light? It means no calls on that line. I suggest you go to your hotel, and I will let them know you came by."

"I didn't come by: I was in there, inside. I only left a few minutes ago, you buzzed me out."

"These men have important duties, ma'am. They're already very busy." He blinked at her, unflappable.

"I know what to do, how to look for him. I need that tablet." The search algorithm spun through her head. Admittedly, underwater video feed would be tough to analyze, but still. If he jumped off that boat on the starboard side, where her ROV was filming, she would have it on the footage, surely Nick's swim pattern would be distinctive, surely she could—

"You sound a little hysterical, ma'am. I know it's frightening to be—"

"You do not dismiss me!" She slammed her hands on the narrow counter, and he twitched back on the other side.

"Ma'am, I suggest you have a seat and take a few deep breaths, maybe call somebody to help you get to your hotel. If you continue to behave this way, I'll need to send somebody out there." He ostentatiously lifted his finger off the intercom, and, after a moment, dropped his gaze back to whatever cartoon show he was watching on his monitors.

She stood beyond the barricade, the duty officer already turning back to his work, pointedly ignoring her. Kyra wanted to shout. She wanted to cry, and she knew that neither reaction would help at all. She knew what to do, and she was utterly helpless.

CHAPTER SIXTY-FIVE

When Kyra's call came through with an address, Irene rose from her chair at the foot of Grant's hospital bed. "I'm sure we'll find him."

Grant's throat tightened, and he gave a nod. "Ma'am, I won't give up until I do." He held out his hand to her. "Thank you for taking care of me."

Her cheeks flushed as she stepped up to accept, her hand warm and strong beneath thin, wrinkled skin like the golden linen of a treasured time. "It was nothing, I'm sure." She blinked a few times, weariness writ plain. "Kyra never lets me, you know. Not since she was eight. And less so since her father passed."

"Irene." He held her gaze. "You are invaluable. I think she's starting to see that."

She smiled bravely and took her leave, both proud and fragile, and he wondered how he was going to ditch her before the flight tomorrow. No way he was taking her into a hot zone.

Grant sank back into the bed. Client and client's mother to alternate location, check. Law enforcement briefed, check—not that they trusted half of what he said, it was, after all, hearsay from a woman he'd married under false pretenses, and they didn't have to know he'd taken her to bed. He needed to get stronger evidence, something tangible to share with the intelligence community to take down both the knights and Shifra. Meantime, get D.A. on the line to finish the conversation that had begun with his new phone number, and ended two exchanges later with her urgent warning to pass on to Kyra before her own boat (maybe) blew up.

D.A. picked up immediately. "Next time you're gonna kill yourself, Chief, would you give HR a heads up? It's pretty inconvenient having to field calls from the New York Times in the blind at one a.m. I think I set the army straight, and got a few more releases out, working to counteract the rumor."

He had told her the plan the night before he executed it—ideal word choice, really. For his purposes, she couldn't immediately contradict the news coming out of Turkey, though some level of official denial always made a rumor sound more legit. They had just underestimated how fast the news would spread. Good new/bad news about the Bone Guard being high-vis on international gossip radar.

"Thanks," he said, then, "There's more." And maybe the tone of his voice clued her in. Every time his thoughts moved to Nick, he tensed with the need for action. Grant stared at the heart monitor, watching the peaks and valleys, the rise and fall of his own life until they moved a little slower, the mountains a little lower.

"Tell me."

Control his tone. Don't let his voice give him away. "Nick is MIA. He was on the ship, running the evac." Where was he now? Was he injured? Had he gotten his medication on time, or gone down that dark passage toward madness? Was he blown to pieces when the bombs went off, scattered to chum the waters, his prosthetic an unrecognized piece of wreckage? Or had he drowned? Was he drifting below the surface, carried on unseen currents, maybe never to be seen again, blank eyes staring toward the distant sky?

"No sign?"

He swallowed. "No sign."

"Oh, hell, Chief." Her voice rasped.

Both fell silent on opposite ends of the connection, opposite sides of the world.

"They'll keep looking. Not many folks on that ship matching his description." He clamped a hand over his mouth, the mountains rising, his ribcage closing in. *Details, not ops.* It was meant to be their fucking vacation. His eyes burned, his lungs burned, and he was blown to pieces as if he'd been on that vessel, expecting a party, unprepared for the fireworks.

"Chief. Grant. I'm so sorry."

Grant peeled away his hand, forced it to relax. He breathed carefully, trying to sink those mountains. "We don't know that he's dead."

"How are you?"

"Calling from the hospital, but I'll get out in the morning."

"What are your injuries?" she asked, and when he did not immediately reply, she growled, "I can't talk to you if you won't talk to me."

"You're sig-int, D.A., so here's the deal. If I start broadcasting my sitrep, I'm just as likely to go off the air permanently." He and Nick had a deal, heads-up in times of trouble out there, or inside. And Nick— He pinched the bridge of his nose, stopping the thoughts that circled behind his eyes. Don't let go, don't let go, do not let go.

Long pause, full of D.A.'s careful breathing. "I copy, Chief," she said softly. "You get out in the morning. What happens then?"

"I know where to go to find the throne. The VP's on my side. She's providing transport for the next phase."

An ominous silence. "You're going through with it, Chief, continuing the search."

"If he got access to the boat, he's got access to the clue. He's not an idiot—he'll figure it out."

"Yeah, okay—so what? I appreciate the client floating you guys through this, or you floating her, but this is pretty far out of the purview of the assignment, even that second contract to search for the throne. Now you've got two secret societies, a major international terrorist incident, Nick is—and you're in the hospital, but you won't say why. You're not ready to talk, and I'm trying to respect that, Casey, cross my heart, I am, but you gotta give me more than the VP's suddenly got the hots for you."

Three secret societies, technically. Grant watched the shifting shadows of the two Secret Service agents outside his room. "If the king gets his throne, he regains his power, the standing he lost tonight when the action failed. Half these guys will call it God's will, Insha'Allah—bringing him to his throne before delivering victory. He gathers more followers—these Shifra guys, they're all in for apocalyptic leadership, they'll die for him, alongside his own knights."

"You're surrounded by fucking lunatics, Casey."

A dry laugh. "Got that right." Unless he'd become one of them. Starting to think so.

"Who's your back-up?"

Honest-to-God assassins who wanted him to set up the king? But they would do no more than that; Bashir had already said so. An unexpected bride as crazy as he was?

"We don't run lone-wolf operations around here, Chief—you're the one who lay down that law."

"We've got a bird on loan from the army. Fly in, find it—document the find and ask for backup from Syria and Turkey." Clue in the assassins to the king's location, and let them take it from there. "We turn over the op, get the hell out before he gets there."

"If he's not there already."

Give it even-odds and a rifle to make the difference. "There's no percentage in letting him win."

"And you're sure this isn't personal. No vendettas, Chief, it's in the contract."

Even for Nick? He didn't have to ask—she would be asking herself that question. "Go to the news coverage, D.A., and watch that ship explode, then tell me you're okay with this guy building his power base across the Middle East."

A sigh on the other end, then she said, "I've seen it. Spent a few years in the Mossad fighting guys like that, sometimes on our own side. I'd like to tell you not to do anything stupid, but this whole operation's pretty marginal in that direction." Deep breath, then, "Do what you have to, Chief. If anyone can stop him, it's you. And Chief?"

A beat to be sure he was listening. "Whatever has happened to Nick, it's on those guys, Casey. It's not on you."

Grant tapped the phone off, and wanted to chuck it across the room. Instead, he dropped it on the blanket.

He pressed the heels of his hands into his eyes as if he could stop the aching or still the tremor that itched beneath his skin. Boots on the ground, get the hell out of the hospital, tear the town apart until he found his wingman. Night diving, morgue searching, fucking dental records, whatever the hell it took to bring Nick home. His breathing hitched and he forced it even. He close his eyes and worked on his breathing, reaching for that repose that, even in on a battlefield, had never felt so far away.

No good to anyone if he could barely walk, if he had nothing left after the last two days. Call the nurses in to give him something strong enough to stop the ache and let him sleep. If only he had a CO who'd take one look at him and confine him to quarters. Trouble was, Grant was the commander, and he was two millimeters short of a meltdown.

Back in Arizona, after saving Grant's ass in the desert, Gooney had tried to convince Grant to take a break. "*At least get something to eat and give yourself a goddamn break for an hour.*"

"*My boss won't like it,*" Grant told him.

"*Your boss is a fucking asshole. Mine, too.*"

Still true. And Gooney had been his CO, back in the Unit. He toyed with the idea of calling him up, asking for orders, just to hear his former CO and some-time employee hoot with laughter.

No CO but himself, and he wasn't listening. No wingman but an aging academic with a fondness for adventure. No back-up, but a prickly millionaire and her technology road show.

He had to get off this track. Had to be something that went right, something in his favor from the long day's work.

Grant scooped the phone off his chest and found the hospital WIFI again, downloading a secure messaging app. That one. Did he want to know? Maybe he didn't. Maybe she'd been captured, the truckload of women seized and raped and slaughtered. Maybe the Nizari couldn't be trusted. Maybe he had already lost her.

He had lost Nick, too—but not forever, Insha'Allah. Breathe, Casey. Keep breathing. Finally tapped out a message.

>*you okay?*

Ten seconds. A minute. Five minutes. He placed the phone on his chest, face down, letting it rise and fall with each careful breath. In, like a ratchet that cranked up the tension. Out, long and slow. Whatever they'd given him for pain began to ebb, comfort inching from his skin and muscle the way that retreating night slowly revealed the carnage of war.

Ten minutes.

Go the fuck to sleep. It used to be so easy.

Low lights and machinery hummed around him. Acoustic tile in the ceiling with a pattern of dots, fifteen up, fifteen across—the vibration jolted him from his contemplation and he lifted the phone.

>*Hey, soldier. Okay. You?*

A rush of exhilaration. He stilled his nerves and answered. >*will be. Doc says good work on the foot.*

>*resting now? Heard about the bomb.*

>*mission objective: 80% Saint Simeon tomorrow*

A longer pause, then, >*idiot*

He certainly grinned like one. >*you married me*

>*as if I had any say*

>*you didn't turn praying mantis and behead me*

>*still might*

He rested his forehead against the slim edge of the phone, the slick feeling of hope against his skin. Always fleeting. He held on. The phone shivered again.

>*soldier?*

>*still here*

>*IFCD*

He frowned, searching his knowledge of acronyms, texting, military or otherwise. >*don't know that one*

>*Intelligent* >*Fascinating* >*Challenging* >*Dangerous*

He traced the words over and over, and a moment later, typed
>*two knights*

>*one horse* >*go to sleep, soldier*

>*Roger that.* Letting his head rest back on the pillow, Grant lay the phone down over his heart. His eyes slid shut as her messages dissolved into peace.

CHAPTER SIXTY-SIX

Kyra stood in the morgue, holding her breath in part from nerves, in part because of the smells. Formaldehyde. Burned flesh. Bowels moved and blood spilled.

"It's not usually like this," the doctor assured her. "Usually, we don't even ask people in to identify the bodies, but we thought you would wish to know. We're aware the role you played last night, Ms. Akbulut, in making sure the loss of life was minimal. Still—" he shrugged and gestured around— "it's not a big city, or a big hospital."

"I understand," she said, trying to sound understanding instead of exasperated. "Please, they said you might have found one of my men."

"A few of the dead had no identification, but are not so badly burned that they might be anonymous, so it seems worth having a look." He beckoned her onward, between a pair of covered tables, to the head of one, and she braced herself, holding back her nausea, hands clasped behind her back. "Don't worry, he's not too gruesome. Drowning is not so bad compared with other ways to go."

Hemorrhagic fever, for instance. Kyra gave a nod, and the man drew back the top of the sheet to reveal a puffy, bloated face. Kostas. His shoulder-length hair and pencil mustache distinctive in spite of the condition of the body. "That's him. Kostas Demosthenes. My pilot."

"Mmm." The doctor took up a tablet and made a note. "He appears to have drowned, as I said. But there's some sign of struggle, as if his boat may have capsized and trapped him, that sort of thing." He drew the sheet back up again. "He was a hero, working with the rescue."

"My assistant can send you his other information, including next of kin." An ex-wife and a few children. A girlfriend. Kyra steeled herself for the question she had to ask. "No sign of the other man, a large Black man with an artificial right leg, mid-thigh?"

The doctor's gaze roamed over the dead. "I will check the burn victims. Both of them have lost extremities. But I don't think either was very large. Some measurements can help us determine height. Do you know—"

"Six foot four, a hundred ninety-three centimeters," said Grant Casey from the doorway. He met Kyra's eye and gave a nod. "Good morning. I... didn't want to leave without checking once more."

She translated his information for the doctor, adding her thanks, then walked gratefully away from the tables with their silent dead. Grateful, too, to see him. Dressed in a tactical shirt and pants with too many pockets, he looked blade-thin and haunted, but better than the last time she'd seen him anyhow. "It's good to see you on your feet."

"I have what I need to keep going." He gestured, indicating she should join him in the hall. They walked to the elevator and he jabbed the button. "The copter is topside, and your gear is already loaded in from the convention center. Irene told me where to find you."

Kyra scowled. "She's not to be here. I told her that, and Adem was meant to keep her home."

"I think she came to see me." He sounded vaguely surprised. "Pity for her that I make a lousy surrogate for Nick." He absorbed the movement as the elevator car started, apparently balanced in spite of his injury. "We need to talk about leaving Irene behind."

"What about it?" she said as they rode up, all the way.

"The last thing I want is to put your mother in danger, but she's also our expert. You and I are good at a lot of things, Byzantine and Templar history are not among them." He kept his gaze fixed on the elevator door, hands at his back, posture erect. "We might need her."

"That's what Google is for."

"Assuming we have access where we're going. Google may know everything there is to know about the world, but would you even know the right questions to ask it?"

She found herself matching his posture, trying on his determination, hoping for an ounce of his courage. "No." She flicked him a glance. "If I am not mistaken, the lunatic and his knights are after us, along with an entire sleeper cell of terrorists."

"I estimate up to 60 possible combatants. Likely they'll reduce their force in the expectation of our own small numbers."

The number made her sway on her feet, and she found him glancing down at her.

"I try to be realistic about these things," he said. "It helps with the mental game."

"You want to bring my mother into a melee involving swords and assault weapons—how on earth would we keep her safe?"

His jaw knotted, and he said, "I do not *want* to bring her, but I am keenly aware that we are at a disadvantage without her. She's a civilian—it's not up to me, and I am absolutely not going to twist her arm. That's why I'm talking to you."

"You're hoping I will twist her arm, as you say?" Kyra folded her own arms.

Dark eyes, almost black without the sunlight. Then the elevator door slid open, and he put out a hand to block it from closing. "Tell her not to come. As I see it, this operation has one of two successful outcomes. One: we get in there, get in fast, and find what we need. For that, we would need your mother. Her level of knowledge radically increases our chance of achieving that mission objective."

But he wanted her to convince her mother to stay behind. In spite of the early daylight, Kyra's skin speckled with gooseflesh. "And two?"

"Two. We don't even look. Forget about the throne. Your mother stays here, you stay with the copter, and I go on alone."

"To face these sixty men."

"You keep eyes on me. We record not the presence of an ancient throne, but the faces of every knight and terrorist who comes after me. They pissed off a lot of people on three different continents, but there's no objective proof of who they are and what they're up to. So. We run a sting, and I'm the target. You get them on film, and the intel community steps in to take over."

She blinked. "Over your dead body."

A single nod, clear and precise. "To save this region from whatever they have in mind? I'll take it." He stepped out into the sunshine. "You did bring that sword?"

CHAPTER SIXTY-SEVEN

From the second seat of the MD 500 Defender helicopter, Grant watched the last of the Mediterranean rush beneath his feet, the surreal calm before combat infusing him, thank God. Half the night, he envisioned having to report to that illusory CO that he was in no way battle ready. Getting some sleep made all the difference. Or at least, enough of it.

"Look at that!" Irene's voice chirped over his headset and he glanced back to the passenger compartment. Could take two more, which meant both women could ride looking forward. Most civilians had some trouble with the rear-facing seats.

Irene wore a Kevlar vest under a linen jacket and over her practical shirt and pants, making her look smaller and more frail than ever. She leaned to stare at the ground below them as the copter's shadow finally touched land at the coast of Turkey and crossed the invisible line that marked the border with Syria. Grant observed her delight, tempered, no doubt, by sheer terror of what came next, and he thought about Outcome Number Two. He could still make it happen. Abandon all pretense of going after the throne and go in as the decoy. Get both women to stay with the bird, if Kyra would agree. Given how fiercely Irene clung to her daughter the last twenty-four hours, he had trouble imagining Irene staying behind if Kyra would not.

A hybrid outcome seemed more likely: Kyra tracked him with her tech, Irene did what she could, when they found what they were looking for, they turned back and he went in alone. Best of both ways, aside from the fact that he wouldn't make it out alive—though he had sent another message early in the morning: Blaise's image, his likely whereabouts, to Bashir. No response, and nothing from Akilah either. *Who's your back-up?* D.A.'s voice echoed in his memory. Still no answer to give her.

"Oh, my!" Irene breathed over the mic. "The Dead Cities! Are you familiar with this region?"

Kyra managed a thin smile. "No, Mother, but I suspect you're about to give us the tour." She held a hard-sided case open on her lap, tiny tools in hand, trying to compensate for the movement of the copter as she tweaked the smallest drone he'd ever seen.

"We don't really know why they're dead, but this is a region once owned by the Byzantine empire. Thousands of people settled here, across these mountains in the border region—" Irene's hand fluttered against the windows, drawing his eye downward as she spoke— "and established olive groves and vineyards. There are still people working them today! In any case, there are hundreds of towns including churches, monasteries, houses, farms and manors dating back to the sixth century, some of them. Within a few hundred years, before the Templars ever came this far, these communities all fled, probably due to the shifting allegiances in the area."

Grant rested his forehead against the bubble, three windows to Irene's two. He should ask the pilot's permission for her to sit up front on the way back. She, at least, would be leaving here or Grant had screwed things up even worse than he envisioned. He gazed down over dry, rectangular fields laid out in stripes of rust, beige and spotty green. Rough fingers of stone reached down from the foothills, digging into the farmland. The uplands and plateaus linking these ridges carried clumps of trees and acres of ruins, hundreds of them. Walls marked ancient boundaries and animal pens, then clustered into the square shapes of houses. Larger blocks of sandstone accumulated into granaries, wineries, and sudden churches. Roofless, they welcomed the sky into hollow arches where the early sun pierced dense relief carvings and draped over topless columns that still marched along vacant naves and framed absent basilicas. Towers crumbled atop the hills, and pyramids of stone defined the roofs of Syrian-style tombs. His mouth went dry, his fingertips pressed to the window as if he could pick up the buildings—but they were too numerous, spreading across the highland plains. Just when he thought they had reached the end of the ruins, another village sprouted from the green clumps of trees showing where the water flowed.

"There you go. Saint Simeon Stylites at your one o'clock," the pilot said.

Grant lifted his gaze. At one time, the complex had been nearly as large as the Hagia Sofia, a cruciform church at the heart of a complex of ecclesiastical buildings. A baptistery stood at the near end, partial domes still rising over the chambers. Crumbled walls linked this with the main church, where arches framed every view, casting long shadows to encircled tumbled columns and richly carved stones. Dense pines filled in at the back of the church and down the slopes to either side. Likely waterway north-northeast, dirt roads to the south, tracking upwards. A few orchards at the lower end, where a group of women carrying baskets turned away from the wind of their descent. Hopefully, the women would be far enough away from the action that they wouldn't get hurt. Shadows shifted among the trees and at the edges of the ancient walls, as if the place seethed with some dark power.

"Word is, the ladies are a diplomatic family earning a special privilege, viewing the ruins like a couple of tourists, and you're their security, but casual," the pilot said. He flashed Grant a sharp grin. "That's why I keep the long guns, in case the story seems suspicious—sorry, buddy. Assad's not really on our side right now."

"Do what you have to, man. We appreciate the lift." Grant carried twin pistols and a fresh knife. Not to mention the longsword in a makeshift scabbard at his hip.

"I'll set you guys down right at the top of the driveway— " the only flat area for some distance— "gonna kick up quite a dust storm and piss off a lot of locals, then I retreat over that ridge." He pointed. "All goes well on your end, extraction point is the same location. All goes south, you make for the ridge and I retrieve as possible and diplomatically feasible." Mirror shades under his helmet. "You know the drill, Lieutenant. I have no authority to interfere, certainly not for any level of hostile engagement. This bird is transport only. Whatever happens on the ground, that's on you, and the Veep denies she ever authorized."

Grant flicked him a salute. "Kyra. Are you ready?"

She gave him one thumbs up as she closed a compartment on a larger drone.

"Me, too, I think," Irene said.

As the bird turned to land, a cloud of dust shifted on the far horizon, a caravan incoming, but at least half an hour away. Less than hour to execute the first outcome. Maybe two before the second outcome executed him.

"Irene. You should stay." He leveled his gaze at her.

She put up her chin, every inch as formidable as her daughter. "Nick went in alone. You don't have to."

Kyra clicked the case shut and turned her hand up in a little shrug.

They touched down, and Grant pulled off his headset, hooking it over the handle. He jumped down from the seat, and opened the rear door, guiding Irene, then Kyra to keep their heads low. Kyra held the case close to her chest as she hustled away from the rotors. Shutting the door, Grant rapped on the side, letting the pilot know they were clear. The bird took off, and Grant ducked away, holding his breath for a minute while the dust swirled.

The Cathedral of Saint Simeon Stylites rose before him, broken to the sky and beckoning like a hand from a crypt. No choice now but to follow.

CHAPTER SIXTY-EIGHT

Once the helicopter's shadow swept its blades over them, and the noise receded toward the Turkish border, Kyra took the lead a step ahead of Casey. They moved through the open gate, entering the walled compound that would have contained all the monastery buildings, the ruined cathedral spreading to her right beyond some broken pavement. She pointed to a smaller cell to one side. "We can leave things here, I think?"

His hand rested on the butt of a gun as he scanned the courtyard, swept the cell with his gaze, and stepped inside to peer through the window on the far wall. Finally, he nodded. "The walls provide decent cover, and I like the window." He tipped his head. "That gives you an escape route behind the exterior gatehouse. If we separate, you come back here. If you get out through the window, signal the pilot. Phones up, and silent, right?"

Mother patted her pocket, then went back to fidgeting with her vest. He had one as well, but it was made to fit a man of his build, and much more comfortable than theirs, Kyra felt certain. Inside the cell, she opened her case against the exterior wall and brought out her own "birds." She beckoned Casey closer and fixed a small pin to his shoulder. "It's a beacon for the drones. Both will target on this, but at different distances. It includes a magnet for the bee-drone if you want it to stay fixed."

"Got it." His hands hung at his sides, not far from the weapons he now wore, holstered, right hip and left thigh, the sword hanging over. His short sleeves bared taut muscle and the bandage that interrupted the tattoos down his arm, ink he had been at pains to conceal throughout their acquaintance until now. The bulletproof vest broadened his chest and shoulders. He resembled a screen test for a Rambo film, angling for Sylvester Stallone's old job. All morning, he carried a charge: she could feel him buzzing like a wire that wasn't properly grounded.

Back in the case, she powered up two of the drones and brought out a small tablet. "And, up."

She stepped back and keyed the signal. These were her top of the line, the electronics made minuscule at great expense to impress visitors to the Turkish displays at the Davos-ME. Look at all the great things Turkey has to offer! Lunatics! Bombers! Technological wizardry that might, Insha'Allah, save a human life. Maybe even his?

The bee-drone hummed softly up to hover just above shoulder level. Casey raised his eyebrows, and the screen showed her a close up of his face, until she triggered the directional re-set.

"It's a fisheye lens so it captures more than you'd expect for its size. This one is secondary, programmed to follow, tracking the movements of your head. It won't move as fast as you, but it will pick up as possible or latch to the pin and act as a bodycam." She slipped a second bee-drone into her lapel pocket, then took charge of a more traditional drone the size of a dinner plate. "I designed the bee-drones for You-Tubers to share their vision more easily. I didn't imagine something like this. I'll be controlling this larger one, but it also has a default patterned flight mode. Both will be transmitting to me and to the back-up in the helicopter, like a remote newscast. The little ones don't have great antenna range, of course, but internal memory will continue to capture images and transmit as able."

He looked around, and the drone panned with him: the open entry gate, the long shadows of arches inside. "Copy that. Irene, what are we looking for?"

He started walking—taking point, he called it, and Mother fell in beside him. "The throne itself? It has six or seven steps, each with a pair of animals facing. The lions are said to guard it—if we do find it, we must be careful. At least two kings are said to have tried to mount the throne, only to fail its tests—not knowing the way." She chuckled. "Kyra's father used to go on about it, and pretend that Kyra was a queen who had mounted the throne of his lap." She mimed holding a child and swaying wildly to and fro.

A sudden sense of movement swept Kyra's memory, and she murmured, "I had forgotten."

Mother's smile broadened. "It all seemed so very unlikely to me. In any case, there are eagles on the throne as well, which were said to spread their wings and call out to herald the king. The throne stands at the top of this, with the seal of Solomon at its back—that circle around a six-pointed star ringed by smaller circles. Above the seal, a statue of a tree to shelter the king. It may have had spreading fronds or branches. All of this was once clad in gold, or perhaps orichalcum, the sources differ. One of the emperors after 966, in need of money for mercenaries, may have stripped the gold and jewels, keeping the mechanisms to be re-clad at a later date. So, at one time, the throne included both sound and movement, but presumably it has not been maintained since Aleume's Day. The animal figures moved, and the throne itself as well."

"What about the clue?" Kyra asked. "It brought us here, but where, exactly, and to what?"

Casey's hand slid restlessly against the handle of his right-hand gun. Or not restless. He held up a fist, then cast them a flash of humor. "That means 'stop' in Special Ops." His eyes tracked the ground around the entrance. She saw nothing of use. In the path of the rotor blades, light dust scattered widely. His hand indicated they could proceed and he walked a little faster. Beyond the entrance, the dirt and gravel showed the tracks of many feet, but it had likely not rained for days, so if he were looking for fresh tracks, he wouldn't find them.

They walked the long aisle up to the golden bulk of the cathedral with its framework of arches. The images they had seen on line barely did justice to its majesty as it rose above them, the work of her nation over a thousand years ago. Deep, geometric carvings rimmed each of the arches, and more stones with shapes like leaves and diamonds filled in randomly where walls had fallen and been rebuilt. At the center of a conjunction of arches, where there must once have been domes, a large base held an irregular, semi-cylindrical stone. Mother regarded it as Casey performed a quick search, gun in hand, carried low. The larger drone hovered, turning in the air to take it all in, while the smaller one looked with Casey into the shadows cast by the vast arches and under the protection of half-fallen domes. Some of the shadows pulsed with irregular movement, an effect the camera seemed unable to compensate for. The contrast too sharp between light and shade as the sun crept higher.

"I hope Aleume did not require us to climb the actual column of Saint Simeon. This is all that remains of it." Mother gestured toward the stone in its place of honor.

Kyra flicked Casey's footage to a smaller window and piloted the large drone in a pattern around the center, under each arch, scanning in either direction, down, and then back to the next arch. Small crosses marked the stonework, and a Star of David, along with a few other, less familiar symbols. "Do these mean anything?" She hovered the drone at eye level with one of them.

Casey came up, placing his back to hers and looked at the screen in quick glances.

"Crosses for Christ, of course, and the Jewish star. This is the chi rho, from the Greek characters for the name of Christ," Mother muttered as she peered at the screen. Her head began to shake. "I see nothing distinctive. So many of the stones have been replaced, you can see how the cathedral has been reconstructed with parts of itself." She waved a hand at the ruins, then let it fall. "I'm sorry, Kyra, I really don't think there's anything for us to find here any more."

Casey froze, his fist raised, head cocked, then he pointed toward the entrance. "Engines. We've got incoming, and you need to get out of here."

"What about you?" Mother asked as they started running.

He met Kyra's eye and said, "Phase two."

She felt ill and suddenly grateful she had skipped her breakfast. But her job was very clear: keep filming, no matter what happened. Capture the images that would let them capture the men, the killers—after they murdered Casey.

Chapter Sixty-nine

The two women broke into a run, picking up on his increasing urgency, and he kept pace alongside, gun in his hand, between them and the gate, the dirt road where their enemy would shortly appear. Irene's description of the throne had almost cast this option from his mind, envisioning its grandeur, being the first man in a thousand years to lay eyes on a treasure of Byzantium, stolen by the Templars, smuggled by the Assassins, hidden away for the heirs of Solomon like something in an epic novel. The heirs of Solomon.

Kyra reached the corner of the cell where they had left the cases for the drones. She turned back, her arm outstretched to her mother. "Come on, come on! We get out through here, and hide." She caught Irene's hand and drew her into the open doorway.

Grant stopped short on the far side of the entrance, pressing his shoulder to the concrete wall that surrounded the compound, gun up, eyes on the growing dust cloud that approached up the road. "Irene! The throne is backed with the seal of Solomon—six-pointed star, right?"

"Yes—inscribed in a circle, and—Oh! Oh, Mr. Casey!"

Sure enough, Irene spun around and started back. He held up his fist. "No. You stay here." He pinned her with his eyes. "I know you'll be watching." He flicked them a salute, and a smile, letting his face go soft and warm, a soldier's farewell to his mom.

Kyra caught her mother's shoulders and brought her around, both of them disappearing behind the wall. Grant took off running back into the cathedral. His left foot, protected by a thermoplastic shield, ached a little, but another round of local anesthetics had taken the edge away without dulling his wits. God knew he was gonna need 'em. He leapt up the steps to the three great arches. Beyond, the apse of the church remained visible, an arch of stone presiding over an empty pavement fringed by grasses. The two drones hummed up alongside, hovering like the presence of old friends. Like the angels of the lost. Grant pointed his gun up, indicating the top of the arch where the deep, geometric carvings framed a keystone inscribed with a six-pointed star. Not just the Star of David, the Seal of Solomon, its circle at the top echoing the arch, at the bottom utterly dissolved by the years. They had dismissed the reconstructions as the work of newer occupants putting back random ancient stones where they didn't belong. Didn't mean the Templars and their Assassin allies hadn't done the same thing back in the thirteenth century.

Grant stepped through the arch, moving fast, acutely aware of the approaching rumble, the thunder of a storm of anger about to break over him. Ahead, down a long-gone corridor, a window lined up with Solomon's arch, another small, rounded echo. This one carried fragments of stone midway, a pair of broken curves that would have completed a circle, maybe the Seal again, outlined in stone. Grant replaced his gun and stalked closer. He let his hands complete the circle, shifting his feet until he could look through it across a tree-marked gully beyond which the rugged terrain started again. The trunks of a few trees interrupted his view. The engines grew louder, then the first one ground to a halt.

Grant scanned the slope, marking the location of a tall tree with a split trunk, memorizing the shape of the ridgeline and the cracks in the stony face, then something caught his eye. The Seal of Solomon took the form of a six-pointed star enclosed in a circle, with the interstices marked by smaller circles. Across the gully, a small round hole, deeply shadowed, marked the slope at ten o'clock. If the small window before him once contained a Star of David, points at around eight and ten would perfectly frame the hole.

Doors slamming, and voices snarling in Arabic. More engines growing near and cutting to silence. More doors, Turkish this time—too many voices to differentiate. Max of sixty. Min of—twenty? Thirty? How many men had it taken to blow that boat? How many men was Nick's life worth?

From here, Grant couldn't see the other circles if, indeed, they even existed. Didn't matter. Didn't matter, either, if he was the one being seen. But not yet. He survived the jaws of the Lion of Truth. He survived the gauntlet at the castle of Limassol. He almost laughed. He had survived Afghanistan, Mongolia and Arizona only to come half-way around the world and find another goddamn desert to die in.

Grant jumped through the window to the slope on the outside. He slithered and jogged down the tumbled stones and scree. Just like any other desert, lizards fled his footfalls and sand-colored rodents shrieked a warning. If his pursuers knew the first thing about navigating the wilderness, they'd zero in within moments. But he'd lay odds they were mostly farmers and city kids like the king they followed. Once they got to the window, his track down scarred the slope like an arrow pointing exactly where he'd gone.

His injuries throbbed a little, protesting the tricky balance of the slopes. He tacked back the other direction, trying to key in on the circle he had spotted, tacking again as he reached the floor of the gully. Scruffy trees grew sparsely around him, letting plenty of sunshine fall to the pine needles and gravel around him. He crossed the rocky channel of a seasonal stream and started up the rise opposite, scanning for the split-topped pine that marked his way. He angled upward again and came to a ledge as broad as an ATV track, concealed from the far view by the rough ground and trees. It sloped down toward where the gully broadened and merged with the scrub land and farms below. He just glimpsed the smoother, straighter trunks of cultivated trees down there, the orchard he had spotted from the air taking advantage of whatever moisture and fertility the stream would bring. Upward, to the left, hard not to imagine carts or horses bringing a heavy load along this same trail eight hundred years ago.

Sunlight bathed the rocky slope ahead of him, and Grant paused, looking back to align the ruin of the church. A little higher, a little further west, he should see...another hole, down low, and the first he had spotted above it, another in between. A grin spread wide and slightly giddy.

Maybe he was going down today, and maybe he wasn't—but first he had one last secret to find.

CHAPTER SEVENTY

Blaise glared at the helicopter flying overhead, chopping them with the shadow of its impotent blades. Not large enough to do much more than deliver Casey and a few friends—if he had any—to the target zone.

The walkie talkie chirped, and Farouk said, "If that's him, I want him."

From the driver's seat next to Blaise, Haldan muttered, "Doesn't everyone," and, for an instant, Blaise wondered if he meant it in a completely different sense than Farouk. "At the very least, my lord, I hope we can get your sword back."

The Viking shifted their vehicle to climb the final slope. One of the Humvees ahead of them—provided by their local allies—kicked up a shower of rocks around a curve, and Haldan jerked the wheel to dodge the fall. "Sorry, my lord."

Blaise swayed heavily, catching himself with the handle over his door, and glanced back to the others. Two knights in rear-facing seats, two more facing forward, bracketing their surprise gift. Blaise felt weary from yesterday's setbacks, but the images of the cross-blazoned column had not been the only treasure they discovered in the lounge on Akbulut's vessel. When Farouk had called down the stairs, Blaise and Chloe thundered up, in spite of their host's protests to stay away. He followed them up, the boat swaying with their movements, but Blaise stopped to marvel at what he saw.

Just inside the glassed-in lounge, a man lay on one of the couches, his feet hanging off the end, one at a slightly off-angle. Big man, Negro, his clothes soaking wet. Two pill bottles stood on the table by his head and an empty glass. Well, well, well. "Come along!" Blaise called back over his shoulder.

Their host scrambled up the stairs and slammed through into the lounge. "Sirs, you don't need to be up here. You have what you wanted, yes?"

"Tell me what he's doing here." Blaise indicated the downed man. "This is the other Bone Guard, am I right?"

The man's hands flapped, and finally he shrugged. "I found him, in the water, or rather he found me—he swam over when he recognized me. I would bring him to the dock, but he's—changed. He looks at me like he holds a gun to my head and says we must come to the boat, now, immediately. He needs his medication, he says, and so we come here. I would call Ms. Akbulut, or his friend, but he says no—you don't see the look in his eyes, he's like a shark, dangerous, so I bring him the pills. He wants to be where he can see, to keep an eye out, he says, and his hands—" the man's own gestures became more specific as if he were holding a gun, aiming it around the space.

"So I get the pills, and I get him a drink. He wants water, I think maybe that's not good, not enough, so I bring whiskey, maybe it settles him, you know? Helps him calm down." He glanced down at the man. "I think maybe he takes too much."

Blaise examined the medicine bottles. "Or the combination of alcohol and drugs has nearly killed him." He dropped to one knee and found a low, slow pulse at the big man's throat. Living still, but he could benefit from medical attention.

The man's eyes flared. "Certainly not, no! I don't harm him. I bring him here, as he wants, he says he will call them himself when he's taken the pills."

"Instead, he fell unconscious, and you called us."

Back to wringing his hands, looking anywhere but at Blaise or the downed man.

"You saw an opportunity and you took it," Blaise supplied encouragingly, letting his voice warm.

"Yes, exactly yes. The man is safe, we call later, it's fine. But you," he looked to Chloe and back, "this is a chance, exactly, and if Ms. Akbulut or that other man come over, then there is no chance."

"I understand completely." The loathsome worm betrayed his employer for money, offered drugs and drink to an addict, not caring when that man collapsed, not caring if the man's companions believed him dead. No, the worm saw this, instead, as a chance for his own financial gain. If he knew what this "chance" really meant to Blaise, he would've asked for more. And perhaps reconsidered the wisdom of letting them so greatly outnumber him. "Chloe. Kill him. Make it look like part of the accident."

"Yes, my lord."

"What?" The man yelped and stumbled away as she turned for him. He fled the room, slamming the door open, slipping on the steps outside. Blaise walked to the back deck to see that it was done as mercifully as might be.

Chloe leapt the balcony to the lower deck, landing just as their host arrived via the stairs. He shrieked and fell back from her onto the dive platform a few steps below. She grabbed his shirt and shoved him onto his back, dropping him down to where water splashed through the metal grate. He struggled, slapping and scraping at her arms, then clawing for her throat.

Chloe sat on his abdomen, one leg straight before her, and shoved his head into the water with her foot, pushing harder as he fought, holding his face under the water. The violence of the fight rocked the boat, letting his mouth sometimes gape into the air. She shifted her position, dragging him further, and pushed harder. He grappled with her leg, and Blaise wondered if the strength of her body surprised him. Men like that often underestimated women's power. The man clawed at her, and she leaned a little forward, grabbing his wrists to pin his hands to the metal grate. Water sloshed against them, rippled by the jerky motion of the man's feet as they finally went still. Just another victim of the night. Chloe rose smoothly, leaving the dead man where he lay, his head in the water, his hands drifting up and slapping down in bleak applause for a job well done.

They took what they wanted from the boat: not much, just the thumb drive and printouts, the laptop from the lounge, and the stricken addict who had clawed his way from the wreck only to falter as he reached safety. A sad tale, and one Blaise and his companions knew all too well. Small matter to load the pilot's corpse into the zodiac he'd come in, and tow it out with Farouk's motor launch, then tip the body into the water and set the zodiac adrift to fetch up where it would. Did the command of such action even require penance? Blaise's understanding of penitence had shifted since he first began his odyssey of personal re-construction and come to share it with others. Chloe stood blameless, of course, pure in her loyalty and noble in her deft action.

"This Casey," Farouk had grumbled, "do we get him in the hospital?"

Blaise shook his head. Casey himself had exercised that gambit—there was little chance he would leave himself open to the same death he claimed to deal to another. At the dock, Blaise supervised the loading of the Black man, now snoring faintly, into the back seat of a car. "The man took some pills and passed out," he told the knights waiting there.

Haldan dropped to check the man's pulse and remained there, kneeling, his fingers lightly at the other man's throat, to address his king. "My lord, did you bring the bottles?"

Blaise shook his head. "We have a clue to unravel, a clue I am sure that Casey and the Akbuluts already have. When we do, we'll know where he's going."

"You don't think he'll just relax in the hospital and let everybody fawn over him?" Farouk yanked a cigarette from his pocket, speaking Turkish so his men couldn't understand him. "You know it's what I would do with his foot like that."

"What do you think, Haldan? Is he likely to give up the chase?"

Haldan's eyes remained on the sleeping man. "No, my lord, not if he perceives you as his rival. Not if he thinks this man is dead because of what we have done. He risked his own life having known me only a day. What would he not do for his very best friend?"

Casey's very best friend now sat like an onyx idol between two knights in the back seat of the Humvee. The Negro noticed Blaise's attention and shifted his dark gaze to match the king's. Since waking, he had spoken not a word, nor taken any action against his captors, though perhaps their sheer numbers and level of armament had dissuaded him from precipitous action. Haldan had taken charge of him, matching the big man's silence with his own soft, firm commands.

"Not everyone who takes pills is an addict," Haldan had told Blaise in gentle rebuke, "Some are just in pain." He gestured toward the Bone Guard's prosthetic leg. Blaise accepted that he might have reacted too strongly to the sight of the bottles and alcohol, but they wouldn't return to the boat, nor would the Bone Guard answer their questions, even regarding his own medication.

The man ate, he walked, he pissed like an automaton, as cooperative and cold as a tiger in a cage. Sometimes, he said "Thank you," in English, apparently not comprehending any other of the several languages spoken around him. It was hard to imagine such a person being anyone's friend, much less that of a personable knight-candidate like Casey.

The Negro's solid, silent presence made the other knights shift in their seats, flinching from him as the Humvee's turn pushed them to one side. Meanwhile, his cuffed hands rested in his lap utterly calm, as if they were on their way to an event he didn't care for, but he didn't care enough to avoid.

If thinking his friend was dead had motivated Casey out of his hospital bed, into a helicopter to infiltrate a dangerous borderland, what would he do when Blaise revealed his friend was very much alive?

CHAPTER SEVENTY-ONE

On the small monitor, Kyra watched over Casey's shoulder as he framed an undistinguished section of ledge between his hands, then jumped out a window and slithered down hill, the drones losing him as he dropped out from below. The breeze-tossed branches of the trees made her jumpy, sure that faces peered back as the bee-drone sank down in pursuit of its beacon.

Casey moved quickly, but Kyra had seen where he was looking. She guided the larger drone on a course straight across the gully.

Beyond the outer wall, heavy vehicles ground to a halt and doors slammed open. "Let's go, let's go! Don't forget your rifle, idiot!" someone shouted in Arabic.

Mother clamped both hands over her mouth, her eyes pinching nearly shut, her breathing rocking her body. Kyra shifted closer to her mother, pressing their sides together. She gave a nod, hoping she looked calm and collected. Opening a memo tab, she tapped, "When they have passed, we go through the window behind us, and up the slope," showing the screen to her mother.

Mother nodded.

More vehicles pulled up, more voices, falling silent for one that sounded calm, clear and commanding, the sort of voice she found it easy to imagine in charge of a courtroom. "My friends," he said in Arabic, then again in Turkish, "our time is nearly at hand. Only a few more obstacles stand between us and our objective. Last night was a setback, and I know you feel this as acutely as I do, but when the throne is mine, with your strength to support me, we shall reclaim our nations." Cheering erupted, and the speaker paused.

On her screen, Casey emerged from the trees, scanning. Spotting the drone, he gave a thumbs up, and she caught his grin, like a boy up to something naughty. Behind her hands, Mother, too, tried a smile, though her eyes washed with tears.

Casey followed the cliff face. From her initial perspective, a clump of thorny brush took up a notch at the center of the area he now explored, and she saw his gaze track upwards, then sweep down to the side, apparently noting a series of holes puncturing the stone, a few to either side of the notch.

"Two challenges await us here, the first is a clue, a hidden secret my knights shall be seeking, and the second is a man." People hissed—mostly men, a few women. "A man who has betrayed us all. From some, he has stolen their wives—" this, in Arabic, then continuing with both languages, "from all he has stolen our honor. I would ask you not to seek retribution for yourselves, but to bring him to bay, to receive his just punishment from your leaders." Cheers, and shouts of "Insha'Allah." How many? Not sixty, certainly. Kyra plucked the second bee drone from her pocket and flicked it on.

She set the larger drone to automatic and carefully guided her new eyes up, up, over, skimming the top of the wall, hovering in a shadow. She turned first toward the gate, the fisheye lens distorting the gathered company as she tried to count them. The king stood at their head, clad in a silver mask. Some of those arrayed before him wore swords, some with swords and sidearms like Casey. Another man stood a half-step behind him, heavily bearded and scowling, chewing on a cigarette, with a gun slung over his back. The men to his side—all men—wore army fatigues and desert gear, and every one of them carried a large rifle. Twenty-three, so far. She panned back toward the cars. Two of the terrorists stood toward the back, looking along the road, one in each direction. No sign of the women who had been working the olive grove. Likely—and rightly—they had fled when the armed men arrived. Between the cars and the wall, another cluster of knights, with Haldan Brunelle among them, and the woman Casey identified as Chloe. And a tall, stalwart presence that made her lips part and her mother grab her elbow with a tremor of excitement. Nick was alive! She had to tell Casey, but how?

Leaving the bee-drone, she flipped back to the larger one as the sound of jogging feet echoed from the walls around her. Thirty-two people, not counting the two left on guard outside, against Casey. Half as bad as he feared, and one of the people was Nick. They'd use him against Casey, of course they would, hurting or killing him with impunity to get Casey to submit. Thirty-two people, forty or more guns, perhaps fifteen swords.

Mother's hand tightened as someone ran by their location, but the people kept going, just two, probably going to check the baptistry at the far end. They circled back again a moment later, and Mother relaxed a fraction.

Meanwhile Kyra scanned the cliffside beyond the gully: Casey was gone. In the last few moments, he had vanished—up the cliff, into the gully, she had no idea. Mother tugged her arm and indicated the window at the back. Their chance had come.

She waved her mother on to mount the tumble of stones from the ancient wall then step through the gap into the space beyond. They'd have to move carefully so as not to attract the attention of the men on guard. Had the knights guarding Nick gone that way as well? No way of knowing without launching again, taking another risk—with her mother already outside their sanctuary.

Kyra eased up from her position, taking a moment to tap out a message to Casey. If he were in range and neither dead nor underground, he would know how many he faced and that his friend was among them. And if he weren't, he'd never know. He would carry out his suicide plan believing he followed his friend to the grave.

Kyra closed her case silently and rose along the wall.

She switched back to the bee-drone she had launched, preparing to summon it home.

In the distorted view of the fisheye lens, an enormous eye stared back. A hand swooped in, and Kyra screamed.

CHAPTER SEVENTY-TWO

U p close, what appeared to be a wrinkle in the stone that divided the circles into two arcs of three deepened away, fronted by a dense growth of something with thorns and overhung by gorse and tough grasses. Eight hundred years. A lot could happen. The khan's tomb had been defended by a false lake, its entrance concealed against animals large and small. Another flake of stone emerged behind the brush, seeming to fill the gap, but if he rested his cheek against the crag, the gap breathed and softly echoed. As he moved in, something moved above him, then let out a shrill call of danger. Hyrax, but the sound sent a jolt through his system, as if he needed another. It shrieked again and he kind of hoped for a hungry eagle.

Grant drew the king's sword and sliced easily through the brush nearest the ridge, just enough to slide past, his hands itching a little where he'd been caught by rose bushes. The bee-drone hovered at his shoulder, but the larger one lingered outside, perhaps confused by the screen of brush that remained. Did he want to be followed? Did he want this place to be where he made his last stand?

Now it came to the point, Grant faced the fact he dearly wanted to live. Too many places he hadn't been, things he hadn't seen. Cece invited him back to the rez for Christmas. And there was Akilah, the Phantom in the flesh. *Intelligent, fascinating, challenging, dangerous.* Nick would be the first person to tell him to live.

And Nick would've been the second person into the breech when he knew how many lives were on the line. Second only because Grant could move faster.

He hacked a few more boughs, deflecting them with the flat of the blade, but whatever space might have existed between the brush and the stone filled with leaves, pine needles and something that crunched beneath his feet like tiny bones. Could be he'd stumped through a badger sett, or the lair of a sand cat.

Light filtered through the branches and the grasses overhead. As he scooted his feet carefully forward, he uncovered a shallow groove, getting broader and deeper, carved to allow the slab of stone to be shoved into the space, making a gap wide enough for a wagon appear to be barely large enough for a man. The pinch opened a moment later, with plenty of space for his shoulders. Wouldn't take much to rock the slab back out of the way, maybe crush the thorn tree at the same time.

Grant replaced the sword. From a pocket by his knee, he retrieved a Maglite and flicked it on. In the passage ahead, small things skittered, claws on stone and perhaps the flutter of wings. The place smelled dry, dusty. Inside the flank of the ridge, stone muffled the sounds from outside.

The beam of his light caught dancing motes that drifted as he moved. The leaves, twigs and bones petered out after a little while. Up ahead, a faint glow drew him onward like a will-o-the-wisp toward his unseen doom. The passage opened abruptly and his light felt small and feeble. Grant flicked it off with nerveless fingers, gazing into the chamber revealed before him.

He had seen the occasional rock-cut church before, and they echoed here in his memory even as his own footsteps echoed within. Expansive as a small auditorium, the chamber's four lobes resembled the cruciform church outside, but of equal size like the Templars cross. Half-domes arched over each of the arms with a larger, full dome at the center, unrefined, but beautifully symmetrical. At each corner, shafts pierced the stone of the ceiling. Sunlight glowed through these openings swirling with flecks of dust, like giant columns, floor to ceiling, of living light veined with gold. Roots and brambles overhung the edges of those holes—they must be the bane of local herdsmen, even as the growth disguised their true nature.

These four columns framed the throne. Mounted on a smaller base, the throne appeared to be hovering almost a foot off the ground. Ancient gold and bronze reflected the low light in channels of worked metal and buttery curves. The shape resolved into a lion about the size of a Maine Coon cat, seated upright with its back toward him, its mane richly coiled, its flanks smooth and gleaming, a tail curled demurely against its back. Grant walked slowly forward, outside the columns. To cut through that light would break the spell.

He walked toward the back, putting off the moment just a little longer. How much longer did he have? Long enough for this, for him to be alone with the Throne of Solomon.

Metal stripped from the back and lower side revealed a wood and metal framework within, meticulously assembled with tiny dovetails, and delicate nails. He glimpsed slender rods inside as he moved. Higher up, the metal sheeting remained, stamped with patterns like ripples on the sea that broke around a central pillar he could likely just wrap his arms around: the plane tree Irene had mentioned. He pinched the bee-drone between his fingers and brought it in closer, recording everything, using his Maglite to illuminate through a slit in the old wood and capture the inner workings he couldn't even see. "Kyra, I hope you can see this. Not right now, I know, but later—you earned all of this. My God, your father was right."

He panned upward along the length of the tree where it towered above him, smaller than the real thing, but maybe not by much. The back of the seat itself was still a good five feet above his head and the tree rose up beyond that, still short of the ceiling. Seamed metal and incautious nails showed where it had been disassembled for transport, and re-assembled here by less careful hands. Where the metal remained at the bottom, it showed stylized figures, hands raised in celebration or supplication, a procession around the base of the throne, approaching the stairs. Six steps, the first one maybe ten feet long, composed of a dozen or more types of wood inlaid with ivory and cabochons of lapis lazuli, malachite and mother-of-pearl. Two lions sat there, gazing fixedly at each other, their expressions stern. On the next step, bears, one of them badly damaged, its face broken away, an empty tube showing that might have carried its voice, or even a perfume or smoke. Above them, griffins clawed at the inlay, their hips raised and wings laid flat over their backs as they bowed before the absent king. Serpents coiled on the stair above, their forked tongues loose and dangling, then doves, roosting alertly, their beaks parted in greeting. At the top step, a pair of eagles stood, their wings unsettled as if they had just been disturbed from their perch, their eyes, at this angle, glaring down at him. One wing on the right rose up too high, shadowing whatever mechanism would make it flap. Grant couldn't see much from where he stood, the throne rising above him.

The sudden shrill protest of the hyrax broke the silence. Grant's heartbeat echoed after, the drum to sound the army's approach.

If the king won. If the next people to enter this chamber were terrorists and knights, and it was here he made his last stand, Grant wanted to complete his record, his final report to his client. Fuck that. He wanted to know the seat of Solomon if it were the last thing he did.

Grant moved toward the center. He must tread lightly, carefully, as a guest and not a usurper.

Across the bottom step, the inlay pattern, and the gaps where it had broken, formed words. He frowned, tracing them with his eyes and the light, the tiny drone still pinched in his fingers. "Anima Justi Sedes Sapientiae," he breathed, then understood. *The soul of the righteous man is the seat of wisdom.* Was he righteous? After everything he had done, could he make such a claim? One way to find out.

He cast a look to the lions on either side, bowed his head, and mounted the step.

CHAPTER SEVENTY-THREE

B laise stared through the window frame. Casey's trail snaked through the pine needles down the slope and up the other side, painfully obvious. What had he seen? What did it matter? He felt the pinch of not having personally solved the clue, but the clues, in this case, meant so much less than the prize he was pursuing. The mask would conceal his disappointment, so long as his voice revealed nothing. "Go around," he called to those behind him. "There's no need all of us climbing out a window."

"I intend to," Farouk muttered, finally releasing his gun and sliding it around to his back. He started forward, but Blaise cut him off and climbed through himself. Farouk followed, along with a few knights and Shifra.

They were so close now to the prize that Blaise felt an itch in his palms. His legacy at last awaited. And, just as close, so did Casey. Birds flapped among the trees and some blasted creature on the far slope cried warning over and over again. Blaise considered asking Farouk to target the creature just to make it shut up, but that wouldn't do. He schooled himself to patience. From inside the trees at the far side of the gully, they found the ledge that became a road, or vice versa.

"If you will permit me, your majesty." Farouk tucked his cigarette into his chest pocket, "he may have established himself in a sniper's nest up there. We should be careful."

They stood a moment, scanning the area, and movement near the ridge caught Blaise's eye. "That—it's a drone." Was Akbulut around here somewhere? The drone moved slowly along the ridge.

Farouk shifted his gun forward. "I could shoot from here, but we then warn the prey."

"If you think he's not already on alert, you are not as clever as I imagined. Do it."

Farouk took careful aim, then fired a single shot. The drone skipped upward in the sky, then slewed down to the ground, twisting like a wounded animal attempting to rise. Farouk grinned, waiting for praise

"It's running a program," Blaise muttered. "If it were under remote command, they wouldn't let it flop around like that. We need some men on top of that ridge." Farouk gave a few hand signals and three of his men took off, running low and parallel. Blaise frowned at the ridge. In spite of the rough ground, most possible hideouts were down low, to the sides rather than along the relatively smooth gully wall. What was the drone doing up there? Not looking for him and his entourage, certainly.

The trees groaned and creaked around him, the forest weighing on his shoulders. Blaise straightened as Farouk's men scrambled into place up along the ridge, working their way back. The nasty creature had finally stopped its cry and gone underg—

Casey didn't come this way at random, he followed the Seal of Solomon. And that meant he had not vanished abruptly either. "The ridge is hollow. We need to find the way in." The bulk of their group appeared to his left at the mouth of the gully, and Blaise came down to meet them. One of the men on the ridge reached for the drone, stumbled and cried out as he apparently tripped over the low grass. The throne would allow him to recruit to a higher standard.

Blaise led the march up the path, and the disturbed earth at the base of the thorn tree was all too clear, as if Casey had ceased to care if anyone followed, but the narrow, dimly lit corridor of stone also made an excellent ambush site. "This tree. I need it gone."

"Yes, my lord." Darius sprang forward slicing the brush with clean, powerful strokes. He and another knight, both wearing leather gauntlets, gathered and mounded the brush to the side, revealing a gap wide enough for only a single person, the way made narrow by a stone inserted some time after the path was made. Still, no shots fired.

Farouk cocked his head, regarding the way. "Two of your men, two of mine, in sequence moving forward."

"Agreed." A few swift orders made it so.

After the first two passed the opening, one called back, "It's wider here, right away! It's clearly a tunnel."

"Go on, then," Farouk shouted.

Blaise pushed past, gesturing his knights after him. The idea of some terrorist getting the first glimpse of his throne since the Templars concealed it—that, he could not bear. Eight hundred years ago, his brethren, the original Templars, carved this very corridor. They walked this path, an idea that resonated through his bones. For these last several years, he had toiled to build coalitions, to draw followers, to walk the footsteps of chivalry. He had reclaimed their temples, and stood in their towers, as if his way and theirs converged. He conjured up the best of their ideals, shaved away the greed that had corrupted them and transformed the order into his own, the Knights Penitent. As Blaise walked the corridor to claim his birthright, the spirits of the King of Jerusalem and of his followers walked with him, a grand procession into the future.

Ahead, the light grew and the four men already inside paused at what must be an entrance. Carvings marked the inner arch, all wrought from the living stone.

"My lord!" Darius turned to him, eyes alight. "It's here."

"And where is Casey?"

The terrorists, more wily than his virtuous knights, scowled into the room, one kneeling, one standing with his back to the wall. "If the dog is here, he must be on the other side of the throne. Maybe in one of the chapels."

Blaise loosened his sword in its sheath and stepped up a little nearer. Using the throne as a shield. The coward—of course he was. Blaise devoured the throne with his eyes, itching to cross the room and mount those stairs, to finally claim the seat so long preserved for him. He stepped back and motioned Farouk closer to whisper in his ear. "Those columns of light. Get your men lined up to them, those will be our sniper holes."

Farouk gave a nod and a grin. "And this, your majesty, is why you are king."

Blaise hoped it wasn't only to direct battle, but still, Farouk's deference gratified him. The man sent whispered commands back along the group. Within the corridor, every sound echoed and redoubled. Beyond it, nothing could be heard.

Blaise strode back to the arch. Bits of dirt and gravel trickled from above and the columns grew more distinct as those on the top cleared away the surrounding grasses.

The king stood, flanked by his knights and supporters, more of them filling in behind him, more of them lurking above like avenging angels. "Show yourself, dog!" he cried out, his voice resounding from the throne room. Shadows shifted on the gleaming throne. Blaise took one more step. "Come, coward, if you would confront your king!"

A gunshot split the silence and thundered in his ears.

CHAPTER SEVENTY-FOUR

Grant leveled his weapon. If he simply picked off whoever popped through the arch, it would take only a few shots before they set up a full-on assault of his position. No point targeting minions, but when the king's shining mask emerged from the gloom, Grant hesitated no more. Take pictures, turn it over to authorities—or take out the lunatic at the top of the heap.

Aim carefully. Heartbeat, the gleam of silver strands in the king's dark hair. Squeeze. Absorb the slight recoil. Sighting along the gun barrel, the strand of silver shifting to a silver flash.

The king's head turned. The sound of the gunshot briefly deafened, followed by the quiet chime of the bullet deflecting off the king's silver mask.

Stone spit out where the bullet struck the wall, and the king staggered slightly, his head jerked with the impact. A streak of blood slashed along the edge of his jaw. A divot bent the metal inward, cutting his face even as it saved his life.

And Grant had revealed his place for nothing. Not like he'd had a lot of choices.

"Get that coward off my throne." The king's voice echoed in the wake of the shot, cold with fury and loud with outrage.

From above, the scrape of metal on stone. Grant caught on not a moment too soon. Shots sprayed down from the skylights, the angle made awkward by the thickness of the stone: the only thing that saved his life in the first thirty seconds.

Grant leapt up from the seat where he'd been crouching. He wrapped one hand over the Seal of Solomon at its back and swung himself behind. From a different skylight, another barrage, pinging off of metal and digging into wood. Grant's right hand burned with sudden agony and the gun tumbled away. He wrapped his arms around the tree trunk, slithering downward, his own blood speeding his course. Already, knights and Shifra poured into the room. Men rushed him from both sides.

"Stop, stop shooting! Don't ruin what we've come here for!" The king howled.

Farouk's voice echoed this. "Take him down, but take him alive."

Grant swept out the sword right-handed, blood streaming from a groove across his hand, his back and shoulder punched by shots that didn't get through the Kevlar. VP had his vote all the way—if he lived to cast another ballot.

Second pistol in his left hand. No caution now, no aiming—no time for that when he had only so many heartbeats left. A bearded man lunged at him, and Grant's shot flung him back into his fellows. A knight's sword darted for his side.

Grant twisted away, his back to the throne, sword on guard too late. Another shot took down the knight, howling and clamping her hand to her wounded abdomen.

The stock of a rifle smashed his temple, knocking him away from relative safety. It drove down again for his throat. He slipped in blood, his left foot twisting under him, by accident more than skill dodging another blow. At least from that direction. Other blows rained down. He fired again, into the throng, then hands grabbed his arm and wrenched the gun away. He sliced the back of the nearest attacker and won an elbow to the face. More hands digging in. Someone kicking him from behind, taking his legs out from under him, right arm bent back and the sword wrested from his bloody grip. They kicked him forward and he rolled hard across the stone floor. A column of sunlight spilled across his face and chest, a glow of apotheosis before the hands descended once more. Two men each gripped his arms, hauling him to his knees in the light. Blood streaked his vision and stung his lips.

Farouk kicked his knees further apart, setting up for the cheap shot. From behind, someone took a deliberate step closer, setting their foot over his left, sole to sole. They leaned in, pressing their weight onto his injured foot, grinding it into the floor.

Grant choked for breath, his ribcage stuttering with the pain. Tearing open Grant's shirt, Farouk yanked free the Velcro that clasped the bulletproof vest and jerked it off, heedless of his face or ears. From the corner of his eye, Grant saw the bee-drone still clipped to its base, the shoulder of his shirt now flapping free. He imagined the fisheye lens spattered with blood like a scene from a slasher film. One in which he tried to be the predator, and ended up as victim number one.

With a little extra torque they could dislocate both arms, broken like a monster invading their Golden Hall. The pain addled his mind and mixed up his metaphors. The bastard behind him grabbed his hair, wrenching his head back to spit in his face.

Grant managed a twitch of his right shoulder, like half a shrug as if he didn't care what they did to him. It earned him the kick he'd been waiting for, an explosion of pain in exchange for the slide of his shirt over his shoulder, realigning the tiny camera with his forward view. One of them, at least, could be doing their job. Minutes passed, an eternity in which he saw nothing but red, tossed on an ocean of pain and struggling for breath.

Feet tramped as the enemy rearranged around him, sending shocks through his bruised knees, every step reverberating through his body as the king approached and stared down into his face.

The silver mask distorted and swam, weeping blood from one side beneath a dent in the metal. Grant's own face, battered and smeared with blood and dirt rippled over that surface as the king examined him. For a moment, their faces aligned, and Grant saw himself hovering above, towering in gray, the Devil's face in the smoke of 9-11, if the devil could bleed. The pits of dark eyes stared back into his own, the damage to the mask warping Grant's reflection like a bullet to the brain.

CHAPTER SEVENTY-FIVE

Casey's body stretched before the king, his arms pulled wide, his face grooved with pain, his chest bared, already streaked with blood and peppered with bruises, lean and vulnerable. Standing as Blaise did in a structure resembling a church, he recognized the resonance in his enemy's posture, and rejected it in the same instant. Any man of flesh could be brought to submission, it did not make him holy or worthy or even important. Blaise turned his back, utterly without fear of this craven, broken thing. "Are we all assembled?"

"Nearly, my lord," Chloe answered. "Two are tending to the wounded, and Haldan's charge is in the corridor."

"Let them come." He urged them all forward with his hand. The prisoner knelt beneath one of the skylights to the right of the throne he had befouled with his blood and his presence. Haldan led the way, his small consort following with the Black man in their midst. As they entered, the man's head lifted, his eyes ablaze, and his voice rolled out with a preacher's power, "Behold the king is come!"

Behind him, Casey uttered the first sound he had made since they entered the chamber. Silent through the shooting, silent through his own assault against them, silent through the beating he earned in reply. Casey cried out, somewhere between pain and longing. Not a word or a name, nothing so articulate. Blaise smiled behind his mask. His enemy had lost even the power of speech. Did his friend's presence give him a nugget of joy, or only a greater despair, knowing they would die together?

Blaise turned about and sank low, again meeting his captive's eye, but this time, on his own level, searching his face. Casey's lips compressed, his breathing shallow and pained, his eyes glittered behind a mask of blood. "I see you do have a heart, my false knight. If I were to bring him to you, if you could see his face, Mr. Casey, would I get to see you cry?"

His lashes fluttered, a quick blink, and he swallowed, a thin line of blood marking his lips. "My lord," he said, and his voice went low and husky, "I believe that you would."

He blinked again, his face a visual struggle with emotion, the habitual blank of the mercenary no longer quite so easy to command. Pain or grief down-turned the corners of his mouth, his nostrils flared a little with the need for breath or the need to suppress. The tattooed lion at his throat appeared to flex its paw with each small gasp.

"Tell me how you climbed the throne," Blaise said, his voice pitched for one man only. Blaise doubted that the throne had any power in it—any but what faith could offer—but he had not come so far without prudence.

Casey's glance flicked up toward the throne and golden dust motes danced between them like the ash from an unseen fire. "I read the inscription, and walked up the steps. My lord, I only knew where I had to go."

To make of Solomon's throne, a sniper's nest. A fool's answer. Blaise let his disappointment underlie his voice. "What if I were to bring him to you to watch him die, and bathe you in his blood, then would you weep?"

"My lord," he said, and Blaise almost thought he heard a smile, "It wouldn't be the first time." The trace of smile fled. "Nor would I be the first to cry."

He was not really trying to deliver a threat, not now, when Farouk stood over him with a machete in one hand and a rifle at his back. Not when five men held him down, and almost thirty more stood waiting only their king's command to slash him to ribbons.

Casey's eyes tracked Blaise as he rose and turned away, directing the knights to bring their man to one of the alcoves. Somewhat a relief, really, not to have to make threats against a man essentially blameless but for following the wrong leader. Knights and Shifra formed ranks before the throne, just beyond the arc of the skylights, respecting his sacred space.

Haldan approached, giving a brief bow. He turned aside a moment, with a scowl. "I'll take that." He put out an imperious hand, and one of the Shifra in the group beyond Casey's humiliation ducked his head and held out the king's sword, streaked with blood from both sides of the short battle.

Haldan received it reverently in both hands, not putting his own upon the hilt, of course. "My lord, it is unfit for you. Let me clean it."

"Thank you, Haldan."

Nearby, Farouk made a harsh sound at the back of his throat. "So, are you going up?" He gestured toward the throne with a blade as long as his arm. "We have a trial to close, and I think you want the condemned to witness."

"Indeed." Blaise released all tension from his body, surrounded as he was by his supporters, even his fallen enemy made to see the true king's rise. The throne itself gave him a moment's pause. He knew the rumors, the way the throne could shed those unworthy to mount it. But Casey had, and none could be so unworthy as he. Chances were, any tricks the throne held were long since ruined, damaged by those who stripped parts of its glory, or simply degraded with the passage of time. He strode slowly to stand before the throne, gazing upon the words Casey spoke of. *Sedes Sapientiae.* The seat of wisdom indeed. Slipping a silk kerchief from his pocket, he took a moment to wipe the blood from his cheek where Casey's bullet deflected from his mask, and said silent thanks to his ancestor, the king of Jerusalem whose mask had inspired him. He stepped between the lions, walked coolly up the stairs, his cape rippling behind him, and turned a smooth pivot at the center. He raised his arms to receive the cheering of his people, then settled his cape and, at very long last, took his throne.

CHAPTER SEVENTY-SIX

Cheering echoed from the passage and Kyra's companions shared a look. Her heart quickened as they stepped into the corridor. Two bearded men led the way. She sweated under a full niqab, certain the whole time she should have stayed away. One task. Stay silent. No matter what she saw, no matter what lay beyond this walk, no matter what she heard or saw. No matter how much blood had already been spilled. Stay silent. All she had to do was to get in range of the bee-drone Casey wore. It would sync automatically, then she could walk away and take the information he had gathered. She had no skills to handle any of what might happen, nothing but the evidence to justify it all. She would turn her back on the smell of blood and the sounds of violence, just like the Book of Job: *and I alone am escaped to tell thee.*

"My lord," called one of the two men as he brought their procession forward. A knight by the entrance turned and frowned. Four women, two Shifra guards—nothing to be concerned over. The two women in front held jugs cradled in their concealed hands.

"Hold," said the knight. "Aren't you supposed to be guarding the gate?"

The man shrugged. "They have rumors about a king, about a time of peace—not my business, eh? But they want to, I don't know—oil him?" He waved a hand vaguely.

One of the women held up her jug of olive oil. "Anoint him," she said softly, with the meek tones of a woman who expected not to speak unless spoken to.

The man growled, but the knight gave a sharp nod. "Anoint him! Of course. My lord." He walked forward, indicating the small group of women should follow. "You two, get back on guard."

Kyra held her mobile in both hands, terrified she would tremble so much the phone simply fell and clattered on the ground, interrupting what was meant to be a solemn ceremony. Of course the mad king would want to be anointed. The space opened out, and she wanted to look up, she wanted more than anything to lift her head and see, but the others all walked heads bowed, and so she followed their example, demure, eyes on her device.

The cheering died down slowly.

In her hand, a new alert blossomed, then pictures flitted by as the drone synced and uploaded in segments. Dark passage, columns of light, close-up on the throne, Casey's grin caught in profile as he guided the drone on a tour, just for her. He used a light and the gaps in the metal to illuminate the workings at the heart of the throne. Rods, gears, smooth curves of metal that would slide together—he gave her exactly what she would have wanted, before she even knew to ask. And she had wanted to fire him. She had only hired him in order to humiliate him and his firm, discarding them as she had so many others. On the way to his death, he had made her a movie. He had made her father's dream come true. Had he and Nick already been united in death? If she did look up would she see not the magnificent throne, but the gruesome remains of two men who had won her trust?

The sync alert blinked and faded, showing a live feed from across the chamber, a skewed and half-tint view as if something obscured the lens. It moved slightly, shivering up and down, up and down, as if it were—no, as if he were breathing. Relief overwhelmed her. Her knees felt shaky. Turn and walk away, retreat a few steps to the archway, then a few steps more—then flee as if her life depended on it, because it did.

"You have come with an offering, good women?"

"We have," answered one of them. "We were tending our grove when we saw the procession of your knights, and we thought at last the king has come."

The camera's view shifted, rising a few inches and growing steady.

A roar of excitement greeted this statement, and the king chuckled. "Please, please. You may leave your offering, and I thank you."

"Of course, your majesty."

In the blurry view, the two women with jugs moved forward, setting their jugs near the base of the throne. She could see two steps, the corner nearest where Casey knelt. Put the phone away. Don't jeopardize anyone else's safety. Phase two had come upon them, whatever happened.

Kyra took a step back. She slid the phone into her pocket, then took another step. She bumped into someone, who said, "Steady there." A woman's voice.

"Apologies," she answered, starting to turn, but the other woman caught her elbow.

"Those shoes. You were working in the orchard in Manolo Blahniks? How do you keep them so clean?" The voice turned hard.

Kyra froze, but the other woman dragged her forward, stumbling in her stupid, stupid shoes.

"My lord!" The knight shouted. With her other hand, she peeled back Kyra's niqab and thrust her, stumbling, into the aisle before the throne. "Kneel before the king," said Chloe.

The Throne of Solomon rose before Kyra, monumentally beautiful, with the king in his silver mask seated at the top beneath a spray of orichalcum branches where once hung ruby fruit. Tears streaked her face. Her father's dream made manifest, and she, too, would die for it.

CHAPTER SEVENTY-SEVEN

The Akbulut woman crouched before him, finally modest, finally stripped of her decadence. "I had to see it!" she blurted. "I had to see the throne, to see if it was true."

She smeared the tears from her face, but they only came anew. "I don't know if you can understand, but maybe you can. You are perhaps the only person who could understand what it is to look for so long, to keep searching when everyone thinks you're—" she stopped at the word, but he knew. He did understand.

When everyone thinks you are mad. He had thought she must be around somewhere, looking over Casey's shoulder with that drone they shot down outside, but he never imagined she would be so bold as to infiltrate this very chamber.

"You women—did you know of this?"

The other niqab-clad women clumped together, two of them clearly hugging each other now. The third turned her veiled head toward Akbulut. "Where's Suya? What have you done with her?" snappish and concerned.

"I paid her," Akbulut said. "I gave her money to take her place." Her gaze returned to the throne as if she could drink it in.

"You have seen it now, what do you think?" Blaise settled back against the Seal of Solomon, spreading his hands. He imagined presiding over courtrooms, respected for his judgment and fairness by all who came before him.

"It's magnificent." Her head shook in wonder. When she glanced toward Casey, her gaze immediately skittered away again, her chin tucked as if embarrassed now by what she was saying. "I would love to walk around it, to examine it—even the broken parts, to see how it's made, and how it works, how it used to work." The women had been speaking Arabic when they entered, and so Akbulut continued in that tongue, her face alight, and he found himself smiling, nodding.

"It will be important to conserve the throne properly of course," Blaise said.

"Conserved? I'd repair it." She stopped herself, her braid slapping her back as if in rebuke. "I'm sorry, I get carried away." She rolled her lips, knotting her fingers together before her. "If I could learn half of what our people knew."

"Indeed," he murmured. How else had he gotten here but by learning from the past?

"What should we do with her?" Chloe asked. Clever Chloe, spotting the other woman's clean, inappropriate shoes.

Farouk growled, "Can we please return to this business?" He jabbed his knife at Casey's side, just short of gutting him.

His impatience grated. Blaise sat here, throned in majesty, with local women bearing gifts and the brilliant and haughty Kyra Akbulut humbled before him, perhaps willing to collaborate—a thought he should really have considered earlier. "Chloe, take her aside." He let his good cheer ring in his voice as he projected. "Let her walk around the throne. She might as well see the whole thing."

Akbulut got to her feet, her face radiant behind the tears. "Thank you, my lord." The two walked away to his right, the other women watching them go, their modesty coverings obscuring their movements.

"So, Farouk. What is it you desire?" Blaise steepled his fingers, elbows on the ivory armrests. The seat was a little broad. Only by staying perfectly centered could he properly use both armrests. A bit to either side and he would resemble a petulant child lounging in his father's chair.

"I want him dead." Farouk stepped before Casey's pinioned figure.

The Shifra at Casey's back gripping his head, forcing him to watch and listen. With his blade slowly tracking each statement, Farouk detailed his plan.

"I want to slice off his genitals for how he stole our brides from us." His broad machete aimed downward.

He brought it a little higher, toward Casey's stomach. "Then I will open his guts like a pig, spilling his bowels onto the floor." The tip of the blade traced over Casey's shoulder and right arm. "I will peel off his blasphemous painted hide.

"I will carve out his tongue, for how he lied to us and betrayed us."

Farouk lifted the gun in his other hand. "I would like to shoot off his fingers one by one, but he might be already dead by then."

He released the gun and seized Casey's head between his hands. "And when he is, I will chop off his accursed head and carry it with me until I can personally deliver it to his bitch whore lying murdering bride."

CHAPTER SEVENTY-EIGHT

F arouk's hands squeezed Grant's skull as he recited his gruesome incantation. Grant's skin felt tight, his muscles bound as his tormentor forced him to envision every step of his punishment. His shoulders throbbed and every breath cut deeper.

Grant stared at Farouk, stared through him, his being focused on revealing nothing. He had tried to play the king earlier, displaying enough emotion to make the king want more. Want to see some suffering? Oh, yeah, bring Nick over. Let the two of them see each other, let them have one, clear line of sight and watch the fucking fireworks.

Atop the throne, the king chuckled, a nasty little sound like stones tumbling down the steps to strike at Grant from afar. Kyra had already gone behind it, would soon emerge on Grant's right, and maybe see the reality of his position for the first time. Desperate to get a glimpse of the throne, maybe willing to cut a deal with a lunatic to walk out of here, free and clear. Who was the mercenary now?

"You want vengeance because I stopped your bomb?" Grant made the question clear and pointed, the tiny camera still at work, to be exhumed later from a shallow grave.

"The next bomb we set will be bigger. Our next target will clear the way for the king forever," Farouk snarled down at him with a wicked glee. "And you will be nothing but dogmeat."

He released Grant's head to draw his huge machete over Grant's face, taking it inch by inch. The gleaming length of it cut the light across Grant's vision.

"My lord, a boon." Haldan walked the aisle, and Farouk snarled as the Viking came alongside. "Today marks a new day in your reign, my lord. Begin as you mean to continue, with both justice and mercy."

"Mercy? For him?" Farouk swung away, the machete still in hand, clearing Grant's view. "After what he's done to us? Not just my people, but yours, too."

Haldan stood before his king, holding the king's sword atop his flat palms. Like the other knights, Haldan dressed well for the occasion with a short cape, his shoulder-length hair topped by a braid, four braids in his red-gold beard. He looked fierce, more Viking today than Crusader, in spite of the sword at his side. He spoke English, unlike most of the others, but his French accent grew more obvious today. Haldan was nervous. "You have always valued sober judgment, my lord. And well I know that you wish each people to be given leave to govern their own."

He slumped a little, his head bowing. "My lord, by that metric, the false knight's punishment belongs to us, to the Knights Penitent. While it's true that he's wronged us all, he was able to do so because of me, because I brought him in. It must have been through the knights he gathered what he needed to attack the Shifra as well. It's my fault, my lord." He swallowed. "I don't know how else to show my true repentance. Unless you would descend and dispense justice by your own hand." He withdrew a step, his toe circling back, a fencer's re-set to face his opponent: Grant, unarmed, already beaten.

"You claim to want to serve for all, but you favor your own kind, it's clear!" Farouk shouted up at the throne.

Haldan lay the king's sword on the ground at his feet and drew his own. "My lord, let it be done. For a failed knight, a knight's death." His eyes, rusty brown, focused on Grant, that slight pinch between them as he set the point of his sword just over Grant's shoulder, ready to sweep off his head. His skin cooled with the touch of steel.

"My dear Haldan, you were my first believer—"

"Aha!" Farouk shouted, and some of his followers hissed their agreement.

"Please, my friends, allow me to finish." The king's oratorical tone rose, swelling to fill the chamber. "Haldan. I understand why you ask this boon. You would deal a merciful death for my own sake, to allow me to begin my rule with clean hands. You would also, I suspect, prefer a man who once saved your life to die with some dignity, and I respect that. However, the crimes he has done to us, to you and I, my friend, and our fellow knights, pale in comparison with what he's done to these, our brethren in the line of Abraham. It is with great regret I say I cannot grant your boon." The king's voice rang, indeed, with sorrow on behalf of his friend.

Energy vibrated the length of the blade, the faintest tremor. Haldan's eyes once more met Grant's. For a moment, he thought he might have an ally, if only to administer the coup de grace. Then Farouk stepped between them, pushing Haldan back.

"You heard the king." Farouk readied his machete. "If you're too weak to watch, then go away—I hate the smell of weakness."

Haldan retreated a half-step, another of those careful moves, lifting his sword away. "Forgive me," he said softly—then his retreat became a quick, slashing movement, his blade driving toward Farouk's gut.

Farouk howled and leapt backward, stumbling over his own men.

Hands slipped and pulled free of Grant's arm as their own leader fell into the men on his right.

Dropped abruptly on the right, Grant snatched the king's sword from the ground and thrust it home into the gut of the first man on his left. The other kept hold of Grant's wrist while he grappled with his gun, trying to bring it around one-handed. Grant got his foot under him and pulled hard. The man overbalanced and Grant's blade skewered him.

"My lord, what aid?" Chloe called out as she rounded the throne at a run, her sword in her hand.

Haldan danced forward in pursuit of his prey, his slice biting the throat of the man who had been at Grant's back. In another step, a lower slice carving into the braincase of another of the captors as the man struggled to free his weapon.

Behind the mess of the dying, Farouk regained his balance and spun about. "You are accursed of Allah!" Arabic. His own men's blood spattered his face and uniform.

Pushing to both feet, Grant slid the thrashing corpse from the end of his blade, then brought it around to clash with an incoming rifle butt. He and Haldan stood back to back now, a circle of deadly steel. They could be attacked from any side, but only by a few people at once.

"Hey, Viking, do you always join up on the losing side?" Grant asked.

"Only when it's the right one," Haldan answered, then his sword rang as he parried an attack. "Give me your left hand."

Grant obeyed, without hesitation. For a moment, their hands clasped between them, and Haldan pressed something into his palm. "The key. He needs it. You're the runner. I've got your back."

From the throne, the king's voice went wild, all control of his tone shattered by this latest betrayal. "Kill the traitor! Kill him and bring me his heart!"

Haldan was in for it now. Fending off another assault, Grant plunged forward, Haldan a step or two behind, fighting a rear-guard action, already keying into each other's sounds and movements. Their prior bout gave each a hint of how the other fought, and they used it now. There: beyond the crowd in an alcove, he caught sight of Nick's bald, dark head.

Another knight swept in before him, this one with a pistol in hand. Grant dropped low and sliced upward, his sword drinking blood. Nice piece of steel, that.

A shot rang out and someone screamed. For an instant Grant believed his own swing had missed, and the knight fired over him, taking out Haldan. Instead, the enemy before him slumped aside, his gun tumbling away as his arm hung crookedly, muscles cleaved by Grant's blade.

"No shooting," the king roared. "Don't kill each other—we can't go mad for two traitors."

The gun, somewhere ahead, fired again, a single shot, and a Shifra collapsed. It wasn't madness, it was precision. A sniper, and he was on

Grant's side.

A gap opened in the crowd as the confusion redoubled, and Grant caught a glimpse of Nick, his wrists chained, a pistol gripped in one hand, that cold stare choosing another target.

CHAPTER SEVENTY-NINE

Blaise sat the top of his throne as his realm descended into blood and madness. Every knight that Haldan struck, Blaise felt the blow, every stroke of his own sword in the false knight's hand sliced chill fury through the king's own breast, and now someone was shooting, and another Shifra fell.

"Stop now! You must stop shooting!" he commanded, in Turkish, in English, in Arabic.

Chloe dove into the fray, pursuing Haldan with the vigor of an avenging angel. Farouk cursed and howled, trying to drive back his own people to let the knights make best use of their weapons, then he swung about with his machete. Yes. Hack Haldan's legs from his body and let him fall. Let him cry for mercy now and receive none.

At the base of the throne, three figures in niqab remained, no longer huddling together. The one who had spoken flung back her cover and raised her arm at the same time: straight before her, extending—no, not a gun, a crossbow, a sight so disconcerting, even to Blaise, that it took him far too long to recognize it.

"Farouk! Behind you—the woman!" Blaise pointed. He had no weapon of his own: Haldan cleaned his blade, polished it on his own cloak and gave it right back to his enemy. The entire chamber seemed to flicker and twirl in Blaise's vision.

On the floor below, Farouk swiveled, machete raised. His eyes flared wide, his mouth spewing a line of invective.

The woman before him stood firm. "If you wish to deliver his head, you don't have far to go." She fired.

A shaft plunged into Farouk's breast. He stumbled, gasping, then swayed forward again. The woman swept another bolt from a quiver at her side, pulled back the string as if she had all the time in the world as Farouk closed the distance.

She fired again, point blank into his throat as he raised his machete against her.

Across the room, Casey shouted, "Nick! Go high!" He threw something, a small flash of metal that tumbled through the air over the heads of those eager to get a blade into him. The Negro, his friend, dropped his weapon—fool—and reached up, snagging the shining thing from the air. He landed in a crouch and the handcuffs tumbled loose. He ignored the pistol instead sliding the rifle from the nearest of his guards already dead. When? How? How could everything go so disastrously wrong just when he had found the greatest symbol of his power? Hagia Dynamis!

Blaise surged to his feet, fists raised. "The traitors must fall! There can be no mercy! Chloe—get around him. Darius—the woman, the one with the burqa!" He leapt to the side, jabbing his finger as if he could aim their blades and their bullets. He must take advantage of his superior height to direct his forces to victory. Against a team of only four, it should be swift.

The two columns of light that framed him, so magnificent in their glow and sparkle, hosted the dance of battle. The one on his right cast the woman's shadow as she re-loaded her weapon and dodged the fury of the Shifra. The one on his left—blood dripped down through the skylight, a sad, gentle rain. Blaise hissed and arched his body, trying to see upward. A hand hung down, the fingers just visible, splayed in accusation, dripping blood.

He spun about to the battle before him, but that image, the impotent hand dripping with blood, stained his vision.

The seat of Solomon groaned beneath him and gave a shudder.

Blaise faltered.

He stepped back to the top, but it didn't help, the throne swayed and pitched. With his every movement, his every effort to remain centered, the throne danced beneath him, rolling like a dinghy in a storm. Blaise struggled for balance and found none. He flailed as the throne tipped again, backward this time, and a bullet whizzed past where his head had been. He grabbed the arm of the seat, and it rolled lazily forward again, the ancient mechanism moaning and grumbling. One of the eagles gave a raspy croak. Its wing lifted and clapped down as the throne dipped like a bested fencer bowing at the end of his fight. Blaise's feet slid out from under him. He clawed at the inlay and slapped at the ivory as he slid down the steps. The damaged bear scraped his hand as he grappled with it, trying to arrest his descent. He landed hard, flung on his side at the feet of his throne.

With a ratcheting chuckle of metal, the first step lifted away from him, and the throne drew back, righting itself in a series of small chimes like delicate laughter. The Throne of Solomon stood tall once more, after expelling its king.

CHAPTER EIGHTY

At the grind and chorus of the throne's ancient workings, Grant flashed a look behind him. In the heart of the chamber, Farouk lay impaled, and the king scrambled to his feet, his mask skewed. He tried to tug it back into place, but the dented silver would not obey, and he flung it aside. Blood streaked his face and his silvered hair. He bared his teeth. A number of the Shifra backed away from him, glancing from Farouk's body to the king.

"Come, come my friends! They are few and we are many," the king insisted, but Farouk's lieutenant shook his head, gesturing with his gun toward the throne.

"You are nobody's heir. You are nothing." At his back, some of the Shifra peeled away, breaking ranks and fleeing for the passage.

"This is not over!" The king shouted. "We shall win and claim our kingdom."

As if her king's words gave her courage, Chloe drove forward. Haldan twisted away from her, leaving his back briefly exposed, and a machete swung toward him. Grant lunged, overextended, but deflected most of the blow. It sliced at Haldan's kidney and slid free, a shallow wound that prodded Haldan a little further.

Chloe pressed her advantage. She swept her foot forward, catching Haldan's ankle and flipping him down. He landed hard, full-length, gaping up at Grant as his still-fragile head struck. Haldan's eyes unfocused. Shit—

oh, shit.

Already off-balance himself, Grant turned his movement into a back-swing, slicing his blade over his fallen comrade.

Chloe's blade struck his as she thrust for Haldan's heart. Her point rang against Grant's and he barely trapped it to the side as Haldan gasped a breath.

A shot buzzed between them, Grant in a low crouch that burned his weary muscles, Chloe bent over him. She drew back, freeing her blade and swinging again in a vicious backhand. Grant brought his sword up, palming the tip to hold it like a bar over them, countering her attack with both arms. The force of her blow sent shockwaves through his shoulders.

Haldan rolled and scrambled out of the way, still struggling for breath. Chloe's blue eyes narrowed and she did not follow.

"How dare you?" Her spittle struck Grant's face. "To cover yourself in shame and defeat, fine—but to ruin a man like him? To reeve him from his king?"

Grant dropped to his back, using the pressure between their blades to draw her closer. He kicked, catching her thigh and knocking her aside. Into the space that opened, Grant rolled to his feet, unsteady, but standing. "Your king is fallen—he was rejected by his own damn throne."

"It is an ancient thing, of sticks and rocks—the king is more, he is greater, and so are we." She attacked, graceful and deadly, the sword an extension of her body and every bit of her power aimed at slaughter. Grant parried, barely deflecting a blow, then earning a slap against his arm, a slice across his ribs. He spun like a dancer, and she stomped toward his left foot. Grant pulled away by an inch and staggered into the wall, his right arm thrown wide, his hand hitting hard.

A perfectly timed cut slashed for his wrist. He pulled back and the blow smote his hand, knocking free his sword to clatter on the ground. Chloe grinned as she brought her sword up for the killing thrust.

"Don't get cocky—my wife's behind you with a crossbow."

"Bullshit, Casey. You're not really married."

"Try telling her that."

The bolt erupted in blood from Chloe's chest and her knees crumpled. Grant side-stepped the falling body and met Akilah's eye. "Damn, but it's good to see you."

Her lips quirked up. "How is it said in America? Honey, I'm home."

CHAPTER EIGHTY-ONE

Blaise grabbed the machete from Farouk's dead hand and a pistol from another corpse. Across the room, Chloe trapped the fucking traitor, on his back before her, only to be dislodged by the false knight, a man so slick they should name snake oil after him. She would succeed, for she was righteous and strong. The accursed Viking couldn't breathe, couldn't even stand but crawled to the wall to drag himself up.

Chloe fixated on Casey: remove the greater threat, but she did not see the Negro converging on their location, still calmly aiming and firing, like a machine made to kill. He worked sidelong until Haldan sheltered at his back as he targeting the fleeing rats of Shifra.

"My lord! Behind you!" Darius shouted, then he ran up as Blaise spun about. Two more women in niqab, and for all of his disdain about men who could not see the power of women, Blaise had forgotten them. Save that they were not women.

The leader dropped his guise and darted forward with a curved knife in his hand, a thin man Blaise recognized. Nizari. Darius fought him back, but the Assassin ducked and dodged, his small frame and quick movements almost taunting the larger man. The last niqab dropped to the floor as well, and the man beneath—clad in mottled, close-fitting garb the shade of sunlight in pine trees—leapt lightly to the back of one of the knights and slashed open his throat. The Assassin dropped away again, his curved blade flicking blood across the column of light as the knight collapsed.

Blaise aimed past Darius's defense and fired, his shot punching the farther Assassin. A second shot smacked him down.

The nearer man dropped back, vanishing in an instant among the Shifra who still jostled for a chance at Casey.

Casey.

"To me, my knights—to me!" Blaise rallied his remaining brethren. "The traitors must pay." His gaze swept the back of the chamber, exposed without his mask, his face felt sticky with sweat and blood. "You, Shifra! Take down the Negro!"

The knights scattered away from the alcove where the Negro and his cowering traitor sheltered. Eight or more Shifra remained, still armed.

"Two knights!" Casey shouted, and the thief he had married answered, "One horse."

Stealing even the Templars' symbol of their strength together.

In Arabic, Casey shouted, "You dogs didn't deserve your wives—I fucked them all!"

The Shifra wavered, the knights still clearing away. The Negro threw aside his rifle and scrambled for another—Haldan the worm got there first, stripping one from a body and tossing it in the air for his defender to catch. Chloe sprawled on the ground between, blood pumping from her stricken heart.

Casey did what Casey had always done. He ran, and his thief ran with him, armed with Chloe's sword, the quiver empty of bolts.

"He's trying to distract you," Blaise barked.

He pivoted, tracking Casey, then lunged after him. Farouk's view of punishment sounded more and more right, mutilating the man who had done so much to destroy the king's reign. Whatever it took to finish him off, but the more painful, the better. Casey and his thief were making for the throne, the scene of Casey's ultimate victory, for he had mounted it and Blaise had been cast down.

Except that someone else already occupied it. Kyra Akbulut stood at the top, her feet braced, a jug in her hands. She hurled it toward the alcove. It streaked oil through the air, then smashed on the ground among the

Shifra, spilling a slick that made them stumble just as they finally came together. That woman held his throne and he could not. How could it possibly be that she—that Casey—that either of them was more righteous than he?

Darius and two others rushed the couple at the bottom of the stairs. Casey's thief dropped to one knee, claiming a pistol while Casey used the king's sword to knock back the blades that came for them. She fired without the discipline of the Negro, but still effective.

Blaise sliced the air with his machete, learning its weight as he stalked closer, then Darius made his attack against the woman. Casey defended, and Blaise plunged into the opening, slashing Casey's back. When Casey twisted to confront him, Blaise pushed forward.

The woman dove out of the way, tucking and rolling to avoid fouling her partner's stance, and leaving him the more exposed. Their blade's clashed, Casey's eyes dark and determined.

Blaise swept back his weapon. "You think you've ruined everything, but you will not win."

"I already have." He thrust.

Blaise parried easily.

Bullets sprayed through a column of light, and Akbulut screamed from the top of the throne.

From the corner of his eye, Blaise saw the Negro's advance, abandoning his protective niche in favor of fighting for his client. At least one of these mercenaries had some sense of honor.

A slash missed Blaise's gut—he was already out of the way, circling back, wishing the column were stone and he could pin this worm against it. Instead, he charged with a flurry of blows, and Casey staggered before him, again favoring his left foot. Shadows moved around them. They danced through the path of light, the back of the throne looming over them, the pillar of the tree rising up toward the heavens.

Casey panted heavily, hard-pressed now, then he swept his blade low, in a weary movement. His foot slipped back and he dropped to one knee in the light of the fourth column, caught in a false halo of golden sunshine.

Blaise lunged after him, low and precise as he passed the rear corner of the throne. The shadows shifted.

A hand caught Blaise's hair and jerked back his head, arresting his forward momentum and drawing his neck taut. The Assassin's curved blade swept so cleanly across Blaise's throat that he continued his lunge, certain the blow had completely missed.

Blood welled into his throat and he gagged. He choked as he fell. He landed on his knees in front of his enemy. Casey's dark gaze held his even as the machete slipped from Blaise's grasp. His best friend betrayed him, his allies disobeyed him, and now his own hands, his own voice abandoned him. Blaise toppled to the floor, staring up at the dancing motes of gold.

Casey touched Blaise's hand, almost tenderly, then rose, eclipsing the skylight with his own darkness. He swept his stolen sword into a final salute, and walked away.

CHAPTER EIGHTY-TWO

The silver mask rocked in a swirl of blood and oil past the throne. Nick stood middle-ground, the rifle nestled in his arms as he scanned the shadows by the arch. The two knights who had backed the king lay nearby, their throats slit. Across the room, something moved, another assassin, this one in sand-stone beige save where his clothes were spattered red. He carried his curving blade backhand, stalking, then seized a man who lay crumpled by the back wall.

"Hey!" Grant ran, then slid across the oil slick that had befuddled the Shifra gunmen. Grant bent his knees like a surfer. "Let him go—he's one of mine."

The Assassin glanced back, Haldan's hair gripped in one hand, the dagger in the other. Haldan's chest stuttered as he breathed, his eyes still wrong.

Grant carried his sword, readying his stance as he reached dry ground. His right arm had gone numb with the fighting, but he managed. He would kill if he had to. "Let him go."

The Assassin gave a whistle.

Grant took a step closer, his left hand reaching, his sword in striking distance.

From the direction of the throne, an answering whistle. The Assassin released Haldan, but slid back just out of reach. Grant caught Haldan's shoulder, interposing himself between the stricken man and the Assassin.

Another whistle accompanied measured steps. The Assassin slipped away his blade then left the room, quick and silent. Grant turned to see Bashir strolling closer, wiping his own curved blade on a scrap of cloth. Bashir tipped his head toward Haldan. "He's not part of the deal."

Grant kept his blade ready. "And slaughtering all of the knights was?" He flicked his gaze over the room, where even the wounded had gone silent, and Nick now stood at the base of the stairs, Kyra crouched on the throne, keeping herself small. Not far away, Akilah caught his glance and saluted with her pistol, indicating the man in front of him, her own ally, but one she would apparently handle if he asked it. During the course of the fight, Grant spotted at least four Assassins: Bashir and the man who had come in with him disguised as women, plus the two guards who had accompanied them. Someone had killed the Shifra waiting above as well, the same men, or others?

"How many of you are there?"

"Same as the number of knives—at least one more than you think."

Grant sank a little, firming his grip. "I'd rather not kill you."

Bashir merely smiled. "I saw what he did for you. If you think you can trust him, I leave him to you." He bowed himself away, tucked the blade at his back and sprinted from the room.

Grant longed to sink down to the floor at Haldan's side, but the whole chamber, filled with the dead, its sole entrance narrow and too easy to block, made him twitchy. He tucked the sword through his belt and squatted. "Hey, Viking."

Haldan's head rested against the wall, his breath reaching toward normal. "Thank you."

A shake of the head. "No more than what you did, and I didn't have to sucker my best friend to do it."

His hazel eyes slid shut, brow pinched, and he wiped a shaky hand over his face.

"What changed your mind?" Grant asked.

"He did." Haldan gestured toward Nick. "I thought I could lure him to serve the king. I told him of the king's excellence of how he spoke and how great he could be. And he spoke to me of you." Haldan blinked and brought his unfocused gaze back to Grant. "Casey is the opposite, he told me. He thinks he does a crappy job. Bad leader, bad boss, bad friend, then he throws himself over for you every time. He does this for me a dozen times, Nick said, and now he's done it for you. He doesn't think of how to look good, or how to be a hero—he thinks it makes no difference. He would throw away his life if it saves somebody else, if it saves a thing worth saving. He'd rather die than fail somebody who's counting on him."

Grant heard echoes of Nick's voice in Haldan's words. "Sounds like he converted you," he said softly.

"The more I watched, the more I saw how different you were to him, to the king. Blaise always said a man who had made a mistake could repent and make a better future." His beard quirked toward a smile. "I hoped it would be true, even if that future were a very short one."

"You ready to move? At least get out to the sunshine and we take a look at that wound?"

His face cleared, and Haldan tried to stand. Taking his hand, Grant slipped an arm around him, supporting him to get to his feet. "You let me know when you need a third chance, Viking. I've got a place for you."

A breath of humor greeted this. "You don't even know who I am, or what I've done."

He did actually, thanks to D.A.'s searching, but he said, "I know what you did today, when you knew you would die right along with me. You asked for a chance at redemption, I'd consider it done. Besides, I kinda like the ink where it is."

"Not to mention the genitals," Haldan replied.

"What the hell're you guys laughing about?" Nick demanded, the rifle resting in his elbow. "And if there's genitals involved, I expect to be informed."

The sound of an engine interrupted, and Grant turned Haldan over to Nick, sprinting for the passageway, Akilah a bare two strides ahead of him. From a body by the door, he swept up a pistol, and darted a glance to her before taking point, dropping to one knee just inside the gap to the outside.

A lone Humvee rocked and ground its way up the ledge, then stuttered to a halt, engine ticking and dust settling.

After a moment, the driver's door popped open, and Irene emerged, squinting into the sunlight and frowning. "Kyra?" She called, then her glance fell to a Shifra corpse not far from the passage, and she stiffened.

Grant stepped from the shadows and tucked the gun out of sight as he walked toward her. "Irene! Kyra's okay—she's inside. Gotta warn you, there's a lot more bodies."

"Oh, dear. I hope she's handling the blood. I imagine there is plenty of that as well, and not just on you?"

Maybe should've taken care of that. "Yes, ma'am. What's with the ride?"

She glanced back to the military-style vehicle she had just driven up. "Ah. When Kyra took off with those people—" her glance flicked toward the gap as, with quiet steps, Akilah moved up beside him— "I couldn't think how to be useful, but they'd already killed the guards, and I thought of some things we needed. There's a pharmacy right in town, you know." She opened the next door and pulled out a plastic case marked with the Red Crescent. "I took a number of first aid kits, and some bandages, as well, some blankets meant for children, but I hope it helps." With a slight hesitation, she revealed something in her hand, two bottles of pills with familiar names. Nick's medications, replicated. "I think they're correct. Medicine is not my strong suit."

Grant took the first aid kit, and closed her hand gently over the bottles. "You did very well. It means a lot to know you were looking out for him when I couldn't."

She nodded, blinking a little, then her gaze lifted away from him and her eyes lit.

Nick emerged from the passage with Haldan, who sank gratefully to the stone and lifted his face to the sunshine. Irene, still dressed in linen and silk, bulked up with her Kevlar vest, ran to Nick and flung her arms around him, heedless of blood or weapon. He shifted his arms, getting the gun free, and glanced in Grant's direction, looking for the order to stand down.

For a moment back there, seeing Nick methodically target one man after another, Grant felt a wave of loss for his friend's transformation, but Nick did not look cagey and fierce—he looked strong, with a self-assurance somewhere between his two selves.

Grant gave him a nod, and Nick shipped the weapon against his back to return an old woman's embrace.

CHAPTER EIGHTY-THREE

Kyra rested back in the throne, alone in the chamber which lay silent at last. She presided over a kingdom of the dead, some of whom she had helped to kill. There was a reckoning she must make for that, but she felt, for the moment, at peace, in spite of the odor of death around her, in spite of the screams, the gunshots, the curses that still echoed in her ears. She sat in the Throne of Solomon. No wiser, certainly, but perhaps more humble. The soul of the righteous was the seat of wisdom, said the words, but a person must first have a soul for such a thing to be relevant, surely. The Order of the Knights Penitent was broken, scattered or slain along with their king, but theirs was not the only pathway toward repentance. Some of the things she had done in her determination to be right had cost others their freedom, their blood, and almost their lives.

"Kyra?" Mother's voice echoed along with approaching footfalls. "Kyra? Oh my goodness!" The footfalls stopped short.

"I'm up here." She shifted her position very carefully, untucking her feet to rest on the top step.

Mother walked around to stand before the throne, eyes enormous in the gloom. "You found it!"

"To be fair, Mr. Casey did, but he needed the both of us to get here."

"What are you doing up there? Are you a righteous man?" She indicated the words of the first step.

Kyra shook her head. "One day, perhaps. Besides, Casey was the first to climb it."

She began her slow descent, carefully centered, perfectly balanced, no movement without thought, until she stood in front of her mother. "He recorded me a tour of the throne, and I got to see bits of it when I came in to sync with the drone. He even thought to show me the inside." She took another step and turned to gaze upon the throne at her mother's side. "I oiled the mechanism. All of these people are fighting around me, and I thought Casey and Nick, and anyone else on our side—I thought they would all be dead, and I couldn't do a thing to be of use. But we had brought the gift of olive oil."

"You have always had your own skills," Mother said softly.

"I thought you wanted me to be like you and Bapi, an academic." Their hands found each other between them.

"No, like me—not like him. He was crazy, remember?" Mother choked up.

Kyra wrapped her mother in her arms and rocked a little, just like Bapi used to do. "No, Mama, he was the seat of wisdom. And so are you."

Mother wrapped her in turn, their bulletproof vests rubbing together and making them laugh, her father's memory crowning them both.

CHAPTER EIGHTY-FOUR

At the open door to the Humvee, Grant pulled out the first aid bundles. Another of those hemostatic dressings would be perfect, maybe a few. He heard a rattle behind him, then the soft murmur of Nick's voice, the higher tone of Irene's and footsteps receding into the passageway. A few blankets lay tossed inside, something to keep Haldan from going into shock. As he reached, his shoulders ached. One by one, each injury made itself known, and he trapped his breath behind bared teeth.

"Let me." Akilah's hand stroked his lower back, then she reached past him with enviable ease and gathered the supplies into her arms. They faced each other for a moment in the open door. "For twenty minutes," she whispered. "You can be human."

"That's about my limit. After that it hurts too much."

Her fingers traced his cheekbone and fell to his clavicle, resting lightly as if afraid to add to his pain.

"Ahem." Nick stood a little shy of their position. "You think maybe some introductions?"

He presented Nick. "Nick Norton, my wingman, my very good friend, and sometime deliverer of a mean ass-kicking, generally well-deserved." Then, with a glance at her, "This is Akilah, better known as the Phantom."

"I am his wife." She put out her hand.

"The imam had a gun," Grant said. "She was bound and gagged."

"As I suspect a woman would have to be to marry you, Chief." Nick's hand engulfed hers.

Akilah smiled, a trace of light. "Very pleased to meet you, Mr. Norton."

"If you need to take over the ass-kicking, you just let me know."

"I'm telling you, that was no wedding. No court in the world would uphold it." Maybe he should just concede the point? No matter—it didn't sit well.

Both of them stared at him, then Nick gathered the bundle of blankets and supplies to his chest. "Right. Let the ass-kicking begin. You come see me when it's done, Chief," he called as he walked away, "Maybe she's fooled about you being just fine, but I'm not."

When they were alone again, she said, "I am not fooled."

Grant wiped a smear of blood—probably his—from her brow at the edge of her hijab. "I know." He slipped his arms around her, lightly, gently— never holding too tight, never pressing too hard. "Will you come home with me?"

Her gaze shifted, and he wasn't fooled either. She leaned in, resting her forehead against his chest.

He kissed the top of her head, then her lips as she lifted her face to meet him. He drew back and pulled something from his pocket, offering it to her on the palm of his hand. "I'll take a knee if you want."

Blood spiraled down his arm, dripping silently to the dusty ground below. Her eyes flicked to his hand, widened, and rose again to his face. "If you do," she said, "will you be able to stand again?"

"I give myself a fifty-fifty shot." He held the ring toward her, the ruby-eyed lion with the sharp ears. A beautiful piece, with a secret power.

She closed her hand around it, around his. "You don't need me now."

"I will. Maybe someday you'll need me, too."

Her other hand stroked his brow, her fingers worked into his hair. "I do. I need to know you are out there, safe and alive." She slipped the ring from his palm into her own. "My fellow warrior."

A fresh ache settled deep, and he looked away, to where Nick knelt alongside Haldan, to where Kyra and her mother emerged from the gap, hand in hand. "Still challenging," he sighed.

"Always dangerous," she answered.

He closed his eyes, the sun warming his face, her touch gliding down his jaw, his throat, his shoulder, trailing along his arm. He put out his hand, and her fingertips brushed his, like a hummingbird touching down then lifting away. He stayed a long moment after, certain she was gone, and finally opened his eyes to her absence. The world was as it always had been, before he had known of her existence. Before he had known her. Like those columns of sunlight in the throne room, that world now filtered through dancing flecks of gold.

Crap—Grant touched his shoulder, and found the bee-drone was gone, the pin base torn away some time during the fighting. Should he be concerned about losing it—or glad the tiny camera hadn't recorded the last few moments like some stealthy kiss-cam?

The bandage on his arm had fallen away, and fresh wounds stung, burned, ached and throbbed.

He limped over to Nick's first aid station and slumped onto a blanket next to Haldan. "What's the strongest thing you got, Nick? I hurt everywhere."

"Chief, I don't think there's any medicine for that."

"Dang."

"Nothing but time," Haldan agreed.

"Maybe space," Nick added, and the two of them shared a knowing smile.

Time and space—and those dancing flecks of gold, each one a moment he might see her again.

If you enjoyed this book, please leave a rating or review wherever you share information about books—they really do make a difference!

Join our mailing list at RocinanteBooks.com to learn about new releases and get special perks for Bone Guard fans!

MORE BY THIS AUTHOR

Have you read the other Bone Guard adventures?

They used to be part of an elite group known only as the Unit—until the brass decided to ignore their intel, and they followed Lieutenant Grant Casey into a firestorm to save a museum, and the people trapped inside. The aftermath leaves Grant and his wingman in the hospital, and the whole team on the outs with the military. But Grant fuses his interest in history with his specialized training, and the Bone Guard is born.

The Bone Guard—where adventure and history ignite!

The Mongol's Coffin

An ancient song sparks a deadly race to Genghis Khan's tomb

When Liz Kirschner discovers a musical map to Genghis Khan's tomb, her scholarly life explodes into arson and gunfire. Grant Casey brings in his team for a race to the tomb—to prevent Chinese authorities from burying it forever. This novel speeds from Cambridge, Massachusetts to Cambridge, England in search of clues—then flies to Inner Mongolia, bringing together a Mongolian singer, Grant's ex-commanding officer and a Hong Kong billionaire with a secret past. Mongolian traditions clash with modern priorities in a high-stakes adventure to save one of the world's greatest lost treasures.

The Nazi Skull

When there's a break-in at the tribal center on the reservation where he grew up, Grant flies home to Arizona only to find himself confronting white supremacists, Nazi eugenics and the tribal elder who refuses to speak his name: his own grandfather.

His family's sacred cache is broken into and an immigrant beaten nearly to death, an ancient bone in his stomach. The search leads Grant to a rogue border militia hunting for the stolen remains of Peking Man. With Grant's life and family on the line, he fights to stay ahead of the shooters as they investigate a Nazi POW camp and uncover a trail that's been cold since the prisoner escape in 1944. Contentious cousins, local heat, and a sunken submarine build up the pressure until the desert night erupts in violence.

Grant must follow the clues from a map of the stars to a graveyard for B-29's. Grant's family secrets won't stay buried in his quest to find the truth and stop the murderous rampage of a neo-Nazi betrayed by the person he trusted the most.

ABOUT THE AUTHOR

E. Chris Ambrose also writes dark historical fantasy novels as E. C. Ambrose: the Dark Apostle series about medieval surgery, from DAW Books. Developing that series made the author into a bona fide research junkie. Interests include the history of technology and medicine, Mongolian history and culture, Medieval history, and reproductive biology of lizards. Research has taken her to Germany, England, France, India, Nepal, China and Mongolia as well as many United States destinations. In the process, E. C. learned how to hunt with a falcon, clear a building of possible assailants, pull traction on a broken limb, and fire an AR-15.

Published works have appeared in *Warrior Women*, Fireside magazine, YARN online, Clarkesworld, several volumes of New Hampshire Pulp Fiction, and *Uncle John's Bathroom Reader*. The author is both a graduate of and an instructor for the Odyssey Writing workshop, and a participant in the Codex on-line writers' workshop.

In addition to writing, E. C. works as an adventure guide, teaching rock climbing and leading hiking, kayaking, climbing and mountain biking camps. Past occupations include founding a wholesale sculpture business, selecting stamps for a philatelic company, selling equestrian equipment, and portraying the Easter Bunny on weekends.

Made in the USA
Middletown, DE
20 January 2025

69847564R00222